AF506939

SPOOKABLE TALES

ANTHOLOGY

www.LiteraryLou.com

Home of Author

Louis Paul DeGrado

Also Available from
Author Louis Paul DeGrado:

Savior

The Round House

The People Across the Sea

The Questors' Adventures

The Calling of the Protectors,

The Legend of Chief

The Calling of the Protectors,

The Mighty Adventures of Mouse, the Cat

The 13th Month

13 Days

Spookable Tales Volume 1

Spookable Tales Volume 2

Spookable Tales Volume 3

Spookable Tales Volume 4

Anna's Art Center

Anna's Art Center Book 2

The Arelis Complex

Finding Christmas Spirit

Foreword:

The first stories I told as a child are those of ghosts and supernatural things. It's only natural I eventually did stories about subjects that have fascinated me my entire life. *The Questor's Adventures, The Roundhouse and Moaning Walls* are all based on my childhood quest to prove ghosts are real.

Spookable Tales started as short campfire stories that would be easy to remember and tell. Hence, the small size of the first volume. It is evident that the stories kept hatching and growing. My quest for variety as well as having some fun with the horror genre appealed to me and so, *Spookable Tales* has kept crawling in my brain.

It has been entertaining for me to cast myself as a character in some of the stories and it also gave me the opportunity to hatch my first supervillain, Doctor Madd, and my first Hero, The Marshall. These characters are in two stories, *The Festival of Fear, The Festival of Fear the Return of Doctor Mad,* that pay homage to a most excellent event, The Colorado Festival of Horror!

This set of stories further led me to publish my first set of plays: *The Vampire Detective Agency,* of which the first two were performed and were a Bloody SMASH! I hope to have all three performed again. If you pay attention, our Vampire Detective appears in other stories I am writing. He will also be back in another murder mystery if I can find a place BRAVE enough to perform these plays!

A Dread Pirate and a curse helped me honor one of my favorite places and events: the Steampunk Festival in Victor Colorado that takes place every fall. You can see the character from *The Festival of Fear,* and *The Marshal,* walking the streets at this festival.

Ghosts, hauntings, curses, vampires, madmen, cult leaders, heroes, demons and angels have all found their way into these brief adventures. It was time for me to present them to you in a combined addition.

Enjoy...

SPOOKABLE TALES ANTHOLOGY

SPOOKABLE TALES VOLUME 1

CONTENTS

Gather Around

though you may despair

there's a tale of terror

in the air

Come not if you are faint of heart

For you might not last

But may depart

Not standing

but lying still

If adventure is what you desire

Then come closer

sit by the fire

And listen well

To the tale I tell...

In the time-honored tradition of telling ghost stories around the campfire, I wrote this story for my friends at Cutty's resort in Coaldale, Colorado. During the last two weekends of the fall before the resort closes for the winter, the resort does a Halloween celebration complete with trick-or-treating and a haunted house! So, in the spirit of the season I wanted to share this story with you. Hope you enjoy...

<u>The Haunted Stare of Jaspar Jones</u>

I'll tell you the story of Jaspar Jones

Who, to this day, is searching for his leg-bones

If you've heard strange sounds after dark and wanted to

go and see

Before you take a single step

you better listen to me

Be warned, be wary

be looking out

Think twice before you wonder into the night

You might find yourself with quite a fright

When you find what is there

The haunted face

of Jaspar Jones

Looking for his leg-bones

with its hollow, lonely stare

It started not so long ago

I'll tell you the tale

When a man

named jasper jones

Came west to Cutty's near the town of Coaldale

Looking for love, looking for land and gold

He found all three right around these parts

Had good luck, so I'm told

But then things went bad

And the story gets sad

When he started to gamble it away

He had plenty but plenty wasn't enough

There was nothing he wouldn't try, nothing he wouldn't bet

No amount was too high, no limits were set

One day he was challenged to outrun the five o'clock train

An impossible challenge

But jasper accepted in vain

He lined up along the track

Despite his love who pleaded

Jaspar knew, there was no turning back

And when the gun rang out, he ran

Fast he ran

But then he tripped and had a fall

Most of his body made it across

Most, but not all

His legs were on the track as the train went past

He looked, but his legs were gone

just below his waist

Unable to stand, he glanced at his love one last time and
dragged himself away with haste

Later that night the townspeople say

They could hear Jasper moaning for all he'd lost

And during the day they'd see the marks of Jasper
dragging himself around

all throughout the town

In the dark of the night

is the only time he'd come down

Out of the hills where he stayed all alone

A hill, well, like that one right there!

If you notice strange tracks on the trail

If at night you hear a moan or a wail

You better stay inside

You better beware

Of Jaspar Jones

Looking for his leg-bones

with his hollow, lonely stare

--The End

Gather Around

though you may despair

there's a tale of terror

in the air

Come not if you are faint of heart

For you might not last

But may depart

Not standing

but lying still

If adventure is what you desire

Then come closer

sit by the fire

and be still

While I tell the tale

of Jeffrey MaGills...

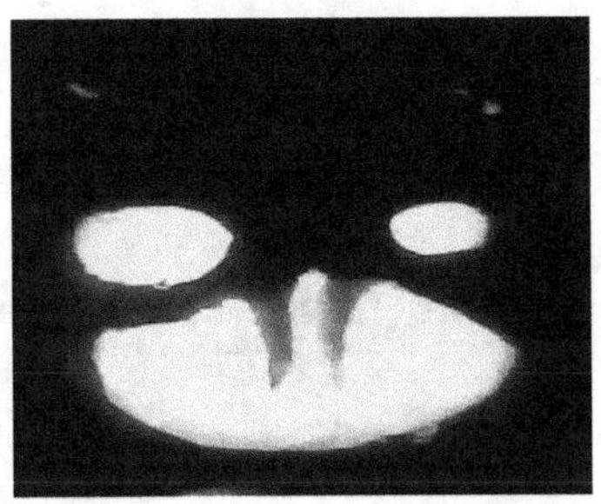

THE LEGEND OF JEFFREY MaGILLS

There is a legend in these hills

About a man named Jeffrey MaGills

He had the fever you see

Not a flu or a cold

But a different one

A fever for gold

His temperature so high

the advice he did ignore

of his friend

Who told him not to venture

On the burial ground

of those who came before

Or he might meet his end

The warning MaGills could not heed

When gold fever set in

Nothing could curb the greed

the cardinal sin

With two other tainted men

MaGills headed out on the trail

Again, he was warned, but to no avail

Some say that is where the story begins

Some say it is where it ends

No one can confirm what happened next

The only one that returned

From that adventure gone bad

Was one of the prospectors

And He had gone mad

He talked of finding riches untold

Talked of treasure, gems and gold

More than he'd ever dreamed

But what he spoke of next

Was incomprehensible

or so it seemed

Tales of shadows and walking dead

Of a cursed burial ground

Or so he said

If treasure he'd found

He had nothing to show

Truth or lie

no one could know

When asked of the others

he raved of something ancient and old

of darkness and terror

that only spared he

who hadn't touched the gold

What of the others

They hadn't fared well

He spewed forth a warning

About the fires of hell

The sheriff formed a posse to go and see

if the prospector had murdered MaGills for the loot

But none would step one foot

into those cursed hills

and so began

the legend of Jeffrey MaGills

Was he murdered

Did he go mad too

No one knows

No one has a clue

Since that time

A few have ventured and return to tell

Of an old man dressed like a prospector from hell

His hands drenched in blood

His eyes fire red

His stare alone

Can strike a man dead

So, if you have gold fever

Don't venture in those hills

For you might run into the mislaid spirit

Of one Jeffrey MaGills

-The End

I WANT MY BONES BACK!

From: *The Questors Adventures*

A man from the city, looking for a better life, moved to the country for a change of pace. There he found a house, the perfect place.

He wondered why the house and land was so cheap and why no one had purchased such fine farm property. He, recently a widower as his family died in a tragic accident, would love to have such a nice property—

something to work with, something to keep him busy. He didn't know he was about to uncover a horrible secret.

The insurance money was enough to buy the land and a tractor. Settling in with only his dog, Max, he started plowing one day. After about three hours, he noticed his dog, which followed him everywhere, was missing. He found his dog sitting in the back of the field standing over something. He got down from his tractor and went over to see what the dog found and noticed it was a bone. Not just any bone, a human bone--a human skull!

He took the skull into his house and puzzled over it. It looked old, ancient. Like the kind you see on those TV shows about mummies. Puzzled, and not sure whether he should call the police, he left the skull on his dresser as when he went to bed. His bedroom was on the second floor of the house.

Late that night his dog started growling and woke the farmer. He looked down at the foot of his bed and could see Max sitting, hair standing on end, teeth showing.

The farmer reached for Max to settle him when he heard the front door open and footsteps coming from downstairs. Someone was in his house!

Before the farmer could reach for his shotgun, which he kept in his room, the footsteps stopped at the base of the stairs and an eerie voice travelled those stairs and froze him; his muscles locked and he couldn't move.

The voice whispered: "I want my bones back. I want my bones back."

He heard footsteps coming up the stairs. Max crawled under the bed. The farmer was frozen with fear. He looked across his room where his shotgun hung on the wall, but something told him it wouldn't do him any good. The sounds came closer, and the eerie voice came again:

"I want my bones back…I want my bones back."

Suddenly, the sounds stopped. The voice and footsteps were gone. The farmer managed to lock his door and get his shotgun, but he didn't sleep all night as his eyes were fixed on the bedroom door and his ears listened for the sounds.

The next morning when the sunlight came through his window, he looked around his room. Max had returned to the foot of his bed and the skull sat on his dresser where he put it. After checking that his front door was still locked and nothing was amiss in the house, he considered that he just had a bad dream. He decided to keep plowing his field because he needed the money from the crops.

He stopped plowing when he noticed Max had stopped and was digging at a spot where he had just plowed. Getting off the tractor, he found Max standing over a whole pile of bones. He worried that if he called the police, they would make him stop plowing to investigate. Given the bones all seemed to be old, he thought they had been in the ground for a long time and was sure no one would be looking for them. Or so he thought.

He decided the bones needed a proper burial and round them up in a bag and took them inside This time he left them down at the bottom of the stairs. Before he went to bed that night, he made sure he locked his front door and put his shotgun by the side of his bed.

Once again, the farmer woke because Max was growling. He heard his front door creak open, but he knew he'd locked it! He heard heavy footsteps going across the floor to the base of the stairs. He hoped the footsteps would stop there because he left the bones downstairs. He tried to reach out and grab his shotgun, but his arms were frozen in fear when suddenly, the ghostly voice came:

"I want my bones back...I want my bones back," the voice called out.

The footsteps started coming up the stairs and the farmer looked for an escape.

"The bones are downstairs," the farmer called out. The footsteps kept approaching and the voice called out again:

"I want my bones back....... I want my bones back."

He looked around his room considering where he could hide when he inhaled deeply in shock as he realized his mistake; he had left the SKULL ON HIS DRESSER!

The footsteps came closer and the voice grew louder. "I want my bones back...I want my bones back!" Both stopped at his bedroom door.

The farmer sat upright on his bed with his knuckles turning white as he gripped his shotgun. Max sat beside him but was silent and still. This time, the farmer knew it wasn't a dream. He kept his position as long as he could, but finally drifted off to sleep.

Happy to wake the next morning, the farmer called realtor over and told him what was happening. The realtor recommended he call the police, but the farmer told him why he didn't want too.

So, the two of them went out and explored the field until they found the bones of three bodies. The farmer thought if they buried the bodies then the sounds would stop because they would be at rest. He told the realtor that the ghostly voice didn't start until he plowed the field and disturbed the bones. The men put the bones in gunny sacks and buried them in the unused stable and said a prayer over them.

That night as the farmer headed to bed, Max refused to come inside and remained outside in the doghouse. The farmer thought he would be safe now that he buried the bodies. This time he put the Holy Bible by his bed because he knew with the forces at work his gun would do him no good. With his front door and bedroom door locked tight, the farmer went to sleep.

In the middle of the night, he woke with a start and sat up in bed. He looked down to find Max and then remembered he was outside. He listened, but there were no sounds. Unable to go back to sleep, he glanced out his window to see the bright moon shining; its light lit his room and he started to feel at ease. Then, glancing around he noticed something…he STILL had the SKULL on his DRESSER! He had forgotten to bury it! How could that be? They had found three complete bodies and buried them.

The farmer realized there must have been a fourth body that he hadn't found. The front door flung open with a crash. The footsteps were louder than before as they pounded across the floor to the base of the stairs. They started coming up the stairs. Then the voice started:

"I want my bones back…I want my bones back." It got closer and louder. "I want my bones back…I want my bones back!"

The next day, the realtor that sold the house and land to the city man who wanted to be farmer, stopped by. He knocked on the door but there was no answer. The car was parked in the driveway and he knew the farmer was home. He went around back to the field. There, he found the farmers dog sitting over some freshly plowed land.

"Where's your owner?" the realtor asked.

Max started digging until the realtor gasped. There, where the dog had dug, was the man's body.

--The End

SPOOKABLE TALES VOLUME 2

LOUIS PAUL DEGRADO

Spookable Tales Volume 2
Copyright © 2020 Louis Paul DeGrado

All rights reserved. No part of this book may be used or reproduced by any means, graphic, electronic, or mechanical, including photocopying, recording, taping, or by any information storage retrieval system without written permission of the author.

This book is a work of fiction. Unless otherwise noted, the author makes no explicit guarantee as to the accuracy of the information contained in the book. Any reference to people or places that may be real is merely coincidental. Just in case the characters in the story come to life, you should beware and lock your door at night.

Special Thanks goes to:

Kyle and Kendra Groves
Kathleen Mack Groves
Ed Groves
The Party People Theatre of Mystery

**Special mention goes to the
Cast and Crew that Made
The Vampire Detective
come to LIFE:**

**Drake Ulah - Colin Stewart
Lacie Starlight - Lexi Deary
Bob - Matthew Coats
Veronica Charm - Martha Page
Freddie Flicks - B Kevin Ritter
Adam Staulker - Jeffery Orman
Director - Pam Kramer
Tech - Caleb Miessler**

Gather Around

though you may despair

there's a tale of terror

in the air

Come not if you are faint of heart

For you might not last

But may depart

Not standing

but lying still

If adventure is what you desire

Then come closer

sit by the fire

And listen well

To the tale I tell

GRAVE ROBBERS

CHAPTER ONE
GRAVEYARD SHIFT

No one could explain what was happening all over the country, all over the globe for that matter. That's what the chief said. Hundreds and sometimes thousands of bodies had just vanished from cemeteries without a trace; the coffins left behind. The scale of the operation would have to be enormous yet, no one had seen or heard anything. That's how the briefing went.

Now, it's Friday night in Canyon City Colorado, and Jeff Denton is just arriving at his post at the Mountain Valley Cemetery. After retiring five years ago from his full-time job, Jeff settled in the town and started working part-time at the Canyon City Police Department; a job that has him working most weekends. Jeff takes out his lunch box and opens it. He puts a cold cut deli sandwich on the seat beside him and pulls out a thermos of coffee and pours himself a cup.

"It's going to be a long night," Jeff says to the empty car. He looks down at his sandwich and considers he would rather be off doing something fun, or at least eating a good pizza at the local joint and having a beer. Instead he is parked outside the cemetery watching for graverobbers. He remembers what led him to this point: The chief called him in. The Chief called everyone in. They were taking extra shifts due to a tip that a group of people digging up graves throughout the country were now in this location and could strike. Although the cemetery had a night guard, the chief thought an extra set of eyes wouldn't hurt.

Jeff positioned his vehicle along the south road that ran parallel to the cemetery. From here, he could see any vehicles approaching from the town below. He started thinking about the reasons someone would want to disturb graves; reasons that ranged from recovering or stealing family heirlooms to digging up buried treasure.

Jeff faded off in his investigative daydream when suddenly, his car started shaking and he sat up straight. "What the?" He shook his head making sure he wasn't dreaming. It was then he heard a low moan coming from outside his car. He reached for his flashlight and readied his weapon. The car stopped shaking but the moaning continued. He turned his head left and right and then rolled the passenger side window down.

It's coming from behind me, he thought as he readied himself to exit the car. He quickly pulled the door handle and stepped out of the car switching the flashlight to his left hand as he reached for his sidearm with his right. Standing about six-feet tall, Jeff was not a small man but had thick arms, broad shoulders, and a body-builders chest. His physique helped him get the job because no one usually messed with him. He took a step toward the back of the vehicle where he heard the sound. The moaning stopped and a faint whisper came from the rear of the vehicle.

"Jeff, Jeff Denton..." the voice called out.

It concerned him that whatever he was facing knew his name. He took another step and could see over the trunk, but nothing was in view.

"Jeff, Jeff Denton, ghosts cannot be shot," the whispering voice called out.

"Alright there, whoever you are come out and put your hands where I can see them!" Jeff commanded. "If one of you guys came out to prank me, this isn't the time."

"Jeff, ghosts cannot be shot, but humans can. Don't hurt the humans, especially one who is an old friend."

Jeff's trained eye spotted the figure as it stood with hands raised and he laughed. A fit man with red hair and blue eyes, dressed in a black coat and jeans grinned at him.

"Louis, what are you doing here?" he said recognizing his friend from Pueblo that he had worked with years ago.

"I should ask you that. Why are you parked outside of the cemetery? Are there some kids daring to go in?"

"No," Jeff said. "We had a warning about some grave robbers. Apparently, there's been a rash in Colorado and some towns in the area have been hit so the chief is worried we might be next."

"Oh," Louis said. "Well, it would be the perfect night for it;" he looked to the sky. "Overcast and chilly. Most people are probably staying indoors."

"Exactly why are you out here?" Jeff asked again. He knew Louis didn't live in Canyon but down the road in Pueblo.

"Research," Louis said. He reached down and picked up a small backpack. "Let's have a seat and I'll tell you what I know."

The two men returned to Jeff's car with Louis taking a seat in the passenger side. Louis took out a thermos and poured some coffee in a cup and handed it to Jeff.

"Thanks," Jeff said. "I have my own." He held up his thermos.

"First, let me apologize for the funny business back there," Louis said. "I just couldn't resist. You should have parked your car where you could watch the back more readily."

"I didn't expect anyone from that direction," Jeff said. "The cemetery is only six acres and has limited access. It's over there I'm watching," he points to the cemetery.

"All those trees don't help," Louis said.

'No, but I figure if someone is coming, they would probably be coming from the south and this is most concentrated part."

"Lots of places to hide out there," Louis said. "I really am sorry."

"Don't worry about it. You sneaking up on me is actually helping me stay awake. Got my adrenaline pumping. You still haven't told me what you are doing out here."

"I'm in town for a ghost hunt at the Abbey tomorrow night. I'm staying with Scott Holiday."

"Oh, how's he doing?" Jeff said. He and Louis worked in the same company with Scott five years ago.

"He's still stubborn as ever. Even with his share of that lottery money he won, he still won't leave his old house or go travelling anywhere. Just kind of sits home on his porch and makes fun of his neighbors that have to go to work."

"That sounds like Scott," Jeff said. "It would be nice to retire early and not have to work. What about you? You said you were doing research. Is the ghost hunt what you are researching?"

"Somewhat," Louis responded.

"You're still writing books?" Jeff asked.

"I am working on some new material," Louis said. "It has a supernatural flare. The ghost hunt is more of a hobby though. You'd never guess who is leading the group."

"Is it Joe?"

"How did you know?" Louis asked.

"Joe Durant, for all his technical mumbo jumbo and hard knocks approach, is one of the most popular ghost hunters in the area currently," Jeff said.

"They invited me out, so I decided to pay them a visit," Louis said.

"They?"

"Joe is leading the tours, but Mari Valdez is the one doing all the marketing and videos. She's the one that contacted me."

"Really," Jeff said. "I didn't know they were into that sort of stuff."

"They weren't back when you worked with them. But they started reading all my stories and watching my posts and next thing you know they are hooked on all that is spooky and supernatural."

"Why are you out here," Jeff asked. "At the cemetery?"

"I'm here for the same reason you are."

"The graverobbers?"

"Yes," Louis said. "Are all the cemeteries being watched?"

"Yes," Jeff said.

"And you are by yourself?"

"There's only so many of us. It's normally a quiet town," Jeff said. "That is until some hoodlums decide to come and tear up graves."

"There's more to these graverobbers than you might know," Louis said. "They aren't some young pranksters you're dealing with."

"No?"

Louis shook his head. "It's more sophisticated than you might think."

"How's that?"

"Tell me what you know and then I'll fill in the gaps," Louis said.

Jeff looked out his windshield and around the surrounding area. "I guess no one told me we had to keep this a secret or anything and it has been on the news. So, here's what I know.

"The chief pulled us in to a meeting and told us about this group of people that were going around digging up graves. Supposed to be going on all over the country. They've hit several towns in Colorado. We had a tip that they were in the area so, we've all been taking shifts and watching the cemeteries."

"Did he tell you if they were stealing anything?" Louis asked.

"That didn't' come up," Jeff said.

"Did he say if they were removing the bodies?"

"Just said that the bodies went missing without a trace."

"Are they digging up specific bodies newly buried or old?" Louis kept questioning.

Jeff shook his head. "We didn't talk about any of those things. All I know is it's illegal to exhume a body without the permission of the family or some type of court order. I guess that's enough for him to put me out here. Now enough with the questions, what do you know, and do you want some of these shortbread cookies my wife made or not?"

"Sure, I'll take some," Louis said.

Jeff took out the cookies and handed some to Louis. He dunked one in his coffee and ate it.

"These sure hit the spot," Louis said. "You know your chief has put you in danger. This thing is much bigger than they let you know. In fact, if I were you, I wouldn't feel safe being out here by myself."

"I don't believe in ghosts and spirits," Jeff said.

"That's not the problem," Louis said as he took a sip of coffee. "This is what I know. There is a someone responsible and they are real."

"They?" Jeff asks.

"Yes, they," Louis responds. "There's more than one and they travel in large groups and seem to be on a schedule when they do strike, in and out in a few hours like a well-coordinated plan. It could have something to do with the fact that they are trying to remain undetected. Anyway, this is more than some high school kids playing a prank."

Jeff suddenly looked past Louis to the cemetery.

"What is it?" Louis asked.

Jeff spotted a figure moving off in the distance. "Hold that thought," Jeff said. He opened his door, grabbed his flashlight. "I need to go check this out." He noticed Louis looked at the time. "Did you need to be somewhere?"

"No, I can wait," Louis said and got out of the car. "What did you see?"

"Over there," Jeff pointed. "Someone is walking over there."

"Let's go," Louis said and started walking to where Jeff pointed.

Jeff quickly overtook Louis and turned around to face him.

"If you get hurt, I'm going to get in trouble, now let me go first," Jeff said.

Louis started following him and Jeff turned around. "Not so close." Louis raised both hands palm out in front. "Okay, I'll stay back."

The two men slowly headed into the cemetery where Jeff spotted a figure lurking. Jeff knelt and watched but the person he was following moved slowly as though looking for someone.

"Maybe I should call this in," Jeff said.

"You think we're in danger?" Louis asked.

"No, I think we're okay. There just appears to be one person. He is acting suspiciously, sneaking around like that. Come on, let's get closer."

The figure, dressed in work boots, a large grey flannel jacket and black cap, moved deeper into the cemetery and eventually stopped at some tombstones and crouched behind them while looking forward into the center of the cemetery.

"Time to find out what you're up too," Jeff said and pulled out his flashlight. "You there, halt."

The high beam startled the man in front of them as they came up behind him. He turned and immediately raised his hands.

"Scott?" Jeff said.

"Jeff?" the man in front of him said as he squinted.

Jeff turned off the flashlight and he and Louis approached a man that had brown hair, a mustache and beard who they both knew as Scott Holiday.

"I thought you were staying with him," Jeff said to Louis.

He is," Scott said. "That's why I'm out here. When he told me what was going on, well, I figured I better get out here and look at the family plot. You know, to make sure it's safe."

"Okay, Louis, now that we've discovered who our mysterious stranger is and that he's not a threat, why don't you finish telling me what you know," Jeff said.

"A few years back, "Louis said, "I stumbled on this group. They called themselves the serenities. At first, I thought it had to do with an old television series I liked so, it piqued my interest. Once I got past the introductions, I found out a lot more."

"This isn't one of your stories is it?" Jeff asked knowing that Louis was an author.

"No, this will knock your socks off and has everything to do with what you've been hearing and more."

"I should probably drive around some," Jeff said.

"I don't know," Louis said. "You have a fairly good view from here. Besides, what I'm about to tell you is barely believable."

"Okay, okay, go ahead," Jeff said. "Let's walk up to the boundary there and back."

The three men started walking as Louis continued telling them what he knew. "These grave robbers that you are talking about, you do know it's much larger than Colorado? In fact, it's a worldwide phenomenon and has only increased over the last decade."

"Really, a decade?" Jeff said. "I hadn't heard about it until recently."

"Yes. Hasn't gained attention because it's not like they are killing people, right? The cemeteries have stopped reporting it because it's an embarrassment to them."

"I guess that could be bad for business," Jeff said. "So, why did it become so important that my chief wanted me out here?"

"People get upsent when someone disturbs their loved ones that have passed on," Scott said.

"Right," Jeff said. "Louis, you don't think what is going on is a prank?"

"That's what I'm getting too, but first, I need to let you know more about this group I met."

"Online?"

"Yes, online."

"Shh," Scott said raising his finger to his lips. "I hear something."

Everyone went silent and the flashlights went off as they came to a halt. Jeff went down on one knee and the other two did the same.

"I don't hear anything," Jeff said.

"That's because you don't have these," Scott said and pointed to hearing aids on his ears. "See, I had to invest in these."

"I hear it too," Louis said. "There's some rustling over in that direction."

Jeff stood causing Louis and Scott to stand. "I guess I can't convince you two to stay behind."

"Nope," Louis said.

"Not a chance," Scott said.

"Okay, just stay behind me," Jeff said and cautiously moved toward the area where Scott indicated hearing rustling sounds. He glanced at Louis, who shrugged his shoulders, and unholstered his weapon before continuing forward.

Suddenly, Jeff took a knee. Scott and Louis slowly came up to him both in a crouched position. Jeff looked forward and pointed. "Over there, two figures just ducked behind those big tombstones."

"Just two?" Louis asked.

"That's all I saw," Jeff said.

"Your hearing might not be good, but you have excellent eyesight," Scott said.

"I had that Laser surgery a few years back," Jeff said.

"I'm glad we are catching up on how old we all are and all the medical procedures we've been through," Louis said, "but shouldn't we be keeping it down? Anyone out there is going to hear us and know we're coming."

"Right," Jeff said. "Stay behind me." Jeff proceeded slowly with Louis and Scott in tow. As they approached closer to the large tombstones all three of them could hear a man and a woman speaking in hushed voices. They could also see light flashes coming from what appeared to be someone checking a cell phone.

Jeff reached for his walkie talkie.

"What are you doing?" Louis asked.

"I'm going to call the station," Jeff replied. "Even if these aren't the people we're waiting for, they are in the cemetery past curfew. I'll probably just scare them off but in case something develops, I want the station informed."

The voices grew louder, and Jeff saw Louis cock his head toward them and then he put his hand across the walkie talkie before Jeff could make a call.

"Wait," Louis said. He took his cell phone out and dialed a number.

From in front of the three men, behind the large tombstones a ringtone from a phone sounded; retro seventies dance music played, and a male's voice could be heard.

"Oh, crap, I forgot to turn my cell phone off," the male voice said.

The tone went off and Louis' call didn't go through. Jeff watched as he hit the redial. This time the caller picked up.

"This is Joe," a hushed voice came from the other side of the tombstones.

"Joe, this is Louis, where are you?"

"I'm, uh, at home of course. Where else would I be at this time of night?"

Louis turned to Jeff and Scott and smiled.

"Just wanted to make sure we are good for tomorrow night," Louis said.

"No problem," Joe said. "The drums will be playing at the Abbey, it's a highly active site. You'll be amazed."

"Okay, see you then," Louis said and put away the phone. "You ready to have some fun?" Louis explained to Jeff and Scott what they were going to do. Scott and Louis took small flashlights out while Jeff stepped forward and slowly moved around the tombstone.

"NOW!" Jeff called out and Louis and Scott, flashlights blazing, flanked two people sitting on a blanket. "Don't move!"

CHAPTER TWO
REUNION

"Mari, Joe? What are you two doing out here?" Jeff asked as a man and woman, both dressed in solid black, stood in front of him.

The man, about five foot nine, stocky with short, black hair, and woman, five-five with long black hair were standing amongst a few backpacks and a cooler, lid open, full of ice and beer.

"We heard about what was going on," Joe said while he used a napkin to wipe his shirt from the drink he spilled.

"Is that all that is going on?" Jeff asked.

"Put your light down," Mari said.

Louis turned his light off while Scott pointed his to the ground. "Sorry," Scott said. "Didn't mean to make you spill your drink."

"We are just business partners," Mari said. "Our spouses don't like all this ghost hunting stuff and if it wasn't for, wait, Louis?

"Yep it's me, and we knew it was you," Louis said. "Well, we knew it was Joe from his ring tone. I though you said you were home?"

"Very funny," Joe said and threw the napkin at Louis.

"Don't you have a ghost hunt at the abbey or something going on?" Jeff asked.

"That's tomorrow night," Mari said.

"What are you doing out here?" Jeff asked.

"You heard, didn't you?" Louis asked.

"We heard about the graverobbers," Joe said. "Wait, is that Scott? Scott Holiday?"

"Hello Joe, Mari," Scott said.

"Isn't this just one big reunion," Jeff said shaking his head. "At least I have back up if I need it."

"Funny we are all out here late at night compared to what we used to do; get up at the crack of dawn and go to work," Scott said.

"Oh, I'm sure glad I don't have to do that anymore," Mari said.

"Is there anyone else that's going to show up?" Jeff asked.

"Not that I know about," Joe said.

"Now that we're all here, what do we do now?" Scott asked.

"Looks like Joe and Mari picked out a good vantage point," Louis said. "Why don't we stay here."

"Okay," Jeff said. "But keep the voices down, I have a job to do out here."

"What's that?" Mari asked.

"They sent him out here to stop the graverobbers," Louis said.

"What do you know about them?" Jeff asked.

"Not much," Joe said. "All I know is that they aren't really grave robbers; they don't take anything. They just dig up the bodies and rebury them without the casket. It's some type of re-bonding with the earth or something like that."

"Sounds like a cult," Jeff said.

"Did you see the speakers?" Mari said.

"Speakers?" Jeff said.

"It's getting dark out and you probably missed them. Dozens of large speakers are along the perimeter pointing toward town."

"Why would someone have speakers out here?" Jeff asked.

"Want a beer?" Joe asked.

"I'll take one," Louis said.

"Me too," Scott said.

"I'm on duty Jeff said."

Everyone settled down on the blankets Joe and Mari laid out. The lights from the cemetery and city below bounded off the clouds creating and eerily clear visibility across the macabre landscape.

"Looks like it might rain before the night is over," Jeff said. "Louis, why don't you continue telling us what you know."

"Okay, I was telling you about this group that is responsible for all of this. You see, they believe in this energy force that makes up the earth and spirit of the earth; that all energy is life and all life is connected. Energy transforms, it doesn't really die. Humans are born of the elements. Those elements must return to the whole or the whole becomes weaker. In this case, the whole is the earth."

How did you get mixed up in all of this?

"That's the amazing part," Louis said. "We all know one of the leaders of this group, cult if you want to call it that. All of us worked with him!"

"Who?" Jeff asked but Louis didn't have time to respond before the entire cemetery went black. Every lamp and every light went out all around them.

"Do you feel that?" Jeff said.

Louis nodded.

Everyone in the group stopped talking as a low vibration came from the ground. Dull green and blue lights came from the direction of the vibration. The speakers emanated a low hum, but that wasn't all that caused the sound.

"It feels like heavy equipment," Jeff said. He stood and the others followed. From the position they were at, they could see across to the north and east of the cemetery and it was there that they noticed movement. Six formations of black clad figures surrounding small tractors started coming toward them. There were six in each row bringing the total number of people they could see below them to seventy-two. Jeff spotted more on the flanks; all in black. He could see they held shovels and rakes.

"Everyone get down," Jeff said as they hid behind the tombstones. He drew his weapon and took a small set of binoculars from his utility belt as Mari and Joe started snapping pictures.

"Make sure your flash is off, so they don't spot us," Jeff said.

"I think they already have," Louis said as he pointed to a group of four of the black-clad figures only thirty yards away that were looking in their direction.

Jeff removed his pistol from the holster.

CHAPTER THREE
AN EARTHLY MISSION

"Do you have seventy bullets?" Louis asked.

"No, but it will only take one to show the others I mean business."

Louis put his hand over to the gun and pushed it down. "I don't think they will harm us if we don't interfere."

"Interfere with what?" Jeff asked. He moved to the edge of the tombstones and Louis followed as they continued watching.

"Look closely at what they are wearing, Jeff," Louis said. "And I don't mean the black jeans and hoods, I mean the advanced night vision goggles."

"You're right about one thing," Jeff said. "This isn't a group of high school kids playing a prank." Jeff went for his walkie talkie and Louis put his hand on it.

"Don't," Louis said. "They think they are running out of time to save the world. I don't know how many officers they have in that police department of yours, but they'll kill you and anyone else that comes to stop them. Believe me, I know."

"What do you suggest I do? Just stand by?" Jeff asked.

"Yes," Louis said. "Just watch. I promise you; they don't steal, and everything will be back to normal when they go."

Through the small binoculars Jeff carried and the amount of light from the workers before them, the group watched in awe as a coordinated operation took place before them.

What appeared to them to be spotters led and flagged specific gravesites. After this, four people would come in and plant a bladed machine that cut the grass out in a grid. The perfect grid was moved to the side. Then a small tractor came along with a conveyor system that pierced vertically into the site and slowly move out horizontally emptying the dirt efficiently into a bucket behind the machine.

"Those tractors must be electric," Joe said. "They're too quiet to be anything else."

"Look at how the blades on the conveyer just move into the ground and dig a hole so efficiently," Mari said. "Where did they get this stuff? It must have cost millions."

"Billions is more like it," Louis said.

The group watched as each of the six machines in their view stopped within minutes of each other. Four members of each group raised what appeared to be cross bows and shot a single arrow into each hole. The rope tied to the end of the arrow was used to pull and raise a coffin which was set to the side. The operator from the tractor came forward and each group knelt before the coffin as in prayer before they opened it, removed the body, and then slowly lowered it back into the hole without the coffin. The coffin was then lowered into the hole over the body and the dirt was put back in. Finally, the grass that had been neatly removed was replaced on top. The group of six people again knelt at the gravesite as though in prayer before moving to the next site.

Amazed, Jeff sat and watched as this process continued for the next four hours.

"I can't believe how efficient they work," Scott said. "Each time something goes wrong at one of the sites whether it's equipment or a digging problem, someone comes along, and the problem is solved immediately. It's..."

"Unreal," Mari said. "I thought our ghost hunts were strange, but this is something I could have never imagined. Maybe we should get out of here."

"They seem to be leaving us alone," Joe said. "Be ready just in case."

"They've already done fifty sites by my count," Jeff said. "And that's just what we can see in front of us. I can tell there's some more lights over there. They just put the bodies back under the coffin. Don't take anything or do anything to it."

"How could they have possibly got all of this equipment here?" Joe asked.

"I have a theory," Jeff said.

Several minutes passed by.

"You going to tell us?" Joe asked.

"Sorry, I was just noticing it appears some of them are leaving," Jeff said. "My theory is that they are using the train. Just two days ago, the Royal Gorge Railway had to shut down for a day. Multiple people reported there was another train on the track just west of here."

"Isn't that track used by the gravel company as well?" Mari asked.

"I supposed it could have been a coincidence," Jeff said. "However, it makes sense that when you consider the amount equipment out there along with the weight of it all, that they are using the railroad to move it around. This is way out of my pay grade."

"Oh no," Joe said. He slumped behind the tombstone. "Get down. There's a group of them gathering and looking our way. One of them is pointing in our direction."

"It's probably nothing," Louis said. "We've stayed put and haven't interfered."

"One of them is walking this way," Joe said.

A figure in a black cloak with night-vision headgear came up the slope toward the group and Jeff looked as close as he could with his binoculars. The person's hands appeared to be free of any tools or weapons. I noticed he's also limping as though he has a bad left leg. The figure stopped about six feet from where the group had been watching. Jeff and Louis stood. Scott, Joe, and Mari did the same so that they were all exposed to the person walking toward them.

The figure moved both hands to its head and removed the goggles and hood.

"Crage? Crage Bryant?" Jeff said. "What are you doing here?"

"Livin' the dream," Crage said. "Thanks for not interfering. It always makes it messier when the local law enforcement tries to interfere." He looked to Louis. "I see you made it."

"You knew about this?" Jeff said as he turned to Louis.

"Kind of," Louis said. "I've been researching the phenomena and well, Crage kind of invited me out to witness the event."

"Thanks for providing the distraction and keeping Jeff and us safe," Crage said.

"No problem," Louis said. "Thank you for letting us watch the ceremony. Hope you don't mind that I invited Mari and Joe along."

"Absolutely not," Crage said. "The more people that understand this whole thing, the faster we can accomplish our mission."

"Ceremony?" Jeff said.

"Yes," Crage replied. "What we are doing is very thought-out and sacred. Everything we are doing has a purpose."

"Which is to save the earth?" Jeff asked. "How? I don't understand."

"You don't believe in our cause?" Crage said.

"I'm not sure I do either," Scott said."

Crage turned and looked at the last few members of his group leaving.

"You have another cemetery to hit tonight?" Jeff asked.

"No, Crage said. "I wanted to make sure no one is waiting for me. We have to load everything and be out of here tonight."

"Speaking of that," Joe said. "How did you get everything here without people in the town noticing. I mean, even as quiet as the equipment was, it's still a lot."

"What do you know about hypnotism?" Crage asked.

Everyone glanced at each other and back at Crage.

"See, there are speakers placed all around the cemetery days ago that are emitting a soft hum that grew louder each night. It was a programmed frequency vibrating in a way that lulled the town to sleep."

"That just blows me away," Louis said. "How come we weren't affected?"

"You are in the perimeter, just like the rest of us," Crage said. "The sound is a very focused wave. Technology I don't even understand."

"I still don't get what you are doing," Jeff said.

"Let me ask you," Crag said. "Do you believe in the effects of climate change, see what pollution does, understand the effects development has on wildlife and the ecosystem?"

"Yes," Scott said. "I understand that I can't keep dumping my sewage in the same place without making a stink. I've got to clean it up somehow."

The group laughed together.

"Okay, maybe I'm coming off too strong," Crage said. "For a long time, people have been looking only at the exterior effects we have on the earth from the things I mention. However, we all know energy doesn't die, it just transforms right?"

"Yes, Louis reminded us what Einstein said; 'Energy cannot be created or destroyed; it can only be changed from one form to another.'"

"Exactly," Crage said.

"So, you think you are returning the energy to the earth by having those people rot in the ground instead of the coffin?" Scott asked.

"They decay and are absorbed back into the host." Crage said. "A complete absorption not possible with some of the casket designs of the day."

"Is there any proof of this?" Jeff asked.

"Sounds like some made up mumbo jumbo so that people like you have something to do when they retire," Scott said.

Crage smiled. "You'd be surprised who knows this is true," Crage said and pointed to the sky. "You think all those satellites they've sent into space are for tv and phones? There're devices up there that measure the earth's ionosphere, temperature, weather patterns and all kinds of stuff. They have the information. And they have data before and after we started doing this. They just don't understand how what we are doing works."

"How long do you think this will go on? How long before someone puts a stop to this?" Jeff asked.

"Oh, heck," Crage said. "We're just a small group and haven't been doing this long. There are seventy or more teams doing this just in the U.S. God knows how many there are worldwide. It will all come to a stop soon."

"How's that?" Jeff asked.

"New legislation will be passed within the next decade that will require all coffins to be made biodegradable," Crage said.

Really? Scott said.

"Yes," Crage said. "It's something we need to do anyway for the environment and space concerns. We can't just keep expanding cemeteries forever. You'd be surprised how high up this all goes."

"I guess then we will just have to worry about climate change and all the other bad stuff we are doing to the planet," Mari said.

The group shared a laugh.

"What am I supposed to tell them at the office?" Jeff asked. The moment he spoke, the lights in the cemetery came back on and as he looked around, there wasn't a soul present other than the group he was standing with.

"Nothing is missing, nothing's out of place. See those guys," Crage pointed to several guys dressed as landscapers raking the grass. "They are going to cover our tracks the best they can. Tell your chief that all you spotted was the landscaping service maintaining the sites."

"What if anyone reports the strange lights and sounds?" Jeff asked.

"Tell them," Crage pointed around to the others in the group, "that it was a group of paranormal investigators doing a ghost hunt."

Louis, Joe, and Mari laughed.

"This is going to make a great story," Louis said.

"It was sure good to see all of you," Crage said. After several handshakes, he walked away.

Suddenly, Jeff's walkie talkie went off. "Officer Denton, this is home base. We have reports of strange lights and sounds coming in from around the cemetery. Is everything okay?"

"I'm out here with some paranormal investigators, they're looking into it as well," Jeff said. "So far, all we've seen is the landscaping service doing their job. I'll keep you informed if I see anything. Over and out."

"It will be light soon," Louis said. "I guess we should get some sleep since we are going to have another late one tonight."

"That's right, we better get going," Mari said. "We still have some stuff to set up." With that statement, Mari and Joe parted.

"I noticed you left your car at the house," Scott said to Louis.

"I walked here," Louis said.

"Do you need a ride back?"

"I'll take him back," Jeff said.

"Okay," Scott said. "I'll try to keep it down this morning so you can get some sleep."

"I'd appreciate that," Louis said.

Jeff and Louis began walking back to the road where his patrol car was parked. "I never expected a night like this. You knew about this all along?"

"Not exactly," Louis said. "I had some information about it and Crage invited me to witness it. I'm going to write a story about it; all fiction, of course."

"Of course," Jeff said. "Why are you looking at me like that?"

Louis stopped walking. "You know, you should come to the ghost hunt tonight. It'll be fun and you'll get to see everyone again."

Jeff started walking, "no way, I've had enough excitement for the weekend and my wife would kill me if I'm out another night."

"Bring her along," Louis said.

Jeff and Louis entered the patrol car and headed down the road as the sun began to rise in Canyon City, Colorado. Deep in the earth, bodies decomposed and gave the essence back to heal the energy that sustained the very life of the planet on which they were living.

51

THE VAMPIRE DETECTIVE AGENCY

I Fell in Love with a Vampire

BY: LOUIS PAUL DEGRADO

The following story was written as a play and will be presented as such. You will be provided a list of characters for your reference. During the story, I invite you to immerse yourself in the experience. Imagine that you are seated in a theatre, the lights are low, you have your favorite drink, some salty popcorn, and someone special by your side. You listen as the play begins and the characters take the stage.

Enjoy...

PS, in the event you are part of a group that wants to perform the play, please contact the author, www.LiteraryLou.com

The Vampire Detective Agency Volume 1 Notes:

Characters Sheet

Drake Ulah (yoolah): Detective, secretly he is a vampire that is over five-hundred years old. He is tired of feeling like he doesn't accomplish anything and has decided to use his skills to solve cases. He feels like no one knows him or knows who he is and is often depressed. He has watched the world he knows change many times and been witness to the death of those he loved. He only goes out at night so he makes excuses of why he can't do stuff during the day. He transforms into a bat when he travels.

Drake dresses in suits and is a proper gentleman. He does not bite people or hunt any longer. He uses fake blood drives to get his supply of blood and is often drinking "juice" boxes (really blood).

Lacie Starlight: Movie star, shining actress but humble in her demeanor. She is in the prime of her career but feels like someone is out to ruin her career. The movie she has been cast in is not a great one. She is starting to tire of the glitz and glamour and longs for love and someone to settle down with.

Lacie dresses like a movie star-extravagant with hair done and make-up

Adam Stauker: Older gentlemen who looks and acts like a slimy salesperson. He is the agent that represents Lacie but secretly, he is stalking her and is infatuated with her. He dresses like a stalker and if he wears a tie, it's a very thin tie. He is creepy, shifty, and uses too much hair gel. He flirts with Veronica whenever no one else is watching.

Bob: Drakes Silent partner (you'll find out why) Bob is an older gentleman who just retired and is not so happy to be out of retirement. He's good at eavesdropping, spying, blending in without being noticed as he's carelessly stealthy. Bob is not happy about his current situation but usually has a jovial and pleasant disposition. When Bob gets upset, it causes poltergeist-like activity.

Bob is always in the same clothes throughout and never changes.

Veronica Charm- Actress and Lacie's understudy. Veronica knows she is worth more than her current position is allowing her to be. She is stuck in a contract but desires to get out. She flirts with Adam when Lacie isn't watching. She is smart, witty, sometimes sarcastic. She dresses upscale and wears silk gloves, necklaces, and really fits the part of a movie star although the has yet to make it big.

Freddie Flicks- (could be guy or girl cast in this role) Movie Director that is nervous and behind schedule. He is currently in a slump and his current project, a Vampire love-story, "I Fell in love with a Vampire" is not going well and had many delays. Freddie dresses in odd colors of checkered suits/short pants and bow ties.

On the set, the Special effects is over budget and the movie has experienced many delays. The market is overrun with vampire love story movies and Freddie isn't sure this one will make the cut. He frets that it might be the end of his career.

Setting: (Remember, Drake only out at night!)

Room 1- Detective Agency: Three chairs and a desk and a file cabinet. A phone on the desk and a bell to indicate the door has opened. Props or furniture in the office is antique as Drake has been alive for Five-Hundred Years!

Room 2- Movie Set: Make up chair with mirror, Director's seat and two other chairs for actors/Actresses. There should also be a table with candles, books, glasses, and a knife (retractable fake knife) in the middle of the set.

Room 3- The street which will be the audience area the players can Interact in.

Scene 1: The Agency

SETTING: (The scene opens with our main character, Drake Ulah, moving a wooden sign inside the detective agency. The sign reads "Blood Drive Today Only. Inquire Inside." The agency is sparsely furnished with two high-back upholstered chairs on one side of a large dark-wood desk. On the other side of the desk is another high-back office chair. The outside door reads "Detective Agency." Drake stores the blood-drive sign and sits at his desk staring at the door hoping for his first client to come through it. His silent partner, Bob, is pacing around while Drake sits at his desk watching the phone and looking at the door.)

Bob: Don't you ever worry that someday someone will get suspicious of your blood drives?

Drake: Would you rather I suck the blood out of someone?

Bob: You did it to me?

Drake: And I am a reformed man. Besides, I could not do it, not these days with all the drugs, perfumes, after shaves and other sanitary issues. The Blood Drive allows me to screen for healthy donors; it's for a good cause after all, I am helping the community by solving cases.

Bob: How long can you keep paying for this office with no clients?

Drake: I've had five-hundred years to save. Plus, I have an extensive collection of antiques to sell if needed.

Bob: Well, I'd get ready to sell some more. Another day is coming to an end with no clients. Maybe we need to hit the street.

Drake: You know I have a sun-allergy.

Bob: Maybe more people would come if you started earlier instead of being open late.

Drake: But I do my best work at night. Besides, more crime happens at night. Lighten up, people just don't know about us yet. Maybe I should take out another add. Or use some of that social media stuff, Facelook or flighter.

Bob: You don't even have a cell phone, when are you going to join the modern age.

Drake: The modern age, (*sigh*). I miss the days when people had time to talk to each other. When lovers wrote letters that took effort and had meaning. I miss, (pulls out a tissue and wipes his right eye)

Bob: There, there, things will get better.

Drake: Does anything I do matter, does anyone care, is my heart alone again, is anyone there?

Bob: I'm here.

Drake: Be quiet, I'm reciting.

Bob: Ah, (puts his hands over his eyes and shakes his head.)

Drake: I cannot see the sun, I cannot feel the warmth of its rays
Oh, how hollow and cold are my days.

Bob: Like your heart.

Drake: Yes (Drake puts both hands on his heart) like my cold, barely beating heart. Have I nothing left to give? Have I no life left to live? What sign is there that I should go on? I hear no calling, I feel no warmth, I am, am...

Bob: Stop. You're depressing me. Why did you open a detective agency? Out of all the things we could have done, why this?

Drake: I've tried about everything: Doctor, lawyer, teacher, priest, executioner.

Bob: Executioner?!

Drake: Yes. The uniform helped hide my identity and the pay, well, let's just say I had all the blood I needed.

Bob: What were you before you became, well, you know.

Drake: A vampire? I was an inspiring playwright.

Bob: Oh, anything I would know?

Drake: You think Shakespeare did all of that himself? I waited tables and worked odd jobs to make a living. I never got anything I wrote on stage before, and then, well, you know.

 Bob: You didn't answer my question; why the detective agency?

Drake: I've always wanted to solve crimes. Joining the police would bring too much attention. Especially now with all the background checks, fingerprinting and stuff like that. Speaking of that, look what I got. (Drake reaches into his drawer and pulls out a fingerprint kit as he stands and walks to the front of the desk. Bob comes over to see.)

Drake: Here, touch this glass. (Drake points to a glass and Bob puts his hand around it but does not lift it off the desk. Drake takes a brush out of the kit and wipes the glass. Then he takes out a magnifying glass and raises the glass looking it over but seems to be unable to find anything.)

Bob: No fingerprint, right? Imagine that.

(The bell rings. Bob opens and Lacie walks in. She notices Drake but cannot figure out why the door opened. She steps forward. Drake turns and looks at her while Bob stands holding the door open.)
Drake: Sorry, the blood drive was last week.
Lacie: Blood drive? I thought this was a detective agency.
Drake: Would you PLEASE close the door.
Bob: Yes, sorry, I don't want to let any light in. With your serious sun allergy.
Lacie: (Turns to shut the door but it is already shut, by Bob)
(Although Bob speaks through the scene, Lacie never acknowledges him)
Drake: May I help you?
Lacie: Oh, there you are. It's so dark in here. Are you the detective?
Drake: (Stands erect and walks around his desk, straightens his suit coat, and puts out his hand) Yes, I am Drake Ulah, Detective. And who do I have the pleasure of meeting.
Lacie: My Name is Lacie Starlight and I need some help.
Drake: (Takes Lacie's hand the old-fashioned way and kisses her knuckle.) Please have a seat.
(Bob and Lacie head toward the same seat and Drake heads Lacie off)
Drake: Please, over here. (Drake motions Lacie to the chair opposite and holds the back until she is seated. Bob sits and shakes his head as Drake takes a seat behind his desk.)
Drake: Now, how can I help you?
Lacie: I think someone is trying to KILL ME!
(Dramatic Music Sound)
Bob: Probably because you tried to take their seat.
Drake: (Ignores Bob) What makes you think that?
Lacie: I am on the movie set for "I FELL IN LOVE WITH A VAMPIRE."
Bob: That explains the Movie Star name.
(Drake looks in Bob's direction with a disapproving look, eyebrows lowered, and then back at Lacie)
Lacie: The movie has had many delays and problems on the set. Just last week, a stage light mysteriously fell at a spot where I was supposed to be standing. Yesterday, the male lead playing the vampire came to my dressing room to talk to me. While we were talking, he said he was

thirsty, so I offered him a drink that was just delivered to my room. After he drank it, he fell dead!
Drake: Dead?
Lacie: Dead!
(Dramatic Music)
Lacie: The drink was poisoned! At least that's what the police have told us.
Bob: Sounds like we have our first case.
Drake: Yes, it does.
Lacie: Yes, it does what?
Drake: Oh, sorry. I mean it does sound like a case.
Lacie: Oh please, Mr. Ulah.
Drake: You can call me Drake.
Lacie: Drake, (Lacie reaches her hands across the table and grabs Drakes hands) Please, help me.
Drake: (Drake looks down at the hands touching, an expression of emotion and loss crosses his face.) I will have to check my schedule. (Drake opens an empty schedule book in front of him making sure Lacie cannot see the inside which is blank)
Bob: Schedule? What are you talking about? This is our first CASE!
Drake: Be quiet please.
(Lacie pulls her hands back as if offended.)
Drake: I'm sorry, I mean I'd be quite pleased to take your case. (Drakes stands) I am booked until tomorrow evening. Would that be soon enough?
Lacie: (Stands) We are back on the set tomorrow afternoon and shooting into the late evening according to our director, Freddie Flicks. I can let the guard know that you will be coming by.
(Drake walks Lacie to the door)
Drake: Don't worry, I can get on the set.
Bob: He can turn into a bat and fly right on in.
Drake: Don't tell anyone you've hired me. That way I can get a look around before anyone knows who I am.
(Lacie Nods)
Drake: I will see you then. And don't worry, we handle this kind of thing all the time.

(Bob snickers in the background as Drake gives him a dirty look and then turns to watch Lacie walk away. Bob gets up and opens the door while Lacie is looking down. She notices the door is open and is baffled)
Bob: Charming young lady.
Drake: I'll say. (Sighs)
Bob: Oh my, are you falling for your first and only client? Isn't that a conflict of interest?
(Drake returns to his desk and pulls out a leather bag and starts filling it full of detective stuff like his fingerprint kit, gloves, magnifying glass, and binoculars)
Drake: No. I am not investigating her, and she is not married. Now, get off that subject. What are your thoughts about the case?
Bob: I think based on what she said, someone may be out to get her. We just need to find out who and why.
Drake: Now that you mention that 'what she said,' I would appreciate it in the future if you don't speak to me while I am interviewing a client. It's disruptive.
Bob: I thought we were partners in this.
Drake: We are but, it's distracting, and I can't focus on the conversation I'm having with the client.
Bob: You know, I don't even have my own desk.
Drake: (Takes out a leather attaché and begins putting things in it like a magnifying glass, fingerprint kit, and some other odds and ends- adlib and have him put something funny in it like a rubber chicken or something like that)
Bob: Are you ignoring me?
Drake: No Bob, I'm just getting ready to go out on my first case. Maybe we can stop and look at desks on our way back.
(Drake stands, grabs a heavy black umbrella, and exits)
END OF SCENE

Scene 2: "I FELL IN LOVE WITH A VAMPIRE."

SETTING: ON the movie set of "I fell in Love with a Vampire."
(Drake is currently a bat and is flying around in the audience as the actor uses the bat prop. He lands backstage and stands, straightening out his suit. Bob appears beside him. They are on the opposite side of Lacie who is there along her understudy, Veronica Charm, and the Director, Freddie Flicks. Freddie is standing while Lacie and Veronica are sitting down.)

Drake: Bob, keep your eyes and ears open. Look around and see if you can overhear or see anything suspicious.
Freddie: (Freddie Flicks notices Drake on the set. And hurriedly walks toward him) Finally, you're here. I have been waiting all day for you. (looks Drake over) I guess you'll do but I would prefer someone taller and more, well, more fit in the upper body.
Drake: Pardon me?
Freddie: Do you have any experience playing the role of a vampire?
Bob: Does he? He's the perfect fit.
Drake: I thought I told you to look around.
(Bob smiles and starts walking around the area)
Freddie: Look around?
Drake: Sorry, I meant, I'm here to have a look around.
Freddie: Aren't you from the acting agency?
(Drake shakes his head)
Freddie: (puts a hand on top of his head and closes his eyes as though he has a headache. Then whispers) Are you the investigator from the insurance company?
Drake: Yes (raises his right hand with his index finger gesturing) I am Detective Drake Ulah, they sent me to investigate.
Freddie: I suppose you'll want to speak with everyone who was here on the set the day of the incident.
Drake: Yes. I need to speak to everyone who was on the set that day.
Freddie: Well, I'll have to round them up. Except for that guy (points to the audience.) He wasn't here the day it happened. I don't even know why he's here. Why are you here? (adlib, banter with audience)
Veronica: (Veronica has been listening to what is going on and finally stands to meet Drake) With the security these days, almost anyone can

get on the set, I mean, do they look like actresses and actors to you (points at audience).
Drake: And you are?
Freddie: Let me introduce you to Veronica Charm. She's Lacie's understudy.
Veronica: (puts out her hand and Drake takes it and kisses her knuckle)
Drake: Charming name.
Veronica: Oh, Darling, it's such a relief to have someone down here from the studio's insurance company. I just don't feel safe here any longer. Do they have any idea who's responsible for the dreadful things happening around here?
Drake: (Stands Erect) That is what I'm here to find out.
Veronica: (Flutters her eyes) Oh, my. You sure you're not an actor with that profile.
Freddie: Gather around everyone.
(Everyone but Bob comes closer to Freddie. Lacie's agent, Adam Stauker, enters but stays back watching)
Freddie: This is Detective Drake....
Drake: Ulah
Freddie: (Raises an eyebrow at the unusual name as he says it) Detective Drake Ulah, sent from the movie studio's insurance company. He's going to ask a few questions and I want you all to cooperate.
(While Freddie is introducing Drake, Lacie raises her hand and Drake puts his finger to his mouth in a motion to have her remain quiet so she puts her hand down)
Adam: (Adam Stauker steps forward) An investigator? It's about time this studio does something. All these setbacks are setting back the career of my star actress. I demand some results!
Lacie: Please Adam (she stands and touches his shoulder as he turns and looks to her with lustful eyes) let this man, what was your name?
Drake: Detective Drake Ulah.
Lacie: Can we just let him do his job so we can get rolling again?
Drake: (Drake steps forward looking at Adam) You are?
Adam: I am Adam Stauker, movie star agent. Lacie is my biggest star.
Veronica: Ha! Falling star maybe.
(The outburst by Veronica attracts attention)
Adam: What did you say about my star?

Veronica: Oh, I mean, ha, look what I found, a shiny penny in my pocket that I didn't know was there. Isn't that good luck or something. (she takes it to Adam who is stern at first, but then raises an eyebrow at Veronica's flirtatious look)

Drake: I'll start my questioning with him. (Drake points to Adam as the rest take seats and Bob mulls around them. Drake takes a small notebook and pencil from his bag that he brought.) You are Adam Stauker?

Adam: Yes, I am.

Drake: Please take a seat (Drake sits in the Director's chair) What is your relationship with Miss Lacie Starlight?

Adam: I've been her agent since she started.

Drake: Have you noticed anything suspicious around here lately?

Adam: You're talking about the accidents? (Drake nods) This movie has been vexed from the start. The day we arrived on set, there was a fire. Then, one of the lights fell on the set and almost hit Lacie. If she hadn't moved offstage to fix her make up at that precise moment, it would have been over. I suppose you're here about the poison in Lacie's drink that killed her co-star?

Drake: Yes, I heard about it. Did they know what was in it?

Adam: It was a chemical mixture of several household items, all found around the set; mixed in a blend that was not bad to taste at first, but the aftertaste was, (pause and look toward audience) TO DIE FOR.

Drake: Interesting.

Adam: I would say there's something suspicious all right. (Leans in and lowers his voice) You know, Freddie's career has been in a slump.

Drake: If his career is in a slump, why would you let your number one star be in this movie?

Adam: (Dismissive) Everyone's doing vampire movies these days. It's almost a requirement to be in at least one.

Freddie has a lot to lose if this movie flops but a lot to gain if it doesn't get made. The studio has insurance on him and the movie. He gets paid even if it doesn't get made. Sounds like they don't trust him, and I wouldn't either.

Drake: How's that?

Adam: As the director, he has access to everything around here, know what I mean. I would start looking closely at Freddie Flicks.

(On the other side of the stage, Freddie is sitting and talking to himself while Bob listens)

Freddie: This movie is going to be the end of me. Sure, the studio will pay me off if it flops, even more if it doesn't get made, but then my career as a director is over. Why'd I ever let that magician Kyle Groves talk me into making a vampire movie?

Drake: Mr. Flicks, I'm ready for you.

(Freddie and Adam Change places.)

Adam: (As stands he whispers) Remember what I said, I'd look closely at Freddie Flicks.

Freddie: (Takes a seat) I hope this isn't going to take too long. We have a schedule to meet.

Drake: I've heard about all the suspicious stuff going on around here: the fire on the set, the light falling, the poison in the drink. That's a lot of strange accidents wouldn't you agree?

Freddie: No one told you about the notes and the flowers?

Drake: What notes? What flowers?

Freddie: Lacie found love notes and flowers outside her dressing room. We suspected Adam but the notes were never signed, and they were all anonymous deliveries.

Drake: What made you think it was Adam?

Freddie: One night, I heard arguing. Adam stormed out of Lacie's dressing room. After their fight, the notes and flowers stopped. That is, they stopped right up until the day before the poisoning incident.

Drake: (Taking notes) What happened then?

Freddie: Another set of flowers came but they were dead roses. I had the security guard bring them to my office instead of delivering them to Lacie. The note on it read, "If our love is dead like these roses and I can't have you, no one can."

Drake: No signature?

Freddie: (looks to audience and uses his hands palms toward audience) *Anonymous.*

Drake: Do you still have the note? I can check it for fingerprints or match the handwriting.

Freddie: Sorry, I didn't keep the horrible thing.

Drake: Lacie doesn't know about the last delivery?

Freddie: Heavens No. She was having enough trouble already and I needed to get this movie on track. (Freddie leans in closer) Did you know Adam took extra insurance money out on Lacie? I also know he studied Chemistry in college. If I were you, I would take a close look at Adam Stauker! I mean look at him. (Drake and Freddie turn and look at Adam) Studied chemistry. The drink was poisoned. He's always watching her like, like a Stalker!

(Drake and Freddie turn and see Adam up against a corner fixated on Lacie as she brushes her hair)

Drake: Is it true, Mr. Flicks, that you make more money if this movie isn't completed than if it is completed and tanks?

Freddie: (Pause) Please don't say that word.

Drake: "Tanks?"

Freddie: No, "Money." This movie is way over budget and now I need to cast a new lead for the vampire. And why would I want this movie to fail? Then my career as a director would be over.

Drake: Thank you for your time. I think we're done here. Miss Veronica Charm, would you please come here and take a seat.

Freddie: (Leans in one more time) Remember what I told you about Adam.

(Veronica and Freddie change places)

Drake: What can you tell me about what has been happening on the set.

Veronica: Mister Drake, if that is your real name, and if you are really an investigator, you would already know what is going on here.

Drake: (Eyebrows raised) I am an investigator and that is my real name. I suggest you cooperate and tell me what you know about all the accidents around here.

Veronica: Oh, I like a tough guy. Maybe we can get together later. (winks) Lacie Starlight is what is going on around here.

Drake: Lacie?

Veronica: Oh, yes. See, she is at the top of her career, darling. But the problem with being at the top is there is only one way to go from there. (Gestures by putting her hand up and then swirling it down like a falling plane) She knows this role will damage her career. Her agent over there, (gestures) Adam, hasn't got her best in mind. He's too hurt because she's spurned him. I have the same problem with my agents. Freddie over there (nods in Freddie's direction) has more to gain if this movie flops, which it will, terrible writing. They should have hired someone better for the writing like that up and coming Louis Paul DeGrado. Anyway, with all this bad mojo (gestures shaking both hands in the air in front of her), no one here really has a chance or desire to make this thing work. It's no wonder so much is going wrong.

Drake: Mojo? You think the set is cursed?

Veronica: Yes. With so much negativity on set well, sometimes I find it hard to breathe.

Drake: So, you think this is all bad luck and no one is out to hurt Lacie?

Veronica: On the contrary, darling, I think everyone is out to hurt her, including Lacie herself. She just doesn't know it.

Drake: Thank you Miss Charm, I think we are through. Just one more thing to ask you. What would you gain if this movie didn't make it or if Lacie was to have an unfortunate accident?

Veronica: I am under contract to be Miss Lacie's understudy. If she were injured, I would be the star of this awful thing. If it were cancelled, I would have to go to whatever project she would take next.

Drake: Thank you Miss Charm. Miss Lacie Starlight, you're next.

(Veronica rises from her seat but leans in and whispers in Drakes ear giving him full view of her neck. Drake's face is turned toward Audience and they can see him glancing and being tempted by her neck)

Veronica: (Whispering) I would be careful around Lacie Starlight.

(Veronica moves back to her seat as Lacie sits in the chair by Drake. Drake composes himself. Bob takes this time to walk over and listen in to the conversation)

Lacie: (leans in) You're working for the insurance company?

Drake: Of course not. It was merely a matter of mistaken identity that I went along with.

Bob: You better hope the real investigator doesn't show up and bust you.

Drake: It's all under control.

Lacie: Pardon me?

Drake: I mean to say it gives me the perfect cover to ask questions without bringing suspicion on you.

Lacie: Have you found out anything?

Drake: Plenty. Just go along with the questioning and we can get together later to discuss the details.

Lacie: (Raises her voice) Yes, detective, how can I help you?

Drake: How come you didn't tell me about the flowers and the notes?
Lacie: I didn't think it was important.
Bob: Maybe she didn't want you to know she had a love interest.
Drake: Who were they from?
Lacie: A secret admirer.
Drake: Not Adam?
(Bob looks toward Adam)
Lacie: I suppose it could have been him, but he never admitted it. He has been acting strange lately and there was that one night…
Drake: The night that you argued?
(Bob turns back to the conversation)
Lacie: Yes, how did you know that?
Drake: I'm an investigator, it's my job to find out what is going on.
Bob: Oh please, someone told you that.
Drake: Would you please be quiet.
Lacie: (Leans back as though offended and then leans forward and talks in a lower voice that Drake can't hear)
Drake: Speak up please.
Lacie: (Irritated) I thought you said to be quiet? Which is it?
Drake: Sorry, please speak louder.
Lacie: Adam would never hurt me.
Drake: Tell me then, is there anyone here who would benefit from you being hurt?
Lacie: Veronica has it in for me.
Bob: Ask her why. Veronica looks like she could go out and be a star on her own. Why is she Lacie's understudy?
Drake: Why Veronica? Couldn't she go out and make her own career?
Lacie: No. She signed a contract to be my understudy. Until I don't have a part, she doesn't have enough time to make a movie of her own. That's why I think we need to investigate her. When we started working together, she was so sweet and…
Bob: Charming?
Drake: That's enough.
Lacie: I'm sorry, are we done?
Drake: No, I mean, I think I've got enough information here. I'll see what I can find out. Until then, I'm going to study these notes and I'll get back to

you tomorrow. (Stands) Thank you everybody. I have enough here (raises his notebook) to make my report.
Freddie: Okay people, let's get back to work. We have schedule to meet.
END OF SCENE

Scene 3: PUZZLING PREDICAMENT

SETTING: (At the detective agency the next day, Drake and Bob are discussing the case. Both are at Drake's desk looking over a pile of notes he took. They have a chart on a dry erase board, or something similar, listing the names of the potential suspects: Lacie Starlight, Adam Stauker, Freddie Flicks, Veronica Charm, Secret Admirer.)

Drake: (pacing, he looks at the notes and at Bob) What did I tell you about being disruptive when I am investigating? The whole time we were there you were a distraction.

Bob: I was investigating!

Drake: You kept talking to me.

Bob: What if I need to ask a question? It's not like they can hear me. I thought we were partners on this! I don't even have my own desk. (Bob is pacing again and appears upset. The glass falls off the table by itself and Drake picks it up and puts it back on the table)

Drake: The desk again? We are partners. Now calm down before you break something.

Bob: Break something? I wouldn't be here if it weren't for you.

Drake: Hey, not fair. How many times do I have to apologize? I was new. I didn't think I took that much blood.

Bob: You killed me!

Drake: For that you decided to haunt me? Why didn't you go to the light?

Bob: I don't know, I was upset.

Drake: And how come I am the only one that can see you?

Bob: When you die, you are given a choice: go to the light or remain behind.

Drake: And you remained as a ghost?

Bob: Yes.

Drake: But there are a lot of ghosts that many people see. How come I am the only one that can see you?

Bob: Oh, that's where it gets interesting. (Bob pulls out a brochure from his pocket, puts it in front of Drake) See, you have a choice; you can haunt a place like a cemetery or building, even a bridge or stretch of road. Then, you can appear to a lot of people.

Drake: I never knew. (Drake looks at the brochure in front of him)

Bob: The drawback is you can never leave; you are bound to that location.

Drake: I'm going to guess that's not what you did since you can move around.

Bob: (Bob puts his finger on his nose and points at Drake) I picked haunting a person. With that, you only appear to that person but, you can follow him or her wherever they go.

Drake: Lucky me.

Bob: Yes, lucky you. You already know about paranormal creatures and aren't even scared of me. My haunting is a waste and I'm stuck here. (Bob sits in his chair and starts crying) Death is so meaningless.

Drake: There, there. (comforts Bob) Although I'm not scared of you, you do annoy me quite a bit, does that count?

Bob: (Sniffling, Nods) That'll have to do.

Drake: I'm lucky to have you; you're the perfect silent partner. Especially for a detective agency.

Bob: (still sniffling) How so?

Drake: No one can see you. You can eavesdrop and no one will know you're there.

Bob: (Dramatic) NO ONE KNOWS I EXIST (starts crying again)

Drake: That's not what I mean. Look, you can enter places without being seen. We don't have to break and enter. I think we got a good thing starting here.

Bob: (Stops crying) You do?

Drake: I do.

Bob: And you are going to get me my own desk?

Drake: Yes, I will get you your own desk.

Bob: With a nameplate and all?

Drake: A nameplate, a chair, even a wastepaper basket.

Bob: What about one of those desk calendars? And a mug with some sarcastic saying on it?

Drake: Can we get back to the case now?

Bob: (nods yes and looks down at the notes Drake has on his desk) That's a lot of notes. Why didn't you use that power thing you do instead of asking all those questions?

Drake: You mean my power to Mesmerize? (strange music sound)

Bob: Yes, why didn't you do the old whammy so you could tell if someone was lying?

Drake: I wanted to do things proper. I am trying to improve my investigative skills. Tell me, what did you overhear?

Bob: Why do you have Lacie's name on the board as a suspect? Isn't she our client?

Drake: Something Veronica said to me made me think that she may be the cause of all of this, and she doesn't know it.

Bob: (looking at list) Freddie Flicks is on his way out. The past two movies he worked on tanked. He only took this one because he's out of options.

Drake: So, he is not a suspect (goes to board and starts erasing Freddie Flick's name)

Bob: On the contrary, he had the studio take out a massive insurance plan on the movie in case it doesn't go forward, they must buy it out. He gains more if they cancel it.

Drake: He's already lost his leading man, easy to replace as he was an unknown, but if he loses his star (Circles Lacie's name and draws a star by it and then write's Freddie Flicks name back on the board)

Bob: That's not all. I found scissors in Veronica's dressing room. I couldn't tell for sure, but it looked to have fibers on it. You know, like from cutting the rope the stage-light was hanging from.

Drake: She is wearing a wig for the set; it could have been fibers from the wig. But (puts his forefinger up and pauses in thought) she did mention that she was ready for a career of her own. Did you get any of the fibers?

Bob: No, but you can fly back there tonight and then we can compare them. Maybe Veronica is tired of living in Lacie's shadow. She is the understudy and Lacie herself was suspicious of her. Why are you underlining Adam's name?

Drake: (At the board underlining Adam's name) Lacie thinks Adam is harmless but he never takes his eyes off her. I've been alive for five-hundred years, I can spot unrequited love. There's nothing worse than a lover's scorn or in this case, a scorned lover.

Bob: Yes, but would it amount to Murder!

(Dramatic Music)

Bob: Maybe you suspect Adam because you are falling for Lacie Starlight, starbrite, kissy, kissy in the night. You should know better than to believe in love at first sight.

Drake: There is nothing more romantic. But what do I have to offer her...?

Bob: Oh no, here it comes. Come on, it's not that bad.

Drake: I suck blood.

Bob: So, I can't eat at all. You got a lot going for you; you are immortal, almost a god.

Drake: Not really, I can't eat stake (holds up the pencil in his hand and motions it towards his heart)

Bob: You have powers: Heightened senses of smell, taste, blood senses. You can tell if someone is lying, and you are exceptionally good at puzzles.

Drake: I cannot heal the sick or flood the world.

Bob: Okay, so maybe not a god but you can fly, and you have super strength. You're like, like, AN AVENGER!

Drake: Yes, that's it. A blood sucking avenger.

Bob: I'm trying to cheer you up.

Drake: I would be happier if we had a definite lead in this case. Right now, EVERYONE we've spoken too is a suspect. Including our client. (Drake circles all the names and then points to random audience member) Even that lady over there looks suspicious.

Bob: I think that's because she was sneaking extra snacks. Yes, I saw you. (points to her and nods his head)

Drake: (puts the markers down and sits at his desk) Oh, just admit it, we can't solve this case. (Drake puts his head down on the top of his desk. The phone rings)

Drake: This is the Night Avenger Detective Agency, Drake Ulah Speaking. (He winks at Bob excited with the new name he's created for the agency)

Lacie: (offstage, voice only) Drake, is that you?

Drake: Yes, Lacie, it is I. I just came up with that new name, what do you think?

Lacie: I think it is, uh, nice.

Drake: Thank you, now what can I do for you?

Lacie: I was wondering if you had any leads on my case.

Drake: (Looks at the board in front of him that's a mess and lies) Yes, we have several leads. I was just getting ready to call you.

Lacie: I'm down at the studio practicing my lines. It's just me here. Do you want to come by?

Drake: I will be there in a flash. (Hangs up phone, Whoosh, bat comes out and Drake flies to Studio)

Bob: (By himself he sits and examines his hands. He slowly notices the audience is looking at him and starts getting nervous. He stands and

moves and notices people following him. Nervous laugh) Huh huh, wooo (spooky hands) and goes off stage.
END OF SCENE

Scene 4: A Horrible Accident

SETTING: (Back on the movie set Drake flies through the audience as a bat and then appears from the back of the set)

Drake: Good Evening, Miss Starlight.

Lacie: (Sitting and reading her script, she turns quickly, surprised) Wow, you got down here fast.

Drake: We are alone, no?

Lacie: Yes. We are alone, now we can talk. Did you find out who could be doing this?

Drake: (Approaches Lacie) As I said, we have some definite leads but not one prime suspect.

Lacie: We?

Drake: Yes, uh, I mean 'we' as in you and…I…as we are in this together.

Lacie (grabs his hands as she stands and moves close to him.) I was hoping you had better news.

Drake: It will be just a matter of days. It seems all of you have a reason to see this movie fail.

Lacie: What do you mean?

Drake: I'll explain. You think Veronica wants you out of her way so she can become the star.

Lacie: I don't know why she just doesn't leave? (breaks free and turns away from Drake)

Drake: She is bound by a contract to be your understudy. Unless something happens to you, she cannot be the star. And that's just the start. Freddie Flicks' career is hanging by a thread. The movie studio took out extra insurance on the movie in case it fails. He can make enough money to get out of the business if the movie flops. Of course, he denies he wants this.

Lacie: If Adam found out, well.

Drake: That's another thing, did you know Adam has doubled his insurance policy on you?

Lacie: (waves Drake's warning off as she turns) Oh, he has insurance on all his big stars. I wouldn't' worry about Adam. He's had an eye for me for a long time.

Drake: Oh, he has?

Lacie: Yes, but I would never mix business with pleasure. (She turns and looks longingly at Drake and steps closer to him) Not at my place of work.

Drake: Of course not.

Lacie: So, if everyone is a suspect, who is your prime suspect?

Drake: We are working on it, but it may take some more time.

Lacie: You said "we" again. What can I do to help?

Drake: Watch for anything suspicious and report it to me immediately.

Lacie: (moves to the table and picks up her script) I don't suppose you have time to help practice the scene I was reading. It's, a love scene. (she hands Drake the script. Bob appears.)

Bob: There you are. I haven't seen you fly that fast since, (puts forefinger to temple in thinking motion) Actually, I've never seen you fly that fast.

Drake: (Glances at Bob and raises his shoulders then turns back to Lacie) Of course I am willing to help. It may even give me insight to the reason someone might be trying to derail this movie.

Lacie: Do you have any experience acting?

Drake: Well, a long time ago when I was in France, I was a playwright and (Bob walks up and smacks him) No, no, not really any acting experience.

Lacie: That's fine. You are playing the part of the vampire, is that okay?

Bob: No problem, he fits the part. He can even do the flying bat scene.

Drake: Would you just stop!

Lacie: Pardon me?"

Drake: I mean, would you just stop right there where you are standing because the, uh, light is just glimmering down on you there.

Lacie: Oh, well, thank you. Here, take the script. I know all my lines.

Drake: (Takes the script and walks over to where Bob is standing to shoo him away. Lacie looks at him as he turns his motions into stretching his arms) Just let me warm up.

Lacie (Lacie closes her eyes as though meditating)

Drake: Is something wrong?

Lacie: No, just concentrating. This is how I warm up. Are you ready?

Drake: (nods. Both move to center stage around a small, round table that has candles, books and a tray of cheese and crackers with a knife. Lacie starts on the opposite side from Drake)

Lacie: I know what you are!

Drake: (Surprised) You know what I am?

(Lacie points to the script)

Drake: Oh, sorry. Give me just a second. (Drake turns his back to Lacie, clears his throat, silently reads the script, and then stands erect and turns around.) Please start again.
Lacie: Can you do an accent?
Bob: Uh, oh, here we go with the accent.
Drake: Accent?
Lacie: Yes, the vampire has a foreign accent.
Bob: Tell him why.
Lacie: It makes it more believable.
Drake: (Turns away from Lacie and grimaces and clenches his fists. When he speaks, it's with an accent for the scene) Very well. Let us begin.
Lacie: I know what you are!
Drake: No one really knows what I am, behind this, this, mask of a man.
Lacie: Everything you said to me is a lie, that is what I know. You've had many loves.
Drake: Yes, I have, you might as well know. How could I not have loved? I have been alive for five-hundred years.
Lacie: Two, it's two-hundred years. (points to script)
Drake: Sorry, two-hundred years. But none of them compared to you.
Lacie: I suppose they are all dead now.
Drake: Yes.
Lacie: Did you kill them?
Drake: Only for the sake of mercy, when they were sick, dying.
Lacie: Do you have someone now?
Drake: Not for a long time. I got tired of falling in love and watching it fade away. That is why you must understand how special you are for me to take that chance again!
Lacie: How could I love you? You're telling me you are a cold-blooded killer. (She puts her hand on his heart) See, no heartbeat. You have no soul. If you are dead, then be dead to me. (Lacie slowly moves around the table closer to Drake and grabs the knife on the cheese tray)
Drake: Yes, I am dead. But my soul aches for you. What can I do to prove my love for you?
Lacie: I want to know it's real. If you are already dead, this shouldn't hurt a bit! (She takes the knife and stabs Drake in the heart. The knife doesn't retract. Lacie tries to move it but its stuck) Oh, my, what have I done?

Drake: (Grabs the knife by the handle) Is that supposed to be a real knife? (pulls out the knife that is now full of blood and examines it)

(Bob rushes to Drakes side)

Lacie: We need to get you to the hospital!

Bob: Did she just try to kill you?

Drake: Don't be silly. You didn't know the prop was a real knife, did you?

Lacie: Of course not! It's supposed to be a prop and retract.

Drake: It's okay (pulls out a handkerchief and puts it over the wound) it didn't go very deep.

Lacie: (looks at the length of the knife and the blood noticing it must have gone deep) You are in shock; we need an ambulance.

Bob: Oh, don't worry about him, he's kind of impervious to stuff like that.

Drake: Shut up, would you.

Lacie: Beg your pardon?

Drake: Sorry, I mean, keep it down. We don't want anyone to hear us.

Lacie: Why?

Drake: This knife is supposed to be a prop, right?

Lacie: (nods) Yes, of course.

Drake: Someone must have changed it to set you up. Understand?

Lacie: No. I don't understand. Are you sure you are not in shock?

Bob: He's fine, barely bleeds at all.

Drake: Did anyone know you were going to be here tonight?

Lacie: I didn't tell anyone on the set. Other than the security guard outside, no one knows I am here but you.

Bob: And me.

Drake: (looks at Bob) Take a look around, would you?

Bob (exits)

Lacie: You want me to see if anyone is here?

Drake: No, stay here with me. From the script we are reading, you did exactly what you were supposed to do. It's my conclusion that someone has switched out the knife for a real knife.

Lacie: But why would someone do that?

Drake: If they can't kill you, they can frame you for murder.

Bob: (enters) Or she is a murderer. There is no one else on the set. You'd be the second lead man to die while working with her. Maybe the poisoning wasn't so...Accidental?

Lacie: (puts a hand to arm to her forehead in shock and nearly faints. Drake helps her to a chair)
Drake: It's clear someone wants you out of the way.
Bob: Or she (points to Lacie) is the murderer! But if you're right and you find the culprit, I'll admit you are a good detective and she's not a murderer.
Drake: And I'll say, "I told you so."
Lacie: What did you tell me?
Drake: I mean, don't tell anyone. What time are you shooting this scene tomorrow?
Bob: I wouldn't use the term "shooting" around here.
Lacie: Eight in the evening. Freddie wants everything shot at night just as it's supposed to be nighttime in the movie.
Drake: Good. All we must do is come up with a plan to find out who had access to the prop and then…
Lacie: Yes? (Lacie stands and comes close to Drake)
Drake: We expose the person who has been out to ruin your career!
Lacie: (Embraces Drake) Thank you! I feel safer already.
Drake: Should I escort you home?
Lacie: Don't you think you should get someone to look at that wound?
Bob: Oh no, it's probably already healed. Part of his vampire magic.
Drake: (raises his voice) Would you PLEASE (notices Lacie looking at him) not worry about me and have a great evening. I will see you tomorrow.
Lacie: Aren't you leaving?
Drake: I'm going to look around. You know, do some investigating before I leave.
(Lacie exits and Drake watches her)
Bob: (Sits down where Lacie had been sitting) Oh my, you really are hopeless. That scene you just did, it was too real for you.
Drake: Yes, Bob. Now I'm hopelessly in love. She really is like…starlight.
Bob: You know this can't end well; you will either suck her blood and kill her or outlive her and watch her grow old and die. Besides, she might suspect something when tomorrow you show up without stitches or any sign that you were stabbed IN THE HEART!
Drake: I am not going to dwell on that right now. If we don't find out who is trying to kill her or frame her, there won't be any Lacie Starlight left to worry about.

Bob: Okay. Remember, you are the second leading man that almost met a deadly fate. We need to be open to the fact that Lacie herself is a suspect.
Drake: Very well.
Bob: All the suspects should be here tomorrow except for...
Drake: Adam Stauker. We will have to call him and tell him that we have some information. That way he will meet us here.
Bob: That should get our suspects here. Except for, (delay) that guy! (point to random audience member and go closer to him) He looks suspicious and you know what?
Drake: What Bob?
Bob: I think he can hear me. (Get closer to the audience member) You know what else?
Drake: What Bob?
Bob: I think he can see me? (Speaks to Audience member) Do you see Dead People?
Drake: I hear Lacie's car in the lot. I must go now.
Bob: Where are you going?
Drake: I'm going to make sure Lacie gets home safe. I'll see you back at the agency.
(Actor playing Drake uses bat prop to fly around the stage and audience here)
Bob: (Addresses audience) Okay, now it's your turn to hear dead people. This is your chance to solve the mystery before the final scene. Take out your clue sheet and fill out who you think is the guilty party.
END OF SCENE and Audience Break

THE VAMPIRE DETECTIVE AGENCY WORKSHEET

Who	Motive (why would they do it)	Supporting Evidence

Scene 5: PREPARATION

SETTING: (Back at detective agency Drake is sitting at his desk looking at a picture of Lacie from a newspaper or magazine article)

Drake: Oh Lacie, you are my shining star, I wish to be with you wherever you are

Your heart is full of blood, fresh, warm, tasty blood. (clears throat) It warms my cool, lonely heart. Yes, I said lonely. (if audience doesn't respond with an "ahh" continue) Really Lonely. Really, really, LONELY.

Audience: Ahhh (hold up "AHHH" sign if needed to get response)

Drake: Thank you. People think vampire's suck. Well, we do, but we are just being who we are. It's a lonely life full of, well, loneliness. I can never relax or rest. Not truly. The world is full of vampire hunters and teenage seductresses with werewolf friends. It's never safe.

Bob: (Appears) Did you see anything last night?

Drake: I saw Adam Stauker

Bob: Lacie's agent?

Drake: Yes, he was outside in the studio parking lot. He followed her all the way home and then sat outside in his car most of the night. He got out of his car and started to go toward her window.

Bob: Let me guess, a bat flew by and he got spooked?

Drake: (laughs) You know me too well.

Bob: That's creepy. I bet you wanted too (Bob uses his fingers to make like a vampire fang going for his neck)

Drake: (pulls out a juice box, fake blood, and pokes a straw into it) You have no idea.

Bob: We still have no clear suspect.

Drake: Yes, but if Adam is stalking Lacie, he may be preventing anyone from getting close to her. I just need to prove my point.

Bob: How are you going to solve this case if you are so distracted?

Drake: Distracted?

Bob: Oh, Please. You are so infatuated with Miss Starlight (points to the magazine Drake was looking at). I knew she had you when you did the vampire accent rehearsing the scene. You know, the accent that every vampire has in every vampire movie that drives you CRAZY.

Drake: Yes, I know, Bob. Not every vampire has an accent. Some of us are from (insert your town name you want too here). But I didn't mind doing it with her.

Bob: How do you plan on drawing out the suspect?
Drake: By doing that scene again with Lacie. Whoever planted the knife will be watching, expecting the knife to be real.
Bob: Do they have a lead for the vampire part already?
Drake: They do now. (Drake picks up the phone) Freddie Flicks please. Freddie?
Freddie: (Voice only off screen) This is Freddie Flicks.
Drake: This is investigator Drake Ulah, we met the other day. Do you have a lead for the scene you are shooting today?
Freddie: No. Not yet.
Drake: (does accent when he speaks this line) Well, search no more. I can play the part and I have read the script.
Freddie: I don't know if we can find a costume in time. The original costume was still on the actor who, you know, died. We could probably do some make-up.
Drake: Don't worry, I have my own attire. One more thing, can you make sure that man, Adam Stauker is there to witness my performance.
Freddie: I will, dear, but you should know, Adam only represents certain types of stars. Those with, how would you say, a bustier profile than yourself.
Drake: Still, I would like him to be there. I will see you tonight.
END OF SCENE

Scene 6: An Accident? Or was it?

SETTING: (We are back on the movie set and Drake has convinced Freddie to let him stand in for the part of the vampire in the same scene he and Lacie were practicing the previous night. Freddie, Lacie and Veronica are on the set and Adam has been called)

Freddie: Okay everyone, take your places. We are practicing the love scene. Let's see if we can get through it tonight.

Lacie: How are we going to shoot the scene without a vampire?

Drake: (Enters with his vampire make-up and cape-he looks the part) I can fix that. (He walks over to Lacie who is speechless)

Freddie: Places everyone.

Lacie: (Goes to Drake and puts her hand on his heart where the wound should be, but he doesn't flinch) How?

Drake: I called Freddie last night. What better way to protect you than to be right here beside you?

Lacie: But you were wounded. I don't understand.

Drake: You will, in time. Just do the scene with me.

Lacie: (Low voice) You never go out at night. You appear out of nowhere, and you can't be killed.

Adam: (comes into view of the audience but stays back from the set)

Freddie: (Sits in his Director's chair.) Okay, everyone clear the set. Drake and Lacie should be the only ones in the scene. Let's roll! (cast still mulling around) I SAID CLEAR THE SET PEOPLE. We have a schedule! (more panicked clearing as everyone, including Adam, steps out of the spotlight)

Lacie: (Closes her eyes as she did before when they were practicing and then opens them looking directly at Drake) I know what you are!

Drake: (Accent) No one really knows what I am, behind this, this, mask of a man.

Lacie: Everything you said to me is a lie, that is what I know. You've had many loves.

Drake: Yes, I have, you might as well know. How could I not have loved? I have been alive for five-hundred years.

Lacie: (Lacie doesn't correct him this time) I suppose they are all dead now.

Drake: Yes.

Lacie: Did you kill them?

Drake: Only for the sake of mercy, when they were sick, dying.
Lacie: Do you have someone now?
Drake: Not for a long time. I got tired of falling in love and watching it fade away. That is why you must understand how special you are for me to take that chance again!
Lacie: How could I? You're a cold-blooded killer. (She puts her hand on his heart) See, no heartbeat. You have no soul. You are, dead. And you are dead to me. (Lacie goes to the table and picks up the knife, hesitates, then turns to Drake)
Drake: Yes, I am dead. But my soul is alive, and it aches for you. (Eyes fixed on Lacie, he pulls her close to him and stares into her eyes, STRANGE MUSIC, until she gets lightheaded and almost faints. Adam rushes to her side and sets her in a chair fanning her. Freddie runs up too.)
Adam: Lacie, oh, my Lacie what is it?
Freddie: Oh my, what next? Is she okay?
Lacie: I'm fine, Adam, Freddie. I just need some air.
Adam: (Stands, addresses Freddie) You are simply pushing her too hard. I insist that this thing be delayed.
Bob: (Comes up to Drake) Why did you do the whammy on her? Is this part of your plan?
Freddie: Oh no, what am I to do? (fretting with hands) We are already behind and over budget.
Drake (Nods at Bob) Can we continue with the understudy (nods toward Veronica) since we are so close to finishing the scene?
Adam: Well, I didn't mean for you to replace her?
Freddie: (Turns and looks at Drake) I don't see why not. Lacie can take a break. Veronica, you're on. (addresses Adam) Please clear the set.
Veronica: (Surprised) Shouldn't we wait and see...
Freddie: Come on honey, we're burning the midnight oil to get this scene ready.
Adam (disgruntled moves off and over by Lacie)
Drake: Don't worry, I'll help you if you need it.
Veronica: (Hesitant, Bob moves behind her and gives her a push, she looks behind her, as she moves closer to Drake)
Drake: You do know the lines, right?
Veronica: (Nods) Yes, I know the lines.

Drake: Let's go then.

Freddie: Take it from "What can I do to prove my love for you?"

Drake: (Nods and turns to Veronica. She doesn't have the knife so he places it in her hand as she is turned away from him) What can I do to prove my love for you?"

Veronica: I want to know it's real. (Turns to face Drake knife in hand) If you are already dead, this shouldn't hurt a bit! (She takes the knife and motions toward Drake but goes across his body without stabbing him.)

Drake: (Grabs Veronica's hand that holds the knife) You're supposed to stab me here. (As he pulls the knife toward him Veronica pulls back and drops the knife.)

Freddie: Okay honey, he was right, you're supposed to stab him. (claps twice) Come on, we simply must get through this scene!

Drake: (Grabs Veronica by the shoulders and stares, Strange Musical sound here!) Look into my eyes. You cannot lie to me. You are the one who cut the rope for the stage lighting?

Veronica: (in a trance-like state) Yes

Drake: (strange music again) And you are the one who poisoned the drink that was meant for Lacie?

Veronica: Yes, it was meant for her. No one else was supposed to get hurt.

Drake: And you were the one who switched the knife? It's real, that's why you couldn't do the scene.

Veronica: Yes, It's all true. She was supposed to kill you. Then she would be out of the way and I could be the star.

Bob: The only thing you'll be starring in is a rendition of Jailhouse Rock.

Lacie: (Stands and moves the chair to Veronica as she starts to collapse and sits down)

Veronica: (Twirling her hair, she has snapped) I just wanted to be a star. Like you (she looks at Lacie)

Adam: (pulls out cell phone) Get me the police!

Drake: I am Drake Ulah, a detective from the Night Avenger Detective Agency. I was hired by Miss Starlight to find out if someone was trying to hurt her. I have found the person responsible. (Turns to Freddie) Veronica Charm is guilty of murder and attempted murder.

Adam: Come on (he lifts Veronica out of the chair) the police are waiting out front. (Turns to Drake) Good work Detective.

Freddie: (Hands in the air) Yes, yes, good work Detective. Oh my, what's next, (follows Adam) this movie's going to be the death of me.
(Drake, Lacie and Bob are still on the stage and Lacie sits back in the chair)
Bob: They called you "detective."
Drake: Yes, they did. (moves over to Lacie)
Lacie: I'm sorry, what's that you said?
Drake: I was just saying, I guess WE solved it.
Lacie: (Nervously playing with her hands) Yes, WE did.
Drake: (kneels so he is level with Lacie) There's something I need to tell you.
Lacie: It's okay, you don't have to say it. (She turns away from Drake) There has been enough revealed today. Don't you think?
Drake: It seems you'll be safe now. Just be careful who you hire as your understudy next time.
(Lacie doesn't respond)
Drake: (Stands behind Lacie and reaches his hands out to touch her shoulders but doesn't) I'll send the bill to the studio. (Drake leaves with Bob comforting him)
Lacie: (Turns at the last moment to watch Drake exit. She stands and looks toward the audience and places her hands-on heart) Oh my, I think I'm in love with a vampire.
END OF SCENE

Scene 7: I FELL IN LOVE WITH A MOVIE STAR

SETTING: ("I Fell in love with a Vampire" Movie has come out. Drake hasn't seen Lacie in months. The Detective Agency is doing well, and Drake has had lots of movie star cases thanks to Freddie Flick's referrals. Bob is happy he has his own desk and is sitting at it trying to make an object move, a mug or something the audience can see. Drake is watching him and is buried in paperwork)

Freddie: (comes out and addresses the audience during the stage change) The movie was not the death of me. Lacie did such a good job, the movie was a smash. I was so happy with that detective, Drake, I sent all my producer and actor friends to him. (Pause. Nods head a few times.) I know, you're wondering whether Drake and Lacie ended up together. (goes to a random couple) Just like these two here who ended up together. How did you two meet? (doesn't let them answer but interrupts) Oh who cares, let's watch the rest of the play!
(Freddie Exits)

Bob: (staring at object/mug on his desk) I just don't understand it. I can only make objects move when I get upset.
Drake: (sitting) I wish I could make all this paperwork go away. Why is it so complicated to run a business?
Bob: Why so upset? With all those referrals from Freddie Flicks, your business is a smash. I can't believe we are in the office tonight without someone beating down the door.
Drake: Lucky at business, not so in love.
Bob: I thought we agreed on this "love" thing.
Drake: My mind tells me not to fall in love but, my cold heart longs for...
(Bell rings as door opens and Lacie Enters the Detective agency. Drake and Bob both stand as Lacie slowly approaches Drake)
Lacie: I wasn't sure I'd find you here. I've come by several times, but you are always closed.
Drake: I've been busy, and I keep late hours.
Lacie: Did you have time to see the movie?
Drake: Yes. It was, good. You were excellent but the guy who played the vampire? Why does everyone try to fake a foreign accent? Can't a vampire be from somewhere that doesn't have an accent?

Lacie: (looking around she notices the second desk) Oh, you got a partner. "Bob" (Reads name tag on desk)
Drake: HE's more of a silent partner. Never really here yet, it's like he's always here.
Bob: Very funny.
Lacie: Oh, I guess that's nice.
Drake: And you, you are doing fine?
Lacie: Yes. But I just wanted to…
Drake: (stands and moves around to Lacie) Yes?
Lacie: I wanted to stop by and tell you, that night on the set (Pause) I know what you are!
Drake: (Gets closer to Lacie, starts with accent like when practicing movie scene) No one really knows what I am, (changes to his normal voice) not behind this, this, mask of a man.
Lacie: Everything you said to me is it a lie? I suppose you've had many loves.
Drake: Yes, I have, you might as well know. How could I not have loved? I have been alive for five-hundred years.
Lacie: I suppose they are all dead now.
Drake: Yes.
Lacie: Did you kill them?
Drake: Only for the sake of mercy, when they were sick, dying.
Lacie: Do you have someone now?
Drake: Not for a long time. I got tired of falling in love and watching it fade away. (Takes Lacie's hands) That is why you must understand how special you are for me to take that chance again.
Lacie: You don't kill people now do you?
Drake: (Laughs) No, I have a way to get what I need that doesn't involve killing. I am helping people.
Lacie: Like you helped me?
Drake: Yes.
(Long Pause as Drake and Lacie stare into each other's eyes.)
Bob: Oh, for crying out loud would you just kiss her!
(Drake and Lacie kiss)
Lacie: I'm done with showbiz.
Drake: (Looks at the paperwork on his desk) I could use some help around here.

Lacie: You would let me help you?
Drake: Yes, of course. I am planning on being open for a long time.
(Lacie turns and eyes Bob's desk and Bob starts shaking his head)
Bob: Don't even think about it lady.
Drake: We can get you your own desk. Are you sure you are okay working with—a vampire?
Lacie: I'm not just working with a vampire. I'm in love with one.
Drake: And you are okay with it?
Lacie: Of course. I've fallen in love with a vampire and I know exactly what I'm doing. I saw it in a movie.
(Drake and Lacie Embrace, hopefully audience applauds)
Bob: Aren't you going to tell her about me.
Drake: No, Bob, I think she's had enough excitement for a while.
Lacie: What's that?
Drake: Nothing, dear. I said we've had enough excitement for a while. We should close for the night.
Lacie: What are we going to do tomorrow?
Drake: Well, tomorrow we are planning a blood drive.
(The End)

Director notes:
1) The audience isn't supposed to know character "Bob" is a ghost until the story unfolds
2) Drake uses his powers to turn into a bat when he needs to get around. Use of a "bat" prop with the actual actor flying it around is recommended
3) Drake uses fake blood drives to get his supply and the first scene starts out with him pulling in the sign. He disguises this blood in in juice boxes. "It's my own blend."
4) The character "Freddie Flicks" can be cast as male or female.

The Vampire Detective is its own book and went on to have three parts/plays. Don't miss your chance to read on and find out how Drake and Lacie's story turns out!

Will it be love, or will it be *MURDER!*

THE NEW MINISTER

CHAPTER ONE
ASSIGNMENT

Bishop Rinaldo stirred at his desk as the phone rang waking him from a light sleep. He reached across and his left hand brought the receiver to his ear as he heard a panicked voice at the other end.

"The man you sent us is dead," an elevated masculine voice said.

"Mister Duran, is that you?" Bishop Rinaldo asked.

"Yes, it's me."

"Reverend Carter is dead, are you sure?"

"Yes, there's no doubt. He was not who we needed. I told you we needed someone strong-willed, with focus and resolution. Our entire town is now at risk. What do you intend to do?"

"I have just the man for you. I will send him right away," Bishop Rinaldo said.

"You better pick someone who is up to the task. Lives are at stake."

Bishop Rinaldo reached across his desk to a file recently placed in his inbox. He opened it and looked through the description. "I think I have just the man for the job."

"We need help now! How soon can he be here?" Mister Duran asked.

"Now, hold on," Bishop Rinaldo said. "You got yourselves into this."

"I know that. But our predecessors made a commitment to help, and you have not provided a way out of this. Are you going to help us or not?"

"I will have him there in two days."

The other end of the line went silent. Bishop Rinaldo pushed a button to get a dial tone and dialed another number.

"Hello, you've reached the rectory, Father Michael speaking."

"Father Michael," Bishop Rinaldo said, "I need you to tell Father Gerald Arriaga that I need to speak with him immediately. Tonight, if possible."

"I will send him to you," Father Michael said.

Bishop Rinaldo hung up the phone and continued to look over the file in front of him. Father Gerald Arriaga was a recent transfer from oversees and he had not assigned him a parish. It seemed he had a mission now and a perfect one for his background; "He studied demonology abroad," he said as he opened his bottom right desk drawer and pulled out a flask of brandy and took a drink. "How convenient that he is here at this moment."

A knock came at the door.

"Please, come in," Bishop Rinaldo said and stood to greet Father Arriaga. "Sorry it's so dark in here, I've been resting." At five feet, ten inches tall, Bishop Rinaldo was not a small man. He was surprised that in front of him stood a man who was at least six foot, well built, and in his forties at best. A face with deep set, brown eyes, a chiseled chin, and black well-trimmed hair looked at him and Bishop Rinaldo suddenly felt he was the lower in status.

"Bishop Rinaldo," Father Arriaga said, "it's a pleasure to meet you." His hand came out and Bishop Rinaldo shook it in the formal greeting. "Is there something wrong?"

"Please, be seated," Bishop Rinaldo said and gestured to a leather, chalus chair in front of his desk. He returned to the chair behind his desk. "Nothing is wrong. It's just, I was reading your file and, with all the travel and experience you've had, I suppose I expected someone..."

"Older?" Father Arriaga said.

"Yes," Bishop Rinaldo said.

"I hope that doesn't affect the assignment you have for me."

"Not at all. In fact, I am glad to see you are in good health. Tell me, are you enjoying your stay here?"

"Yes, I never knew Colorado was so beautiful. The mountains are breathtaking."

"You have never been to Colorado before?" Bishop Rinaldo asked.

"Yes," Father Arriaga replied. "Only the south-eastern part where it is much flatter."

"Is there a reason you have not been settled at a parish and remained?" Bishop Rinaldo asked.

"I have always been put on special assignments; none of which have allowed me the pleasure of remaining in one place for long," Father Arriaga said.

"Does that bother you?"

"Not at all."

"I've been told you are a problem solver," Bishop Rinaldo said.

"Yes, I've been called that."

Bishop Rinaldo picked up the file on Father Arriaga and glanced at it. "I also see that you studied demonology,"

"Yes, I found it interesting," Father Arriaga said.

"I have a problem with a small parish in Dyersville and I need someone to go there immediately. It's a small, mountain town that would be a perfect place for you to witness more of Colorado's beauty. These small towns are where we have some of our most committed and faithful patrons. The city council there has always supported our church and its efforts. We must protect them."

"Protect them?" Father Arriaga asked. "I'm not sure I've heard it put that way before."

"Let's just say they have certain beliefs there that your background in demonology might help you understand. You will learn more about what I am referring too after you've arrived. The community church is small, adequate for the task. There are no accommodations so you will be staying with a host family, the Duran's. When you arrive in town, Paul Duran will greet you at the church."

"Is there currently no one at the parish?" Father Arriaga asked.

Bishop Rinaldo hesitated before he answered. "There was a Father Carter there. He had a crisis of faith. Perhaps the remote location had something to do with it." He stood causing Father Arriaga to do the same as he headed toward the door. "I need you there as soon as possible."

"I can leave tomorrow," Father Arriaga said.

"Good," Bishop Rinaldo said. "I will arrange transportation."

"Will there be anything else?" Father Arriaga asked.

Bishop Rinaldo looked to the floor before responding. "You will need to discover what is there on your own terms, Father Arriaga. Once you do, I am hoping some of what you referred too as 'problem solving' skills will be of use. If not, I can find someone to replace you if you wish to leave."

CHAPTER TWO
MEETING FAITH

Father Arriaga observed closely from the backseat of the car he rode in as he entered Dyersville. The town before him included one grocery store, a small school that, according to the sign, combined all grades. One gas station and a main street lined with businesses ended at the modest church. Though only a few houses were in town, he could see many houses lining the hillside sticking out of the mountainous forest. These houses, large and modern he noted, were not those of a poor, mountain town but spoke of wealth.

"I would make sure you stock up before winter," the silver-haired driver who'd met him in Denver told Father Arriaga as they arrived at the church.

"Once the snow sets in, it's almost impossible to get up here. And coming down the mountain is impossible."

"I'll keep that in mind," Father Arriaga said.

"You sure you want me to leave you off at the church?" The driver said. "I was instructed to take you to the Duran's house."

"The church will be fine," Father Arriaga said. "I want to see it before I go anywhere else. I can call the Duran's when I'm ready."

"You'll have to use the phone in the church," the driver said. "There's no cell service here. Well, here we are."

The driver carried Father Arriaga's bag into the church and then parted. Father Arriaga looked around the church which contained modern, padded seats instead of pews and a brightly lit alter area. The microphone, sound system and lighting were all state of the art. "Not a town in financial need," he said to himself.

He went to the alter and the podium where he would deliver his messages and looked out at the empty seats in front of him. He paused for a moment and visualized giving a sermon.

He went into the small ready room to the side of the alter where priests kept their garments and sacraments. It was in the small room where he found a desk and browsed around. He browsed through the side drawers only to find a few files of counseling sessions.

He opened the middle drawer and it appeared empty until he started to close it and it jammed. Upon examining it, he found a journal lodged between the back of the drawer and the desk.

Father Arriaga moved the drawer back and forth several times and worked the journal into a position where he could reach it and pried the small book out. He opened it to find it was a log from Father Carter, the previous minister. As he read the journal, he grew concerned by the story the writing told.

"I have found an evil here more real than I ever imagined," Father Carter wrote. "I was not prepared to have my faith tested so, but the town has confided in me secrets; unimaginable secrets of a pact made to save it from destruction. Although warned, I have decided that this cannot continue, and I have chosen to confront this sacrilege."

The writing stopped and there were no entries after this. Father Arriaga heard the door open and footsteps in the church. He put the journal back in the drawer and headed out through the side door and found a tall, dark-haired, middle-aged man in the church. He wore designer jeans and a dress shirt with a sport coat.

"Father Arriaga?" the man before him asked.

"Yes, I am he," Father Arriaga said. "Mister Duran?"

"You can call me Paul," he said and put out his hand.

The man who presented himself was dressed in a brown, causal suit without a tie, stood a good foot shorter than Father Arriaga but was in shape. He noticed he had city hands, callous free and soft.

"Did you just arrive?"

"I've been here a few hours," Father Arriaga said.

"The Bishop acted quickly then," Paul said.

"Was that important?"

"What did he tell you about our town?"

"Just that the previous minister had left; something about a crisis of faith and that you had requested someone to fill in." He decided not to mention anything further and let the rest be revealed to him by the actions of those he would meet. Besides, Bishop Rinaldo hadn't given any direct information, just a comment about his skills. He was sure to learn the town's secret soon enough.

"Well, I guess I better fill you in," Paul said. "But not before you had dinner and we get you settled. There's no place to stay here at the church so we've set up a room at the house. Is that your only bag?"

"Yes," Father Arriaga said.

"Sworn to poverty," Paul said. "I don't know how you do it."

The two men exited the church and went to a gray jeep. Paul put the bags in the back and the two headed out of town.

"Tell me about your town," Father Arriaga said.

"We are a rural people," Paul said. "A small community, but tight in our values. The town was founded in the eighteen-hundreds, a mining town. It nearly died out in the early nineteen-hundreds. Several fires struck the area. That along with the mines drying up led people to start leaving. Only a few families remained."

"Yes, I've heard about the old mining towns in Colorado. Some of them have found new life with the casinos and gambling," Father Arriaga said. His comment drew a stern look.

"No gambling in this town," Paul said. "There's always something bad that follows that type of industry. We might be small and sometimes barely getting by as a town, but we have values."

"I meant no offense," Father Arriaga said. In the back of his mind he was thinking about the journal he found at the church and couldn't help but wonder what evil Father Carter was speaking of when he wrote his final entry.

"Here we are," Paul said pulling into a large, two-story wood house that looked modern with its stained wood and huge windows. There were multiple cars parked in the driveway leading to the house.

"Do a lot of people live here?" Father Arriaga asked.

"No. Just my family is here. We invited some of the town council to meet you," Paul said.

"Oh, I wish I'd had time to clean up a little."

"You look fine, Father," Paul said.

Paul parked the car and the two men went inside. Father Arriaga met three families that were on the town council and Paul's wife, a thin, blonde woman named Debra. They ate dinner that included fresh trout from the area, baked potatoes, salad, and rolls. Father Arriaga answered questions when asked and spoke about his travels. Most of his time he tried to listen and observe. The people around the table were friendly and welcoming; happy that he arrived so soon.

After dinner, he went into the living room where the conversations continued. He noticed family pictures on the large mantle of the fireplace, and it was his question that darkened the mood of the room.

"I see you have a daughter, Paul. Is she away at college? She looks about that age."

Multiple eyes in the room looked to the floor as though searching for a lost pair of contacts or money and the rest turned to Paul who shifted his weight from leg to leg but didn't answer.

"Well, we should be going," one of the men said and then the others followed until all the families left, leaving Father Arriaga alone with Paul and his wife.

"I'm sorry," Father Arriaga said. "Did I say something wrong?"

"Oh, no," Debra said. "Why don't you have a seat in the living room. Would you like something to drink? Brandy, wine, beer?"

"No, I'm fine," Father Arriaga said.

Debra left and brought back a glass of wine for herself and what appeared to be a whiskey for her husband who stood by the mantle looking at the picture that included the girl Father Arriaga assumed was their daughter.

"I should wait until you've had a good night rest to tell you," Paul said as he drank half of his whiskey. "The truth is, we are running out of time to save her."

"Your daughter?"

"Yes," Paul said and finished his drink, putting the glass down on the coffee table, he took a seat in a leather recliner. "You better sit down."

Father Arriaga took a seat on the brown, all leather couch while Debra sat at the other end.

"Please don't judge us in what I am about to tell you. We are a God-fearing people and we've done what we thought we had to do. Everyone in the town knows and everyone has agreed to keep it a secret. What I'm about to reveal to you has been a curse on our town for decades. That's why we asked for you, a man of stronger faith. Father Carter, well, he wasn't up to it."

Father Arriaga leaned forward. "Tell me. What is it that has you so worried?"

Paul's eyes shifted to the empty glass and then back to Father Arriaga. His eyes were fixed forward when he asked, "Do you believe in demons?"

CHAPTER THREE
THE DARKNESS IN THE BASEMENT

Paul sat in his chair and stared forward as he recounted a story of how the town elders, faced with an out of control fire and certain doom made a pact with a demon to save the town from destruction. The deal was that the demon could possess a member of the community and exist among them. However, once the town was saved, the person the demon possessed was thrown into a cage and the local minister tried to exercise the demon only to fail.

The demon took it's revenge by drying up the mines and causing the town to descend into poverty. The church managed to control the demon and keep it from affecting the community any further but it still managed to possess a member of each generation and families fled the area never to return.

"The last person the demon possessed was my mother," Paul said. "The girl in the picture is our daughter, Susan. When my mother passed, the demon went into my daughter. That was just a few weeks ago."

"Did Father Carter know about all of this?" Father Arriaga asked.

"Yes, but he didn't truly accept it. You see, my mother was a strong woman and fought the demon. Most of the time she went about her business and seemed normal; no one could tell she was possessed. When she died and the demon moved into my daughter, things changed; her faith wasn't as deep, and the demon has all but taken control of her. Father Carter tried to help, but he wasn't strong enough."

"So, he left?" Father Arriaga asked.

"Not exactly," Paul said. "It's kind of hard to explain."

"I see," Father Arriaga said. He decided to give up on finding Father Carter's where abouts and focus on the girl. "Where is your daughter now?"

"We keep her in the basement," Paul said. "You should really get a good night sleep before you meet her."

"I'm fine," Father Arriaga said. "I wish to see her now." He stood causing Debra and Paul to stand. "I insist."

"Please, help her," Debra said.

"I don't think he believes us," Paul said.

"Why would I doubt you?" Father Arriaga asked.

"Very well, come with me," Paul said, and the two men headed down a hallway to a solid door that was padlocked. Paul took out a key and opened the door. "If you don't mind, I'm going to stay up here. I don't think I can bear to see her right now."

Father Arriaga put his hand on Paul's shoulder. "I don't mind, now I'm glad I got here so fast."

"Be careful," Paul said. "She lies."

"It's okay, I've dealt with this before," Father Arriaga said and headed down the wooden staircase. He emerged into a well-lit large, single room basement. In the room was a ping-pong table, air hockey, and foosball table. In the corner of the room, by a karaoke machine, the girl from the picture, young with brunette hair, sat alone. In front of the chair on the floor was a significant pile of ash.

"Hello, Father Arriaga," the girl said.

"Hello, Susan. Am I speaking with Susan?" Father Arriaga asked.

"Of course, I'm Susan. You don't believe all that stuff they told you about demons, do you?"

"How do you know what I was told?" Father Arriaga asked.

"The vents allow sound to travel," Susan said.

"Why would I doubt them?" Father Arriaga said.

"You think demons are real? You're as crazy as everyone else around here. At least untie me so I can get out of here. What kind of priest would allow a girl's father to keep her tied up in a basement?"

Father Arriaga approached the girl and could see she was strapped to the chair. He examined the pile of ashes on the floor. He knelt and made the sign of the cross and said a prayer.

"Oh no, you know." Susan said.

"Yes," Father Arriaga said and stood. "Why did you do this to Father Carter," he looked at the pile of ashes.

"He tried to make me leave," Susan said. "I don't want to leave."

"Why don't you want to leave?" Father Arriaga asked. "You don't belong here."

"I made a deal and as long as the town is here, I get to be here, see," Susan said.

"I've heard about this deal," Father Arriaga said as he walked around the chair. "Why did you pick Susan?"

"I didn't," Susan said. "The family had a choice. When grandma died, I needed a host. None of them wanted to allow me in, so I told them I would pick Susan. She was too young to resist and I knew she would be around for a long time. They let it happen."

"That wasn't nice of them," Father Arriaga said. He continued to move around Susan.

"I agree," Susan said. "I will make you a deal preacher."

"What is that?"

"You think this family brought you here to protect them, they didn't. They brought you here because I told them too. I told them I wanted a stronger vessel to inhabit; one that would allow me access to certain places."

"I have been baptized in the name of the trinity. You cannot inhabit me. I am protected," Father Arriaga said.

"I can if you allow me entry."

"Why me?" Father Arriaga asked.

"I need someone who could get me places only a priest can go," Susan said.

"Why did you not try this with Father Carter?"

"I did. He was too weak to take the bargain."

"Bargain?"

"For the girl," Susan said. "His soul for the salvation of the girl. Father Carter thought he could break the deal. He didn't really understand."

"Why would you want me? I would be a terrible host. We wouldn't agree on much," Father Arriaga said.

"I have questions that need answers," Susan said.

"Questions?"

"Why I am what I am. Does He," she glanced to the ceiling, "really exist."

"That is fascinating," Father Arriaga said. "I never thought I would see this day."

"You don't believe me, do you?"

"Why wouldn't I believe you?"

"Father Carter didn't, not at first. He thought this was mental illness; brought on by the family's superstitions. You don't believe demons are real, that I am really possessing this girl. You probably think it's puberty, adolescence."

"Actually, I fully believe," Father Arriaga said. "You would be surprised how much we have in common."

"What are you talking about?" Susan said. "What could we possibly have in common?"

Father Arriaga kept circling Susan as he spoke. "You said people don't believe in you, that they don't believe your kind exists right?"

"Yes," Susan said.

"Well, I have the same problem," Father Arriaga said. "People don't believe in me either, not my kind anyway."

"You're kind?" Susan said. "Would you stop circling you're making me dizzy."

Father Arriaga came to a stop in front of Susan and went down on one knee to face her directly. His eyes became a bright, white light as he reached out and grasped Susan's hands. A halo of gold light appeared above his head as he spoke. "I will answer one question for you, so you know."

"I don't believe it," Susan said. "You're real?"

"Yes, and so is He. Your kind have betrayed His law of life; that you are not above others, and it is not yours to take. That is your question and I have answered. Now, I command you to leave."

"What about the deal?" Susan said.

"The deal is over. You take your revenge, but you cannot take this girl," Father Arriaga said. "Don't test me."

Susan's head tilted downward, and she went limp.

The halo over Father Arriaga's head disappeared and his eyes returned to normal. He stood and went to the back of the chair. He undid the straps that held Susan and lifted her out of the chair.

"I've got you," Father Arriaga said and carried her up the stairs.

"Is she?" Debra said as Father Arriaga came through the basement door.

"She needs water," Father Arriaga said as he sat her down on the couch.

Debra left the room as Paul knelt by his daughter.

"How can I ever thank you?" Paul said.

"We need to leave, now," Father Arriaga said. "Does your school have a bus?"

"Yes," Paul said. "Just one."

"That will do," Father Arriaga said. "I need every child in town on that bus in the next hour. We have very little time."

"You think the demon will come for them?" Paul asked.

"No, but we should take precautions."

"Yes, of course," Paul said. "We probably need to get her to the medical center. I'll start the car." He left the house as Debra came back with a wet rag and put it on Susan's head. Susan moved back and forth and drank some water as she opened her eyes.

"Mom?"

"Yes, Susan, it's me." Debra said.

"We need to leave, now," Father Arriaga said and helped Susan stand.

"You," Susan said as she looked to Father Arriaga. "You were in my dream."

"Yes," Father Arriaga said. "And just like in your dream, you must listen to me now."

"I don't know if we should go anywhere tonight," Paul said as he entered the living room. "There's one hell of a storm out there. I've never seen lightning like that, not this close to winter."

"We need to go, now," Father Arriaga said as he escorted Susan to the door and into the jeep outside. Debra and Paul followed.

They entered the jeep with Susan and her mother in the back and Father Arriaga in the passenger's seat as Paul Drove. They started to pull away when a bolt of lightning struck the house causing it to explode in flames.

"My God," Paul said.

"You can say that" Father Arriaga said.

As they drove down the main street, many buildings were ablaze from lightning strikes and the trees surrounding the town were on fire.

"I don't know if we can make it to the emergency center," Paul said.

"We can't," Father Arriaga said. "We need to get to the school. Keep going, it's no longer safe here. Once we get to the school, we will leave town tonight."

The car sped down main street and to the edge of town when suddenly, a large tree full of fire fell in front of them and blocked the road. Paul slammed on the brakes

"Lord, forgive these two, they did not know how to deal with the evil of their kin," Father Arriaga said. "This family is asking for a second chance. Pray with me."

Paul, Debra, and Susan all prayed as Father Arriaga left the vehicle. He went to the tree and moved it out of the way. When he returned to the car, the family was silent.

"I suggest we go," Father Arriaga said.

"Yes, of course. Go," Paul said as he and his family continued down the road to the school.

"What the hell is going on?" a man yelled at Paul and Father Arriaga when they exited the car at the school. "The entire town is on fire."

"This is principal Meyers," Paul said.

"Yes, we met at dinner," Father Arriaga said.

"Are the children loaded on the bus?" Father Arriaga said.

"No, most of them are in the school," Meyers said.

"We need them in the bus now!" Father Arriaga said and the principal turned and ran to the school. Soon, a row of children followed and entered the bus.

"The driver is not here," Paul said. "And we are missing some of the kids."

"We will have to take what we can get. We are out of time," Father Arriaga said. "I will drive." He looked at Paul. "You and the rest of the parents can follow, but I cannot guarantee that I can get you out. It was you who made a deal with the demon, not these children."

"Let's go then," Paul said as he and Debra yelled out to the other parents to get in their cars and follow.

Father Arriaga entered the bus and started the engine. He turned to the children. "Anyone know a good song that everyone can sing?"

A kid sang out and the others joined in as Father Arriaga hit the gas and moved with haste down the road. He watched behind him as lightning struck and school building lit up. Then, one by one the cars behind him were struck till only the bus remained and continued its path down the road to salvation.

Somewhere in Colorado, a town once named Dyersville, consumed by flame, no longer exists.

The END.

Now that you've finished
Now that you're through
Don't let the fear
Take hold of you
Don't worry about grave robbers
Vampires or demons
Or other creatures of the night
Just say your prayers
and sleep tighty tight
but don't rest before
you check under the bed
in the closet
and lock the front door

SPOOKABLE TALES VOLUME 3

LOUIS PAUL DEGRADO

Spookable Tales Volume 3

Copyright © 2022 Louis Paul DeGrado

All rights reserved. No part of this book may be used or reproduced by any means, graphic, electronic, or mechanical, including photocopying, recording, taping, or by any information storage retrieval system without written permission of the author.

This book is a work of fiction. Unless otherwise noted, the author makes no explicit guarantee as to the accuracy of the information contained in the book. Any reference to people or places that may be real is merely coincidental. Just in case, you should beware and lock your door at night.

The Festival of FEAR

Table of Contents

Why do you come here

Do you come to be scared

Is it because you have no fear

Or is it because you've been dared

A single

A double

A triple dog dare

What would you do

To get out of it now

To go home where it's safe

If only you knew how

You had a bad feeling

Something would go wrong

You had a premonition

But still, went along

Now your complacency

Your need to feel belonging

Will bring you great dread

Nothing to worry about

You'll soon be dead

FESTIVAL OF FEAR!

FESTIVAL OF FEAR!

Screams! Screams in the night outside my door. Something has gone wrong! I am disoriented as I wake, not just from the late hour and the unfamiliar room but, from the vodka I had before bed. We stayed up late celebrating a special event, the Festival of Fear, which had taken place at the hotel where we were now staying. I sat up in my double bed on the sixth-floor hotel suite. I wondered if I was dreaming, if someone was watching a movie, or if it was the alcohol. I looked to the twin bed next to mine where my friend, Sandy, lay asleep. She hadn't stirred. Maybe, I was just dreaming; the nights events, all centered around what causes us fear, catching up to me. Perhaps there was some after-party that was taking place and the guests were drunk and out of control. I hesitated before getting out of bed hoping it would pass.

Then, the screams came again from beyond the door of our hotel room. It wasn't a single scream, but multiple from different people yelling that stirred me from by bed. I reached for the lamp and hit the button. Now, I could see the room better; Sandy, my black-haired, brown-eyed friend whose shared interests brought us to the festival, remained sound asleep. Dressed in sweatpants and a black t-shirt with the word "Author" in white across the front, I slipped my feet into my untied shoes and walked out to the living room. I closed the bedroom door most of the way behind me, doing my best not to disturb Sandy. I went to the door of the hotel room and peeped through the small hole but couldn't see anything. I slowly opened the door, the dimly lit hallway stretching to the left and right of me lay abandoned. I made my way to elevators, two that were opposite each other with a hallway in the middle. It ended at a balcony that overlooked the lower floors and the lobby, and that's where I was headed. The balcony had a high railing with glass reinforced bottom that I surmised was to keep kids from fitting through and falling off. From here, I overlooked the other floors and down into the lobby and restaurant area. It was there the noise of panic and dread poured forth, filling the hallways and rest of the empty, eerie spaces of the hotel.

The hotel itself had a unique design: the front check-in lobby opened to a larger lobby that held a large social area and another room segregated as a dining area. This huge inner rectangle of open space went all the way through the center of the hotel while the occupancy rooms were located around the perimeter, forming as a castle wall around the inner core. The rooms were accessed by a front and rear stairwell to each side, or through two sets of glass elevators located on opposite sides midway of the inner lobby, the elevators were directly across from each other. On this particular weekend, the lobby had been decorated with all things horror: mannequins of vampires, werewolves, zombies, witches, and all creatures of the night, along with movie posters, spider webs, fog machines, and dark settings-- leaving no area free of horror.

It was from this overlook, where I had gazed dozens of times during the day, watching people come and go through the lobby, watching people eat and socialize as they unknowingly became my entertainment. I created stories in my head about who they were and what they were doing at the hotel; what drove them to desire a festival based on fear? What fanaticism drove them to pay to be encompassed in darkness and death? Now, from this same position, where I had carelessly judged others, I found myself looking down to a very different scene where all judgment fled.

The costume contest at ten was the last event of the evening and more than half of the audience, all staying at the hotel, was pouring down drink after drink. Like me, they were glad to have a room that didn't require driving to get to. As I looked at the lobby, I could easily make out the same crowd that was there at the costume contest, still dressed in their outfits. There were more gathered in their pajamas and sweatpants. Could this be an after-hours party?

As I looked on, I realized there was something wrong...there were people on the floor, and they weren't there because they were drunk. Those dressed in costume were attacking the others. I scanned the other floors and spotted more horrific scenes on the second, third and fourth floor. People were being stabbed by slashers, bitten by vampires, and chased by clowns! CLOWNS!

BING! The elevator rang behind me and I swung around as the door opened. I looked across the elevator entrance to my hotel room and safety wondering if I could run there before the occupants had time to exit. I began to move forward but came to a stop when two young, black-haired women in cocktail dresses and a man in a dark hopsack blazer with denim pants, stepped out. *Maybe they won't notice me*, I thought, but they looked right at me!

"He looks normal," one of the women said. "Can you hear me?"

"Of course," I said. "What is going on?"

"We need to get out of here, all of us," the man said.

I recognized the middle-aged man who spoke from one of the panels I had visited during the event. His long, black hair and beard, slightly graying, were easy to spot even in the dull lighting. He had introduced himself as a paranormal investigator.

"Ryan the ghost hunter, isn't it?" I asked.

"I prefer Paranormal Investigator if you don't mind. And you are?"

"Louis DeGrado, the author."

"Like your shirt says," one of the ladies remarked.

"Yes, Mister DeGrado, I remember we spoke after one of my presentations. I prefer the term 'Paranormal Investigator' because I do so much more than investigate ghosts. That might not matter now. It appears some of the attendees have decided to make this a true festival of fear. They are acting like the characters they are portraying in their costumes and it's all too real."

"You mean what I'm hearing and seeing down there is real?" I said.

Ryan nodded.

"I just witnessed someone in a hockey mask holding a knife thrust it into another person who fell to the ground screaming."

"I'm afraid it's not a gimmick," Ryan said. "Everyone wearing a costume has gone berserk. The front of the hotel is overrun with killer clowns. In the panic, we fled the lobby via the elevators. That might have been a bad choice as I'm not sure how long we'll be safe up here."

"Can we try the stairs?" One of the women said as the four of us stepped away from the elevators and into the hallway.

"Wait," I said. "I need to get my friend." I turned to my hotel room and slid the electronic key across the sensor to open the door. "Why don't you step inside and get out of the hallway." Ryan and the two ladies stepped into the living area and closed the door. I went to the bedroom, not sure of how to wake my friend or what I would say to her that wouldn't sound crazy. "Sandy?" I gently said and touched her shoulder. "You need to wake up now."

Sandy stirred from her sleep. She brushed her fine, black, hair back as she sat up on the edge of the bed. "What is it? Is it morning already? How come it's still so dark?"

"No, it's not morning but I need you to get up. There's a problem in the hotel and we need to evacuate."

"Evacuate? What is it?"

"I don't want to create panic, but something is wrong. Can you get dressed as quickly as possible and meet me at the door?"

"I'll be right there," she said.

I exited the bedroom and headed to the door where Ryan kept watch. I stopped and took a moment to tie my shoes. The sounds of screams and violent struggles crept up from the lower floors.

"The elevator is quiet, and the hallway is clear," Ryan said. "The front lobby was overrun and might be dangerous, but the back area where the entrance to the kitchen was still clear. I think we should try to reach the back stairway. We could at least get down to a lower floor. Maybe, make it to the kitchen and exit."

"I'm for the stairs," I said. "That way we can see what's coming toward us."

"I'm ready," Sandy said as she came to the door dressed in slacks and sweatshirt with tennis shoes on. She stepped back with her eyes fixed on Ryan. "Who's this?"

"This is Ryan Conner the ghost, I mean, paranormal investigator."

The two shook hands.

"Please to meet you," Ryan said.

"Oh, you're the one that does the presentations and real haunted houses," Sandy said. She looked at the two ladies sitting on the couch and back at me.

I looked at Ryan who shrugged his shoulders in apparent admission that if he'd known the two ladies' names, he'd forgotten them.

We didn't have time for more introductions as a loud scream came from below.

"What was that?" Sandy asked.

"You don't really want to know," Ryan said. "Let's go." The two ladies with Ryan followed us down the hall.

"Sandy," I said and grabbed her arm. "There is something going on here, something dangerous. It may seem part of the theatrics but, believe me it's real."

Sandy stopped. "You're scaring me. Is this a stunt?"

"No," I said as I glanced down the hallway behind us and noticed the two ladies were now following us. "It seems something has gone wrong. I don't know what happened but, people are acting out."

"Acting out?" she said.

"They are becoming the characters their costumes portray," I said.

Sandy stepped to the edge and looked over the railing to the lobby area down below.

"Oh my God!" Sandy said. "Is this real?!"

On the lobby floor below, we counted more than twenty bloodied bodies on the ground. I glanced left toward the main entrance where a set of stairs led to the check-in area and the reception lobby, and there were multiple costumed characters roaming about.

"What are you waiting for?" I heard Ryan say.

"You're right," I said. "I don't think we can make it to the front door. There's too many of them."

"I agree," Ryan said. "At the base of the elevators there's at least five Michaels, three Jasons and four Freddys. That doesn't even account for the clowns by the check-in desk."

"Look there," Sandy pointed toward the middle of the group. "It's a mixture of vampires, werewolves, witches and zombies."

"And one really cool looking warlock who's looking this way," I said.

"I've always been partial to zombies," Sandy said.

"Why is that?" I asked.

"Simple life," Sandy said.

"Quick," I said and put my arms out to pull Sandy back. "That weird character is looking this way!"

Ryan and the others stepped back as well. "I don't think he spotted us," Ryan said. "I like zombies too. They are straight forward and easy to predict; they are going to eat you. All the other slashers and killers have all kinds of different motivations. Most take after specific prey but, others have no preference and just outright kill anybody."

"You've got to love the tenacity of a killer that keeps coming forward," I said.

"True," Ryan said. "That was true of the supporters as well."

"What do you mean?" I asked.

"Check any low-budget movie that almost didn't get made and you'll find a list of those who supported the movie that just wouldn't give up."

"That's so one dimensional, "Sandy said. "Stab, stab, stab. I can't believe people keep lining up for that kind of movie. Why?"

"It's to get close to girls," I said.

Sandy shook her head at me.

"Let's continue to the stairs," Ryan said. "I'm sure there's a back exit we can try if we get down to the first floor."

We kept close to the inner doors of the rooms that lined the perimeter of the building and away from the railing as we hoped to remain anonymous to the macabre partiers below.

"So," Ryan asked, "Sandy, what's your favorite scary monster?"

"Demons," Sandy said. "Especially the kind that can change form and jump into someone you know. And then you have to kill that person or be killed. It's quite the twist when suddenly you look like the murderer."

"A true moral dilemma," Ryan said. "Actually, the slasher movies were never expected to succeed as much as they did. That's why so many of them have sequels that are moronic; they weren't well planned."

We stayed close to the inner doors as we approached the stairwell. "Why do you think they were popular?" I asked.

"People enjoy the adrenaline rush of being scared," Ryan said. "Horror movies expose a dark side of our human mind—a depth that remains unexplored and is capable of so much more. We have only scratched the surface."

"Clearly," I said. "Which may be why we are witnessing the horror of this night." I heard the elevators opening behind us as we made it to the stairs, noticing the two girls that had been with Ryan were no longer with us.

"Ready?" Ryan asked as he grasped the handle to the heavy, fire door that opened to the stairs. An opening we hoped would lead to our escape.

I looked to Sandy, and she nodded.

"Let's go," I said.

Ryan opened the door, and I took a quick look on the other side before heading down. I only got three steps before I heard voices from below.

"Hurry, they're right on our tail," a male's voice sounded. I spotted two men coming up the stairs in a hurry. The first one, a stocky middle-aged man with dark hair in a Thor costume with a hammer, and the other, average height in a brown, sport coat, wearing jeans with bright red sneakers. The Thor character spotted me while the other, carrying a baseball bat, walked backwards up the stairs in a defensive position.

"Ed, I see someone up ahead. He doesn't look affected, you," he pointed at me with the hammer. "Do you understand me?"

"I can hear you but, I don't understand why your friend would wear those shoes with that outfit," I said.

Sandy gave me a fist bump. "Nice to see you still have a sense of humor under pressure."

"Very funny," the man said. "You better hurry back up the stairs and find something to block that door if you know what's good for you. What's coming up behind us is no joking matter."

I turned around to find that Sandy and Ryan had already exited the stairwell. The three of us went into a small conference room and began grabbing furniture and hauling it out toward the stairwell door.

"Where'd the two girls go?" Sandy asked.

"I spotted them running back down the hall toward the elevator," I said.

"That's the worst thing to do," Ryan said. "In every scary movie you are supposed to stick together. That's like rule number one."

"You're comparing what's going on here to a movie?" Sandy asked.

"Sorry," Ryan said. "I guess it's the way I'm coping. It's just, surreal."

"Hey there," the man dressed in the sport coat said as he emerged from the stairwell behind his friend and closed the door. "I'm Ed Panteleon. This joker here dressed as Thor is my buddy, Jose Medina," he said as all of us continued the process of blocking the door.

"Nice costume," I said to Jose. "I'm Louis, this is Sandy, and this is..."

"Ryan?" Jose said. "We know him. We're part of the event. Well, not part of this mess that's going on now. Are there any more of you up here?"

"We had two ladies with us a minute ago," I said and turned to Ryan.

Ryan shrugged his shoulders. "I didn't really know their names."

"Are you an author?" Ed pointed to my shirt.

"Yes, as a matter of fact," I said. "Do you read much?"

"No," Ed said.

"Is that blood on your bat?" Sandy asked as everyone backed away from the door.

"Yes," Ed said. "I was at the bar talking with some baseball fans when we were attacked by those lunatics. Several of the fans had bats they'd bought at the game. It seemed the right weapon at the time and, the guy who had it won't be needing it anymore."

"I recognize you," I said. "You're one of the artists from the fair earlier."

"Yes," Ed said. "I'm currently doing some artwork for the Vampire Detective Agency plays. They're in high demand now. Is this floor safe?"

"There's no fanatics up here," Ryan said.

"Well, they're moving up the stairs," Jose said.

"That stairway is secure," I said, "but, we still have the elevators on both sides and the front stairwell to cover."

I turned toward our room just in time to spot a hooded character with a knife standing over the two ladies that had accompanied our group. I looked at Ryan. "Guess you were right."

"Rule number one," Ryan said.

"This can't be real," Sandy said.

The hooded figure looked in our direction and began running at our group.

"WATCH OUT!" I yelled.

"I got this," Ed said. Bat in hand, Ed wound up and swung as the figure came in range. The swing hit the hand carrying the knife and smashed both it and the knife against the wall. The knife fell to the floor while the attacker, stung by the force, stopped.

Ryan sprang into action and using his shoulder, slammed into the attacker, and launched him over the railing. I stepped forward and watched in horror as the person fell to the lobby below and spattered across the floor barely missing a table.

"Good one," Jose said as he looked down.

I turned to see Sandy who was shaking. "Are you okay?"

"What is going on?" Sandy said. "Did we just?"

"We defended ourselves," Ryan said.

We didn't have time to consider the implications. As the four of us looked down the lobby we were greeted by masked figures staring back.

"Uh oh," Jose said as he continued looking over the railing. "I think our secret's out. The sixth floor is no longer safe"

"At least the stairs are blocked," Ed said.

"They're heading for the elevators," Ryan said.

"Hurry," I said. "Let's try the front stairs."

The five of us headed down the hall past the elevator and to the front stairwell but before we got to the door a herd of zombies emerged blocking the hallway.

"There's too many," Ryan said.

We watched an unfortunate couple come out of their hotel room and right into the zombie apocalypse.

"Oh my God," Jose said. "Look, they really think they are zombies; they're eating those people."

I shouldn't have looked. One of the zombies tore into the neck of the person being held down who was still alive. Blood and skin came out in the oblivious creature's mouth and spattered against the wall. I stepped to the railing and bent over, hurling all I'd eaten that day. As I watched my lunch and dinner fall, I took pride in the fact that several of the demented creatures slid and fell in the vomit and were temporarily disabled.

"Ha, take that!" I yelled down as I wiped my mouth on my sleeve.

More costumed characters emerged from the stairwell in front of us. We began our retreat the way we came when: "BING!" The elevator door rang from behind us!

"Quick," Ryan said. "Take a position. As they come out of the elevator, push them over the railing. It's our only hope."

"I- I don't know if I can do that," Jose said.

Before the rest of us could get into position, the door opened, and several masked people emerged. One with a knife stabbed Jose in the right shoulder.

Screaming, Jose backed away and, in a flash, Sandy executed a perfect spinning roundhouse kick. The mask flew off the character who attacked Jose. I spotted a frightened face as the person hit the railing and then fell to the ground in front of us.

"What a paradigm shift," Jose said. "The beautiful girl hero saving the boy. I like it!"

"This hero's with me," I said and took a position by Sandy checking my surroundings.

Ryan and Ed were busy pushing the other two characters over the ledge. No screams rang out from them as they fell to their fatal doom. Two more masked characters came toward me and were about to grab the knife that fell on the floor. With both distracted, I grabbed on to one and Sandy the other as we heaved them over the railing. I turned back to see Ed getting ready to hit the stabber Sandy had kicked to the ground.

"Wait," I said. "I think Sandy's kick knocked some sense into him." I approached the man on the ground. Ed stood close with his bat ready to swing. The elevator door opened again, this time from the opposite side. Two men came out. Ed, Jose, Sandy and I formed a line between the hallway and railing, ready to push the next attackers to the railing. Meanwhile, Ryan had Jose against the wall behind us and was trying to stop the bleeding from his stab wound.

"Wait!" the first man who emerged from the elevator yelled holding his hands in the air.

The two men weren't in costume; both wore baseball jerseys and sneakers.

"You two understand us?" Ryan asked.

"Hey, that's my bat!" the taller man said and started to head toward Ed.

"Sorry," Ed said and handed the man the bat. "I thought you were dead."

"Who are you?" I asked.

"I'm Mike Keys and this is Chris Vanzuela," said the first man who was a medium build with a black crew-cut and baseball shirt. He walked with a slight limp indicating bad knees.

"Vanzuela?" Jose said. "Is that Canadian?"

"Dang, this bat is ruined," Chris said. "And no, it's not Canadian."

"Sorry," Ed said. "I'll buy you another one if we make it out of here."

"Obviously, the man had to use it to defend himself," Mike said.

Chris had a muscular build and wore a short sleeve shirt exposing tattoos on both arms. His most notable feature was a mohawk with spiked black hair and red tips.

"That's a no brainer," Chris said as he looked at Ed. "Look, I understand you needed to use it. That's okay. Glad we ran into you guys and by the looks of it, you've been dishing it back. I plan to get out of here alive so stick with me."

"I suggest we do something quickly," Ryan said. "The zombies look like they are almost done eating those people and there's more characters behind them waiting to get through.

"You just came from the elevator," I said. "Does that mean you couldn't go down?"

"The lobby all the way to the front exit is over-run with those characters," Mike said. "Too many to get through. That's why we headed up here."

"Well, the back stairwell is blocked," I said. "And the front stairway is full of zombies."

"Great," Ed said. "Looks like we've struck out, game over! What are we going to do now?"

"Follow me," I said. We were close to our hotel room, so I pulled Sandy along and stepped to the entrance and scanned my key. "Everyone in here quickly until we can come up with a plan."

"What about him?" Ed asked as the stabber still struggled on the ground in front of the elevators.

"Leave him," Ryan said. "We can't take any chances."

I held the door until everyone was inside.

Bing! The elevator doors rang again, and I didn't wait to see who was getting out. I closed the door behind me, and Ryan and Chris barricaded the door with the chairs and loveseat.

"That should hold them," I said. "Does anyone have a cell signal?" Phones came out and went back with no one having any luck.

"What the hell is going on here?" Chris said. "We were just here for the game today. We were staying at this stupid hotel. What's going on with all the costumes?"

"Welcome to the Festival of Fear," Ryan said in a raised voice as he grabbed a beer from the small refrigerator, opened it and took a drink. He turned to the group. "We have it all for those who enjoy the horror genre. If you dress in black and like the macabre, look no further you have found your people. Here are the slashers, thrashers, killer clowns, zombies, and ghouls, all around. Nostalgic past mixed with future gore. Come one come all for what's in store." He paused as did the rest of us as he looked around the room. "Does anyone name their kid Jason, or Michael- or Freddy anymore? And has anyone counted the sheer number of slasher movies? Only outdone by zombies mind you. We have it all here for you to enjoy."

"Don't forget vampires," Jose said. "Lots of vampire movies."

"Ryan," I said. "Maybe you should sit down. You seem a little exited."

"Am I?" Ryan said. "People have gone crazy out there and we are stuck in here. This had to be planned. Especially with the phones being down. How could this be kept hidden? Where are the police?"

"I agree," I said. "This had to be planned. I only hope that it is confined to this location and the whole world hasn't gone mad."

"Oh my," Ryan said and clenched his hands. "I never thought of that. A global pandemic of fear."

"Sorry I put that in your head," I said. "Until we figure something out, let's remain calm. We don't really know what set those people off and maybe it has something to do with how excited they got. The best thing we can do is remain calm and not make any rash decisions."

Ryan looked at his hands which were shaking and had some blood from Jose's wound. "You have a point," he said and headed to the bathroom while Mike and Ed came out of the bedroom.

"So, this is some kind of convention for people that like horror movies, lucky me," Mike said.

"I guess that's why everyone is wearing black," Chris said. "I mean, everyone. Even the girls have all dyed their hair black. I mean, come on, that's so been done before...get some new material people."

I watched as Chris caught Sandy looking at him. Her hair was black as were her nails, eye makeup and lipstick.

"I mean," Chris said, "it looks good on you."

"That's because it's my color," Sandy said. "Besides, black is always cool and never goes out of style."

"We checked the windows," Ed said as he and Mike came from the bedroom. "They are too small and high for us to get out of. There's no ledge or anything to leverage us getting down the wall."

"I think we are safe in the room for now," I said. "Where's Ryan?"

"He's lying down on the bed with his arm over his eyes," Ed said.

Everyone stopped and looked toward the door as scream rang out from the hallway.

"I'm going to turn the lights out except for that back room," I said and moved to one lamp while Sandy went to the other and in a second the room grew darker. We could still each other in the light coming from the back bedroom.

"Anyone want a drink?" Sandy asked. "We have beer and vodka."

Everyone but Ryan, who remained lying on the bed in the back room, stood and went to the small fridge where Sandy served drinks.

"Jose?" Ed said. "You don't drink."

"I do tonight," Jose said as Sandy handed him a plastic cup and poured vodka. "Make it a double."

Everyone settled back down on the chairs on the floor and grew quiet as the sounds of murder and mayhem from outside the room continued.

"Did you notice their faces," I said. "When we knocked them over the railing they didn't scream when they fell."

"What do you think that means?" Sandy asked.

"They were void of emotion," I said. "Robotic like. Almost as if hypnotized or on drugs."

"Like they are being controlled?" Sandy asked.

"Precisely," I said. "It just doesn't make sense that all of the sudden this many people turned psychotic."

"You may be on to something," Sandy said. "If it were a single person or maybe even a small group of them doing a coordinated stunt, I might believe different. But this...this is...madness."

"She's a professor of science," I said as the others looked at her.

"I know a lot of those people," Ed said. "I'm an anime artist here for the event. They might be odd but not psychotic."

"I'm a legal assistant," Jose said. "I do cosplay on the side." He referenced his Thor costume as he said this. "Guess I should have skipped this event."

"I'll say," Mike said. "Chris and I weren't even here for this festival of horror or whatever you call it. We came to watch the game and now we're stuck with all these freaks who've watched too many scary movies and now are acting as if they are in one."

"Wait," I said. "You just said something that makes perfect sense."

"It'd be the first time," Chris said and chuckled.

"What do you mean?" Mike said.

"Only the attendees what are in costume are acting out," I said. "That's at least one common thread."

"So," Sandy said. "Something has caused those dressed in costume to snap."

"And act like the characters they are portraying," Ryan said. "Think about it...the slashers were slashing; the zombies were eating people and the clowns were chasing people."

"What triggered it?" I asked.

"Well, since it didn't affect everyone, I think we cross off out the hotel food, water, drinks, ventilation or elevator music from our list of suspects"

"Right," I said. "It had to be something that affected those in costume. What about makeup?"

"Not everyone is wearing makeup," Sandy said.

"I think I witnessed what happened," Jose said.

"You think you did?" Ed asked.

All of us gathered around Jose as he sat on one of the two remaining chairs at the table. The other furniture was being used as a barricade for the door. We all glanced briefly at the door noting the chaos and screaming continued outside and had reached the sixth floor.

Ryan emerged from the bedroom and went to the front door where he turned back to the group and listened. Sandy sat on the remaining chair as I stood by her. She held out her hand which I tightly grasped.

Jose started relaying what he'd witnessed. "It was that guy," Jose said pointing at a shirt I had hanging by the sink close to the coffee maker and small refrigerator.

"That's the shirt I wore today," I said. "I took it off to wash out some fake blood I got on it. It's a shirt from a melodrama theatre."

"The person I saw downstairs looked like that character on your shirt," Jose said.

The shirt had the picture of a character in Victorian suit tails with a top hat and mustache.

"The top-hat guy?" Ed asked.

"Yes," Jose said. "I told you there was something off about him. He was dressed like a character out of the late twenties- black cloak and tie, greasy, wavy black hair, mustache, and goatee. A wicked smile with very red lips that framed rather unusually long, sparkling white teeth. He might have even powdered his face."

I must have given Jose a surprise look.

"Hey, I'm a cosplayer, I know a little about makeup," Jose said.

"Yes, I know the one you are talking about," Ed said. "I saw him at the costume contest. He had an entourage of young people."

"That was him," Jose said. "He was surrounded by six young people, three girls and three guys, all dressed as fifties university students. They had the same teal and beige sweaters and pants and had similar, small backpacks. Even the same haircuts; the girls were all shoulder-length and wavy while the boys were crew-cut. Anyway, at the end of the contest, he took the stage with these people. I thought it was part of the festival."

"It wasn't," Ryan said as he came into the room and stood by Jose. "I was one of the judges and the contest was done. That's why I left and went to the bar."

"Yes," Jose said, but many people were still in the lobby, and they too thought it was part of the show. Music started playing and the mustache man and these young people started some weird, ritualistic dance. I walked away and went to the bar. But it was not long after that I noticed the strange behavior of those watching."

"You think this man and his entourage hypnotized them somehow?" Ed asked.

"After what we've been discussing, yes, I do. And there was something else I noticed," Jose continued, "those on the stage were not affected."

"What do you mean?" Sandy asked.

"The boys and girls around him that I said were dressed in beige and teal, they were acting the same as before, which still wasn't normal, but not like those dressed in costumes."

"The plot thickens," I said.

"You'll have to forgive him," Sandy said. "He's a writer."

"Yes, I am," I said pointing to my shirt and the 'Author' title on it. "This is the perfect plot. The festival was pre-planned as were the events that accompanied it. Anyone living in this area or in touch online could have known, not only of the event, but of the costume contest. If this man dressed as so," I pointed to the character on the shirt, "wanted to enact an experiment in terror, they'd have the perfect audience just waiting for them at this venue: The Festival of Fear!"

"You're not serious," Mike said. "You think those people were hypnotized by this man? I was under the impression that people wouldn't do anything they didn't want too under hypnosis. Like, murder?"

"Maybe they don't know they are hypnotized," I said.

"Music combined with certain rhythmic motions are used all over the world in ceremonies," Ryan said. "Many of these ceremonies put those participating in a trance-like state," Ryan said.

"Yes," Sandy said, "And as you pointed out, Ryan, the slashers are slashing, the vampires are biting, and the zombies are, uh, well, being zombies. They aren't just homicidal; they are acting as if they are the characters they are dressed to be. Just like someone has convinced them that they are these characters."

"How? Why? I don't get it." Mike said.

"How is any of this going to get us out of here?" Chris asked. "Shouldn't we be making a plan to escape?"

"If we understand what is happening," I said. "It might help us piece together a way to deal with it."

"If they are under some type of suggestive trance and they are acting like the characters they are dressed to portray, they may very well be unaware of their actions" Ryan said.

"That's how they get around the morality part," I said. "Subconsciously, they don't know they are actually murdering people. They might think they are just acting out a part."

"There's got to be more to it than that," Sandy said.

"Much more," Ryan said. "Those who have attended this event have spent all day analyzing the categories of horror, the science and science fiction behind it all. The motivations of the writers and the stories portrayed were explored in focus groups. These people dressed up as characters they have followed and known from the movies, they watched and idolized. All around us we are surrounded by what is surreal. We have moved into a time where our identities are so intermixed with the characters we worship, and our individualism so intertwined with them that we are adapting their personalities instead of having our own. The fact that someone dressed up as a zombie, a vampire or a slasher demonstrates that they were associating with that personality in the first place. Add the costume and you are now queued up for such a transformation."

"That's why I stick to baseball," Mike said. "Not so complicated."

"Are we that weak?" I said. "Are we that hollow that we have no real substance other than what we are fed by the news and media and that we live our lives through the celebrities we follow? Is that why we line up for the tabloids, need so much social media and see every news cast filled to the brim with the latest celebrity gossip?" I suddenly realized the room was quiet and all eyes were on me. "Sorry, I might have overanalyzed there, and I didn't mean to say that out loud."

"It's a good thing we're out of alcohol," Sandy said.

"It's an accurate analysis," Ryan said. "We've lost balance of separating reality from fantasy. That's why kids live in the basement and play video games; a life away from the reality of life is better than the life in front of me. It will only get worse with the further introduction of virtual reality."

"We won't leave the house except for food," Jose said as he looked at Ed.

"What?" Ed said. "So, I have a few virtual reality games."

"Stores deliver everything now. Anyone that really wants too can stay home indefinitely," Ryan said.

"That's kind of creepy to think that it's come to this," Sandy said. "Instead of using our advancement to improve the human condition, we've used them to give us a method to make ourselves more comfortable in our mediocrity."

"You're right," I said. "Most people only achieve to get more possessions, wealth or stature. Few are motivated by an unselfish drive to better the human condition."

"You are getting really deep and philosophical right now," Ryan said.

"Is that bothering you?" I asked.

"No," he said stirring from his sitting position and standing. "What bothers me is that this is the type of analysis and discussion that happens during a movie right before a traumatic event."

"A traumatic event?" Chris asked.

"He means, something bad is about to happen and..." I was cut off as a loud crash sounded from down the hall. Everyone looked toward the door.

"What was that?" Chris jumped up from his seat and tried to look through the peephole in the front door.

"Sounds like someone is bashing doors in," Ryan said. "We might not be as safe as we thought we were."

"Man," Chris said. "I knew I should have stayed home and watched the game on tv. No travelling, no lines, cheaper beer. If I make it out of this, I'm buying a bigger screen tv and staying home!"

"Let's check out those windows again," I said. A group of us headed into the bedroom. Jose was to my left and Sandy to my right as we pulled the curtains back and looked down to the parking lot below.

"Look," Jose said and pointed.

I followed the direction and spotted a group of young people standing around the perimeter of the hotel property about twenty feet apart.

"They are dressed the same as the students that danced around that doctor," Jose said.

"Doctor?" I asked.

"Yes," Jose said. "That's what he kind of reminded me of. A doctor out of the late eighteen-hundreds."

"A mad doctor," Sandy said.

"Doctor Mad!" Ryan said as he came up behind us. "Now I remember...some time ago there was a man who tried to get a character he developed into the horror movies. It was a character dressed as the one you described Jose. He used hypnosis on his patients to kill others and get his way. He was basically a cult leader."

"What happened?" Sandy asked.

"Cult movies and hypnosis were not in vogue," Ryan said. "He tried for years but no one took his character seriously. The character wasn't ominous enough."

"Bet they'd rethink that now," Ed said from behind us.

"Wait," I said and pointed. "Look, there's someone who isn't in costume trying to get to a car. It looks like one of the hotel staff."

We looked on as we watched a young man who had an injured left leg hobble toward a blue sedan. He was almost there when two of the sweater-dressed people closed in on him.

"Maybe they are going to help him," Jose said.

As two of them got on each side they both put their arms under him to support him.

"See," Jose said.

Our brief moment of hope turned to horror as we watched a third person go behind the man and hit him on the back of the head with a wood club.

"Ouch, so much for that idea," Jose said.

"So, even if we get out of the hotel somehow," I said, "we are going to have to deal with the parking lot gang."

"Parking lot gang," Sandy said. "That's catchy."

"This just keeps getting better," Ryan said.

"Surely, someone on the outside must be noticing something is wrong by now!" Ed said. "Someone hasn't arrived home on time, someone hasn't called and checked in or someone driving by has to be noticing that something isn't right! Has this hotel suddenly disappeared from reality?"

"Might I remind you," Ryan said as he turned away from the window. "We are in a remote hotel north of the city. There really is nothing close to the hotel open currently and we aren't along any busy roads or in a residential area with houses close by."

"Doctor Mad knew what he was doing," Sandy said.

"All speculation at this time," Ryan said. "We don't know if this character exists or something else has gone wrong. However, if he does exist, I want to go on record as the first to refer to him as Doctor Mad." He exited the bedroom.

"And I get to play him at the next event," Jose said. He and Ed were heading toward the front room.

"What are you talking about?" Ed said.

"He's a unique and fascinating character," Jose said.

"Obviously," Ed said. "But don't you think we should focus on getting out of here first?"

"That's a no brainer," Ed said. "So, what do we do?"

"Come on," I said to Sandy, "let's join them and figure out what our next step should be." We all headed back to the front room. "Well, the way I see it is we have one box of tissues there in the bathroom."

"Tissues, what does that have to do with anything?" Sandy said.

I looked to the group. "We can all sit here and cry about this or it's time we do something," I said. "Sandy, you have that bottle of hairspray, right?"

"Yes," Sandy said.

"Hairspray?" Jose asked.

"It's the only way to get this hold," Sandy said pointing to her fascinating hairdo that could support a cinderblock on the top.

"Thor," I said, "I mean, Jose, get your hammer ready. And you two, get those bats ready."

Mike and Chris grabbed their bats, and I led the group into the bathroom where we could be in full light. I grabbed Sandy's lipstick. "Do you mind?" I asked.

Sandy shook her head.

I turned the holder on the to get a good amount of the blood-red emollient sticking out and drew a map on the mirror.

"We head to the north stairs. We use the bats and weapons to fight through and get to the stairwell. You three," I pointed to Ed, Mike, and Jose and drew three stick figures on the mirror, "take the front. Sandy and I will take the rear. Chris and Ryan, you two will be in the middle where you can step in where needed. Once we get to the stairs, we can use our uphill advantage to push anything in front of us down the stairs. There is a side exit at the lobby that leads to the presentation room. I'm hoping it's not as busy or guarded as the front."

"Hoping?" Mike said. "That's a lot of assumptions with our lives on the line."

"It's either this or we stay here praying we can wait this out," I said.

A scream rang out from the hallway causing our attention to be directed toward the front door. A crashing sound came from the adjacent room.

"Sounds like someone beat the door down in the room next to us," Sandy said.

"We don't have much time," Mike said. "Please continue."

"We break out through the side and head to my car here," I said. "Don't trust anyone dressed in costume or as a student with a backpack. Everybody good?"

"One more thing," Ryan said. "We need to commit to this. Everyone."

"What do you mean?" Ed asked.

"I mean, no one stops fighting. Don't give up and no sissies," Ryan said. "This isn't a game, and we won't get a second chance."

"Right," Chris said. He put his hand out in the middle. "Just a while ago, I didn't even know most of you. Now, we're the best chance for any of us to survive this. Good luck everyone."

We each put our hand on top of the other and then we lined up at the front door. Mike and Ed started moving the furniture back and clearing the way.

"I'm sorry I suggested we go to this event," Sandy whispered into my ear as we prepared to exit the room.

"Hey, I've had the time of my life," I said. "We're going to make it."

She grabbed my hand and squeezed it tightly.

With the last barrier at the door removed Mike turned around. "Look, I know I am not a part of this festival, but I've watched plenty of horror movies in my time. Before we go out there, I need to get a few things off my chest. What I remember about horror movies and the parts I hate is when, you know, when the killer is attacking someone, and the other person just freezes and watches instead of helping. Well, don't do that."

"Good point," I said.

"Wait," Ed said. "When one of these attackers approaches with an axe or knife raised, don't cringe in fear saying the pathetic 'no.' Like that is going to work. They mean to kill you and you better defend yourself."

"Right, I hate that," Chris said.

"What's you point?" I asked.

"Can we all agree to not do any of those things?" Mike asked.

I looked around the room as everyone nodded.

"I know I'm not ending this way," Chris said.

"We've got to fight back," Jose said. "It's us or them."

"Look," Ryan said. "These are not the real monsters of the movies, like they exist anyway. I mean, these are flesh and blood humans. We have a chance if we play it smart. Based on what we know of how these people are dressed, they will act accordingly."

"So, given that," Sandy said, "we should avoid the slashers and head for the zombies, werewolves and Frankenstein's who are not carrying weapons."

"Exactly," Ryan said.

"And we now know how Doctor Mad's helpers are dressed," I said. "Like students with backpacks."

"So, we are sticking with that name, 'Doctor Mad'" Ryan said.

I nodded. "Mike, Jose and Ed, you go forward with your bats and hammer and clear the path and we'll take our positions. Sandy and I will watch the rear. Stay close in case someone needs help. Everyone ready?"

"Batter up," Mike said.

The door swung open, and we were surprised to find the area in front of the room clear. There were characters to both sides down the hallway and six more in front looking over the balcony to the lobby below. The path to the elevator was clear.

Mike put his index finger to his lips, "shh," he whispered.

We all nodded as we walked toward the elevators. It wasn't our original plan but suddenly appeared feasible. We made it to the fist elevator and Mike reached out and pushed the button.

"Bing," the doors flew open. The sound was enough to stir the monsters looking off the balcony and they started coming our way. We crowded into the empty elevator before they could get a hand on anyone. Jose smashed the one single hand that did reach in before the door shut causing its owner to withdraw.

"Do we go all the way or to the second floor?" Ed asked as he ended up by the buttons.

"Try the lobby," Ryan said, "but don't get out right away until we make sure it's clear."

We all watched each floor through the glass doors as we went down.

"The second floor is pretty clear," I said. "Maybe we should get off there."

"It's too late, we're already at the ground floor," Ryan said.

"We keep our positions when we exit," I said. "No gaps."

"Right, but don't exit until we know it's clear," Chris said.

The glass doors that allowed the rider to see out on every floor were covered on the first floor as the car settled into a walled room. I held my breath as the door opened and Jose and Ed went out. The rest of us started to follow but didn't get far before we were shoved back in.

"Not clear! Not Clear," Ed shouted coming back in. Mike and Jose swung away as multiple Michaels and Jason's slashed at them. One got a piece of Mike with a blade to his right forearm which he pulled back to his body as his bat dropped to the ground. The doors closed and for a moment we were safe again.

"Hit two," Ryan's voice rang out. I found myself closest to the buttons and pushed the second floor as Ed and Chris attended to Mike.

"It's much worse than it looks," Mike said about his wound and laughed.

Jose pulled a patch off his robe and used it to wrap Mike's arm. Sandy reached down and picked up the bat but Mike grasping his arm shook his head. "You keep it. I'm not good with my left hand."

Sandy handed Mike the ice pick she was carrying and grasped the bat tightly.

The door to the elevator opened on the second floor and there were now five characters clustered outside the door.

"AHHHH!" I heard the battle cry as Ed put his bat out in front of him with both hands and used it to push out and engage the attackers. We all exited and watched as he continued forward and one by one the villains fell over the railing to the lobby. The final one grabbed onto Ed's bat as he pushed forward causing him to follow over the railing as he fell to the first floor. I jumped forward to the balcony and spotted Ed as he landed on the other bodies that broke his fall. He rolled off keeping his bat in hand. He stood and looked up at me.

"Wooo hoo!" Ed yelled out and smiled. It was a short-lived moment of triumph as several slashers came at him. He fought valiantly but there were too many blades.

In a desperate moment, I considered jumping from the second floor to help Ed. If I landed on one of the attackers, it would break my fall. I stepped forward but a hand grasped my right shoulder and held me back. I turned to see Sandy. Our eyes locked in dread.

"It's too late for him, but we still have a chance," Sandy said. We turned to the reality before us. Jose and Mike were in the hallway motioning us forward.

"Where's Ed?" Jose asked. I shook my head.

"Remember the plan," Ryan said. "Let's head to the stairs."

"We got your back," I said and turned to look down the hall as Mike, Jose and Ryan began moving toward the stairwell entrance. Sandy stood beside me, and we glanced back to see two clowns and a hippie engage Mike and Jose while another clown came at us from the rear. Sandy caught the clown with a round kick to the side of its head causing its wig fly off as it crashed to the ground out cold.

"Wow," I said, "you knocked her out. Hope I don't ever make you mad."

The clowns in front didn't have it as easy; broken noses and flying teeth were on display as Jose and Mike swung their weapons and continued to the stairs. I helped Ryan with the hippie character. He punched the character hard in the stomach and when he bent over, I finished with and elbow to the side of the head and backhand knocking the misfit to the ground.

"Hippies," Ryan said, "who needs 'em."

At last, there were no masked monsters between us and the entrance to the front stairwell. We moved toward the doorway stepping over bodies of hotel guests. The sigh of relief was short lived. The door opened and two killer clowns, a scarecrow, and three zombies emerged, heading right toward us. We engaged but there were too many. Mike tripped over the bodies as we were pushed back, and Chris tried to reach him but was struck several times by the clowns; one carried a mallet while another had a knife.

"Get out of here," Chris said as he swung wildly and blocked the way so the rest of us could get down the hallway.

In a moment of final glory, I watched Mike grab the ankle of one of the clowns following us. He tripped it and Chris followed by smashing its head with the bat. It would be their last stand as he succumbed to the monsters.

"Back to the elevators," I yelled out as I fought off two witches that came up behind us. I gave one a right cross and the other my left elbow and watched them drop.

"Go!" I heard Jose say as we ran to the elevators. When we turned the corner to the waiting area, we were met by several masked figures and had to fight our way to the elevator. Sandy reached out and hit the button. The doors opened on the right, but the elevator wasn't clear. She managed to kick the exiting freaks back in as the elevator door shut with Jose, Ryan, Sandy, and myself inside with three costumed characters. After a few backhands and kicks, the characters we all unconscious or dead on the floor of the elevator.

"Now what?" Sandy asked.

"We can't keep losing people," Ryan said. The elevator doors came open and he and Jose moved out.

I exited and cleared the area to the left of us by pushing two screamers off the balcony. I could see Jose and Ryan engaging multiple characters while Sandy kept between the elevators making sure nothing else would come out and flank us. Suddenly, the elevator behind us opened.

"It's Empty!" I shouted. "Get in!" I pulled Sandy across as Jose and Ryan stepped back trying to fend off multiple attackers. Jose tripped and two clowns toppled onto him. Ryan tried to help but as soon as he turned, he was ambushed from behind. I pushed one of the attackers off Ryan and we simultaneously hit the other one who fell to the ground. As we turned, we watched Jose being shredded with knives and bitten by zombies. His eyes locked with mine and pled for help.

"Get in!" Sandy shouted.

"Wait," Ryan said. He leaned down and ripped the mask off one of the clowns. I understood what he was doing and fought my way to get two more masks. I took one from an unconscious character lying on the floor and the other I ripped off a character attacking Jose. Surprised at my own strength, in an adrenaline-fueled rage I grabbed from the back and twisted the head hearing the neck snap before I tore the mask away.

Jose, barely standing and in shock did not move toward the elevator. I could see he was bleeding from multiple stab wounds.

"Come on, we need to get inside," I said pulling Jose behind me.

Jose started to move toward me when two more slashers attacked. He was stabbed from behind by one as the other came toward me. I executed a move and dodged to my left as I blocked the knife arm with a left inward block. I grabbed the attacker's arm with my right hand on his wrist and pulled it against my left forearm breaking the attacker's arm at the elbow. The attacker fell to the ground. The character engaging Jose knelt over him and stabbed him repeatedly. I kicked the attacker to the back of the head knocking him out. I checked my surroundings and knelt by Jose.

"Come on, get up," I said as I put my hand out. I could see blood flowing from his mouth. He spit some out as he talked.

"Obviously, I'm not getting up from this," Jose said as he struggled to speak. "It's a no brainer that you need to leave me. Go."

Ryan came up behind me and put his hand on my shoulder. "We need to go," Ryan said.

"Take this," Jose said and handed me the hammer. "And do me a favor." He squeezed my hand.

"What favor?" I asked.

"When you write your story about all of this, make sure," Jose struggled to continue as he spit blood.

"I'll make sure you die a hero in a glorious way," I said.

He smiled, coughed once, and went limp.

Ryan pulled me up and we stumbled into the elevator as Sandy held the door open. A slasher character came up behind me and I turned, grasping the makeshift hammer that Jose had carried, and swung it with a mighty force at the head of the machete wielding maniac. A thunderous crack sounded as the wood handle snapped with the impact and the attacker flew backwards, crashing down on the floor.

"Ooh, that hurt," Ryan said as we both entered the elevator. The door closed and we each breathed a sigh of relief for a moment. Sandy held her hand on the close button and kept the elevator from moving.

"I have an idea," Ryan said. "Put this on." He took one of the masks I held and gave it to Sandy.

"You think this will work," I asked.

"I think we're out of options," Ryan said. "I don't know about you, but I'm beat and there's too many of them."

"Can we make it back to the hotel room?" Sandy asked.

"We need to get out of here," Ryan said. "Let's go back out with these masks on," Ryan said. "Act like they do and don't engage them. We should know very quickly if it's working. I'll go first."

"What if it doesn't work?" Sandy said.

"Then we'll try to get back to the hotel room and hold out as long as we can," I said, "Agreed?"

"Agreed," Ryan and Sandy said simultaneously.

I noticed Sandy looking at my shirt and I looked down at myself, seeing blood on my front and sleeves as well as my jeans. "It's not fake blood this time," she said.

"I guess not," I said. "Ruined two of my favorite shirts in a day. Are you still able to kick?" I asked.

"I'm going to kick some ass if anyone comes close," she said and pushed the button to the lobby.

We put the plastic and latex coverings on and prepared ourselves as the elevator door opened. Ryan stepped out right into three costumed characters. They were ready to attack but hesitated as they looked at him. I exited with Sandy and, noticing they didn't attack, nudged Ryan. The three of use headed down the hallway and took a left to go out the side exit. It was still night but the lights in the parking lot were enough for us to find out way. We headed toward my car and got inside. I locked the doors and breathed a sigh of relief before turning the key to start the engine.

Several of the students took notice and headed our way as the engine roared to life. With Ryan in the backseat and Sandy in the passenger seat, I gunned the engine and headed for the exit. As we moved across the hotel entrance area, I spotted a black hearse and the character that everyone had described; a man with a black suit, top hat, beard, and mustache, was getting into the back of the hearse. I slammed on the brakes.

"What are you doing," Ryan asked. "Let's get out of here."

The gallant man getting into the car must have heard the screeching of the tires and glanced toward us. He stepped back from the car, remove his top hat, and took a bow before entering the hearse. The vehicle circled around the lot and took a right turn out of the parking lot. Tempted to follow, we were confronted by three people dressed as students with their goofy backpacks blocking our way. I hit the gas and drove straight for them without slowing down. Two of them jumped to the side but the third one was not so lucky and didn't clear the driver's side mirror. The mirror caught her arm and knocked her to the ground.

I hesitated only a moment at the end of the parking lot still tempted to follow Doctor Mad. Assessing our situation, tired and in no shape to fight, I took a left toward the highway. As we pulled out of the center and started toward the on-ramp, we passed multiple emergency vehicles on their way to the hotel.

"Should we go back and tell them?" I asked and looked over to Sandy and then checked the rear-view mirror to see if Ryan had heard me. My cell phone beeped, and Sandy's went off as we all finally got a signal.

"No, don't go back to that hellhole," Ryan said. "I'll give them a call."

I headed down the highway with no destination in mind just glad to get away from the terror of the hotel. I listened as Ryan spoke to the police and gave them our information. Ryan offered to allow us to crash at his house the rest of the night, and we accepted his offer. The next day we went down to the police station and gave our statements. We also asked if they could get our luggage for us as no one was ready to go back to the hotel. This took another day, so we remained at Ryan's house.

A Detective Jennings came by Ryan's house to deliver our luggage and gave us a debrief. We were told that when the police arrived on the scene there was loud music playing over the intercom system and the costumed characters had all fallen asleep. A toxicology report was done on several of the suspects but came back negative. The footage from the hotel cameras had been erased and any recording of the event had been taken. We each gave our description of Doctor Mad to which Jennings grinned at the name we'd given the character.

"Doctor Mad?" Jennings said. "A man dressed like that and driving around in a hearse shouldn't be too hard to find."

Once Jennings left, Sandy and I packed the car, said goodbye to Ryan who we promised to keep in touch with, and headed home.

"Glad to be going home?" I asked as Sandy fastened her seat belt.

"Yes," she said. "I'm so sorry about all of this. I guess next time I'll think twice about inviting anyone to something with 'fear,' 'horror,' or 'terror,' in the name."

"Don't worry," I said. "There was no way you could have known this would happen. Besides, as terrible as this ordeal has been, I probably wouldn't have made it if it wasn't for you."

She smiled and then her phone wrang.

"This is Sandy Sullivan," she said as I pulled onto the highway.

"Hey," Sand said. "It's the director of the Festival of Fear."

"Really? What does he want?"

"He says he wants to apologize for what happened and claims they were not involved in any way, nor did they have any prior knowledge or warning of what transpired."

"I would hope not," I replied. "Why would they want to kill their attendees?"

"There's more..."

"Yes?"

"He says they are already getting calls for next year's festival and they are worried they are going to sell out. They wanted to make sure they give anyone that attended this year free tickets for next year's event."

"Ha! I imagine the demand for that won't be high. They won't have many returns as most of them are dead and the rest are in jail," I said. "Anyone who made it out of there would be crazy to return."

"Just a minute," Sandy said to the person at the other end as she held the phone in her hand and a moment of silence passed between us.

I watched the road in front of me carefully suddenly valuing each precious moment I was experiencing with the knowledge that I, we, had been so close to a curtain call.

"So," she said, "are we going?"

"Free tickets?"

"Yes?"

"Does that include free hotel?"

"Does that include the hotel?" Sandy asked.

"He says the hotel is included as well," Sandy said.
"Tell him we'll be there! Oh, and insist we get a room on the sixth floor."

Prologue:

Two months after the colossal event, Detective Jennings called Sandy and I and debriefed us on the investigation. Those involved in the costume mayhem showed psychological trauma brought about by suspected hypnosis and mind conditioning.

Although the hotel cameras footage was erased, the police were able to recover some personal videos taken by victims and footage from local businesses including a view of the hearse we had sighted.

The hearse and Doctor Mad are still at-large as are the numerous accomplices that we described being dressed as university students. The hotel is planning an increased security presence as well as increasing background checks on the participants of this year's festival which is still scheduled to take place.

Detective Jennings advised us not to attend.

The End

READERS NOTE: THE ABOVE SECTION WAS CALLED A "PROLOGUE" ALTHOUGH IT APPEARS AT THE END OF THE STORY FOR THE VERY PURPOSE OF INDICATING THERE WOULD BE ANOTHER STORY."

Do you believe in ghosts
What about a haunted house
Would you be scared to go
Or would you line up to be first
Would you be at your best
Or be at your worst

As the tour starts
Beware of ghosts
Those who remain behind
For the tale I tell
Starts as a friendly haunt
With warm feelings
And happy ghosts
That appear to be your friend
But as the night wears on
You might find
The happiness will end

For there are no friendly ghosts
Only those stuck here to wander
And making them aware
Is surely a big blunder
For once they realize their fate
That they are no longer in a living state
What is left is
Sadness, madness, anger and hate

THE THOUSANDS

CHAPTER ONE

INVITATION TO A HAUNTED HOUSE

Do you believe in a hereafter? A heaven or hell or whatever it may be? It is fact that energy does not cease but is only transferred. This is something you must understand before you read any further; it is only through the understanding of this transformation that this story will make sense. There are many among us that believe the soul or spirit is the energy or lifeforce within flesh and tissue, and the body is merely a transportation device for this force. The energy that is stored within the vessel is not lost when the body dies, it's just transformed.

It was Ryan Conner who invited me- *me*, an author of many works and a confessed fanatic of everything horror, supernatural or science fiction related. I wanted to believe in ghosts, spirits, aliens, ESP and magic. However, my business profession and duties as a parent often took me far from my imagination and kept me firmly footed in the world of reality. That's why I was delighted when he called and invited me along on a case; you see, Ryan is a paranormal investigator that I met at The Festival of Fear in Denver, Colorado. It's important to him that you do not call him a ghost hunter, which he feels demeans his profession. It was that profession that got him invitations to places others would not dare go.

I heard the car pull into my driveway and wheeled my bag outside locking the door behind me. Ryan, vehicle still running, exited the driver side. A few inches shorter than me, at five eight, Ryan had long black hair and a beard; both were graying a bit. His large arms and hands spoke of a past in weightlifting-- although he'd never mentioned it.

"Well, I didn't expect to see you so soon, not after that last event," I said as he opened the back to his blue Ford Explorer and I placed my bag inside. Then I turned and shook his hand.

"I thought it would be best if I took some time off after that last event," Ryan said. "This case is too interesting to pass up. Come on, we should get going. I'll brief you on the way. If we don't run into heavy traffic, we could be there mid-afternoon."

"Let's go," I said and climbed into the passenger seat as we headed out of town and down the highway to our next destiny. Soon, we were on the highway heading northwest to our destination.

"So, what have you been doing with your time?" Ryan asked.

"I've been catching up on my favorite shows. This digital age is great; they've got episodes of everything made from my childhood"

"So, what have you been watching?"

"Battlestar Galactica, the original. The rest is a rip off," I said. "It's kind of cheesy now that I'm older but, still good."

"Geez, I forgot about that show," Ryan said. "Haven't seen it forever."

"All kids in my neighborhood watched it. It was new and exciting and full of adventure," I said.

"I remember they killed it with season two," Ryan said.

"Then they did a remake that was so different from the original that they should have just made it a new show," I said.

"End of the seventies and into the eighties. What an original time," Ryan said.

"I like to watch some of the shows from my youth. It gets my mind back to my adventurous age when life was, well, full of endless opportunity! Speaking of opportunities, tell me, where are we going?"

Bryan smiled from under his mustache and beard. "We are going on an exciting tour! Exclusive access to one of the most active haunted houses in Colorado; the Wendel House."

"Wow, exclusive access," I said. "Does that mean we are staying the night?"

"Of course," Ryan said. "Which that alone surprises me."

"Why?"

"The group I run tends to spend more time and do thorough research when we are invited. Not like these fly-by-night firms that go in for a few hours at night and merely scare themselves to impress an audience. We like to stay a few days and really get to the bottom of things. Last time I was there, they didn't seem happy with letting us stay the night. Our results were not as conclusive as they wanted and they didn't exactly invite us back,"

"Not conclusive," I said. "Did you tell them that their haunted house wasn't haunted?"

"Our results were inconclusive," Ryan said. "However, I will tell you that it is one of the most peculiar places I've been. I mean, we've seen some coincidences and some strange occurrences we can't explain. In this case, we wanted more time to prove our conclusions."

"Always the skeptic, right?"

"It's our reputation," Ryan said. "Unfortunately, they would not allow us more time and we were not willing to rule the experience unexplained."

"Ah, an impasse," I said.

"If we don't keep an open mind and do thorough research, we become one of those hyped shows on television; good for the fans and pocketbook, but not good for science."

"So, what happened?"

"I pressed for more access and was denied," Ryan said. "I don't know if it was too personal or if the director feared I'd publish results not favorable to the tours."

"Why did that matter so much?"

"The only way the house stays operating is through donations and due to the tours. You have been there of course?"

"Actually, it is too far north for my usual expeditions," I said. "Besides, now that you know I haven't visited the place, I can be a skeptical observer as well."

"Right," Ryan said. "Then there is something you should know. The house is claimed to be the most active haunt. This does not mean it's evil. In fact, they pride themselves that the house is full of friendly ghosts."

"Really?" I said.

"I know," Ryan said. "Not the usual story or reason people are driven to see a haunted house. They've turned the story into a romantic one: a husband and wife so loving with their family that they all want to stay together in their happy home for eternity."

"That almost sounds like a horror story in itself," I said. "Spend eternity with your family," I laughed. It almost sounds like something parents can use as a threat to get children to do homework."

"Or chores," Ryan laughed. "Just don't tell the director, Miss Cassandra Krage, that."

"Did you say Miss?" I asked.

"Yes," Ryan said. "I think she is in her forties, never married. She's been there at least twenty years and I would say she has indeed been touched by the house, if you believe in that sort of bond."

"Interesting," I said. "Who else will we be meeting there?"

"Stephey Lake is a tech assistant I've brought in to help us. She lives close to the location, and she's been there before so she's familiar with the surroundings. I wanted a larger team but, Miss Krage wouldn't agree to it. There is another surprise you might find entertaining; you will have the unique opportunity to meet someone who is on the fringe of science: Mr. Rick Niley, psychic investigator extraordinaire!"

"A psychic investigator," I said. "This will be a treat." I took out a small notebook and started to jot a few things down.

"Paper and pencil?" Ryan asked. "No laptop?"

"Pen," I said. "I'm old fashioned that way. Now, how long till we get there and what's for lunch?"

After a short stop along the way for some wood-fired pizza, we soon found ourselves gliding over the high mountains in the middle of the state. The house we were visiting stood in an old mining town and was one of the oldest houses in a place that had seen tragedy a time or two. Fire had consumed much of the town on more than one occasion. The inhabitants that remained lived through the gold and silver rush to a time when the mines went dry. The current residents thrived off of what was left of a single gold mine and the proceeds from gambling casinos courtesy of the late twentieth century. The house itself was one of the many attractions in the scenic mountain town that was full of mining and other historical tours and tourist shops. The quiet town was a great place to get away from it all and enjoy some fresh air.

"I'm just hoping that's not all there is here," I said not realizing that I said this out loud.

"All there is to what?" Ryan asked.

"All there is to this story," I said. "We share one thing in common, we are both waiting for something more exciting to happen: a brush with the unknown, the supernatural. I'm not young anymore and I just wonder if that is ever really going to happen."

"That's a bold statement coming from a man who makes his living the way you do," Ryan said. "I mean, *The 13th Month*? That was a great story. I thought it would be a movie by now."

"So did I," I replied.

Ryan moved to the back of the car. I had a single bag, so I helped him with his equipment.

"I wasn't sure if you'd really come with," Ryan said, "after our last adventure together."

"I'm hoping that was a freak coincidence," I said. We were both referring to *The Festival of Fear.* It was an event where we met and became friends but barely survived. That's another story for another time. "I couldn't pass up the opportunity," I said. "A chance to see the famous Wendel House along with the opportunity to put my investigative skills together."

"Oh," Ryan said. "What are you investigating?"

"Same thing you are, the strange happenings and the cause behind them."

"Well, here's to hoping we both find something here that's worthwhile," Ryan said.

"As long as it doesn't turn out like last time," I said. Little did I know as we approached the door to the Wendel House that our next adventure together would be similar to the first: full of dead people!

CHAPTER TWO
WELCOME TO THE FRIENDLY
HAUNTED HOUSE

We approached the front of the large, stone house which, according to the website, had been constructed in 1889, right when the railroad started coming to the old mining town. The windows had been modernized and the surroundings were definitely not what they had been at the time the house was built. The lawn, lush and green, was bordered by tall, ponderosa pine trees, probably not even saplings at the time the Wendels moved in. Two big wooden doors opened in front of us as we walked up the wide stairwell to the front of the house. There we were greeted by two ladies at the front door: Miss Cassandra Krage, who looked straight out of the Victorian Era with her lavender dress hemmed and trimmed with egg-white lacing. Her hair done up where it was tucked under a fancy black hat with purple flowers. Her companion, Nora, a shorter lady with long, brown flowing hair, was dressed as a maid and took our jackets before she helped direct us to a large living area.

"Welcome," Miss Krage said. "I have set up some cots for you in the living area and set up a table for dining. Please, do not disturb any of the displays in the house or go behind any of the closed areas without first checking with me.

"Has Rick arrived yet?" Ryan asked.

"Mister Niley has not arrived at this time," Miss Krage responded. "Would you like a tour of the house?"

Bryan started unpacking a bag of equipment and was setting stuff in order when she asked. "I've been here before," he said. "Mister DeGrado may want a tour. You know, he's an author."

"Yes, I know," Miss Krage said. "I've seen two of your melodramas at the Golden Rush theatre here. They were both enjoyable. Would you care for a tour of the house?"

"Yes, I would love to look around," I said. "I've always been fascinated with history and the supernatural."

"Oh?" Miss Krage said. "Well, we like to consider this house a friendly haunt."

"Yes, I've heard," I said as I checked my phone battery and turned it to camera mode hoping to snap some shots.

"Please, call me Sandra," Miss Krage, Sandra, said. She came beside me and put her arm in mine as she took me on a tour of the first floor.

"Why do you call this a friendly haunt?" I asked.

"See, years after the gold rush started, this town was booming. However, it lacked a proper doctor. So, some of the wealthier families recruited a top-notch doctor; Doctor Wendel."

"Looks like they treated him very well," I commented as we went to the dining room.

"They did," Sandra said. "They built him a small house and he set up shop here."

"So, this wasn't his original home?"

"No, he fell in love with the daughter of one of the wealthiest families. It was her father that built them this house as a wedding gift. Although not completed until about eighteen eighty-nine, construction on this site started twenty years earlier. The original stakeholders sold to the mining company who then gave the house to the doctor as a wedding gift. Mister and Missus Wendel had two wonderful children, and his son was a writer. Short stories mostly. It was suspected that his sister actually did most of the writing and used his name because, you know."

After touring a study, a music room and Doctor Wendel's office where he would see patients, we went into the large living room. The living room contained a couch and chairs from the period but also held several modern chairs that sat in front of a large, sixty-inch television. On the screen, a video played about the history of the house. Across from the seating areas, a long mirror lay along a wall that led to the stairway entrance; it's where Sandra led me up to the second floor.

"Why do you think the family has remained in the house?" I asked being careful to stay away from the term "haunted," not wanting to offend my guide.

Sandra led me to a family portrait hanging at the top of the stairs. "Doctor Wendel had to travel for his practice. He wrote letters when he was away from home. Many of the letters he wrote were later found in the house. They were beautiful letters, some of which are on display in their bedroom. All, a testament to the love he had for his wife and children."

Sandra's eyes lit-up and she glanced into a distant past while her lips turned to a half-smile and continued the tale.

"They were so in love that they both committed to being together forever in this home," Sandra said. She then focused back to me.

I managed as smile. She blushed.

"I'm sorry," Sandra said.

"No need to be," I said. "What clues have you come across that you think it is their ghosts in this house?"

"Those who visit the house often smell the tobacco from the pipe Doctor Wendel smoked. They also smell the perfume, an expensive and exclusive lavender that he bought for his wife, in the hallways and in the music room. She loved the cello. Sometimes at night, the cello plays. We've had several investigators that have told us the whole family is here; come back to live forever in what was their happiest moments."

We stopped in both the children's rooms and were now in the Doctor and his wife's bedroom. "I noticed your tours are only during the day," I said.

"Yes, we try to be respectful of the family," Sandra said. "After all, it is there home we are trouncing all over. Plus, we've had less favorable clientele at night. There's more to see, especially the theatre room but, I heard the door which means Mister Niley is probably here. We should get back to the others."

"Of course," I said. "Lead the way."

Sandra put her arm through mine again and led me along the empty corridors down to the first floor. This time, I felt a presence; hers. In the midst of the period pieces and history, I felt the warmth and passion of someone lost in a different time. My guide seemed quite at home in the past and with the family she had come to know.

While coming down the stairs I spotted a tall, middle-aged, lanky man with short, black hair wearing a brown suit with a vest. Upon his face a thin mustache and his small, brown eyes were darting about from behind thick-framed circular glasses. He smiled when he spotted Sandra.

"Ah, the owner of the house," Niley stated causing Sandra to blush.

"Just the caretaker," Sandra said. "It's a pleasure to see you again. May I introduce Author Louis Paul DeGrado."

I shook Rick Niley's hand. He appeared unimpressed with me as his eyes quickly darted away. He walked in a half circle around the entry and then back to the base of the stairs. He looked toward the second floor. "I can understand why you called...there is a disturbance. Yes, something is very wrong here."

I glanced around the room noticing everyone had stopped what they were doing and focused on Rick Niley. Suddenly, a crash sounded from the reception room. We hurried to see what had happened. Had the disturbed ghosts communicated their displeasure with us? Was this a hint to leave? What could have caused the sound?

"Sorry, I accidently pulled the monitor off the table while trying to get the cord to reach that outlet," a scrawny kid with short but thick black, hair in a black leather jacket and shirt looked at us.

"This is Stephey Lake," Ryan said. "My technical assistant who will be setting up the cameras and monitoring them throughout the night." A young lady about five foot five, with black eye makeup around both eyes, greeted me. She wore a black leather jacket with a rock band t-shirt underneath.

"What's going on?" Ryan said.

"Don't mind me," Stephey said. "Just adjusting some equipment. I'll be sitting in this room monitoring the equipment. That's my job. Just a fly on the wall."

"Well, welcome to the Wendel house," Sandra said and put out her hand to greet Stephey. "If there's anything you need."

"Some food would be nice," Stephey said. "I haven't had anything to eat since this morning."

"Yes, of course," Sandra said. "I will be serving dinner shortly after we have a tour and discuss why I've asked for all of you to come here. You're more than welcome to join us in the living area to eat."

"Oh, no thanks," Stephey said. "I prefer to be watching the monitors. Just pretend I'm not here, hu, hu. Unless, of course, you hear a scream from here or something…hu, hu, just kidding."

"We'll keep an eye on you," Ryan said. "Thank you for coming so soon. Now, Miss Sandra, where do we start?"

"Dinner's here," Nora said coming in the front door with several bags.

We retired to the back porch where a picnic table had been set up for us to eat. A meal of fried chicken, mashed potatoes and green beans was served with iced tea and lemonade to drink.

The conversation lagged during the meal, so I started asking questions.

"So, Mister Niley, how do you know Ryan Conner and Miss Krage?"

Ryan smiled pleasantly at Sandra. "My talents have allowed me to travel and meet some wonderful people such as Miss Cassandra Krage. I visited here for a tour once and was invited to use my expertise to estimate the age of family members that still resides here." His smile disappeared as he turned to Ryan. "Mister Conner and I inhabit the same circles due to our professions. With respect, we have differing views on many subjects, but I could not ask for a better investigator when it comes to getting to the bottom of things."

Ryan took a drink of tea and put his glass down. "I would say we have many similar beliefs. I, like you Mister Niley, believe that there is something that exists after we die. The energy that makes us who we are, has to go on somehow after death. I can say that I really want to believe this. However, my approach has been scientific and my data, unfortunately, has not supported what I've hoped to find." Ryan turned to Sandra catching her in mid-bite. "To tell you the truth, I was surprised to be invited back here."

Sandra quickly swallowed her food and wiped her lips lightly with a paper napkin.

"I believe your disbelief will be put to rest tonight," Sandra said. "Of that, I am sure."

"I look forward to it," Ryan said as he raised his glass. "A toast, to all of us who seek wonder and adventure."

We clinked our glasses together and the cloud lifted from above us. I was sure it was still there, just higher. I noticed Niley glancing my way.

"Mister DeGrado, exactly how do you know Mister Conner?"

"It's a long story," I said. "We met in Denver at the Festival of Fear."

"Wasn't there something in the news about that?" Sandra said.

"Yes," Niley stated. "Some of the participants were murdered by other attendees if I'm not mistaken. Only a few people were said to survive the ordeal."

Ryan pointed to himself, to me, and back to himself.

"Oh my," Sandra said. "Did they find out what caused those people to go, well, crazy?"

Ryan and I locked eyes for a moment.

"Not exactly," I spoke. "The investigation is still ongoing." Ryan and I knew the truth about the villain the police were now hunting, Doctor Mad is the name we'd given him. The police asked us not to give him any publicity fearing it would only tip him off that they knew of him. They didn't want him to get publicity and desire more.

"Well," Niley said, "what do you expect from a group of people that throw themselves so deep into their fantasies? Sooner or later, they can't tell what's real and what's fake. All proof that nothing supernatural, other than perhaps God, is good."

I watched Ryan's expression as Niley's words hung across the table. His eyebrows raised as he looked like he was about to say something but instead, reached for his tea. Perhaps, it was the fact that our psychic didn't believe the supernatural were up to any good that surprised him. It surprised me as well.

"Well," Sandra said, "I hope you are ready to keep an open mind about the Wendel House. Here, we have a family that's decided to stay together after death. That's what I said. Is it so hard to believe that a family, so happy together in life, is committed to never leaving each other and thereby remain bound together in this home?"

"Makes for a great story," I said.

"A sad one," Niley said. "Imagine never experiencing what is beyond."

"If you've never been beyond, you wouldn't know," Ryan said.

"And that is your prison," Niley said. "You are trapped in what you believe to be the best you've ever known but you don't know that because it is all you've known."

Sandra smiled as though amused at all the talking but somehow, I caught a glimpse of her romantic side believing in the story she wove of love and happiness.

"I'm sorry to say," Niley spoke, "but I have never experienced what you are speaking of—a happy ghost. There is no such thing. The very sense of being stuck and unable to move forward to what is next is an indication that something is wrong. The very reason for your current disturbance and change may be that this once 'happy family,' as you say, has finally realize the contrary. It's not natural for them to be remain behind. The longer they stay, the more they move away from what they were."

"What do you mean, 'from what they were?' I asked.

Rick Niley took a slow drink from his glass of tea. He looked directly at Sandra before answering. "I'm not used to being the bad guy, I have heard that is your job, Ryan."

Ryan laughed. "Yes, I'm usually the one telling folks that there is no evidence that ghosts really exist. Yet, I still hold out for that day I might discover something truly unexplained."

"I can tell Mister DeGrado is still wanting an answer," Niley said. "We often project our human behaviors on ghosts. This is in err, they are not human anymore."

Sandra suddenly stood from here chair surprising the rest of the group. She blushed and then looked around the table. "Is there anything else we can get for you before we start clearing the table?"

No one indicated a need so her and Nora began clearing the table while Ryan and I helped. Niley went inside the house.

"I hope we didn't offend our host," I said to Ryan as the two of us overlooked the back yard. I noticed an outhouse and a well among the flowers and grass that were all in pristine condition.

"I don't think any of us can come between the bond Sandra Krage has with this house and the family," Ryan said. "It wouldn't surprise me to find that in her afterlife she decided to remain here with the ghosts of the family."

I knew Ryan was just being playful with his words and didn't mean any disrespect. He himself wanted to believe in an afterlife however, his years of investigations had turned up no proof that anything beyond existed, no voices, no apparitions, no contact with the unknown. My thoughts were interrupted as Sandra came through the back door.

"Shall we begin?" Sandra said.

The four of us gathered at the base of the stairs. Rick Niley, Ryan Conner, myself and our host, Miss Cassandra Krage, Sandra. Nora continued her cleaning and preparation duties while Stephey, with earphones on, sat behind a multitude of monitors and merely gave us a thumbs up as we passed by.

The tour of the first floor was uneventful and we headed up the stair when Niley stopped midway and looked down.

"You just met Little Alice," Sandra said. "Little Alice has been known to tug on visitors' ankles in a teasing way. A few people have stumbled on occasion."

"Little Alice?" I asked.

"Yes," Sandra said, "She's the five-year old daughter picture here," she pointed to a picture of the family on the wall midway up the stairway.

"I thought the children had all grown," I said.

"No," Niley said. "The couple's children both died but not in the house. That is part of the mystery. It is believed that the members of this family exist as ghosts during the happiest period of their lives. For them, it was in this house as a family."

"Sounds like the perfect place to put some of your equipment," I said to Ryan.

Ryan pointed to a camera mounted on the banister.

"My tech Stephey is already on it."

"I tell you the story of how we pick our guides," Sandra continued, "because I believe that may be where some of our problems begin."

"How so?"

"Please, have a seat in the room here," Sandra said. She led us into a large, open room about twenty feet wide by thirty feet long with seating for at least twenty or more people and a large screen against the far wall.

"This room was the family's theatre room," Sandra said. "An uncommon feature for most homes of that day and one of the reasons they were so popular. They would put on plays and perform music on the piano, cello, violin. In fact, many times we've heard music here at night." She pointed to the instruments that were set on stands throughout the room.

We sat in the chairs while Sandra went to the front and sat in a single chair by the small stage. She reached over and picked up the cello and started playing it. When she finished, we applauded.

"Thank you," Sandra said. "What I just played for you is a selection that we found in this house. Some of the staff over the years have claimed to hear it when downstairs at night. This is one of the many occurrences we've come used to."

"Most of what you are speaking of occurs in the evening, correct?" Niley stated.

"Yes," Sandra said. "Which is why we prefer not to have tours during the evening. We don't want to disturb the family."

"You mentioned the little girl," I said, "I was under the impression that no tragic events actually took place at the house and that it was, forgive my term, a happy haunted house."

Sandra smiled as she put her hand up to her face trying to cover her reaction. "Well, if there is such a thing, this would be the place. You are correct; there was little to no tragedy here at the house. However, both children were killed at a young age during a flood. They were travelling south on a train and caught with their nanny. As a remembrance, the parents hosted many children's activities and supported family events. You could say it was to make up for the loss of their own children."

"Now, back to the reason I believe there has been some unsettling events," Sandra continued. "You see, one of our younger guides, the daughter of a friend of ours who we hired because of her relationship, decided to meet her boyfriend here at the end of her shift. Instead of leaving, they stayed after hours. He turned out to be one of those amateur ghost hunters. One of our friends caught the videos he took on that checkmate channel. We wrote them and had them all taken down of course."

"How did the parents die," I asked.

"Excuse me?" Sandra asked.

"The parents in the picture," I said. "They remained in the house and had all the events you speak about but how did they meet their end?"

"Oh," Sandra said as she stood and went to a small bookcase. She removed a book and brought it back handing it to me. "The story is right here," Sandra said. "But, to save you from having to read the whole book, they died together on the cold night of September twenty-third, nineteen thirty-two."

"Together?" I asked.

"Yes, they were found in bed together. It was the first really cold night of the season, and the story goes that they did not want to bear another cold winter at their age. One could not live without the other, so their spirits passed together."

"Sounds suspicious," Ryan said.

"Yes," Sandra said. "However, there was an investigation but, no one profited from their demise, so it was never given much thought. They constantly gave to the community and had no enemies."

"That love is what you say kept them here in this house together?" I asked.

Sandra nodded.

"I would hope that when I depart, I won't still be at my house," Niley said. "I couldn't imagine what that would be like." He turned to me. "You've written about ghosts; how do you think they would feel?"

"I never thought about it. I mean, do they sleep? Do they need rest? Do they care if it's day or night?"

"Well," Sandra said, "I think they put up with tours during the day because they have some historical value as well as telling their story; to inspire others." She looked at me. "I believe that is one of your sayings isn't it Mister DeGrado. To 'Exist to Inspire.'"

Ryan nudged me. "Looks like she did her research on us as well."

We are taken by surprise as the violin and cello both fell of their stands simultaneously. Ryan stood and went over to the instruments, and I followed.

"This is the kind of thing that has been happening," Sandra said. "It's like they're unhappy."

"They are," Niley said. He stood and moved to where Ryan and I were investigating the instruments.

Ryan took the cello and placed it back on the stand. He put his hand on the instrument and moved it back and forth. "This stand is secure. Someone might have placed it where it wasn't balanced properly."

"They did that to the violin as well?" Niley said. "A little coincidental don't you think?"

"This type of thing has become common," Sandra said. "There have also been several incidents on the stairs and a few in the bathroom."

"What has happened in the bathroom?" Ryan asked.

"Visitors who place stuff on shelves have their stuff go missing," Sandra said. "We find it later somewhere in the house. It's led to a lot of complaints."

Niley walked around the room as though he was searching for something. We all watched as he wondered around. He stopped by the entrance. "I suggest," he said, "we all go downstairs."

"Why? The action is up here?" Ryan asked.

"To get to the bottom of this," Niley said. "We are going to perform a séance."

CHAPTER THREE
SEANCE

"It was a dark and stormy night," Ryan said in an ominously low voice as he entered the kitchen. "The guests, with their host, sat around the dinner table not knowing it would be their last meal. Ooohh."

"I think someone is not allowed to have wine with his meal," I said smiling as Ryan sat down.

"I was just offering some help on the story you're going to write about all of this," Ryan said. "So, are we ready to start?"

"Mister Conner," Niley said. "Please take a seat and be calm. I have a feeling that tonight might be your lucky night."

"Why is that?" Ryan asked.

"You may finally witness what you have been waiting for; proof that life continues beyond our corporeal existence."

We sat at the dining room table that Sandra and Nora had cleared for the séance. They lit candles on the table and turned the lights off in the room. Seated were Sandra, Niley, Ryan and myself. Stephey stayed at the monitors, and Nora went to the kitchen area and was making coffee for the long night ahead.

"Now," Niley said as he carefully moved his chair into a position that appeared to suit him, "we will try to make contact with the inhabitants of the house. If I'm successful, we can ask them questions. We all contain energy and will disrupt the spirits if we move about. I ask that you please remain seated while we do this, and that you hold hands to contain our inner circle of energy. If we break that circle it will make it harder to stay in contact." He sat and we all held hands.

"Is it true that the inner circle is also containment for the spirit that we are communicating with and protection for ourselves?" I asked.

"Protection for us, perhaps," Niley said. "Our contact will keep us from wandering off or being distracted. That is more in the case of malevolent spirits which I do not believe we will find here. Regardless, our physical contact will keep us aware of each other. It will not contain the spirits around us. That is only in the movies."

I sat across the table from Niley while to my right was Ryan and my left, Sandra. Her hand was warm and soft. She gripped my hand tightly as Niley spoke.

"We are here to communicate with the spirits in this house," Niley said. "We mean no harm to them or this house but are here to help." He closed his eyes and sat still.

I glanced at Ryan and noticed, like me, he had his eyes open and was scanning around the room. Sandra held her eyes closed. The house grew eerily silent as we sat there. I found myself watching the flame of the candle bounce. Quite hypnotized by its motion, it took me a moment to notice Niley's eyes had opened and he stared at me; no, not at me, but beyond.

"I am getting a feeling I have not had here before," Niley said. "It is not what I expected. Sandra, you thought the family was upset due to your guides late night tour. Although the two people were here at night and past what is normally closing hours, the family didn't seem to mind that. In fact, I get the sense they were entertained by the new lovers."

"You're in contact with them?" Ryan asked.

"Yes," Niley stated. "Wait, there's disappointment here. Something is wrong and disturbing them. But they are not the ones responsible for the objects being misplaced and accidents during the tours."

Niley went silent.

"Niley," Ryan said. "Are you still listening? What is it? What do you hear?"

I noticed Sandra increased her grip and it was becoming uncomfortable. Her eyes were closed tightly and her head slightly twitched left and right.

"Oh my," Niley said. "Oh my, oh my," Niley said and started rocking back and forth. He was visibly disturbed as his chest bumped against the table until the table started moving. His motions became uncontrolled as he shook back and forth in a manner that seemed impossible for him to do by himself while seated. I glanced at Ryan who fixated on Niley.

"Stephey," Ryan called out.

"Yes," Stephey responded.

"Are you getting all of this?"

No response came.

"Stephey? Please, tell me you're recording!"

I heard a sound beside me and noticed it was Sandra humming. "I recognize that song," I said.

"It's the same one she played earlier on the cello,'" Ryan said. He moved his chair back as though he was going to stand.

"Sorry," Stephey said. "I hear you. But you've got to see this."

"Don't break the circle!" Sandra said as her eyes came wide open, and she glared at us.

I looked in her direction and mouthed the word *sorry*.

"We're almost done here and then I'll take a look," Ryan said.

"I've never seen anything like this before," Stephey said from the other room.

"What is it?" Niley said. His body stopped shaking and he sat erect. "Tell me, what is bothering you?"

Niley's eyes remained closed as he spoke.

"Who is here with you?" Niley continued. "Many? How many? Thousands? Thousands. Thousands!"

The table shook and the candle went out as Niley opened his eyes and the light came on.

Ryan and Sandra, still gripping my hand, were both standing. Niley looked directly at me.

"You did well," Niley said. "They did not feel threatened by you and your presence here helped calm the mood."

"Thank you," I said still digesting what had happened. I let go of Ryan and Sandra's hand as the two of them stepped away from the table.

"I'll be right back," Ryan said and left to the side room where Stephey sat.

"Pardon me," I said and followed Ryan. The overhead light was off leaving the glow from the monitors the only source of illumination. Ryan moved to the side of Stephey and looked at the monitors lined up along the rectangular plastic table. I stayed on the opposite side and could not see what they were looking at.

"I don't understand," Ryan said. "I thought you said you had something. There's no electric, no magnetic reading, no sound, no temperature differences on any of the readings. Stephey, what are you talking about?"

"Watch this," she said as her hand moved over the computer mouse. "Watch the camera as it panned across the mirror."

"I still don't see what you're talking about," Ryan said. "Is that a reflection in the mirror? What is that?"

Stephey stood and grabbed the portable camera that sat on the table. She headed to the living room as Ryan and I followed. She took a cord from the back of the camera and hooked it into the television used for the house's video. She turned the television on and started to display the video on the large screen.

"Watch the screen," Stephey said. She pointed the camera at the mirror along the wall in the living room. At this time, everyone had gathered in the living room including the house maid Nora and Niley.

"Oh My," Sandra said as the rest of us looked at the screen.

Figures, outlined in a soft, white light could be seen in the mirror as a procession of them went through the room. From what the camera displayed, the room itself seemed empty and the ghostly apparitions only appeared as a reflection in the mirror.

"What are we looking at?" Ryan asked.

"It's a live feed," Stephey said.

"There's a whole bunch of them, more than twenty and they seem to be moving along as more come into the room," Sandra said.

"It must be a trick of the lighting or something," Ryan said. He looked around the room and then moved over to the lights.

"That's what I thought," Stephey said. "But follow me." She detached the cord and, camera in hand, led us upstairs into the master bedroom. Ryan, Sandra and I followed while the rest remained downstairs.

We entered the master bedroom where against the wall across from the bed stood a large dresser mirror. Stephey pointed the camera at the mirror and turned the display so we could see it.

We each stood facing the long mirror. There was nothing apparent where we were standing or in the mirror when we looked at it but, in the camera screen, multiple figures appeared in the reflection as though they were in the room with us.

"What does it mean?" Sandra asked with her hands going up to her face. She turned and left the room.

From where I stood, I could not get a good look at the camera's viewer as Ryan and Stephey remained staring into it.

"May I," I said not sure I wanted to see a closer view. Stephey handed me the device. I faced the camera away from the mirror and could see nothing but the physical furniture in the room and Stephey and Ryan. When I faced the camera back to the mirror, I witnessed a procession of softly outlined people moving across the room. Ryan came up beside me.

"Is this the proof we've both been looking for?" I asked.

"I'm not sure what is going on," Ryan said. "Hold that so I can see it for a minute." Ryan closely watched the small viewer. "Look closely. These are not forms of people from the past. You can see the outline of what they are wearing."

"What, what do you mean?" I asked.

"They are dressed in attire from recent times," Ryan said. "This may be a playback, somehow, of all the visitors to this house. Captured by the mirrors. That's my conclusion. If we were seeing the actual family that is supposed to have remained here, then I would think differently. But these are a reflection of modern times."

"Oh, so no ghosts?" I said.

"Although it's interesting, I'd have to say inconclusive to what it means at this time," Ryan said. "Just like most of what I find. Come on, let's head back downstairs."

I followed Ryan and Stephey down the solid wood stairs to the large living room where Niley stood at the mirror. He put his hand up to it and closed his eyes.

"I am speaking to those who inhabit this dwelling," Niley said as the rest of us remained silent and watched. "Tell me what it is that is keeping you here."

Suddenly, the mirror began to vibrate, and a crack appeared at the end opposite where Niley held his hand. The crack grew in size and started running along the length of it. Ryan stepped forward and grabbed Niley and pulled him back just as it reached his hand. The mirror shattered and all of us turned away as small pieces of it flew out.

"Thank you," Niley said

"Is anyone injured?" Sandra said as she walked around checking everyone.

No one appeared to be injured but we were all in shock, not sure what caused the mirror to explode. The swirl of a powerful night wind howled outside and blew a cold breeze into the room as it penetrated the walls.

"This isn't finished," Niley said. "We must go back to the table and restart the séance if we are to get answers."

Drinks were served and we took a moment to reflect before we gathered back in the dining room at the wooden table. Stephey was back at the monitors while Nora swept up the glass from the mirror in the adjacent room. We held hands and Niley closed his eyes.

"I am speaking with Mr. Wendel now," Niley said.

"Ask him who these people are?" Ryan said. "Who are we seeing in the mirrors?"

"They are the departed, recently departed. They are all around. I can see them. Stuck here, in this house. They cannot get to the next realm."

"Next realm?" Sandra said.

Niley opened his eyes. "Yes, I am being told that this house has become a path for those going from this place to the other. Many travel through here but the way is blocked now. That is why they wander."

"Who? Who wanders?" Ryan asked.

"The departed," Niley said. He closed his eyes again. "They are many. They are intruding on our lives. There are many. There are many."

"What do they want?" Ryan said.

"They are in our house. They are stuck. There are many," Niley said.

"How many?" Ryan asked.

The air in the room went still and the power went off. The candles on the table were the only source of light. I could still see Niley's face. He moved slightly back and forth. Then, he came to a sudden stop as his eyes opened.

"There are thousands!"

CHAPTER FOUR
THOUSANDS

Around us in every corner of the room and in the entrances, white glowing figures roamed in the darkness. Their phosphorescent outline made visible by the lack of light. After a few minutes, the power returned, and the figures faded.

The circle was broken as Ryan and Niley both stood. Ryan went to the side room, and I could hear him talking to Stephey.

"Please tell me you got that," Ryan said.

"Nothing," Stephey said. "That wasn't a power outage, it was more like an EMP wave. It knocked out everything, including all battery back-ups. I'm trying to restore power now. Luckily, it appears there's no permanent damage."

Niley walked around the room with his hands out as though feeling the air for something. He turned to Sandra.

"This house is a conduit for those passing to the next realm. The family that chose to reside here attracted the others to them. Like many places where there are being stuck between places, this place has become a pathway to the other side. Something has gone wrong, and the conduit is blocked. They keep coming but they are stuck."

"What is blocking it?" I asked

"I don't know," Niley said.

Ryan turned the lights on and came to the table. "If this gets out, that after we die we are all just stuck in limbo here on earth, what a slap to religion. One of my drives in investigating was to find out if there is anything more. When I didn't find concrete evidence of hauntings, ghosts or the afterlife, I thought, *that's okay, that means we go on and it's a mystery*. This is the ultimate slap in the face. To find out something exists after death, but it may be nothing more than being trapped here!" He sat down.

Sandra leaned forward and blew out the candles.

"I don't think that is the case," Niley said. "We are talking about passageways that allow energy to go from perhaps one dimension to another. That's what this house and so many other supernatural places are: transfer points."

"What you're saying is this one is blocked," I said.

"What if it's not just here that has the problem? What if this is occurring everywhere?" Sandra said.

"Then Heaven is full," Niley said.

"Well," Ryan said, "whatever energy is left in those things we witnessed, it doesn't seem to be harmful. They didn't seem to mind that we were here."

"Don't forget the mirror," I said.

Ryan nodded.

"They are simply lost and wandering," Niley said. "Some of the trapped energy is not positive and getting, well, angry. It will only increase as will the negative events and feelings."

Sandra's elegantly content and happy face lacked color and her eyes were sullen.

"There goes the happy haunted house," Ryan said. He stood. "Louis, I have an idea. Come with me."

We left the room and went upstairs to the master bedroom. "Help me with this mirror," Ryan said as he hoisted the large, antique floor mirror.

I grabbed on to the other side as we carried the mirror downstairs and put it by the large television. Ryan took the camera that Stephey had used earlier, put it on a stand, and pointed it at the mirror. He turned the television on, and we watched the screen. The eerie figures appeared in the reflection and were captured by the camera.

"Amazing," Ryan said.

Niley came into the room behind us and the three of us watched the screen observing the progression of spirits across the mirror.

"What do we do now?" I asked.

"Miss Cassandra went to lie down," Niley said. "It is after two a.m. I don't know if there is anything we can do. Unless, you know how to communicate with spirits."

"I was under the impression that was your job," I said.

Niley smiled at me, and Ryan laughed.

"I suppose we should all get some rest," Ryan said. "I think I'll plan on setting up for a longer stay. This phenomenon has to be observed."

The three of us made ourselves ready for bed and then slept on the cots in the living room. Stephey stayed at her monitors throughout the night while Sandra and Nora slept off in a guest room. The night passed quickly as most of us were stirring by seven.

"There's coffee and croissants in the kitchen," Sandra said as she peeked her head in the living room. I noticed Ryan was out of his cot and looked around to find that he was watching the television screen. I stood and went over to it as Stephey emerged from the kitchen and handed both of us a cup of coffee.

"They've been there all night," Stephey said pointing at the ghostly figures on the screen. "They just keep shuffling around. At least they don't seem to mind us."

"Yes," Ryan said. "Let's hope it remains that way. Louis and I are going back today. I'm going to take some of the recordings and analyze them. I'll return when I have some ideas, if any, of what to do next."

The rest of the morning, Ryan and I helped Stephey pack the cameras and various monitoring instruments into a van. Although some amazing things happened in the past twenty-four hours, no one seemed eager to stay at the house. The idea of all the spirits roaming about didn't sit well and became more creepy than amazing. Even Niley was at a loss to explain the reason the entities seemed to be stuck. He did offer to stay longer which made the rest of us feel a little better as we weren't leaving Sandra by herself.

I thanked Sandra for her hospitality and informed her I would be returning with Ryan when he came back if that was okay with her. We drove away from the house without answers to explain what was happening and unsure if we would have any in the future.

CHAPTER FIVE
THE LONELY CELLO

Weeks went by and a month passed before Ryan called me and invited me back to the Wendel House. After doing some research, both Rick Niley and Ryan were ready to get together and discuss their theories on the occurrences. During our call, Ryan informed me that more events had occurred at the house since the last time I was there and with the increase in activity, it was time to return. I agreed to go with him.

I travelled to Ryan's house in Denver this time, and we took his vehicle from there. Ryan updated me on the new events along the way; he informed me that Stephey and some of the other team members of his paranormal research group visited other hot spots to see if they could replicate the figures in the mirror as was taking place at the Wendel House. While they did get some small representations, they were fleeting at best. Ryan and Niley concluded that the Wendel House alone was where the energy was blocked. Ryan wasn't sure he believed in the conduit theory as Niley did but, he admitted, "It does make sense that lost spirits would be attracted to places like the Wendel House."

Speaking of the house, he informed me that the tours had all been discontinued. People reported a heavy feeling and problems breathing. The atmosphere of the place had changed so dramatically that tourists were getting sick merely stepping into the house. Apparently, a heaviness filled the air, and a sense of dread overcame the tourists. The local towns people claimed that the feeling had spread outward from the house to the town. Some were leaving the area.

"So, why are we going back if we might get sick?" I asked.

"Niley and I have some clues as to why there is a problem in that house," Ryan said. "He has continued to be in contact with the family there. He claims that the family has been there so long that their spirits are stronger than the newly departed. Strong enough to keep the others there."

"Why would they do that?" I asked.

"Imagine this," Ryan said waving his right hand in the air to indicate something big. "Niley said the little girl, Alice, started noticing all of the other, well, spirits or ghosts or whatever, and her spirit has realized it's not correct for her to remain in the house."

"So, she is blocking the path somehow?" I asked.

"No," Ryan said. "According to Niley, it's the parents blocking the way."

"Obsessed with keeping the family together," I said. "Sandra said that was the place they felt the happiest. Now they can't let it go and face the unknown."

"Perhaps," Ryan said. "By the way, you should prepare yourself for Sandra. She's not the same."

"What do you mean?"

"She has refused to leave the house and become sickly; she's lost weight and has grown pale.

"Her dream is coming apart," I said. "It's only natural it would be having an effect on her."

"She's tried many times to communicate with the family to no avail. The toll of all this is going on is having an adverse effect on her health. Given that, we will not stay at the house long. We will be staying at a small hotel down the road."

"It's that bad?"

"Yes, I'm afraid so," Ryan said. "I've felt it myself. The feeling in the house is spreading to the town. People are leaving due to health reasons. No one in the town suspects their problems might be related to the Wendel house. We need to be careful what we mention when we are out and about. It's all speculation, of course. There's no hard evidence."

"Still," I said, "I wouldn't recommend debating it. As advanced as we claim to be, I could just see people heading for the house with torches."

Ryan laughed.

"If only we could find a solution," I said.

"That's why I brought you along," Ryan said. "I'm hoping with our combined imaginations and intelligence we can figure something out."

"If we don't?" I asked.

"The torch idea may not be all that far-fetched," Ryan said.

I didn't respond to Ryan's last remark partly because we both knew he wasn't kidding. Throughout history, fire had been used to deal with the unknown; perhaps due to the fact that it also held energy and transformed things. The effect was destructive, and I didn't want to consider it. It bothered me to consider Cassandra Krage, who was so passionate about the family and the history of the house, was losing her dream while we were helpless to intervene. I slowly drifted off to sleep as we started climbing the winding mountain pathways that led to the town where the Wendel House stood.

I awoke to an uneasy feeling and looked over to Ryan who kept his eyes on the road. We had come down the last climb and were descending into the town heading toward the Wendel House.

"You can feel it already, can't you?" Ryan asked.

"Yes," I said. "I can't describe it fully but, it's like when I'm sleeping at home and something has caused me to wake; a sound, a change in temperature or..."

"A feeling like someone is in your house?" Ryan said.

"Yes," I said. "That's it."

We pulled up to the house and spotted Niley speaking with a well-dressed older gentleman with gray hair outside as we parked the car. I left my bag in the car while Ryan pulled out some equipment cases. I grabbed one to help him as we headed for the entrance. Niley spotted us and smiled.

"Ah, the author has returned," he said. "Good to see you," we shook hands.

The other man speaking with Niley turned to me. "Doctor Cavalli, please to meet you."

Ryan and I greeted the Doctor who pardoned himself quickly noting there were many house calls to make.

"I'm afraid Sandra collapsed last night," Niley said. "Doctor Cavalli had a look at her this morning and is recommending she get some tests done. But I haven't been able to convince her to leave this house."

"Maybe we can help," Ryan said.

Niley opened the door as we went inside. I immediately noticed the heaviness as we crossed the threshold, and in turn, Ryan and Niley noticed my hesitation as they stopped and waited for me.

"You'll get used to it," Niley said.

"It's like a thick humidity without the sweat," I said.

"That's a good way to describe it," Ryan said. "Make sure your write that down for the book."

"Book?"

"I'm sure you're going to write about this experience," Ryan said. "You'd be a fool if you didn't"

I walked a few steps into the living room and stood looking at the large television screen which was still sitting there displaying the reflection from the mirror. However, the bedroom mirror was gone and the one on the wall had been replaced. The new mirror ran the full length of the wall facing out into the living room and ended at the entrance to the stairway. I felt a touch on my shoulder and turned to see Stephey.

I shook hands with her.

"The figures are not moving at all," Stephey said. "They are shoulder to shoulder and just stare into space. They are in every corner of the house."

"They've kept coming then," I said.

"Yes," Stephey said. "They are attracted to something here. They are all around us."

I put my hands out and watched the screen as I moved around to see if my motions had any impact on the figures whose outline was reflected in the mirror; I simply passed through them.

"That's pleasant," Ryan said as handed the equipment to Stephey. "Here's the extra phase protection you requested."

"Thanks," Stephey said. "I've been trying to guard all of my equipment with EMP shielding. The pulses have grown in frequency and I'm tired of having to reboot. The energy in this house is increasingly unstable."

"I believe their energy is what we feel when we walk through the house," Niley said. "The heavy feeling, as Louis described, is why we feel uneasy and get sick. The longer one is exposed to it, the harder it is to breathe, and it becomes hard to hold onto thoughts. The interesting aspect is that Sandra is not as affected as we are."

"What do you mean?" I asked.

"Come and see," Niley said and led us into the side room where Stephey had his equipment set up.

We rounded the plastic table where extra monitors were keeping track of various rooms in the house. The one we focused upon was streaming a shot from the guest bedroom. Sandra was sleeping on the bed.

"Now, watch this," Stephey said as she panned the camera to the large mirror on a vanity dresser. The ghostly figures reflected in the mirror and were concentrated throughout the room with the exception of the bed. There, a lone figure stood by the bed poised as though looking down at Sandra. The outline was that of a lady.

"Notice the dress," Niley said pointing to the figure on the screen. "Unlike the modern clothes of the others, this figure has on a Victorian era dress. I believe we are seeing the image of the lady of the house, Misses Wendel."

"Extraordinary," Ryan said as he stepped beside me.

"She seems to be protecting her from the others," Niley said. "It's not enough to keep all the effects from her, her health is failing, but she appears to be able to move about with less effort than the rest of us."

"You have been in touch with the family of this house?" I asked.

"Yes," Niley said. "It's not as direct as our séance but, since I made contact on many prior occasions, I can now communicate to them without so much effort. It is still restrictive with only a few images here and there. That's why we need to have another one."

"Another one?" I asked.

"Yes, another Séance," Riley said.

"Lunch is ready," Nora said as she entered the room.

We all headed to the patio where Nora served some lemonade and sandwiches. She sat away from us as we spoke.

"Another séance?" Ryan said. "That's what you recommend?"

"Yes," Niley said. "Tonight. We need to find out who or what is blocking the pathway in this house."

"Surely Sandra cannot participate," Ryan said. "Not in her current condition."

"No, but Stephey can," Niley said.

"I glanced sideways at Stephey who grinned and appeared pleased to be asked to sit at the table instead of being behind his monitors.

"Very well," Ryan said. "Tonight, it is. Let's try to put this to rest. For Sandra's sake."

"Can I see her?" I asked.

"I'll take you to the room," Niley said. "But don't wake her if she's sleeping."

"Understood," I said.

"We'll go to the hotel after," Ryan said. "Rest there for awhile and then come back this evening."

Niley and I went to the guest bedroom while Ryan and Stephey went into the room with all their equipment. When we moved toward the bed, I felt a change in the air; it felt lighter as I stood beside Sandra. She was sound asleep with her head turned away from me. I reached down and touched her hair.

"Maybe we should just take her out of here," I whispered. "Take her down to the hotel where we are staying for her own good."

"I've thought of that," Niley said. "If we can't figure out what is going on tonight, maybe that's what we will do."

The door to the room shut behind us. The sound woke Sandra who looked up at me.

"Hello," she said. "You've come again?"

"Yes, of course," I said. I watched as Niley went to the door and tried to open it with no success. "I wanted to check and see how you were doing."

Sandra moved to the side of the bed and sat up. "I am fine, I assure you. Don't listen to these scoundrels that would have you believe I'm not." She started to stand and stumbled right into my arms.

"I'm sorry," she said as I helped her back to a seated position on the bed. "I just need something to drink. Niley, would you bring me something?"

Niley tried the door again and this time was successful at getting it open. He glanced at me, and I didn't miss the message he conveyed; the presence in the house might not let Sandra leave.

"I've had time to read your latest book, *The Meadow*," Sandra said. "Do you have some time to talk. I really liked the songs and poetry throughout."

"Thank you," I said and sat on the bed beside her. We talked for about an hour before she drifted back to sleep and Ryan came in looking for me. Ryan and I left the house and headed to the hotel room that wasn't far away in the small town.

After checking in, I took some time to write a few things down. It occurred to me that Ryan was correct that I should write a story about the occurrence even if I had to change some names and locations to keep the identity of the place and people secret; a respect I owed them to keep the curious from harassing those involved. I had done so before in one of my previous books, *The Questors' Adventures.* Inevitably, someone would try to get locations or names out of me, and I would just state that I am a science fiction writer and would not admit to how much of the story is true versus fiction.

With our bags put away and taking some time to rest, we headed out on foot to a nearby diner where we ate before heading back to the house on foot. The short walk gave us time to talk and stretch our legs. Although it was mid-summer, the high-mountain climate gave us a cool setting for our walk as the sun began to set.

"I'm taking your advice," I said to Ryan. "To write stuff down for a possible story."

"That's great," Ryan said.

"Of course, I'm going to change character names and disguise the location. I might even throw in some of my own philosophical beliefs and messages. I always do."

"You're the author," Ryan said. "I think that's fair."

"You've been quieter than usual since we arrived," I said. "Is there something on your mind?"

Ryan stopped for a moment. He looked to the sky. "I bet we're going to see thousands of stars on our trip back."

"Thousands," I said. "That word rings an ominous tone."

"Oh yes, of course," Ryan said. "When we asked how many were trapped, Niley said 'Thousands,' didn't he?"

"You are avoiding the question," I said. "Is something on your mind?"

"Not avoiding," Ryan said. "Just thinking. You are right, there is something on my mind. I've finally found the proof that I was looking for: there is something beyond. It is evident that we have documented an event here we cannot explain. Proof positive that there is something beyond." He started walking again.

"So, you should be happy," I said.

"Yes and no," Ryan said. "I'm glad I know there is something beyond but, we don't really know what it is."

"I don't think we're supposed to know," I said. "Imagine if the mystery of the beyond, good or bad, was exposed."

We both paused to hear a crow sounding off in the distant. It was answered by others.

"Wow, that was odd," Ryan said.

"I didn't think they lived this high up," I said.

"They are supposed to be spiritual messengers," Ryan said. "It was right on queue with what you were saying so please, continue."

"If the hereafter was revealed pleasant," I said, "there are those who might be in a hurry to get there. The whole of humanity already lives in a fog of trying to discover life's mystery. If we already know the destination, we might cut the journey short and miss the purpose."

"Which is what?" Ryan asked.

"I believe we spend too much effort trying to find purpose. The purpose of life is elusive because it's already been given to us: it's life itself. Live it!"

"You mean I should just live it up and not worry?" Ryan said.

"No, I'm saying live with respect. Every religion has certain tenets of a moral life that includes key principles such as respecting and not transgressing others. If we'd just follow these guidelines and agree on some values, we will find the elusive peace."

"Sounds so simple," Ryan said. "What if what is beyond is not good. What if it's a place we find we'd rather not go to?"

"Then, life would be miserable," I said.

"Why's that?"

"Imagine living with the knowledge that sooner or later you are going to die and what's waiting for you is horrible? You'd be afraid to live—always worrying of what might happen to end your life."

"I guess you're right," Ryan said. "We'd probably all be addicted to drugs and alcohol, in constant denial."

"So many people are already afraid and unsure of themselves that they don't really live," I said. "They cling to something that will never be but give up what is meant to be." We arrived outside the Wendel House.

"That's it!" Ryan said.

"What?"

"Cling! Follow me," Ryan said.

We did not go to the front door but went to the back entrance where we found Sandra, Stephey and Niley out on the back porch sitting at the table. After a short greeting, we all sat down as Ryan told us his idea.

"I think there is someone that is ready to move on," Ryan said. "One of the family members from what you are telling us, Niley."

"Yes," Niley said. "After years of being together and watching others pass through this portal that we cannot see, little Alice's soul is ready to move on but, the family is holding onto her. They are clinging to their existence here as a family."

"They are afraid," Ryan said. "They have been together for so long in this place, they are afraid to face what is after. It's possible this family does not want to take a chance that what is after is not better."

"Brilliant theory," Niley said.

"It was his," Ryan said and pointed to me.

"Yes," Niley said. "The author and philosopher. It makes sense that the storyteller would be able to put this all together."

Sandra smiled and looked at me. "So, what do we do to help them?"

I shook my head.

"We must convince them it's time to go on," Niley said. "It's what is meant to be. By hanging on they are interfering with the natural order, which is why the others are probably stuck. If we fix this, if we get them to move on, the rest can go as well." He looked at his watch. "We can start now."

Sandra slowly stood with Niley helping her. She scolded him claiming she was fine as she headed inside. He turned back to us.

"I think we need to get to the bottom of this tonight for her sake," Niley said.

"She needs to leave the house no matter what happens tonight," Ryan said. "Agreed?"

"I don't think it's that simple," Niley said.

"Why?" Ryan asked.

"When we were up in the bedroom," I said, "I made a comment about carrying her out of the house. The door shut on us."

"It wouldn't open until Sandra woke," Niley said. "I think the family is scared and will not let her leave."

"Hmm," Ryan said. "That family sure has a way of holding on to things." He turned to me. "That torch idea is starting to sound more like an option," he winked.

"Torch idea?" Stephey said.

"He's just kidding, I hope," I said.

"Gentlemen," Ryan said as he stood. "Let's take our places inside and get this going."

After sitting outside for a while, entering the house took a tremendous toll on all of us. The heavy feeling on the body drained my energy. As we took our places around the table, Sandra lit the candles and turned off the light as she moved out of the room.

We took hold of each other's hands as Niley started to recite his usual greeting but stopped short.

"It is too heavy in here," Niley said. He stood and went to the other room for a moment. He came back carrying a chair. Sandra entered the room behind him. "Please, sit here." Niley said and put her chair close to the table but not at the table. Then, he took his seat. "I believe we will have more success while she is in the room."

He was correct. The heavy feeling abated. Just as in the bedroom earlier, it appeared that Sandra was somehow protected, and the area she was in was less crowded by the spectral beings. The lighter feeling helped us concentrate.

After his opening, Niley began to reach out to the members of the family asking to speak with them. He kept his eyes closed for what seemed like an hour and then two. My hands became sweaty, and I grew tired. I glanced back at Sandra, and she smiled at me. When I returned my attention to Niley his eyes were open.

"I have made contact with all of the family members except little Alice," Niley said. "This confirms my suspicion that she is involved."

"Involved how?" Ryan asked.

"Originally, I thought she was the one ready to move on and the rest of the family was not ready. I had it wrong. The child is confused. That may be why the rest of the family has stayed around so long, to look after her. It was her, not Misses Wendel, that closed the door in the bedroom when you suggested to move Sandra out of the house."

"What?" Sandra said. "You were going to remove me from the house?"

"Yes," I said. "Everyone thinks it's a good idea. You need to take a break from this place."

Sandra didn't respond to me but stood and went by Niley. "Can the parents convince her to move on?" she asked.

"I don't know," Niley said. "She's a stubborn child and she's not listening to them any longer."

"Then, maybe she'll listen to me," Sandra said and walked out of the room.

Immediately I felt the heaviness return and smother me. Niley mumbled some stuff and told us we could take a break as he left the table. Ryan and Stephey followed into the living room, so I stood and made my way there. Sandra was calling for Alice as she started up the stairs toward the little girl's room. Niley was just a few steps behind her.

"Look," Stephey said as he pointed to the television.

We all watched the screen as the ghostly figures that had been standing still were no shuffling around and appeared to be moving to the stairway. We couldn't see any further as the mirror ended.

"Go get the portable camera," Ryan said.

Stephey moved went to the side room to get the camera. As I watched him, everything started moving slower. My thoughts were paced and the voices I heard were distorted. I could barely make out Niley's voice from the top of the stairs, but I was aware enough to notice the panicked tone.

"Someone call the doctor," Niley said. "Hurry!"

Beside me, Ryan had gone down on one knee and breathed heavily. He scrambled for his phone and pulled it out and hit the button to dial before handing it to me.

"Yes, sorry, I need the doctor at the Wendel house. Yes, Doctor Cavalli, I'm sorry to bother you, this is the author you met earlier at the Wendel House. Yes, it's Sandra. Yes, we will get her out of the house at once and get her down to you. We'll be right there." I handed the phone back to Ryan and helped him to his feet.

He put the phone away, closed his eyes tightly for a moment and opened them. A fierce look, angry and defiant, came forth. "Come on, we are going to get Sandra and take her to the office down the street."

We made our way up the stairs. We looked in the master bedroom and in the children's room before we finally found Niley kneeling over Sandra in the theatre room. Niley was struggling to get to his feet, so I bent down to lift her.

"It's too late," Niley said. "She's gone."

I immediately started CPR.

Ryan came beside me. "That's not going to help. We need to get her out of the house," he said and helped me lift her. We went down the stairs. At the base of the stairwell, I stumbled and went down on one knee. "Sorry Alice, I'm taking Sandra," I said aloud.

Ryan helped me to my feet and out the door. We crowded into Niley's car and headed down the street.

Doctor Cavalli tried several times to revive Sandra, but nothing worked. He led us to a waiting room while his assistant attended to Sandra's body. It was then that Doctor Calli told us about Sandra's cardiomyopathy, a weak heart condition that had caused her fatigue and stress. He went on to say she'd had it for some time and that her work at the Wendel house had given her peace. Not lately, though. She had been struggling to cope with the problems at the house. There were no questions when the coroner arrived about what we were doing at the house that night or implications that any of what we were doing caused her issue.

"She was already living on borrowed time," Doctor Cavalli said. "She had a degenerative condition. Her only option was a transplant, and she wouldn't leave the house long enough to be eligible. The only thing that kept her going was her love for that house and the history behind it."

We returned to the house to find that Nora had left and informed Stephey she would not be returning. Her fear of the house had overcome her need for employment there.

"I'm going to get Stephey," Ryan said. "I think we should pack it up for the night and head back to the hotel. Tomorrow, I'll talk to Doctor Cavalli and find out who we can contact about what has happened to Sandra and what do with the house."

"Give me a moment," I said standing in the living room with Niley. I was trying to process all that was happening. Somewhere in my brain, with all that was going on, there was an idea occurring, a concept, a little voice. I just had to focus on what it wanted to tell me.

Ryan went to help Stephey set up monitoring equipment for the night.

I stood directly in front of the television screen and watched the display of ghostly figures captioned by the camera feed. Earlier, the room had been packed and none of the figures moved even when I waved and tried to disrupt them. Now, however, I noticed they were moving. All of the shapes turned in the same direction, toward the front door. "Something is coming," I said to myself. I was correct as a new figure came forth across the mirror. It was the outline of a lady in a Victorian dress. I thought I was seeing the lady of the house, Misses Wendel, until the figure stopped and glanced right at the camera; something none of the other ghostly figures did.

"Oh, my," Niley said.

I stared at the screen and felt the thump of Ryan's cell phone at my feet as he dropped it to the floor. The three of us were staring into the face of Cassandra Krage who looked at us in the mirror as the image was captured by the camera. She smiled and then turned and walked toward the stairs.

"Get the camera," Ryan said as Stephey stepped into the living room only to run back to the side room to get the camera.

We all followed Stephey upstairs as he scanned the mirrors in the rooms to see if we could spot the figure of Sandra again. We were not able to locate it, but we did notice all the spectral outlines were moving into the theatre room. We continued checking mirrors for the next four hours until we were out of energy and settled in the living room. Delivery pizza and beers were served as we kept watch on the large screen. The house was clearing, and the figures once stuck appeared to be moving on to whatever came next.

"I believe she did it," Niley said. "She passed from this world and found her way to this house and somehow helped the family move on."

"You think it was her that unblocked the portal or whatever it is that allowed the others to move on?" Ryan asked.

"Yes," Niley said. "There is a way to be certain."

"No," Ryan said. "No more seances. Not tonight, not any night."

"Well," Niley said, "I hope she finds her peace. I'm heading to the hotel. Do you gentlemen want a ride?"

We left the house together and returned the next day to gather Ryan's equipment. We stayed in town long enough to attend Sandra's funeral. It was during the eulogy I realized that in the end, Sandra did go home; to a place she's always been and a time she felt at ease; the Wendel House.

EPILOGUE

A year went by before the Wendel house found a new host and was once again opened to the public. Although the story of the family and the history of the house remained a predominant theme, ghost hunters and psychics no longer spoke about the presence of the family at the house. Instead, they spoke about the presence of a lady wearing a Victorian dress who played the cello.

THE END

When the body
has left the physical plane
It's not natural to remain
What's left not the same
Without the physical frame
It might act out to get a response
Not understanding or knowing
What has happened
And it's time to be going

A shadow or reflection a spirit
Others will not comprehend
Some will fear it
It is best to let go
And move to what is next
It is what is meant
Let it be so

THE LOSS OF MY SOUL

I waited in the dark. The moment had arrived, the night of my revenge. Quietly and alone, I waited. He would be coming to bed soon and would find me there ready to torment, ready to take everything from him. For I had watched and waited. Although I lacked the form and energy for direct intervention, with slow and dreadful purpose, I have executed my plan.

Distant were the memories that I was human once and had a family and a life. It takes too much concentration to remember what I was and all that has been lost. The kind mind once mine has given in to thoughts of madness. The loving heart that once committed to matrimony and raising two children, now lies full of such darkness I could not recognize myself and would be a stranger to those I used to love; of whose names I can no longer remember. I have a distinct impression that what I once was is not what I am now.

Pain and rage bore me into this new existence. Shock and gall proliferated my thoughts when I reflected on what was done to me. My rage and thoughts *How dare you do this to me!* You see, I was murdered. The how and why has left me but the who, well, he's going to get what's coming to him.

It was enough for me to pull myself with all my energy back from the light that sought me. It took so much effort, so much concentration that I'm sure there were things I lost, parts of me no longer present. That's why I can't remember. In the end, I will win. I'm almost there; as I get stronger, he weakens.

Tonight, is the night I will break him. How do I know? There are signs. The medication on the table that has been used beyond the recommended dose. The unmade bed, the clothes thrown across the floor, the broken alarm clock. The disturbances, caused by yours truly, have increased as I've gained strength. Small moments have turned into full restless nights.

At first, it was just enough to wake him and make him look around. Then, it became routine and the look on his face turned from curiosity to terror. There are stains of tears on the pillow from the weeping man who doesn't understand what is happening. Oh, how lowly my heart has sunk when I find joy in the terror of another. It seems only just, given what he did to me, took everything, my life.

I don't remember how I found him, the one who did what he did to me, but I did. After I turned from the light, what was left of me knew its' purpose and like a hound, sniffed the scent of the man I was going to kill. Yes, I am going to kill him! No one will understand. It will look like it was his heart, or that he couldn't breathe or something. It doesn't matter as long as the result is there.

Long nights have I spent in this room penetrating his dreams and waking him in terror. I almost had him last night. The gun in his nightstand was so close and I could tell he thought about using it. Who wouldn't? Tormented by something unseen to the point people will think you are the one that is crazy.

Aha! I hear him now. He's come home late again. No doubt already full of liquor. This is the medicine a hopeless man has turned too after the woman left him several days ago: my doing. At least, I think it was several days ago. She accused him of going mad. He was rather in poor spirits or, should I say, had a spirit haunting him--driving him mad. Doesn't matter.

I wait until he's done with his nightly routine. I watch him as he checks his room as though he thinks he will find something. Under the bed, behind the curtain, under the covers. Yes, do check. This only adds to your misery when you can't explain what is about to happen.

It takes some time for the troubled man to fall asleep. One last shot of bourbon from the bottle on his nightstand is what he thinks will help. A memory flashes that I too once drank the same drink. The bottle looks familiar. Damn you! Drink it down already so we can get on with it, will you!

Finally, he's gone to sleep. Oh, the alcohol has done its thing and put you out. No matter. It's time to start. Now, I sit on his chest. I focus and put my energy down into it. I can tell he's having trouble breathing as the sweat beads start on his forehead. He tosses and turns as I concentrate and penetrate his REM sleep to be RIP sleep. Although, it's not really going to be "Rest In Peace", but "DIE FOR WHAT YOU DID TO ME!" No peace. Not tonight, not ever again until I've had my revenge.

His heart is racing. Screams in his dreams. He's running but there is no escape. Darkness! Coldness! Aha! I've found you! It's different this time. He's afraid, terrified. I strike and strike again. The dream is too real for him. Suddenly, he wakes. I think I've failed again until he looks at me. I can tell tonight he sees me; I can tell by the terrified look that is in his eyes and the fact that he is not trying to get out of the bed. His perception that I am really on his chest is holding him down. He seems surprised. His heart races and his breath is shallow as he clutches his chest. His eyes, tearing in pain. He looks directly at me.

"Brother?" he says. Then his eyes close and I watch the essence drain from him. I have my revenge.

A long time passes, and I sit on his body; His dead body, for there is no movement in it. For me, I look around. There is only darkness, there is no light. I've had my revenge.

Now what?

The End

SPOOKABLE TALES
VOLUME 4

THE RETURN
OF
DOCTOR MAD

Spookable Tales Volume 4

Copyright © 2024 Louis Paul DeGrado

All rights reserved. No part of this book may be used or reproduced by any means, graphic, electronic, or mechanical, including photocopying, recording, taping, or by any information storage retrieval system without written permission of the author.

This book is a work of fiction. Unless otherwise noted, the author makes no explicit guarantee as to the accuracy of the information contained in the book. Any reference to people or places that may be real is merely coincidental...OR IS IT!!

WHY DO YOU KEEP READING
AREN'T YOU AFRAID
DO YOU THINK YOU CAN HIDE
IN THE BED THAT YOU MADE
LIE YOU DOWN TO REST
IN A COFFIN WOULD BE BEST
TO SAVE TIME YOU MIGHT
WHEN YOU DIE OF FRIGHT
FOR THE STORIES ARE GRIM
AND THE PATH AHEAD
IS DARK AND DREARY
BUT DON'T WORRY
ABOUT WHAT I'VE SAID
YOU'VE MADE IT SO FAR
AND HOW WELL YOU'LL FARE
WILL BE KNOWN AT THE END
WHEN YOU'LL BE
FULL OF TERROR

Louis Paul DeGrado

THE FESTIVAL OF FEAR
RETURN OF DOCTOR MAD

TABLE OF TERROR CONTENTS

Prologue:

If you haven't read *The Festival of Fear,* you are likely behind from where we need to start. However, you will still want to read the story I'm about to tell if only for one reason; to know who survives. For, at the time I started documenting my next run-in with Doctor Mad, yes, that's my name for him, I wasn't sure he wouldn't kill me next since I survived his first debacle and tried hard over the past two years to expose him. I've left instructions for my friends, Ryan and Rob, to finish this story if I fall to the despicable villain.

Now, where were we? It's been two years since the Festival of Fear where Doctor Mad appeared with his deluded followers and convinced the participants of the costume contest that they were in a movie. Each proceeded to act as the character they portrayed and the massacre began.

The hotel has been closed, the festival suspended, and the police denied the existence of Doctor Mad instead calling it a case of mass hysteria. The authorities attributed the massacre to a bunch of overactive fans acting out their fantasies. Three survivors, Sandy, Ryan Conner, and I know better.

Sandy, tired of my obsession on finding Doctor Mad and worried about being targeted by a killer, has understandably went her own way. Ryan, still living in Denver and heading up a paranormal research group, and I still remain in touch.

Since I survived and profited by writing about the events, I have become one of the prime suspects even gaining a shadow from the FBI, Agent Valentine. We've become friends over the past year and I've grown used to him being everywhere I go. It actually gives me a sense of security in case the real villain returns.

The Director of the Festival of Fear, Brent Stein has succeeded in getting his festival off the ground this year and has consulted me multiple times to ensure he's taking the precautions. Why, so people don't get killed but also, due to the massacre and our macabre fascination with horror, the Festival has now reached epic proportions and the reservations indicate a record-breaking attendance. September has arrived and the festival will take place in three weeks.

I will be going...

CHAPTER ONE
THE RETURN

"Author Louis Paul DeGrado sat in the limousine waiting for the crowd in front of the bookstore to clear so the driver could take him back to the hotel when his phone rang. He looked at the number, smiled and answered."

"Excellent timing, I just got done for the day," I said into the receiver.

"I don't think you're done," I recognized Ryan Connor's voice on the other end. "Turn on HNR news."

"Oh, sorry Ryan," I said. "Took me by surprise, I thought you were my agent checking on my signing. It went well by the way." I reached over and found the remote for the small television and turned on the news.

"Back to the hotel?" the driver asked and I nodded as the car started moving forward.

"What's so important on the news that I need to know?" Okay, "I've got the channel."

"Just listen," Ryan said.

I watched as the break finished and the desk reporter came back in view. The camera focused on her as she looked into its gazing eye and continued her story.

"The police now confirming the existence of Doctor Mad. That's right, Doctor Mad, the name coined by Author Louis Paul DeGrado to describe the villain behind the massacre at the Colorado Festival of Fear. Doctor Mad has struck again and the police are now revealing a rash of incidents at local universities tied to the Doctor including the murder of prominent researcher, Gene Archer. We will be covering more on these stories this week and reaching out to the author to get his reaction."

I turned the television off.

"Well, that should help your book sales," Ryan said. "That is, unless he's going to target you."

"No, I don't think that will happen," I said. "This is what he's wanted all along, more publicity for his cause. He's going after young people."

"Why do you think he's back?" Ryan asked.

"I think he wants to be a supervillain. He wants to create influence and confusion. What better way than to go after a group of people, our students, who are already struggling with identity crisis? I would like to know the connection to the lady mentioned, Gene Archer. Do you think you and Rob can use some of your investigative skills and find out more about her? It may give us some insight on why she was targeted."

"Sure," Ryan said. "You're still coming to the memorial, right?"

"Of course," I said.

"Then, let's plan on talking while you're in town. I'm sure you're busy, I just thought you'd like to know the story has been revealed."

"Thanks," I said. "Hey, before you go, are you still in touch with Brent?"

"Yes, we've talked," Ryan said.

"Is the festival still on?"

"Yes, still on for Friday the Thirteenth," Ryan said and paused. "You think this Doctor Mad character will try to make an appearance at the festival?"

"I think we should be prepared for anything," I said. "That's why I wanted to speak with Brent. You know, since that night, I get a shiver down my spine every time a black limousine pulls up. It reminds me of the black hearse he rode away in. Not a good thing with what I'm doing now."

"You really think he would take a chance to make an appearance at the festival? Do you think he's that predictable?" Ryan said."

"Not predictable, but bold," I said. "That's what worries me. I just don't know if it will be a cameo appearance to let me know he's out there or if he's got something more sinister planned. We need to be prepared either way. Talk to you soon." The call ended.

The car rounded the turn to the hotel I was staying at. The driver turned his head back toward me. "Looks like your secrets out," he pointed toward the entrance where dozens of reporters waited.

The phone rang again. It was my agent.

"Paige?" I said.

"Yes, are you okay?"

"Fine, but I can't go back to the hotel."

"I have a ticket for you on the next flight to Colorado, head there now. I'll have someone get your bags from the hotel."

"You're a blessing," I said.

"Do you want me to release a statement for you?" Paige asked. "That might help."

"Yes," I said. "The police have confirmed what I have already known and told them all along. It should be no surprise that evil lurks among us and we must be ever vigilant in our actions. What we do matters! That's the theme in *The 13th Month* and it applies to everyday life. Doctor Mad should not be celebrated. He is an evil man. I will be cooperating with the authorities to bring this criminal to justice. Did you get all of that?"

"Yes," Paige said. "Very good. To the point and nothing controversial. There's still a lot of suspicion that you cooked all this up in the first place. Some deny the massacre ever happened. Are you really okay?"

"Actually," I said, "I'm afraid of what this character will do. I don't think he's out to get me personally but, I fear for those he's targeting. To stay hidden this long and out of sight, he's too cunning for my liking."

"Good thing you have an alibi that separates you from the murder scene," Paige said. "Hundreds of people lined up to see you at your appearance and hear you play your songs. Let's hope this clears you of any suspicion."

The line went dead.

"To the airport," I said to the driver.

Luckily, my agent had booked me on a flight that left immediately and, since I had no luggage to check in, I went through security quickly. I sat in the first-class seat by myself and turned on the news.

"Police now confirm the existence of Doctor Mad," the reporter said. "The name used to define the villain was coined by Science Fiction Author Louis Paul DeGrado who blamed the massacre at the Colorado Festival of Fear on the villain despite denials by the authorities."

"Well, Jen," another reporter said, "authorities are stating that they couldn't reveal the details due to an ongoing investigation."

"I would say they owe an apology to the survivors, Brad, for hiding the truth so long."

"Yes, Jen," Brad said. "And we can only wonder what Louis DeGrado is thinking now that his nickname is being used to describe this villain. Doctor Mad may take an exception to being called, well, Mad."

"Bring it on," I said and turned the screen off. I sat back in my seat.

The plane started backing away from the gate when I happened to glance around and notice there was no one else in the small, first-class seating section. Then, a man, black suit and tie, city shoes, walked through the curtain. He headed right for me and sat down across the aisle. I nodded. He pulled out an ID badge and showed it to me as he spoke.

"Mister DeGrado, I'm agent Valentine, Federal Bureau. I've been assigned to you."

The agent looked like a middle-weight boxer who was going out on the town with his gold watch and shiny shoes. I smiled.

"You look like an agent with that suit and tie," I said. "It also appears your fit and ready to fight. I've always wanted a bodyguard."

Agent Valentine laughed. "I'm not your bodyguard."

"I've had someone checking in on me since the events at the Festival of Fear," I said. "What exactly do you mean by being assigned to me?"

"For your security," Agent Valentine said. "We've known for some time that you were not responsible and have been looking into this Doctor Mad. Now that his identity has been confirmed and the news is linking it to you, we feel you might be in danger."

"So, you're like a bodyguard?"

"Think of me as your shadow," he said. "I'm more here to catch the bad guy then protect you."

"Great," I said. "That means a lot to me," I shook my head. "Is that your real name," I asked.

"Kirk Valentine," he said.

"Kirk from?"

"Yes, my parents were big fans," he said.

"Well, at least it won't be a boring flight now," I said. We both buckled in as the plane took off and climbed to cruising altitude. I offered to buy Valentine a beer but he declined. He did eat dinner with me as we talked some more.

"So, you've been tracking me for over a year?" I asked. He had revealed the case file he'd compiled on the events at the Festival of Fear.

"Not so much you, as our interest in the concept of the villain you are portraying as responsible," Valentine said. "I mean, there are some at the bureau that have gone as far as stating you invented the entire thing to help your own career."

"I lost friends there," I said. "And it hardly helped my career being ostracized. My main genre is not horror, but inspirational juvenile works. It's hard to be an example and inspire with something like this hanging over me."

"I suppose so," Valentine said. "Still, your survival of the mayhem that happened that day made you a suspect. Your story was difficult to believe."

"Story?"

"That the victims were hypnotized," Valentine said.

"They were, it was obvious," I said. "You see, I've studied it more since the event. A person must first be susceptible to be hypnotized right?"

Valentine nodded.

"Then, it's stated that the person cannot be made to do anything against their own morals," I said.

He nodded again.

"However, it's my theory that these people, who were dressed in costumes of their horror icons, were convinced they were in the movie of their character and therefore, thought what they were doing wasn't real."

"Mass hypnotism carried out by one individual?" Valentine asked.

"Oh, he wasn't alone," I said.

"Yes, that's right," Valentine said, "the kids dressed as college students with their satchels."

"They weren't kids," I said. "They were just dressed in a manner that reminded me of college students. See, I worked on a campus for a few years. The sweaters, backpacks, satchels or whatever they're called, and other attire that was prevalent on campus is what they were wearing. They were all dressed in a similar fashion like a cult. You don't have to believe me, but I was there."

"On the contrary, I know of many cases around the world where, through some type of ceremony, be it dance or song, this type of behavior exists. People with compromised constitutions will follow the behaviors of others or a leader without much provocation. It's what is meant by mob mentality and has been around for centuries."

"So, what evidence was uncovered that exposed him, Doctor Mad I mean?" I asked.

Valentine reached into his bag and brought out a small notebook. He looked around the plane before turning it on. He pulled up a file.

"While monitoring protests at the universities some of our agents started putting a profile together of these followers, as you might call them. People dressed in similar garb; the attire and backpacks from the late fifties, sixties and seventies so to speak."

"His followers," I said.

"This connection led us to his identity," Valentine said.

"Identity? You know who he is?"

"He's a former professor," Valentine said. "He spent thirty-years at various universities." He clicked on a picture of a man in a suit and tie at a university. The picture was dated to be twenty-three years older than the current date but, as I looked at the face, I could see Doctor Mad!

"A colleague of his came forward," Valentine said.

"Let me guess, the murdered Gene Archer," I said.

"Yes," Valentine confirmed.

"His real name is Doctor Darius Pool."

CHAPTER TWO
LETTERS FROM A MADMAN

Being an author in a generation where people want to watch videos more than exercising their brain to read has its advantages; the general public lost interest in me relatively quickly. Doctor Mad remained a hot item but the writer who named him, me, was out of the spotlight and back at home. I had just finished breakfast when there was a knock at my door.

"This is for you," my neighbor Heather said as she entered my house and handed me an envelope. "Got any grape jelly?"

Heather, a five-ten, blonde yoga instructor and veterinarian, was my closest neighbor. She had been engaged twice but never married. I enjoyed her company as she always treated me like family.

"In the cabinet," I said. "It's kind of early for the mail to be delivered." I examined the plain, white envelope that was sealed. "Hmm, no stamp or return address. Great, another invitation."

"You should be flattered that so many people invite you to events," Heather said as she sat down on the couch.

"Make yourself at home," I said somewhat jokingly. Her backyard and mine shared a fence and we had gotten to know each other over the years and often watched scary movies together.

"I couldn't wait to see my neighbor who is all over the news now," Heather said. "You've got the whole neighborhood group talking about you."

"Neighborhood group?" I asked

"You know, the one you always ignore that send you letters every month to join. You should join, it will do you good to get out more."

"I get out plenty," I said.

I began opening the letter. "Well, when I first started writing, I couldn't get offers to anything. The local zoo wouldn't carry my books. The playhouse wouldn't do my plays. I always thought people would warm up to and support an author from their own hometown but that didn't happen."

"No?"

"No, quite the reverse. It's like the people of my hometown assumed no talent could exist here." I stopped talking when I read the first line of the letter. It was handwritten and in bold, black lettering.

"Is it an invitation?" Heather asked.

"No," I said as I continued reading.

"Did you know there's a man parked at the edge of the cul-de-sac in a black SUV?"

"Yes," I said. "He's watching me."

"Why, are you a suspect?" Heather asked.

"No, he's protecting me."

"From whom?"

"From him," I said as I finished reading the letter and pointed to it.

Heather put her toast and coffee down and came over to me. She took the letter and read it out loud.

"Dear Mister, DeGrado, or would you prefer I call you Author Louis Paul DeGrado. Yes, I know who you are and where you live. Don't worry, I have no ill will toward you."

"I can't say the same about you," I said.

Heather continued: "You have made me famous, or infamous. 'Doctor Mad,' as you've so easily coined me. Every supervillain needs a good name. Even if it is inaccurate. After all, who is mad here? The author who writes about good and evil, who kills millions of people on the planet Arelis in his book or who hunted for ghosts as a kid? Or should we ask who isn't mad when we consider who people vote into office these days.

"Why am I writing you? You were smart enough to evade my first appearance at the Festival of Fear, and now you are the one who insisted that I exist. I guess it's only fate that I go by the name you use for me. Name aside, I am pleased. It's time the world got to know why I am out here. Isn't that what all us supervillains want is the world to understand our twisted plans? That may be what you think but, trust me, I could care less about public opinion."

"Trust me?" I said. "Why would I trust him?"

Heather ignored me and continued reading:

"We are so underrated, us supervillains. It's the slashers that get all the credit and for what? Simple murder? No real thought about it, just stab slash, hack and kill and you're guaranteed dozens of sequels and your face on a shirt. No why or real meaning behind what you are doing? Society knows it's not real but celebrates the villain anyway. I'm real, and if people really understood me, they'd be terrified!"

"What are you doing?" Heather asked as I headed for the front door.

"I'm going out there to face my fear, if Doctor Mad is out there, I'm going to confront him."

Heather put her hand on my shoulder to stop me.

I smiled, "Just kidding. agent Valentine should know about this."

"Valentine?" Heather said.

"Yes, and don't make fun of his name or he'll get upset. And don't tell him I told you about him or..."

"He'll get upset," Heather laughed. "Well, he's not doing a very good job being so visible."

"Actually, I think he wants to be noticed," I said. "Which makes it even more troublesome that someone was able to get this letter to my doorstep."

"Oh, I guess I didn't tell you, it was delivered to my house," Heather said. "I found it outside my door."

I walked across the room to the kitchen and pulled out a mug from the cabinet, poured some coffee and headed to the door.

"Where are you going now?" Heather asked.

"I'll be right back," I said. "You can watch through the window if you want."

The cull de sac I resided in had been a quiet and secure neighborhood. I enjoyed living close to the downtown historic area and the zoo which were two of my favorite places to visit. Valentine had parked his car across the street in front of a vacant house that was being refurbished. As I approached his SUV, the window came down.

"Who's the girl?" Valentine asked.

"She's my neighbor that lives behind me, Heather," I said. I noticed his laptop sitting on the passenger's side was open to my webpage.

"Doing some research there," I said as I handed him the mug of coffee.

"Thanks," Valentine said. "Just learning as much as I can about the case I'm on and the parties involved. I didn't realize how many books you've written."

"I'll have to bring you one to read," I said. "In the meantime," I handed him the letter from Doctor Mad.

"No way he got this past me," Valentine said.

"He didn't," I said. "He left it at Heather's doorstep. That probably means he knows you're out here."

"Handwritten with a calligraphy pen," Valentine said. "He's sure full of himself."

I looked around to see if anyone was watching our conversation. "I probably shouldn't stay long. I'll come back for that later."

"Bring me a book when you do," Valentine said.

"Which one?"

"Surprise me," he said. "Hey," he waved me back and I moved closer to the vehicle. "You wrote about the events at the Festival of Fear, are you going to write about all of this as well?"

"I might," I said. "Depends on who's standing in the end."

"What do you mean?" Valentine said.

"Doctor Mad is amused with me right now but, my goal is to get him," I said. "He's probably in the area to cause trouble at the Festival of Fear. Eventually we will come head-to-head and only one of us will remain."

"I'm here to make sure it doesn't come to that," Valentine said.

"I hope so," I said. Internally, I was already considering how intelligent Doctor Mad might be and how connected. The challenge of finding him before he acted might be a task bigger than either Valentine or I could handle. I would have to be vigilant.

"One more thing," Valentine said. "Are you going to put me in your book when you write about all of this?"

"Yep, and I'm going to make you a Black Guy named Valentine who wears sunglasses and has the build of a boxer but dresses like a pimp."

"I am a black man named 'Valentine,'" Valentine said.

"I know, it's a perfect disguise. No one will ever suspect I used your real identity!"

"You need to make sure you keep me informed of your whereabouts from now on. If I'm not around then I won't be any good at protecting you."

"Wow," I said. "I'm touched by your concern. First, the authorities ostracize me saying this Doctor Mad is all in my imagination because I'm a science-fiction author and susceptible to exaggeration. Then, when you realize I was right, suddenly you want to know what I know and think, bring me in for questioning, no compensation for my time, I might add. And, who told the press what I named him? I didn't. So, if I have a target on my back, whose fault is it?"

"Like you said, he's amused by you right now. You bring him the attention he desires," Valentine said.

I leaned back and took a good look around the neighborhood. "He might be watching me now. Not him exactly, that's below him, but one of these people around here doesn't belong. Perhaps the mail carrier, the lawn service guy over there, the dog walker there, or even that person riding the bike." I laughed as Agent Valentine strained to see everyone I pointed out from his seated position.

"Go ahead and laugh," Valentine said. "He needs you for his plan now. However, in my experience, he will tire of you if you criticize him or do something he doesn't like and then..."

"It's curtains," I said.

"Curtains?" Valentine asked. "What does that mean?"

"You don't know that saying? Geez, how old are you?" I said. "Curtains means you've met your demise."

"Oh," Valentine said. "And the killer uses the curtains to wrap up and disguise your body during the removal. You know, a way to hide the evidence."

"Hmm," I said. "Interesting theory but, I think it just means that it's the end. You know, like the end of a show and the curtains close."

"Speaking of curtains, your lady friend is watching us through the curtain over there. How well do you know her? Maybe she's the one working for him. It was convenient that she brought the envelope," Valentine said.

"I'm going to send her out here with a book for you," I said. "Then you can question her. Oh, and she's single." I laughed as I walked back to my house.

CHAPTER THREE
THE MEMORIAL

It was two weeks before the Festival of Fear and I had travelled to Denver for the memorial that would be at the hotel where the horrible massacre occurred. The hotel was closed indefinitely and the investigation is ongoing. In the parking lot, a large, fifty-foot-long marble tombstone has been erected with the names of those who perished on small placards attached to the stone. The memorial was the idea of the director of the festival, Brent Stein, and the hotel with further donations from families of the deceased.

I had booked the weekend at one of my favorite haunts, an actual haunted bed and breakfast located downtown by capitol hill. Agent Valentine was also booked there and, since Heather shared my fascination with scary stuff and we both knew she was being watched by Doctor Mad, she came along.

On an overcast day in the middle of the afternoon, we rode to the site in a black limousine. We picked up the others on the way.

"There's more of a crowd then I expected," I said from the back of the limousine that ferried Heather, Brent, Ryan, Rob, and myself. Agent Valentine had taken his own transportation and intended to stay in the background.

"It's become a popular item in the news," Heather said. "Especially with the recent revelation of Doctor Mad."

"Yes, but the police told us they would be restricting access to survivors and their families today. I guess I just expect so many people to show. I'm worried."

"Why," Ryan asked. Ryan, who stood about five nine, was fifty-eight years old and had long, black, graying hair, was one of the three survivors along with Sandy and me. "For the last two years we've been painted at fault in a way. Brent for having an event that celebrates horror and me for writing about it. All of us for sticking to our story and narrowly escaping being suspect. We should be regarded as survivors and respected for our courage."

"Good point," Brent said. "I'm not going to be ashamed for celebrating who I am. I enjoy the horror genre. Watching the movies makes me feel the same as when doing extreme sports; it's my adrenaline rush."

Brent, sixty-two years old with short, black hair, stood six four and was nicknamed 'the tall man,' by the rest of us in reference to a classic character from one of my favorite horror tales. He always knew where to go and who to speak too when it came to the horror genre that had been his passion.

"What happened is not your fault," Ryan said.

"It's a proven fact that we want that rush, crave it,' Rob said. "That's why people line up for it at the box office. That's also why, I'm sure, we have some extra people here today. They are fascinated by the horror of what happened."

Rob was Ryan's partner at the "Rocky Mountain Investigators of Paranormal Experiences", AKA "RIPE." He had degrees in astrology, physics, psychology and specialized in alien and supernatural phenomena. The most technical of our group, Rob tended to wear his hair long and dressed like a hippie.

"Yes, well, I like to be scared and enjoy the suspense," I said. "But, as some of the critics say, some of the stuff has just gotten out of control. When writers and directors are simply trying to go for shock value instead of a good storyline or true suspense, it's just not appealing. There's no real art in that. It's been done."

"Yes, just the shock value alone needs some story, even if it's demented," Brent said.

"It sells tickets," Ryan said. "People are easily entertained by a few jump scares and some skin. Fascinated by how far the movie will go and how gruesome the kills can be portrayed."

"But does it numb us to the reality of true horror?" Rob asked. "I mean, does it make us less sensitive because we are exposed to it so much?"

"Anyone ever tell you that you over analyze things," Ryan said.

"You do," Rob said. "All the time."

I laughed along with the others. "All good points for our conversation later. You are all invited to join us for dinner tonight."

Everyone nodded back.

"Let's just hope this crowd doesn't hold us accountable in any way for the events that happened two years ago," I said.

"People need to be held accountable for their actions," Rob said. "What happened was the delusions of a madman brought to life. No one is accountable but him and those that helped him."

We exited the car and headed to the memorial which was located at the hotel entrance. To get there, we walked through a parking lot that still had vehicles parked from the fateful festival; those that were unclaimed by the victims that didn't make it out alive.

It was in this very parking lot where I had escaped with Ryan and Sandy and glanced over to see Doctor Mad tip his hat at me as he left in a large vehicle that appeared to be a cross between a hearse and limousine. The black top-hat, black mustache, beard and cape he wore still fresh in my mind as was the evil smile he held.

"I'll knock that smirk off his face the next time I...." I suddenly realized I was speaking out loud as the others stopped walking and turned to me. "Sorry," I said. "Let's continue."

We cleared the final row of the parking lot and went toward the hotel front. There stood a barrier the police had erected years ago to keep looky-loos away. We cleared the entrance and found ourselves surrounded by the few survivors and the family members paying tribute. I could tell I'd been noticed. The result turned out to be favorable as applause followed.

"He's the one that told us the truth," one of the people in the audience cried out. "He exposed Doctor Mad."

"Say something," someone shouted out. Suddenly, I found myself at the center of the crowd while Ryan, Brent, Heather and Rob had backed away. Out of the corner of my eye I spotted Agent Valentine at the edge of the crowd and knew he'd have my back if things got rough.

"Thank you," I said. "We have all come here today to remember those we loved and those who survived. What happened two years ago on that day should have never taken place. Those who gathered did so to celebrate and enjoy a pastime and interest that probably caused them much grief at some time or another. They came to this festival to find acceptance without being judged from others who shared the same fascinations. It's easy to say that we shouldn't honor those who went to such a festival but, they were doing what they loved and being themselves."

Cheers rang out.

"Please post what I am about to say on every social media you can find. The tragedy that took place here two years ago was orchestrated by a madman. Someone who was not smart but insecure with himself. He preyed on those weaker than himself and used them to carry out a cowardly act that had no meaning other than to inflict harm and fulfill his deranged delusion that he somehow would leave a mark in this world."

Applause rang out. I caught Agent Valentine's eyes and could tell he wasn't pleased. I was doing the very thing he'd counseled against by challenging the evil Doctor Mad and insulting him.

"Doctor Mad has tried to convince me he's intelligent and deserves credit for masterminding what he's done. He thinks of himself as a supervillain. But he lives in the shadows like a cockroach and is too insecure to show himself; afraid that he'd be squashed. Well, I say, go ahead and continue hiding. The rest of us are going to move on and live and celebrate. You can't scare us; we love being SCARED!" I shouted out and the crowd went wild. I took the bouquet of flowers and laid them at the memorial and thanked those who cared to come up and shake my hands as they did with Ryan, Brent and Rob.

We soon found ourselves back in the limo and heading downtown to one of my favorite restaurants that had a piano bar and plenty of history. The joint had been many things over the years including a bank and still had the vault room. An upscale restaurant, it was located close to the capitol and, yes, it was also purportedly haunted. I'd made reservations in advance and we went to a back table where we could have some privacy.

"First round's on me," I said and headed to the bar. I leaned against the bar right next to Agent Valentine who calmly sat drinking his club soda.

"That was quite a show back there," Valentine said. "Do you know what the term 'poke the bear' means and why it's not good?"

"Kind of let the moment get away from me," I said.

"Well, keep it up and we'll catch our villain when he comes after you. Hopefully before he kills you," Valentine said.

"Oh, come on," I said. "We're both too smart to let something like that happen. I was gaining the upper hand. True psychotics have an emotional gap in empathy so we can't appeal to his humanity. But they also don't like to be seen as stupid."

"Or mad?"

"Or mad."

"You think you can unbalance him and make him act out?" Valentine asked.

"Yes," I said. "The closer we get to the festival, the more I worry about not knowing where he is or what he is up too."

The bartender took my order and table number and I headed back to the table where the group was discussing this year's theme for the festival, classic monsters. Trays of breads, olives and cheeses were spread throughout and I grabbed some olives as I sat and listened to the ongoing conversation.

"No, no, here me out," Brent said, "The first classic monsters weren't evil."

"How so?" Heather asked.

"The Werewolf origin is not explained well, but it was probably used to keep children home after hours," Brent said.

"As were many of the tales over the years," Rob said. "Fables to show what happens if you don't follow certain rules. Like not being out at night."

"Similar to religion," Ryan said.

"Not my exact point," Brent said "I was more talking about the originals. See, the man who becomes the wolfman didn't bite himself. The Mummy didn't unbury himself; Count Dracula was trying to save his land and, Frankenstein's Monster didn't create himself. So, no one can claim they started with evil intent in mind. We might even say there was horror inflicted upon them and then, in what they became, they inflicted it on others."

"Point well taken," I said and offered a toast as the drinks arrived. "To horror writers, artists, creators, directors, producers, actors and fans!"

"Here, Here!" the others said.

"Yes, the real monster in Frankenstein was the doctor in which case we have many monsters running around now under the guise of this profession doing evil," Rob Said.

The food arrived and we all started to dig in.

"It makes you wonder how the first scary stories were inspired," Brent said. "Our generations were exposed to books, movies, art and television on the supernatural and unexplained. Naturally, that exposure led to interest or disinterest of the subject. However, there was none of this in ancient times. Who told the first horror stories and were the meanings simple warning such as don't go out of the cave after dark or you'll die? What were they exposed too? What nightmares did they have? Are all the zombie fears really a remnant of ancient cannibalistic tendencies? Have you ever thought about that?"

"I think," Rob said, "you also need to consider the lack of science at the time. Everything in the ancient world from bad thunderstorms, eclipses to animal attacks were not understood. The lack of lighting at night made this time of the day particularly scary. Imagine what was heard but could not be seen or explained back then. So, imaginations ran wild."

"And, with the advent of science, we've become less scared of explainable things," Ryan said.

"More scared of what we can't explain, human behavior," Rob said. "A huge amount of movies are now focused on human terror."

"I can think of no greater terror than those in authority having the power to start a war that affects thousands, millions of people," Brent said.

The group fell silent.

"Which is why we celebrate the imagination more than the actual," I said. "That's what the Festival of Fear is really about, right Brent? The creative side that entertains us and makes us feel alive."

"Right," Brent said. "We always need to keep the distinction that what we celebrate is the creativity and not the true horror that exists."

The conversation slowed when a waiter came up to Ryan and whispered something. Ryan nodded.

"I have something for all of you," Ryan said and stood. The rest of us, some with drinks in hand, followed him down a hallway to a back room that could seat a small party. A leather couch and two leather recliners were in a semicircle around a wooden table. On the table a television was set-up with a laptop hooked up to it.

"A horror movie?" I asked.

"I think I'm done," Heather said. "I can find my way back to my room."

"You sure?" I asked. She nodded.

"Go ahead and take the limo and tell the driver we're done for the night," I said. "I'll walk back."

The others said their farewells as Heather left.

"Take a seat," Ryan said. "Rob and I have something to show you."

Brent and I sat on the couch facing the television while Rob and Ryan went to the front and sat on either side of the screen.

"You asked us to use our investigative skills to research Doctor Mad," Ryan said. "This is what we have so far. Don't worry about taking notes, I have a copy of all of this for you. Rob?"

"As you know from your FBI friend," Rob said, "Doctor Mad's real name is Darius Pool, or Doctor Darious Pool. He started as a professor at a community college teaching basic psychology over forty years ago. However, from the start, Doctor Pool had an interest in human behavior. We have video from his classroom."

The television came to life with a video shot from the back of a classroom. A man at the front was spinning a hypnotic spiral. He was speaking to the class but the audio was too low and the quality too poor to understand him.

"Look at the students," Rob said. The setting was a college-classroom with about thirty students sitting in five rows. "By their attire, I imagine this is late eighties, early nineties?"

"You're correct," Ryan said. "Our Professor is just getting started with his experiments. He goes on to get his Doctorate in Paranormal Psychology and Psychiatry. He becomes unpopular due to his use of hypnosis. He's obsessed with it and is turned in by his fellow faculty on numerous occasions for abuse of both funds and student assistants, several of which committed suicide."

"He's doing an experiment now, isn't' he?" I asked.

"Yes," Ryan said. On the video, a few students stood and left the room while the others remained seated. "See, he had those not susceptible to his hypnosis technique remove themselves so he could refine his group to those he could control."

"How long did he teach?" I asked.

"That's where it gets interesting," Rob said. "We think we know, but he may have changed names a few times so, our data might be incomplete."

"What we have so far," Ryan said, "is that he started in nineteen eighty-seven at a junior college, and last taught at Great Land Polytech in two-thousand fifteen. Our investigation turned up evidence that he was at over fifteen different colleges touching an estimated four-thousand students from what we've found so far. If he had a private practice as well, there may be more he influence."

"How is it possible that no one noticed his record?" Brent asked.

"He was driven out multiple times but no one had the guts to put that down on his record so, he kept getting hired," Ryan said.

"I suppose he was a brilliant teacher," Rob Said.

"Most psychopaths are above average intelligence," Ryan said.

"The students probably had no idea they were being programmed," Rob said.

"His followers could be anywhere," I said.

"Precisely," Ryan said. "Many of them have worked their way into certain positions where he's just waiting to trigger them. It's no wonder he hasn't been stopped."

"The only way to be safe would be to track down all of his students and try to deprogram them," I said.

"An overwhelming task it seems," Rob said. He and Ryan took seats in the recliners.

"Can we start the search in the local area?" I asked. "Start with people you know who are involved with the festival. I'll help by looking into the background of people I know."

"You don't really think he would try something at this year's festival?" Brent said. "I've hired extra security including some of my friends will be undercover."

I looked at every member of our small group and made eye contact. "I don't think we have the luxury of predicting the mind of a maniac. We should take every precaution."

"Do we know anything about his motive?" Brent said. "Why target our festival of all things?"

"He's been targeting activities that involve the younger generations," Rob said. "The college protests for example. He might be behind the mall shootings and crime sprees. His motive may be to create chaos or just demonstrate he has control."

"He might be testing the span of his control and preparing for something bigger," Brent said.

"Unsatisfied with the status, the hunger inside of him would grow and desire more. It follows a pattern of escalation," Rob said.

"More of what?" Ryan asked.

"More power, more control," Rob said. "That's the motive of a supervillain."

"I was thinking about supervillains in the horror genre," I said. "They aren't usually a stand-alone character but have a nemesis."

"There aren't too many specific to horror actually," Brent said. "Those that exist are more sci-fi, thriller, drama or, unfortunate to say, non-fiction. Our own world history is full of these characters. Many become dictators and hold some possessive ability of their direct follower while they terrorize the general population. If only people would learn how to bond together and stand up to these people faster."

"We focus on the wrong history lessons and therefore are doomed to repeat the tragedies," I said.

"Isn't Satan kind of a supervillain after all," Ryan said.

"I guess if you roll up the characteristics," I said.

"Which would be?" Ryan asked.

"The need to control or destroy," I said. "They want control or to seed destruction of what they can't control."

"Extremely one-dimensional," Brent said as he drank his bourbon. "They see themselves as implementing controlled chaos or anarchy to destroy the status quo by convincing others they lack power and freedom. Then, they take that power and freedom from them."

"Interesting," I said. "So, in tearing down society, it's like our supervillain is mad that he or she isn't in control and therefore trying to control the destruction of the system of control. However, it is in the lack of structure that they find the need to destroy further; when those that follow them don't follow the new system of control."

"What system is that?" Rob asked.

"Do what I say or I kill you," I said. "What I cannot control I destroy and the rules I make for you don't apply to me. That seems to be the inner workings of the supervillain."

"Wow, you guys really know how to bring the mood down," Ryan said. "Shall we return to civilization?"

We walked back to the main room. I noticed the crowd had thinned and the musicians had left. I was ready to get back to my room and change into something more comfortable as I'd been in a suit all day.

"Well, it's time for me to go," I said. I looked and spotted Valentine at the bar speaking to a good-looking woman and figured I'd give him a break. Besides, I thought, the haunted bed and breakfast was just down the street and it was a nice night.

I walked outside and took a deep breath of the night air feeling refreshed. The interesting conversation had been a workout for my brain and I was looking forward to less stimulation. Suddenly, a black limousine pulled alongside me and the driver exited, opened the door and motioned for me to get in.

CHAPTER FOUR
A RIDE WITH MADNESS

The driver, dressed in a black suit, let his coat hang open enough to show me his revolver in the holster strapped across his chest. I obliged him and stepped into the back seat where I found myself sitting across from Doctor Mad. The door closed and the driver went around to the front of the vehicle, entered and we headed down the street. The windows were dark so I was unable to tell where we were going.

Doctor Mad sat still and his eyes, narrowed and unwavering under the black top-hat, were focused directly on me. A slight smile lie upon his lips that sat under the waxed curled mustache. His face had make-up, powdery, white with a little blush, on both the cheeks and what I could see of his lower forehead in the manner suited to a theatre performer. He clenched a cane in his hands which was positioned across his right knee and went down under his left leg to the floor.

"I've always been fascinated with writers," Doctor Mad said. His voice melodic and soothing with a slight English accent. "Not so much with non-fiction but science-fiction and fantasy authors. They create whole worlds inside their minds full of characters, events, philosophies and societies. Truly, a marvel of intellect must be behind this ability. Wouldn't you say?"

"No amount of flattery or keen discussion will distract me from what you did or who you are, Professor Darius Pool."

His left eyebrow raised.

"Yes, I know who you are, or who you were, Professor."

"Doctor, I achieved that status. Besides, it goes along with your nickname for me, 'Doctor Mad.' I'm sure you must be proud that all the news outlets are using that name. Are you making any money on it?"

"No," I said. "But there is a reward for you so, if you're worried about my well-being, let's just go to the police station. I'll get out first and make sure they don't shoot you. Then I can collect the reward and make money which I can then donate to the victims of your massacre."

"Oh, come now," Doctor Mad said. "I thought it would be a thrill to get to know you and talk to you. I've been behind so many things, countless events. You not only slipped away but noticed me in the process. You know how enjoyable that was for me to finally be recognized? Now my secret is revealed. Surely you must be as curious about me as I am about the man who outsmarted me. Don't you have any questions?"

I didn't answer. His hands moved from the cane momentarily to a cabinet on his left where he opened the door to display a bottle of wine, bourbon, and vodka.

"May I offer you a drink?"

"I'll pass," I said. "Your motivation. That's my question. What is the motivation behind what you are doing? Surely, you must have justified some type of reason or purpose if only to yourself."

"You want it to be something simple like I want to control things, or I want to destroy things, is that it?" Doctor Mad said.

"No, I want to understand. You see I've always misunderstood why people that are so genius or so potentially inspirational do bad things. Why not inspire good? Why not hypnotize people to do good deeds? Can you imagine if terrorist organizations won over their enemies by doing good deeds or if gangs had morals and values that led to the betterment of society."

"You have something there," Doctor Mad said. "That would be true power. But no one gets remembered or credited for that type of stuff."

"You're kidding me," I said. "What about the Nobel prize winners, Ghandi, Mother Theresa, all the compassionate heroes throughout history."

"Sidelines at best," Doctor Mad said. "They are not half as idolized as the villains. Have you ever seen anyone dressed up as these people for a costume party? Well, maybe Ghandi but, you understand my point. Besides that, haven't you been following the trends? Our misguided youth now find a way to turn any hero into a villain and any villain into a misunderstood victim. It's almost made being a bad guy, well, not bad."

"You might be right but, this trend will pass," I said. "Inevitably, good people will stand up when they've had enough."

"Oh, I hope so," Doctor Mad said. "Without the constant battle between right and wrong there would only be boring order and progress. People like me are irrelevant if we keep celebrating and even electing villains to office."

"So, you'd rather be remembered among the monsters of society than someone who achieved something heroic?" I asked.

"Monsters? It's you and your friends that celebrate monsters." Doctor Mad said. "Why do you celebrate the horror genre. Maybe my lesson is that we need to abandon this gruesome celebration of such a traumatic topic. You do know that they glorify the slashers and the killers. You talk about why I don't do something good and yet you celebrate the industry that creates art and movies about HORROR?"

"Everyone enjoys a good story and scare," I said. "The difference is distinguishing between real and fantasy, good and evil."

"Yes," Doctor Mad said. "A distinction that is blurred and played right into my plan. You see, I learned that I could make people think they are in a dream and their actions aren't real. That is how I defeated the morality when I have them do something they might have doubts about. A moral compass that has grown cloudier and a veil that is nearly invisible. You see, with the movies and games these days, death and impartiality to cruelty is all around us and all I have to do is convince them they are in a game. I merely encourage the monster to come out, isn't that what all the movie makers, the horror fans desire?"

"It's that simple?" I asked.

"Bystanders to death is what we've become," Doctor Mad said. "That is why you cannot defeat me. You yourself, Louis, believe evil exists because we let it! You are right, it's in all of us and it's winning! Look at the language, the gangs, the stores having to lock everything up! Armed guards in public places and bars on every window. The inevitable is already in motion, I'm just enabling the natural trend."

"The trend toward chaos?" I said.

"No, not just chaos, violent chaos to tear down the fabric of what is and lead us to something different. It might not be perfect but it is time to have someone else take the wheel, don't you think?"

I didn't answer.

"The hate is already there, I merely open the door to let what's inside come out, you cannot deny it! People act out and it's only after that they turn and realize they want order. I will be there in the end to give it to them."

"You're insane," I said. "A mad plan from a madman."

"I read your business book and you said, 'you get the behavior you allow'. How right you are. What was allowed grew to be accepted and now, all is accepted. I have many followers waiting to push the buttons when I tell them! Aren't you tired of it all? Aren't you ready for a change?"

"Not if that change requires so much death and destruction," I said. "There's got to be a better way."

"I'm teaching you the way," Doctor Mad said. "I am, after all, an instructor. I am not showing you anything that isn't already there, I'm just exposing what lies beneath. The ill intent we all have for each other that lies just beneath the surface."

"I think history is already a testament to that lesson," I said. "While I agree we need a refresher to our moral compass, there are other ways to go about this instead of harming people. If you are talented, you wouldn't be doing these things. You are evil true and pure and there is no honor in that. You have done nothing to change my opinion and only confirmed that my name for you applies, Doctor Mad."

"That's really how you feel?"

I nodded.

"Shame, I was going to ask you to join me as my biographer. I mean, there's so many things people won't even know about me like the years I spent being a chiropractor."

"Sorry," I said. "I'm a science-fiction writer, not a biographer. I prefer to create worlds where the good guys win and the world's a better place than the one we live in."

"You are a dreamer," Doctor Mad said. "Driver, stop here."

The car pulled to the curb and stopped. The driver walked over to open my door.

"I'm going to find a way to stop you," I said. "Since the authorities don't seem to be able to do it, I will."

"You'd be safer going home," Doctor Mad said.

"Is this goodbye?" I asked.

"Oh, I hardly think so. You amuse me," Doctor Mad said. "But, I will warn you. Dreamers often die broke and alone."

He tipped his hat as I exited I took a good look at the driver who watched me closely. His face, expressionless with a chiseled jaw and nose that had clearly been broken a few times. While he had one hand on the door, the other was clearly on his revolver and I firmly believed he had killed before. It was the determined look on his face that I would remember and later reflect back upon.

The limousine drove away and my thoughts drifted to the driver and his actions. It was then I realized, the driver didn't seem to be under the influence of hypnotism as he bore no sign of it. That meant, in addition to his hypnotized students that might be incapable of knowing what they were doing, Doctor Mad had willing supporters. This made him more dangerous than I'd anticipated.

I noticed I was just about a block from the mansion where I was staying. I walked down the street and turned once to see the limousine pull away. Words from Doctor Mad echoed in my mind"

"Encourage the monster to come out, isn't that what all the movie makers, the horror fans desire?"

I headed toward my destination when I noticed a group of people standing at the curb of the mansion all staring at me. It was the nightly ghost walk and the host was someone I had met before and who I had given a copy of my *Spookable Tales Anthology.* I waved at the group of fellow ghost seekers and headed up the stairs to the haunted bed and breakfast where I was staying. I barely cleared the doorway when Valentine was in my face. He looked at me and down at his watch.

"He's here," I said to valentine

"How do you know?" Valentine asked.

"As you might have noticed, I've been gone awhile."

"Yes, I thought it took a long time for you to walk just a few blocks?"

We headed into a reception room where I poured two shots of bourbon and sat down in one of two wing-backed chairs that lie around an antique coffee table.

"I love staying in places like this," I said delaying the heaviness of the conversation we needed to have.

"Why's that?" Valentine entertained.

"The eloquent ambience, quiet and warm comfort of these historical places soothes ones spirit. I also enjoy the lack of electronic devices which distract us from focusing on enjoying conversations with each other."

"Yes, I guess it is part of the allure," Valentine said. "Now, tell me what happened. What did he want?" he sat across from me in the other chair, leaving the bourbon untouched.

"He had a lot of information. He's been planting seeds for three to four decades," I said. "There's no telling how many students he's influenced or where they are now. There might even be someone close to me he's influenced and I, and they, don't even know it."

"Because of being hypnotized?" Valentine asked.

"Yes," I said. "That's what he was doing all those years while teaching. He was building his army. He might have people with the police, even within your organization. He seems to know my every move. Plus, he drives around in a big limousine yet the police can never find him. Don't you think that's a little hard to explain?"

Valentine sat back in his chair without a word. I reached over and took the glass of bourbon I poured for him and drank it.

"He asked me to be his biographer," I said as I stood. "I declined. Then, he told me I would be safer if I left and went home."

"So, you think he's planning something for the festival?" Valentine asked.

I nodded, all while thinking, *someone's got to stop him*!

After I talked with Agent Valentine, I went to my room still shaken from the events. I took a breath and focused on my feelings. It wasn't fear I was feeling but aggravation, anger. I was determined to take action. It was then I realized, I had to become something else. I had to change. I could no longer be a bystander, but needed to be someone that took action.

I sat down at a small desk in the room and wrote out my idea, a concept of my own; a hero that appeared when needed to make things right.

"If only it were that simple," I said to the ghosts in my room before going to bed. I stood to go to the bathroom and brush my teeth when something caught me from the corner of my eye...the closet door was open.

Now, I've always counseled people, for fun but on a serious note as well, that if they think they have an intruder in their house or room that the first thing they should do is prepare to defend themselves. That usually means getting some type of weapon or, if it's dark, a flashlight. It is also during this moment you need to take stock of your options: whether fight or flight, meaning run, is the best thing to do. I would say freezing in fear is your worst option but, if you were one of those types, you wouldn't be reading this story.

However you decide to handle the situation, you should not do what I did next and give away your position.

"Hello, is anyone there?" I called out.

No one answered. If there had been a stalker or someone who was going to harm me, I had just given my position away. I slowly opened the closet fully by sliding the door and noticed a wrapped bag on a hanger as though a suit had been dry cleaned and hung. On the bag was a note.

"Thought this would suit your concept for the upcoming Steampunk Festival. Hope you like it...Heather."

I undid the bag and took out the costume trying it on. The black trench-coat with the leather cross-stitch design would do perfectly. I would need some accessories.

CHAPTER FIVE
THE MARSHAL

The next day, I headed to the Steampunk Festival in Victor Colorado. It was an annual event I attended since it started years ago and didn't want to miss out. I enjoyed the atmosphere of the town and its people. It was another town I frequented and usually found myself staying at the haunted Victor Hotel or the famed Colorado Grande hotel.

I strolled down the street eating my chocolate chip cookies and drinking an iced coffee when I noticed Brent and some of the other organizers at a booth for the Festival of Fear. I walked up to the booth.

"Wow, what a costume!" Brent said. "I think you have the most authority here."

Brent was referring to my self-made costume. Over the years, I had collected badges from every small town or city I visited. I currently was the Sheriff in no less than twenty-five counties, including Tombstone and Dodge City, and a federal marshal among other military badges. I had taken the black, cowboy trench-coat Heather found for me and lined each side on the front with the various badges. I also had adorned my brown, gear-decorated hat with badges. Worn, brown cowboy boots with spurs completed the ensemble.

"Check out these glasses," I said as I took off the metal frames and handed them to Brent. "If you move the lever on the side you can zoom in an out. Who needs binoculars?"

"Where's your gun?" Brent asked.

"That's classified," I said and winked. I really hadn't put much thought into a gun or any type of weapon for my costume and his observation made me consider the option.

"I didn't know you were going to be here today," I said.

"A friend of mine told me this was a great place to visit," he smiled at me. "Besides, you can never do too much marketing. It's going to be a record turnout this year. Partly due to the stories attached you know, the tragedy and the possible appearance of Doctor Mad."

"Well, let's just hope it will be uneventful," I said while considering the plan I was hatching to make it so.

"You continue to have suspicions about it?" Brent asked.

I motioned Brent to follow me to the side of the booth and lowered my voice.

"What is it?" Brent asked.

"After our dinner, I had a run-in with Doctor Mad. He's in the area and I believe he's up to no good. So, I've asked Ryan to look into the background of all those you keep in your inner circle. You see, Doctor Mad has a lot of connections as we've spoken about."

"You think he has someone on the inside of the Festival of Fear?"

"I'm not sure, but we need to be cautious if we're going to avoid another catastrophe and, if you think back, it makes sense that he had inside information about all your events that night."

"I don't know, it was well advertised an all over the internet," Brent said. "I don't want to believe someone close to me would be capable of such things."

"It may be someone he's programmed over the years who doesn't even know they are helping him," I said. "Which is part of the problem, it could be anyone he came into contact with."

"Which is why you asked Ryan to do the background searches?"

"Yes," I said. "There's more. See, I don't just want to stop the doctor from another foul deed, I want to put an end to his reign of terror."

"How?" Brent asked.

"By setting a trap," I said. "All I need is a place and a way to lure him there."

"How about an exclusive pre-event party with celebrities at a haunted location?" Brent said,

"Perfect!" I said. "Well discuss the details immediately before. I don't want to give anything away in advance. And Brent, keep this to yourself."

"Trust no one," Brent said and nodded. "Where are you staying tonight?"

"Oh, my brother and I are staying at the Victor hotel, fourth floor."

"The haunted floor?" Brent asked.

"Of course," I said. "Wouldn't miss an opportunity. Besides, I know the owner, Christine, and have been coming here for years. Are you staying for the party tonight?"

"No, I have to get back," Brent said. "Lots going on with the festival getting so close."

"Well, you're going to miss a spectacular event," I said. "The parade at the end culminates with everyone marching up that hill to burn the effigy of the Dread Pirate."

"Pirates? In Colorado?" Brent said.

"Yes," I said. "It's based on a true story of some of the last pirates who were hunted and they trekked all the way to Colorado to hide their treasure. Only one survived and he was killed for his gold."

"So, he haunts the town. Is that it?" Brent asked.

"Only if they don't follow through with the tradition and pay tribute," I said.

Brent looked up at the sky and so did I. There wasn't a cloud to be seen.

"Seems pretty dry up here for a fire," Brent said.

"I know," I said. "I'd hate to see them break from tradition." Mike came down the row of vendors and joined us as I said this.

"Then the pirate will come out and haunt the town, is that it?" Brent said.

Mike's eyes went wide. "Haunt the town? What I miss?"

"Oh, nothing," I said. "Just the story about *The Dread Pirate.* But we'll save that for another time."

After an eventful night at the Steampunk Festival, I went home for the week but was headed back up to Denver the following weekend. There I met with the organizers of the Festival of Fear to go over a plan I hoped they'd support; a plan to lure Doctor Mad into a trap. It would consist of several parts and I would be going over some parts with all of them and other parts with just individuals. If the plan failed, I would know who among us, if anyone, was under the influence of the Doctor.

Agent Valentine accompanied me to Denver where I checked into my favorite haunt and headed out to the mall where I was going to meet by brother, Mike, who lived in Denver, for lunch. I invited Valentine to dine with us but he declined. I went to a few of my favorite stores before meeting Mike at the food area.

"Did you sleep well or did the ghosts disturb you?" Mike asked. "You know, you can always stay with us."

"The ghosts left me alone again, I'm sorry to say," I said. "It's safer for me to stay away from you and your family at the current time until this festival is over."

"After what we went through last weekend at the Steampunk Festival, I agree," Mike said.

We stood in line at one of the food vendors and then settled in the middle of the large seating area to eat. The food court was by the entrance and exit with doors to one side of us and the hall and stairway to the three-story mall on the other side.

"Hey," I heard Mike say as he looked at me. "Are you hearing anything I say?"

"Sorry," I said. "I'm having trouble focusing. I felt a nagging sensation; my own internal senses telling me something wasn't right. I listened and started taking stock. What was out of place? My health seemed fine as did my guests, the weather had changed and a light rain was coming down outside but nothing more.

I scanned the crowd and that's when it hit me! There, in the background I spotted some young adults riding on the animal rides that kids usually are upon. Not one, but more than a dozen. It wasn't just that they were on the silly electric methods of transportation but the way they were dressed as university students with backpacks that alarmed me.

I reached out and touched Mike's hand as he reached for a French fry. The effect worked as he immediately stopped speaking and looked at me. "What is it?"

"I need you to go to a safe place and hide. Maybe the bathroom in one of the stores and don't come out no matter what hear," I said.

"Why?" Mike asked.

"It's, Doctor Mad!"

"What are you going to do?" Mike asked.

"I'm going to get help," I said looking around for Agent Valentine who I could usually spot but couldn't locate at the current moment. I went into one of the side stores and went to a changing room.

When I exited, I found that the minions took their position by the exit and the mall music increased in volume and changed to an eerie, circus sound. I took out my noise cancelling earplugs and watched. It was there it happened in front of me.

A man, wearing a long trench coat and a western hat emerged. The hat was decorated with badges as was the jacket all the way down the front on both sides. His gun was drawn and I spotted the two students blocking the doors go down with the figure smashing the lock they had put on the doors and motioning people to exit the mall.

Several bad guys started heading for the hero who shot brilliantly. I noticed there were no bullets flying but instead, darts. They must have been tranquilizer's as the targets started dropping to the floor quickly after being struck. One got behind the hero and wrapped his arms around the man. His hat fell off as he executed a move to throw the villain down and hit him with a left punch to the jaw disabling the opponent who, after being struck, looked surprised and ran.

"This Way!" I heard the hero yelling as people echoed his command and they exited the door.

I got close enough to see the badge on his hat read 'Marshal' as I passed by and went into the mall where I looked over the railing to the lower floor. Several men with knives out were walking and trying to find targets. The Marshal was quickly beside me and with marksmen skills, put the knife wielding attackers on the ground.

"I see we have a fly in the ointment," the voice rang out over the intercom.

"Where are you going?" I asked The Marshal. "To find out who is behind that voice."

I went along. As we approached the mall offices, we could see multiple students lined up and behind them, I spotted the black-suited Doctor who was heading toward the door.

"It's Doctor Mad," I said to the Marshal.

Suddenly, I spotted Valentine in the middle of the walkway to our right. He looked confused. The Marshal got beside him. "Agent Valentine, take these," The Marshal said and handed him a pair of noise-cancelling earplugs. He then slapped Valentine across the face and that seemed to do the trick as a coherent Valentine looked around.

"Don't shoot the people dressed as students if they have a glazed look on their face. They are under hypnosis and don't know what they are doing," The Marshal said.

"Right," Valentine said.

Several students came from behind The Marshal and Valentine but soon found themselves on the ground as fists and darts flew. Doctor Mad was making a run for the door. The Marshal fired several shots in his direction but all were blocked by the mesmerized students. However, he did get the Doctor's attention as he turned and looked in their direction. This time, the smile wasn't so pleasant and he pointed at the Marshal tipped his hat and then motioned those around him to attack.

Valentine pointed his revolver in the direction of the oncoming students but the Marshal reached over and lowered it as he quickly reloaded and shot. The attackers fell to the ground.

"What was that?" Valentine asked.

"Tranquilizer," The Marshal said. "These people are hypnotized and don't know what they are doing. We shouldn't harm them."

"You made an automated dart gun?" Valentine asked.

"Somebody had too," The Marshal said. Then I started, I mean The Marshal ran toward the door with Valentine only to see the villain escaped in his limousine.

"Damn," The Marshal said. "Well, it was a pleasure to meet you, Agent Valentine." He threw something down that caused Agent Valentine to look down. A flash emanated that temporarily blinded him. When he regained his eyesight, the Marshal was gone.

After a few moments of the smoke clearing, I approached Agent Valentine. "Are you alright? Here, let's take a seat." I moved to a bench as the police began to arrive. "You better get your FBI badge out."

"Your brother?"

"Let's go find him," I said.

The police were soon all over the mall as I returned to the food court to locate my brother who I found being questioned.

"There you are," Mike said.

"Don't worry," I said. "I have and FBI agent stalking me. I was perfectly safe." Agent Valentine came up behind me as I spoke. "Here he is now. Agent Valentine, my brother, Mike."

"Yes, we know all about your family," Valentine said. "Are you really a cable guy that hunts ghosts on the weekends?"

I laughed as my brother's face went blank. "Come on," I said as Mike started walking away. "I'm just kidding."

Mike said goodbye, wished me well and headed home while Valentine and I met with the police in charge.

"I can't believe you can't find it. It's a big black car!" I said standing outside the mall security office where the police were looking at the camera footage.

"We know what a limousine looks like," the officer said. "The problem is that the cameras were down throughout the entire incident."

"A cover-up," I said.

"Is there something you're not telling us?" the officer asked.

"Doctor Mad has connections," I said. "Anyone on the security team here at the mall who may have come in contact with him at any point could be compromised. I would check to see if any of them attended college in the last thirty-years and had an instructor or a chiropractor name Darius Pool."

"A chiropractor?" Valentine asked.

"Yes, I forgot to tell you about that," I said.

"Are we done here?" I asked the police officer.

"One more question," the officer said. "Some people said they were helped by someone dressed as a Steampunk Marshal?"

"I didn't see anything," I said and glanced at Valentine. He remained quiet. "Look, officer, these people were being influenced by someone who uses music and motion to induce hypnotic trances. They could have been convinced of a lot of things. I'd be careful trusting what they say they witnessed."

"Wait a minute while I check if we're clear to release you," the officer said leaving us alone on the bench.

"A Steampunk Marshal?" Valentine asked.

"You were probably having delusions as well," I said. "We just did that Steampunk Festival last week so that was probably on your mind."

"I suppose so," Valentine said. "But..."

I didn't give him more time to consider. "Where the hell were you when all this started," I said. "I thought you were watching me. I looked around and you were nowhere to be found."

"I was getting ice-cream down at the other end," Valentine said. "I did manage to stop several of them."

"Did you see this character the others are speaking about?" the officer said as he came up to us again. "We have several witnesses that said they saw someone in black with badges on his or her hat wearing steampunk glasses. Apparently, they were the reason this wasn't worse."

"Oh, like a hero?" I said.

"Maybe," the officer said. "But we don't want to encourage a vigilante."

Valentine looked at me, then back at the uniformed man.

"No. We didn't see anything like what you described," Valentine said. "But I did see the students and knocked a few of them out. Didn't feel right to shoot them."

"Why weren't either of you affected by this music?"

"Well, since the last time I ran into this hoodlum, I've been taking precautions," I said and pulled out my noise blocking earbuds."

"Smart man," the officer said. "Well, I understand you helped get a lot of people to safety, thank you. We'll let you know if we find anything."

"You said the cameras were off?"

"Yes," officer said.

"This Doctor Mad has many followers, I suggest you check the employees who work here that have access to the security cameras. Especially any of them who are a college graduate."

The police were done with our questioning and the mall was closing for the night. We headed for the exit.

"What do we do now?" Valentine said.

"I have someone I need to talk too," I said. "I'll keep you informed."

I turned away from Valentine as I started to form my plan which excluded him from knowing specifics. My actions that day had awaken senses that I'd long forgotten how to use. One of those senses was telling me there was something wrong with Agent Valentine and my logical reasoning side agreed.

"Valentine is never around when Doctor Mad appears," my little voice said. "He was stunned when the attack began."

I would have to be wary.

CHAPTER SIX
MISTER "E"

Do you believe in Magic
I won't change your mind
In Magic amazement and surprise
Is what you will find
The smile and laughter
is their real magic they bring
Do you believe in magic
It's a real thing

After the mall incident, I returned to the mansion where I was staying and invited the others over where we met in the dining room. It was late evening and the other guests had turned in. I shut the door to the room as everyone sat down in the comfortable wing-back chairs. It was here I was going to lay out my plan.

Rob and Ryan were in attendance but Brent couldn't make it. This was good for me because I didn't want to share my total plan with anyone. I also didn't let Valentine participate.

"I need to contact him," I said. "It's clear we need to figure out how to break the programming he's used."

"The magician?" Rob asked.

"He was first a hypnotist. He was so good at it, it scared him. He swore to never do it again."

"You know, most experts on the study of hypnotism will tell you that the hypnotist can't make someone do anything they don't want to do or is against their values," Rob said.

"Mister E told me that's not true," I said. "Do you think people really want to act foolish, bark like a dog or cluck like a chicken? He told me that the experts say those things about not being able to truly control you to turn people off of the practice because it's too dangerous. Mind control can easily be turned malicious if not in check. Every hypnotist is on some type of watch list and, believe me, the government keeps tabs on them."

"What about Doctor Mad? Why hasn't he been caught then?" Ryan asked.

"For all known purposes, he may have people in the government working for him," I said.

"So, what makes you think this Mister E will help us?" Rob asked.

"Other than his shared distaste for criminals, he swore he was the best that's ever been. He's not going to tolerate someone using this gift for evil. Can I borrow your cell phone?"

Rob hesitated and I wasn't sure he understood me.

"Can you let me use your cell phone to call Mister E? I'm afraid mine may be compromised."

"Here you go," Rob said and handed me the phone.

"Hello," I heard the voice from the other end of the line and recognized Kathy's voice. She was the wife of the marvelous hypnotist and magician, Mister E.

"Hello Kathy, it's Louis," I said.

"Oh, hi Louis. We got that last book you sent us and it was stupendous. Thank you."

"That's good to hear," I said. "You two will always have a special place in my heart. Now, I need to talk to the magician please."

I heard Kathy hand the phone over and tell him it was I on the phone.

"Hello, Louis," Mister E said.

"Mister E, I know you said you retired, but I have a favor to ask. What if I told you there was someone out here doing hypnotism that, not only thinks he's better than you, but is using his gift for EVIL purposes!"

The phone went silent for a moment. I looked at Rob and Ryan who remained silent. I checked the phone to make sure I was still connected.

"Yes, Louis, tell me how I can help," Mister E. said.

I laid out my plan and listened to Mister E recommend a way forward.

After our meeting, I thanked Rob and Ryan for coming by and escorted them to the door. I turned around to go back to my room and found Valentine waiting for me in the lobby.

"You know, this is the second time you've made me stay at this haunted mansion. If I see a ghost or something I'm really going to be cross," Valentine said.

"Take it as another experience to knock off your bucket list," I said. "Besides, I haven't seen anything all the years I've been staying here."

"You sound disappointed."

"I am," I said. "Life can be so boring. A little adventure goes a long way."

"Well, good luck with that. Goodnight," Valentine said and turned to walk away.

"Agent Valentine," I said. He turned back to me. "I've always wondered about the moral dilemmas of being a lawman. I mean, you are supposed to bring the bad guys in and let the court system decide their fate."

"I suppose that's right," Valentine said. "What's your point?"

"Don't you ever just want to give them what they deserve?"

"That depends," he said. "What they deserve is not supposed to be up to me."

"But, if you really know they are bad, evil and did the things they are accused of doing, wouldn't that be enough evidence?"

"Some people say that you can't undo what's been done," Valentine said.

"You can make sure it doesn't happen again?" I said. "You get the behavior you allow. If we let evil walk upright, it will grow. Sometimes, we need to put it in the ground, permanently."

"You mean like this Doctor Mad?"

I nodded.

"What did you have in mind?" Valentine asked.

"Let's just say, I have a plan. You can be part of it or, you can just look away."

"You do understand that if it's not in accordance with the law and anyone were to find out , I'd have to be in full denial," Valentine said."

"I understand," I said.

"I have a question for you," Valentine said.

"Go ahead."

"You say you spotted Doctor Mad at the memorial?"

"Yes."

"Later that same night after dinner, he came by when you were walking to the hotel picked you up and took you for a ride in his limousine, right?"

"Yes, I've told you all of this."

He stepped away from me and started walking toward the exit. Then, he turned back to me. "It's just that, I was selected for this mission because I'm considered to be observant; nothing gets by me. However, I've never seen this Doctor Mad. Every time we check surveillance, we can't catch this huge, black limousine that he takes everywhere. Nor do I ever get a glimpse of him when you say he's been somewhere."

"You're doubting his existence?" I asked. "What about the henchmen at the mall?"

"I'm not doubting he exists or that he has followers," Valentine said. His eyes shifted to my feet and then back to me as he met my gaze. "I'm just starting to question 'who' this person could be. I mean, do you suppose a person with a great imagination could create someone like Doctor Mad and define him so well that they actually become that character?"

I didn't respond right away. Part of me wanted to walk away from Agent Valentine. I didn't need him! I could take care of myself. How dare he!

"You're eluding to the initial theory the FBI had, that it was me?" I said. "What about the name I've given you? The background checks you've done and information you provided?"

"You could have researched that professor and framed it so it looks like he's the one," Valentine said.

"Have you tried to find him?"

"Actually," Valentine said. He paced a few steps toward his room. "We found his ex-wife. She claims he's dead."

The revelation caught me off guard and I didn't respond immediately. My head started to reel from the bourbon and the late hour.

"Well of course she does," I said. "She's probably his first victim. No doubt he hypnotized her and convinced her of all kinds of stuff."

Valentine's hand went this his chin and he clenched it momentarily with his thumb and index finger. Then he pointed toward me. "Let's just make sure we stay in better contact for the next few days. We don't need any misunderstanding. Why are you smiling?"

"I'm putting all of this in the book," I said. "Your theory is ingenious. The author being the bad guy because he created a character so well it becomes real to him and he doesn't even know that it's him that is doing the crazy things. It'll be a marvelous twist if that becomes the truth."

"Now you're starting to scare me," Valentine said.

"Oh, the only thing you should be scared about is the fake name I'm going to use for you when I write about all of this. You know, so I don't have to get permission and all."

"With all the buttons your pushing, I'm just hoping you're alive to finish it," Valentine said.

"Don't worry," I said. "I have a plan."

"I expect a free copy," Valentine said. "We should both get some sleep.

I agreed.

CHAPTER SEVEN
THE TAILS TURN

With our Imagination's we can do great things. Pretend to go places we've never been, create wonderous worlds, inventions, even solve every problem that afflicts us. We can also create monsters, demons, ghosts, and unthinkable creatures. The real quest we should put our imaginations too is to envision a world without evil and make it true. LPD

It was Thursday and I was at home rounding up the last few items for my trip. The time had arrived and The Festival of Fear was only a day away. I walked into my living room to find Heather sitting on the couch.

"Oh, hello there," I said. "To what do I owe the pleasure?"

She looked at me, her eyes solid and her lips tight. She stood and her hands went to her hips. "When were you going to tell me?"

I sat down in my rocking chair and took a deep breath. "Heather, I'm afraid I have a lot of secrets that you may not know. None of them I intentionally keep to harm anyone but, you're going to have to be more specific for me to know what you're talking about."

"I've read the news of what happened while you were up in Denver at the mall," she said.

"Yes," I said. "I probably should have told you more, but I didn't want you to worry. We were fine."

"There were reports of a cowboy figure that came in and broke up the plan," Heather said.

"Yes, I know, The Marshal, as they call him. Supposedly used a gun and all. I tell you, I was there, it's a rumor. People were probably being gassed and with the hypnotic music they were being subjected too, they probably saw a lot of things that weren't there."

"It wasn't just a gun this character had, it was a tranquilizer gun," Heather said.

"Really?" I started to get concerned at how much she knew. "How do you know that?"

"Oh, because when the police tested why all those student minions, as you call them, were knocked out, they did a toxicology. Seems there was some tranquilizer fluid in them, the same used in large animals."

"Really," I said. Heather's posture hadn't changed and she stepped closer.

"Yes, so they started looking at how someone got their hands on this stuff and, since I am a veterinarian and you were at the location, they questioned me."

I sat up in my chair, concerned. "Wow, they just won't get it that I'm the victim and not the criminal here. What did you say?"

"I told them that I didn't know anything which is the truth. I even have witnesses through the whole event to back my alibi that I wasn't anywhere near the area."

I sat back. "That's good. To think that they suspect you as being this cowboy character. I guess now they'll leave you alone."

"It's not me I'm worried about," Heather said. She paused. The front of her right foot lifted and then came back down tapping the floor. "Well?"

"Even if I had seen this 'Marshal,' it would be in both our interests to protect his identity," I said.

"You admit he exists?" Heather asked.

"If I were to tell you anything," I said, "it would only make the world a more dangerous place for you."

"Give this Marshal character a message for me," she said. "When you're dealing with bad guys, you should just put them away."

"Well, maybe he felt those helpers were unknowing victims. Some of them were programmed from a young age who didn't really understand what they were doing."

"That I can understand but, Doctor Mad, he needs to be put in the ground. If your Marshal friend needs help, I carry a Thirty-Eight Special in my purse."

"I'll relay the message," I said. "You still riding up to Denver with me?" I stated.

"Of course," Heather said. "I just put my suitcase in the back of the car."

"Great," I said. "Then what are we waiting for?"

"I hope you know what you're doing," Heather said. She walked past me toward the door. "You owe me two-hundred dollars, that stuff's not cheap. And you better be careful. You can still kill someone with tranquilizer if they're allergic or if you use too much."

"Like I said, I think this whole thing is made up. But, if it weren't, I would relay your message to The Marshal."

We were soon on our way to Denver with Agent Valentine tailing us in his black SUV. As I'd requested, Brent sent out a message to special guests to meet at the Harra hotel; a resort that had been under construction for years and was purportedly haunted. The added flare of a haunted hotel for a pre-event was to fool Doctor Mad and give every appearance that the invitation was authentic.

We met at the Ghost Rider Café for dinner and drinks. Here, in a small banquet room, we discussed the plan. Prior to the meeting, I had asked Ryan to use his investigative skills to run background checks on everyone who would be invited to the early event including those in our immediate group.

"That was a good meal," Brent said. "Now, I believe you wanted to discuss something with all of us before we head to the hotel."

"First, a toast to a most wonderful group of friends and horror enthusiasts," I said raising my glass. Around the table were Rob, Ryan, Brent, Brent's wife Jenny, and Heather. "Now that we've done that, Rob, Ryan, I asked you to do some tasks. Have you uncovered anything?"

Rob stood first. "Well, I didn't know you had asked Ryan to do anything, but I was asked to look into the background of everyone here and who will be administrating the event in any way. I checked everyone's background to see if anyone could have come into contact with Doctor Darius Pool while he was employed at the various schools where he worked.

"Darius Pool?" Jenny asked.

"Yes, sorry," Brent said, "we found out earlier that this is the real name of Doctor Mad. I should have let you know. Rob, please continue."

"I passed a few of the names to Louis that were of concern but no one in our immediate group was suspect," Rob said and sat down.

Ryan stood. "I did the same search apparently to make our author friend more secure that neither of us," he pointed to himself and then Rob, "were in on the ploy. I had the same findings." He stared at me for a moment and started to say something else but bit his lip and sat down.

"Now that's out of the way, here's my plan," I said and told everyone what I could without giving away the entire plan. Key to execution was keeping some parts secret.

"That's all you need from us?" Brent said. "It seems too simple."

"I hope it is," I said as my phone went off and I answered. "Ah, the cars are here. I will see everyone at the haunted hotel."

"You're not going with us?" Rob asked.

"No, I'm going with my FBI friend, Agent Valentine," I said.

We finished our drinks, paid the bill and grabbed our jackets. On the way to the door, Ryan tugged at my arm and pulled me aside.

"There's something else I discovered in my investigation," Ryan whispered.

"What? Tell me," I said.

"Your FBI agent, Valentine. Prior to being accepted into the program, he was at the university where Doctor Pool taught. His curriculum had a lot of psychology classes. I didn't get his transcripts to check his instructors but, I would be cautious."

"Thanks, Ryan," I said. "That explains a lot." I reflected on the conversation Valentine and I had the previous weekend about not being present together whenever Doctor Mad appeared. If Valentine were under the influence of Doctor Mad, I would have to take one more precaution. I pulled out my phone and punched in the number.

"Mister E," I said, "you can bring the car around and, my suspicion was correct. Agent Valentine will be joining us."

I headed out to where Valentine sat in his SUV waiting to follow us and walked up to the car.

Valentine looked forward for a minute and then rolled down the window. "You're not supposed to come right up to me," he scolded.

"Look," I said. "If you're trying to remain inconspicuous, I have a better plan. Have you ever ridden in a limousine?"

Agent Valentine rode with Heather and I in a limousine with a special driver. As I suspected, Valentine insisted on riding in front. This allowed the driver and Valentine to get to know one another.

The Hotel we were heading too was an old, wooden three-story structure built in the early nineteen hundreds by some rich European settlers. It had gone into ruin and been reopened countless times and was purportedly haunted by the ghost of its founders.

The property was surrounded by a tall, black metal fence with signage indicating the area was closed and under construction. The new owners had embraced the legend of the haunting and were making it an attraction for all things paranormal. The rooms were to be decorated with horror props and paraphernalia throughout with the main interior copying movie sets from the horror genre.

We had to enter through a gate and headed down a semicircle drive to the front entrance where there was a drop-off area and a small parking lot.

Most of the others had already arrived and we noticed a few other guests that hadn't been at the dinner were arriving as well. We all headed to the front door with the exception of Agent Valentine, who exited and wanted to do a security check of the grounds, and our limo driver who left the premises.

Heather and I approached the front doors. The hotel was lit only by candles and lanterns on this special night. Mummy's and skeletons lined the front entrance and effigies of classic horror figures greeted us in the lobby.

A security guard checked our passes as we went down the hallway and followed the others straight past the unmanned check-in counter and out through a side door. Here, a bus was waiting under a renovated coach house. I walked Heather to the bus.

"Don't worry, you'll be fine," I said. "Just stick with the others and I'll see you later." I headed back into the hotel and went to the check-in area and dismissed the security guard.

Several of the guards were sleeping; an indication Doctor Mad was going to appear. I had Mister E perform an orientation with the on-site staff. This orientation included a deprogramming of anyone that could be under the spell of Doctor Mad. Mister E simply put in a suggestion that they go to sleep.

Agent Valentine came up beside me and looked down the hall. "What's going on? Where'd everybody go?"

"Everything is going to plan," I said. I turned to see he had changed into the uniform I'd provided. He was dressed as a limousine driver in a black tuxedo with tails and a drivers cap.

"I see the clothes fit, are you ready?" I asked.

"Funny," Valentine said. "I don't remember the ride here. I only remember arriving. I don't even remember changing into this uniform."

"You remember the plan, right?" I asked.

"Of course," he said. "Where are the others?"

"Secret," I said. "See, I didn't tell anyone of you the entire plan. That way, I could ensure nothing would go wrong or, if something did, I would know the culprit."

"You're sure Doctor Mad has someone on the inside and is going to make an appearance?" Valentine asked.

"I'm counting on it," I said.

We exited a side door and went to a large luggage rack with a trunk on it. Valentine opened the lid and I got in.

"You sure you want to do this?" Valentine asked while the lid was still open.

"I'm afraid the driver would recognize me if I don't disguise myself enough," I said. "He doesn't know who you are. It'll work, trust me."

He still hesitated.

"Are you still holding on to that suspicion that I am actually Doctor Mad?"

"If you come out of that trunk in a black tuxedo, I'm going to shoot first and ask questions later," Valentine said and shut the lid. I had only a few moments before we'd be out front.

The low lighting and the dark night helped us keep our disguise as we moved out into the front of the hotel.

"How the heck did that get there?" I heard Valentine say and then we started moving. "Another limousine just pulled in and a man with a top hat just exited and headed to the front of the hotel. Okay, get ready."

When Valentine opened the trunk, he held out his hand to help me out. He had placed the long luggage hauler in front of the limo and pulled his revolver as he quickly moved to the driver's side, opened the door and pushed the driver over as I hopped in the back. Valentine hit the control and slid the window down that divided the front and back seat.

The driver looked at me and I immediately recognized Doctor Mad's chauffer.

"You're too late," the driver said. "He's already inside."

"Good," The Marshal said. "He'll be out shortly when he finds the place abandoned. You see, I had someone come into the hotel prior to the guest arriving that met with the staff. He was a hypnotist that deprogrammed all of your helpers."

I then pointed. "All of the guests are being evacuated in that bus over there pulling away." The large bus emerged from the other side of the hotel and headed out of the gate. "They'll be taken to safety while we wait here for the good doctor to return. You see, it is I that have the upper hand."

"What about him," Valentine asked. "You can duck down back there, but if he sees two of us in the front seat, don't you think he'll get suspicious?"

I shook my head.

The driver smiled at Valentine who immediately slugged him with his left hand across the jaw knocking him unconscious. He looked at me and shrugged his shoulders. "I thought it might be best," he said.

We both quickly exited and moved the driver out of the car. Valentine handcuffed him and we put him in the trunk on the luggage rack.

"Boy, if we get pulled over, me dressed like this, you like that," Valentine said.

"Don't worry," The Marshal said. "We're the good guys."

"There he is," Valentine said. "He's coming up on the right side.

I kept crouched and watched as Doctor Mad opened the door and quickly jumped inside the passenger's side of the vehicle. "Let's go driver," he said.

The doors locked immediately and Valentine started the car and began heading to our destination.

"I wish I had a camera to catch the look on your face right now," The Marshal said as he pointed his gun in the direction of Doctor Mad. "Don't try anything. I have enough sedative in the gun that it might kill you. If that doesn't stop you, my friend there in the front seat surely will."

Valentine glared back at the Doctor and nodded.

"Well, you have improved your game, I'll give you that," Doctor Mad said. He comfortably put his cane across his lap. "What makes you think you have a chance here? I have people everywhere. In fact, I have a surprise for you, right, Agent Valentine?"

The car kept moving in the planned direction as Doctor Mad looked toward Agent Valentine who then turned.

"Yes, teacher," Agent Valentine said. "Where should we go?"

"Head to the Sahara Palace," Doctor Mad said. "See, I hold all the cards."

"I'll let you believe that for a moment, just to keep you calm," The Marshal said.

"I'm curious, how far will you have to be pushed before you have to use a real gun someday? As I said, I have people everywhere. Agent Valentine was once a student of mine. It is I who requested he be assigned to you, not the FBI."

"I suspected that," The Marshal said. "It was just too convenient that he was never present every time you appeared. I was also suspicious how you knew my every move and how you planted letters on my doorstep while he was right outside."

The car went past the turn Doctor Mad indicated.

"Valentine, you were supposed to turn left there," Doctor Mad said.

"Who says I haven't," The Marshal said.

"Haven't what?" Doctor Mad asked.

"Who says I haven't used a real gun," The Marshal said. "I simply prefer no harm come to those who are innocent and being manipulated. My sympathy lies not for the real criminals."

The doctor glanced down at the weapon and back to the front of the car. He started chanting some words, "blue skies, nothing but blue skies, do I see."

"It won't work," The Marshal said. "I had Agent Valentine deprogrammed by a friend of mine after I discovered he may have come in contact with you. A friend we are heading to see. Just sit back and enjoy the ride. We can keep talking or I can have you sleep," The Marshal tapped the gun.

"Are you at least going to tell me where we are going? To jail I suppose?" Doctor Mad said.

The Marshal thought about shooting him. Doctor Mad's smirk had returned and was almost too much to bear.

"I told you, to see a friend of mine who wants to meet you," The Marshal said.

Valentine pulled into a dark alley in a shady business district on Colfax avenue to the rear entrance of the Wolf's Den bar. Valentine used a large zip tie on Doctor Mad's hands while the Marshal kept the gun pointed at him. The men entered through the back door and went into a small room with a single table and a chair at either side. A man sat on the opposite side from the doorway and stood as they entered.

"Hey, isn't that our driver from before?" Agent Valentine asked.

I smiled. "Agent Valentine, please have your friends at the FBI search the Sahara hotel for more of Doctor Mad's cronies. And don't forget his driver back at the hotel we left in the luggage rack."

"You're okay here?" Valentine asked.

"Yes," The Marshal said. "Doctor Mad, let me introduce you to a friend of mine, Mister E."

The man introduced was dressed in a black suit with a dark, maroon vest. The suit, covered by a long black cape, was complemented with white, silk gloves and a large, blue bow tie. In his hands, Mister E held a long, alder-wood wand tipped with a sapphire crystal.

"Sit down," a commanding deep voice emitted from Mister E and surprised me but had its effect as Doctor Mad sat down.

Mister E, hands out flat with each end on the wand, brought them together in front of him and directly in front of Doctor Mad collapsing the wand. When he separated the hands, a blue flame appeared and slowly morphed into a large, blue, sparkling amulet. He proceeded to take the string of the amulet in his hand and held it in front of Doctor Mad as it spun. Soon, Doctor Mad's eyes glossed over.

"Marshal," Mister E said, "don't look at the amulet. Follow my lead"

Mister E kept spinning the amulet hanging by the string in his left hand while he started to snap his right fingers. He looked toward me, I mean, The Marshal and we both started snapping our fingers. He then broke into the lyrics of "Strange Magic" by the Electric Light Orchestra.

After we finished the chorus he stopped snapping his fingers and pulled the amulet up into his left hand which he shook, and then opened showing the amulet had vanished.

While Doctor Mad stayed at the table looking forward, Mister E motioned The Marshal to the door. "I will need a few moments with him."

"What are you going to do with him?" The Marshal asked.

"We, magicians, have a strict code," Mister E said. "Magic is never to be used for evil purposes. When I'm done, the professor here will be a penitent man. Now, give me a few minutes and you can return with your agent to arrest him."

The Marshal went outside with Agent Valentine. "Looks like we've got the situation under control now. You shouldn't be needing me any longer," The Marshal said and there was a flash of smoke and The Marshal was gone.

I came down the hallway to greet agent Valentine. "Are they still in there?' I asked.

"Yes, how did you know," Valentine said and smiled. As we listened outside of the door.

The room had gone silent so I knocked on the door. There was no answer. "Don't worry," I said, "this is the only way in or out."

Agent Valentine and I looked at each other and hurried into the room where we found Doctor Mad sitting by himself.

"Where did Mister E go?" I asked.

"I am almost finished," Doctor Mad said. He had his head bent down and was furiously writing on the papers in front of him.

"Finished with what?" Agent Valentine asked and we both looked down at the papers on the table. "It's a confession," Valentine said. "It's not only his confession but he also gives us a list of names of his accomplices: Mike Johnson, Chad Wright, Shannon Dietz."

"Wow, people you'd never expect," I said. I guess we'll have to start rounding them up."

"We? Agent Valentine said. "You better let the authorities handle this. Besides, it will take a while. Do you know how many Mike Johnson's are in the phone book?"

"A lot?" I said.

"A lot," Agent Valentine said.

"I guess this puts a wrap on Doctor Mad."

"So, it seems," agent Valentine said. "However, you can never tell with supervillains. They always seem to come back."

"You know, you should come to the Festival of Fear with us," I said.

"Not a chance," Agent Valentine said.. "And no more haunted hotels."

We both laughed.

The next day the news would carry the story of how Doctor Mad had directed his driver to take him to the police station. There he surrendered himself and provided ample evidence for a conviction. He has not requested a lawyer."

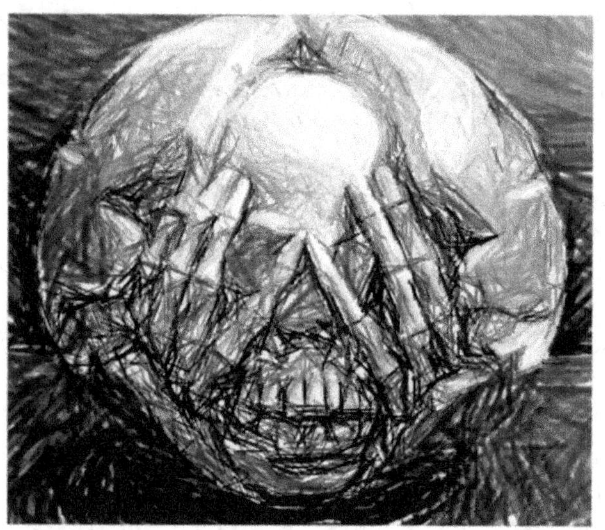

CHAPTER EIGHT
A FESTIVAL TO REMEMBER

The Festival of Fear is always a GREAT event. Attending the festival is a true adventure and you never know what to expect but here are a few givens:

The color black is IN. Black shirts, black jackets, black jeans, black accessories, make-up, hair, jewelry, and art will all be in style.

If you don't know your movies or trivia, don't pretend. People here know their facts. They know stories behind the stories. It's all part of the passion for the genre. There's an amazing level of respect among those who attend and tolerance for celebrating something that, in another time, would probably have led to a person being burned on a stake.

Imagination and creativity are off the charts as you will meet all types of artists of many crafts, Rooms are filled with special effects artists, designers, movie makers, producers, cosplayers, paranormal researchers, ghost hunters and writers! Vendors sell imaginative creations that are sure to inspire nightmares.

Oh, and the fans love to dress-up!

This brings us to our final chapter and the revelation that I survived! It was Friday at three, we checked in at the front desk, received our bottle of wine, and went to our rooms to change into our costumes for the night. Yes, the Festival of Fear was happening and in our own way it was a celebration of who we are, were and will be; those who love the thrill of being scared. After the events of the night before, we could enjoy it without having to worry about Doctor Mad.

Despite his misgivings, Agent Valentine escorted Heather and I to the festival. While I waited for Heather, I made a trip to see Agent

Valentine who was right down the hall from me. I knocked on his door and he answered.

"I have one more favor to ask," I said.

"You're running a little short on requests," Valentine said.

I took out my hardback of *13Days* and handed it to Valentine. "It's autographed," I said.

"Okay, what is it," he said as he took the book and looked inside.

"We're about the same size right?"

Valentine looked at me, then at his big arms and back.

"Well, close enough," I said.

"What did you have in mind?"

"Heather is in her room waiting for me to come by, and..."

Heather heard a knock on her door and opened it forcefully, "It's about TIME...." She stopped midsentence and looked upon the figure in her doorway.

Dressed in boots, a black trench coat and wearing a steampunk hat and glasses The Marshal stood before her. On the front of the hat was a large badge that she could read the name 'Marshal' across it.

"I just wanted to stop by and let you know, Doctor Mad has been detained and is no longer a threat," The Marshal said. "And that the good guys will always win in the end. Now, enjoy your night."

"Wait," Heather said. "Who are you?"

The man looked at Heather. "I'm The Marshall. I'm here to teach the world that they still need honorable good men."

The Marshall tipped his hat and threw down something that was in his hand. A popping sound followed by smoke in the hall caused Heather to shut the door. She locked it.

She was startled when her phone rang.

"He, hel, hello?"

"Heather?" I said. "Are you okay?"

"Yes, of course," she said. "Just watching a scary movie while I'm getting ready."

"That's why I called," I said. "I'm running late and wanted to know if I should come by or meet you there."

"You can come by," she said. "See you then."

I knocked on the door and Heather answered. She was dressed as a movie star. She blinked and waved a fan in front of her face. "Is there something the matter?"

"No," I said. "I thought you were going as..."

"Lacie Starlight, movie star," Heather said. "And you are?"

"Drake Ulah," I responded. "Vampire Detective at your service." We both laughed as we headed down the hall to the elevator.

"I know it's not you," Heather said.

"What?" I questioned.

"The Marshal. I know it's not you. Although, I'm still suspicious that there's a connection."

"What do you mean you don't think I'm The Marshal? I suppose you don't think I'm tough enough. Is that it?"

"No," she said. "Although, I did find him handsome."

"The Marshall? You've seen him," I said.

"Yes. That's how I know you're not him."

"He wears a disguise; How could you be so sure?"

"Uhm, because he's black."

"Oh," I said. The elevator opened and we entered. The door started to close and I reached out and stopped it. "Come along Bob. We don't want to be late."

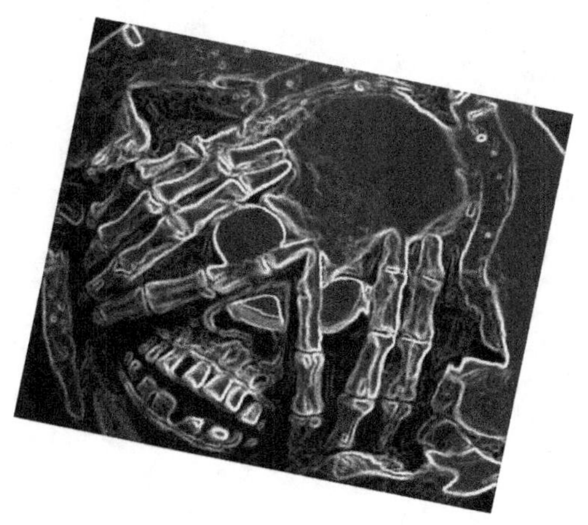

Prologue:

That weekend was the greatest Festival of Fear I'd attended with fantastic guests, an awesome costume contest and plenty of spooky movies and tales. When I returned home that Sunday, an envelope with no return address was attached to my door. It was addressed to "The Marshall."

I scanned the neighborhood and didn't spot anyone watching me. I stepped inside the doorway before opening the letter. It was handwritten in calligraphy with a maroon color.

"Dear Marshall, I am a big fan, of HORROR that is. I especially like bloody scenes. We will be in touch shortly. Watch for my sign.

Sincerely,

Blood Lust"

THE DREAD PIRATE

Table of Contents

CHAPTER ONE

STEAMPUNK

It was mid-September in the high elevation town of Victor and I pulled over the last hill in my four-wheel drive jeep spotting the town in the distance. It was the annual Steampunk festival and I hadn't missed it in five years. I started going with my daughter years ago and did the last two years on my own. This time, I had convinced my brother, Chad, to come along. His wife was away on a trip for her business and he never hesitated to get away to a mountain destination. The caveat is that I had to climb one of the states fourteener's with him the day after the festival. A feat I wasn't sure my body was ready to do but my spirit was willing.

I pulled into the town that was bustling with traffic and had RVs and tents set up all about the park with vendors lining the street. My consistent visits to the town over the years made me familiar with some of the locals. I knew one of the owners of the hotel, Christine Combs, who also worked there at the restaurant and bar. Spaces were reserved in front of the hotel for guests and I noticed Chad's truck, a blue dodge ram with lift kit and huge tires that was hard to miss, parked in front.

The four-story brick hotel, built in the late 1880s, was a monument to the gold-rush days and stood as a cornerstone among two of the town's busiest streets. The interior still held onto the antique, rustic furnishing in the lobby and in the rooms which gave it a classy appearance.

I took out my small suitcase and headed in the front door where I spotted Chad sitting at the bar speaking with Christine. Christine was a beautiful brunette with long hair, dark, brown-eyes, and a face that belonged in the movies. I walked over as they noticed me.

"Ah, the adventurer returns," Christine said as she poured me a beer. "Welcome back. Where's your daughter?"

"She's transferred to the big city this semester," I said. "That's why this guy is here," I referenced Chad. "Christine, this is my brother, Chad." I set my suitcase on a chair and took a seat on a stool at the bar next to Chad.

"Yes," Christine said. "We've met. He was telling me all about your ghost hunting days when you were kids."

"Oh, was he?" I smiled. "Well, glad you could make it."

Chad, six foot one with broad shoulders and a sleek build, looked every bit like a seasoned hiker with his fluorescent-green windbreaker, soft-soled hiking shoes and tiny backpack.

"I hope you brought clothes for the festival," I said. "You'll look ridiculous going out like that and, although this town is fairly free of crime, you'll probably get mugged."

"I brought other clothes," Chad said. "They're up in the room."

"Oh, where'd you put us this time?" I asked Christine.

"On the haunted fourth floor," she said making quotations with her hands. "I hope you brought clothes as well, if the mayor sees you…"

"What about the mayor?" Chad asked.

"Oh, the mayor doesn't like me since I did that piece on the hotel here," I said.

"Let me guess," Chad said. "You told everyone it's not haunted and found explanations for all the strange happenings? The town wants the hotel to be haunted for better business and they see you as ruining that."

"I can't help it if I logically concluded that vibration from the elevator is what caused furniture to move and that a faulty water heating system is what caused the rapping sounds on the floor. And, as for the dead people on the fourth floor, well, I hate to tell you this but, people die everywhere every day. If all of them became ghosts, every building in old towns like this would be haunted."

"Do you want something to eat?" Christine asked.

"Sure, what do you have?"

"The usual," Christine said and left the bar to go back to the kitchen.

I leaned over to Chad. "That's not the only reason the mayor and I don't get along. He's Christine's husband and part owner of the hotel."

"Oh," Chad said.

Christine came back with two Reuben sandwiches and placed one in front of each of us. "That's ex-husband," she said. "Rick and I divorced this summer."

"Does that mean you're…" I started to ask.

"No, he's still part owner," Christine said.

"Sorry about that," I said.

"It's okay," Christine said as more customers entered through the front door. "He lets me run the hotel how I want. He's busy enough being the mayor and all. Well, let me know if you need anything else." She left to go wait on the other customers.

"This is good," Chad said as he took a bite of his sandwich."

"I know right," I said and we both ate and caught up with each other's recent activities. It wasn't long before we were finished with our lunch.

"Well, should we go put our luggage away now?" Chad asked.

I checked my phone for the time. "Sounds good. We have a few hours to kill before the events start." I left money on the table and waved to Christine who was tied up with all the people coming in. "Come on, let's go to our rooms. We can ride up the haunted elevator to the haunted fourth floor."

"It's haunted?" Chad asked as we headed to the metal box that served as the elevator. "I should have known."

"Why do you think I picked this as the place to stay," I said.

We pushed the button for going up and the gate unlocked. The elevator, a historical piece of its own, was a large metal basket with a retractable, expanded metal gate in front of the doorway. We entered.

"Well, someone died building the elevator. He fell down the shaft and they say he haunts it," I said.

"At least our rooms aren't haunted," Chad said and looked at me. "Oh…Don't tell me."

"Funny thing," I say," we're staying on the fourth floor. It has all kinds of stories about being haunted and why. It was a makeshift hospital and maternity ward. But, my favorite story, well, let's just say in the winter the ground is frozen so, they needed somewhere to store bodies until the ground thawed so they could bury them."

"Gross," Chad said. "What's on the agenda tonight?"

The elevator door closed and I pushed the button for the fourth floor. The slow ride allowed me time to explain to my brother what was about to take place.

"The opening is tonight at eight at the Black Raven Bar. There we will kick off a toast, with the mayor…"

"The mayor who doesn't like you?" Chad asked.

"Yes, exactly. We will toast the start of the festivities. Tomorrow, there will be vendors, costumes, a circus and a parade."

"A parade?"

"Oh yes, that's one of the most important parts," I said as the elevator came to a stop and we exited down the hall to our rooms. "The parade is what pays homage to the entire event and commemorates why it was started."

"Then, we'll have to go," Chad said.

"That's if we make it through the night."

"What do you mean?" Chad asked.

"I mean, this is the most haunted floor of the hotel," I winked. "You never know what could happen."

At the time, I had no idea that Fate was about to deal us and the entire town a wild card.

CHAPTER TWO

LOOK AT ALL THE STARS!

We ate dinner at the hotel and changed into our costumes before heading to the bar. I had a long, black trench coat completely decked out with every badge and metal button I'd collected over the years. To top it off, I wore a large, dark brown cowboy hat adorned with metal gears with a huge Marshals badge on the front. Of course, under my jacket I had my skeleton key fastened to my belt. Chad had an aviators cap and jacket decked out with gears and wires.

We headed to the door and right before the elevator I stopped and pulled out my cell phone and took a picture showing it to Chad.

"Wow, we hardly look like ourselves," Chad said as we stepped back into the metal transportation device that glided us down to the first floor.

We entered the Black Raven and found ourselves in good company with over fifty guys and gals in costumes toasting and cheering. We sat down at one of the last open tables and watched as the mayor put up his hands and asked everyone to be quiet. He then spoke about the town and the upcoming activities while our waiter served us some stout beer.

"What's with the priest?" Chad asked.

"That's where it gets interesting," I said. Then I noticed someone coming our direction. It was Christine and she came right toward us still dressed as she had been at the hotel.

"Mind if I sit here," Christine said.

"Absolutely not," I said and stood to pull out her chair. It was then I noticed Mike, the mayor and Christine's ex-husband glance in my direction. He recognized me as I took my seat. I simply raised my beer in his direction and nodded.

"I was just telling Chad here the reason there's a priest at tonight's ceremony but, I'm sure you could do better."

"Well, Christine started, "in the town's history, there was a pirate on the run with his booty, so to speak, that came up from Texas around eighteen hundred and twenty. That was well before the town was established. That pirate and his band built some cabins, well, somewhere right about where the town is now. They lived off the land and only one, The Dread Pirate Harry, a wild old man with long, white hair and only one front tooth left, was the only one alive when the miners struck gold."

"Wow, is that really true?" I asked. I noticed another person in the bar had overheard Christine's story and taken interest, Trevor Towny. Trevor ran the local museum and had been known to weave a tale or two and had even published some books on the local history. A young man, Trevor rarely shaved or bathed and always wore an old miner's cap pulled down over his thick, busy hair. The cap had the logo for his gift shop on it.

"I don't know if it's true," Christine said. "I'm just telling you the tale as I know it." She took a long drink of her beer and continued. "So, the story goes that the miners found out this old man was likely sitting on some treasure so, a couple of boys went to get some information and, well, they supposedly roughed him up and somehow started his cabin on fire. Apparently, he cursed the town and the gold he left behind which still hasn't been found to this day."

"It's true, it's all true," I heard a voice from behind Christine as Trevor stepped up to our table.

"Hello, Trevor," I said. "Don't know if you remember me."

"Sure, the author," Trevor said and shook my hand.

"This is my brother, Chad," I said and Chad and Trevor shook hands. I offered him a seat at the table and immediately caught the look between him and Christine as she narrowed her eyes and held her lips tight.

"I'll just tell you what I know and be on my way," Trevor said. "They buried that pirate in the place where his cabin burned down. We built the town right over it. Right over his cursed grave. The hotel was built there and it burned down. So, they dug up his bones and buried him somewhere else thinking it would solve the problem."

"Did the curse go away?" Chad asked.

"No," Trevor said. "Five men died that year on the anniversary of the pirates death. The same number of men who had burned him in his cabin. Then, the town elders dug up his bones again and buried him in hallowed ground with a ceremony. They hoped this would stop the curse."

"Did the curse go away this time?" I asked.

"They didn't get all his bones. See, he had a peg-leg so one of his legs, not sure which one, was missing."

"I don't suppose you're going to tell me a shark was responsible for the missing leg," Chad said and laughed.

"I'm serious!" Trevor said and the mood around the table changed. "That pirate lost his leg alright. But he kept the bone with him everywhere he went in a box. That box also held the map for the gold he hid somewhere beneath where the town now lies."

"Trevor, over here," a voice called out from another part of the bar.

"Come by the museum tomorrow and I'll tell you more," Trevor said and left.

"That was a good story," Chad said.

"Yes, and we caught him at a good time," Christine said.

"How so," Chad asked.

"Early enough that he isn't drunk yet," Christine said. "As much as we all like Trevor, he has a drinking problem. You want to hear some whoppers, just stay around after ten and he'll really get going."

We all laughed.

"So, what did happen?"

"The town brought in a medicine man," Christine said. "And he told them the pirates spirit wasn't at rest. He still thought the gold was his and would harm anyone who got close to it. He told the town elders that they needed to remind him he had passed. So, every year, the town burns and effigy of that pirate to honor him and keep the curse from repeating."

"Really?" Chad asked.

"Absolutely," I said. "They put a fake skeleton in a wood coffin and set it to light at the end of the parade!"

"Want to see him?" Christine asked.

The three of us stood and walked around to the other side of the bar where a skeleton had been positioned at the end of the bar. Someone had put a pirates hat on its head and the long, bony hand was across the bar cupping a beer.

"To the DREAD PIRATE!" Trevor said as he passed in front of us and clang his glass to the pirate's glass and the crowd cheered.

"Must be the elevation," Chad said and smiled.

We stayed at the Black Raven until midnight and stumbled out to the street and headed back to the hotel. Chad stepped off the sidewalk to the middle of the street and stopped walking as he looked up at the sky. I went over to him.

"What? What is it?" I said.

"WOW! Look at all those stars!"

"Much better than Hollywood, right," I said.

The night was quiet other than a few people making their way back to the hotel or to the various campsites that were set up around the town. We made our way to the elevator and went to the fourth floor. It was there I had a good laugh.

"Did you see that?" Chad said as he exited the elevator.

"See what?" I asked.

"That figure down the hall," Chad said. "It was there, and then, it disappeared.

"Let's go see," I said and started walking down the hallway when a hand grasped my shoulder.

"Maybe tomorrow, when it's light outside," Chad said. "For now, let's live it alone and we'll leave it alone."

CHAPTER THREE

THE PARADE

"You still have the projector up on the fourth floor?" I asked as Christine put a breakfast burrito in front of me. Chad was still in the room sleeping so I came down to get an early breakfast and hear the chatter about the room.

"Of course," she said. "It's triggered when the elevator door opens. Is it not working?"

"No," I said, "it got Chad last night and I didn't tell him the truth so he's a little spooked."

"It's all part of the experience," Christine winked and went back to the kitchen.

I smiled and turned my head as I watched her walk away. My smile faded as I turned back to bite into my burrito and spotted the mayor watching me from a table across the room.

"You have a thing for her?" Chad said as he sat down in the booth facing me. He followed my gaze. "Oh, I see the mayor, or should I say, her ex is here."

"I hope you're amused," I said. "And yes, I've been fond of her for many years. I just never thought I'd have any chance to, you know. Plus, she lives up here and this hotel is her life. And her ex-husband is the mayor."

"Wow, can you come up with any more excuses?" Chad said.

"I just don't know if I have the courage to…"

"To ask me out," Christine said as she approached out table and put another breakfast burrito in front of
Chad.

"You knew she was coming up behind me," I said to Chad as he smiled back.

I looked at Christine who smiled.

"I'm glad you are both amused at my expense here," I said.

Christine looked over to where her ex was sitting.

"Is everything okay?" I asked.

"Christine sat down beside me for a moment. "Yes, it's just the whole town is worried about the fire danger today. With all the people from out of town, Rick has had to do extra checks to make sure no one has an open fire. He's also worried about the ceremony tonight."

"You mean the ceremony where we march up the hill and burn the fake effigy of the pirate?" Chad said.

"Yes," Christine said.

An awkward moment of silence crossed the table.

"So, are you going to ask her out?" Chad said.

"Well, maybe later when I'm not so busy we'll have some time to discuss this situation," Christine said, stood and walked away.

"Ready?" I asked as we finished our breakfast and headed outside.

The streets outside were packed with artistic displays and gifts of all types. I bought several paintings from one of my favorite artists and a new steampunk hat. Since the hotel was right where all the action was happening it was easy for us to haul our loot back to the room and head back for more.

We watched a few freak shows and some acrobatics at the main park as the day passed and the evening came. It was now time for us to head to the main street and watch the parade. There, anyone who was dressed in costume could participate.

The parade started with a loud gong and many costumed figures came down the streets marching to punk rock songs accompanied by at least one person playing bagpipes.

"Is that an ostrich?" Chad asked as we sat on the sidewalk taking pictures.

"I believe it's an Emu, similar but not exactly the same."

"And a hearse?"

"Yep," I said. "And following that is the wood coffin with the Dread Pirate!" We fell in line with the rest of those who went out to the hillside where the parade ended. This was the site where the annual coffin burning took place at sunset. The mood in the crowd was jubilant as food and drink was served from the tables set up in the area and live music played.

Suddenly, the music stopped and an argument could be heard coming from the area where the coffin had been kept.

"You don't know what you're doing," a familiar voice rang out. It was Trevor.

Chad and I looked on as did the rest of the crowd who'd grown silent. Trevor, who was waving his arms as he cursed and yelled was addressing the mayor, Rick Combs.

The mayor looked out at the crowd and someone handed him a microphone. "Sorry folks, we are not going to finish with our usual bonfire tonight. The fire danger is too high and we can't risk it. There's still plenty of food and drinks for everyone and the band will be here until ten. Please make sure there are no open fires as you go back to your campgrounds."

Suddenly, Trevor grabbed the microphone. "Don't stay, get out of town. It's not safe here. The Dread Pirate will get his revenge. Five people will die in the next twenty-four hours if we don't burn the coffin."

Members of the crowd came forward and worked with the mayor to restrain Trevor as he shouted. "You don't know what you're doing!"

They finally got Trevor to calm down and he sat at a picnic table.

"Well, that was disturbing," Chad said.

"I guess so," I stated as I looked around and noticed a lot of people walking back towards town. "Looks like there won't be much of a party tonight. Sorry."

"Oh no, this has been a great time," Chad said. "I had fun today. Let's stay out for a while, it's such a nice night."

"I agree," I said. "Maybe they'll be less calamity now that everyone's turning in."

Suddenly, someone starting yelling in front of us. "Fire, there's a fire at the campground!"

Men rushed by us and the towns single fire truck came out and headed down to the campground that was one street over from where Chad and I were walking. We rounded the corner and could see a trailer on fire. We cautiously approached as many people were already crowded around.

"Looks like nobody was inside," one of the firemen called out.

Chad tapped my shoulder and pointed to our right. I looked where he pointed and spotted Trevor Towny moving quietly back toward town. He spotted me looking at him and put his finger to his lips in a gesture to be quiet. He then motioned us to follow him.

"Let's go," I said to Chad as we followed Trevor into town and to the museum he owned. We entered to find Trevor standing behind the front counter.

"I need you two to help me," Trevor said.

"Help you with what?" I asked.

"Help me stop it before someone really gets hurt," Trevor said. He took out a large, leather-bound book and placed it on the counter. "Here is the closest thing I have to a reference."

"I'm not sure what you are talking about," I said. I noticed Chad had become preoccupied at the door and was staring out at something.

"In order to stop what is taking place, we need to find Dread's missing leg and burn it on the hill. We must follow the tradition and put him to rest."

"Louis?" Chad said from the door.

"It was last seen in this area," Trevor pointed. "I can only imagine it was lost in the fire of the Hotel. "I opened this museum and collected many things hoping one day I'd find it."

"Louis!" Chad's tone increased and he looked at me eyes wide.

"What?" I said.

"People are heading this way," Chad said.

"So?"

"The police are leading the pack and they have that pitchfork and torches look in their eyes.

"You have nothing to worry about," Trevor said. "They are coming for me. Now, take my keys and hide in the back there."

I took Trevor's keys and Chad and I went to the back of his museum. The police came in with the mayor and we overheard the conversation:

"Trevor Towny, you are under arrest for arson," the police officer said.

"Were you trying to kill someone or just trying to up your book sales," the mayor said.

"I was trying to drive people out of town," Trevor said. "They're going to get hurt staying around here and you know it."

I positioned myself to look over the display of mining tools we hid behind, keeping my head down I would see the deputy, Jason, behind Trevor.

"Take him to jail," the mayor said.

"You sure Rick?" Jason asked.

"Yes, he could've hurt somebody and he destroyed property," Rick said.

He glanced around the store and I remained as still as I could while ducking behind the counter where I spied from.

"It was my own darn trailer I burned down," Trevor said. "That's why I parked it where I did so no one would get hurt."

"Well, no one got hurt but a bunch of people are leaving town now. The vendors and townsfolk aren't going to be happy tomorrow when there's no one here for the rest of the festival. And what do you think that will do to our town?"

The lights went out and the door shut behind the men as they left the building.

"What should we do now?" I said.

"First thing is we get out of here," Chad said. "This old museum is probably full of all kinds of haunted things."

We waited until the street outside was clear before we exited the old museum. There were still a few activities going on in the main park and down at the Black Raven, but much of the town grew silent in the evening hour. We headed back to the hotel, cleaned up and changed out of our costumes. We ate dinner at the hotel which was fairly empty as everyone else was still on the hill or at the Black Raven.

"At least we don't have to worry about finding a seat," I said as we headed toward what looked like a comfortable booth off to the side.

"It's kind of dark back here," Chad said as he sat down.

"I know," I said as I pulled out the book Trevor had given us. "This way no one will notice us as we look this over and decide our next steps."

"Oh no," Chad said. "My next step is to get some food, maybe something to drink later and head to bed for a good night sleep."

"Oh, come on, where's that adventurous spirit?"

Christine walked up to our table with a couple of beers for us. "Is he trying to drag you along on one of his adventures?"

"Yep, and I'll have none of that," Chad said. "Did you know he drug us along when we were kids to go to haunted houses?"

"I did," Christine said. "He gave me a copy of *The Questors' Adventures*."

"Sure, got quiet tonight," I said.

Christine sighed. "That stunt Trevor pulled scared a lot of people away. I'll be fine because most people pre-paid but I'm worried about all the vendors tomorrow. Many of those in town count on this festival for their income."

"Right there," Mike said and pointed to a section of the book.

"Christine," I said, "Does this hotel have a basement?"

"Sure," Christine said. "Why? Hey, is that Trevor's book?"

"Yes," I said. "He gave it to us right before he got arrested.

"Well, you won't find what you're looking for in this hotel. You see, this isn't the original hotel. If that old pirates shack was where the hotel was built, it would have been across the street there," Christine pointed. "See, that's the location of the first hotel."

"What happened to it?"

"It burned down," she said and her hand went to her cheek. "It burned down in the late eighteen hundreds. Almost the entire town burned down see. Buildings back then were made of wood."

"Then everything was replaced with brick," I said. "But the fires continued didn't they?"

"Yes," Christine said.

All three of us were silent for a moment as the thought crossed my mind and Chad said it out loud:

"The pirate's curse," Chad said.

"While I was touring the town earlier, I couldn't help but notice the signs of fire on many of the buildings," I said. "I guess I've noticed it before but didn't think much about it."

"Not a lot of investment has been going on here," Christine said. "Some of those fires happened a long time ago."

"How many have happened since the festival started?" I asked.

"I'm not sure," Christine said. "I'd say there haven't been many fires for about five years now."

"Since the festival started," I said.

Christine looked around the restaurant which still had very few customers. "Scoot over," she said and sat beside me. "Now," she looked at me, "From what I know about you, you don't believe in any of this superstitious stuff. Not really. You'd like to but nothing has ever happened that confirms your desire to believe. Am I right?"

I had taken to twisting my napkin and looked at Chad who had a patient look on his face as though he'd wait all night for my answer.

"I guess we know each other more than I thought," I said to Christine. "What's your point?"

"You're not buying into this curse stuff are you?" Christine asked.

I took a long drink from the glass of beer in front of me. "I think it's more likely that someone is after that old pirates gold than anything else and they are using the curse as a cover. Just in case and, because we've got nothing better to do, who do we need to see to get into that building," I said and pointed across the street.

CHAPTER FOUR

THE SECRET DIG

Christine asked her associate to watch the bar while she, Chad and I went to the jail to check on Trevor. Once there, Sheriff Mike Johnson told us Trevor was to be kept through the weekend so he couldn't interfere anymore with the festival. We asked if we could visit with him and, seeing no harm in it, the sheriff obliged.

"Well, you've come back to hear more," Trevor said as we looked through the bars at him as he lay on a cot against the far wall of the jail cell. "That means the fires haven't stopped. Has anyone died yet?"

"Look," I said to Trevor. "We may not believe in the Pirate's curse, but the lost gold is real and we know that. Christine told us something interesting and we wanted to confirm it with you."

Trevor sat upright but remained on the cot. "What that?"

Christine moved closer to the bars as she spoke, "you told them the hotel was built over the place where the pirates cabin had stood. That would put it under the town storage building, not under the hotel. Remember, the first hotel burned down and it was rebuilt in its' current location."

Trevor's right hand went up to his forehead. "Oh, my, how could I have missed that," he said. "You're right. Which means that's where we should look for it."

"The gold?" Christine asked.

"No, the pirates leg," Trevor said. "Unless we bury the leg bone, his curse will remain on this town."

Christine shook her head and stepped back. "I give up," she said.

Trevor rubbed his chin. "I suppose the gold could be around there as well. I mean, it's possible. Everyone assumed that when they couldn't find it that the pirate buried it in the hills somewhere. People been looking for years and ain't found nothing. Maybe he buried it under his shack after all."

We didn't have time to discuss the situation further. Sheriff Johnson came back to where we were standing. "I need you to leave, there's another fire across town. I need to get over there to support the chief."

"I tried to warn you," Trevor said.

"You just sit tight there," Sheriff Johnson said. "And you better hope we can't tie this to you in anyway or you're never getting out of there."

We exited out to the front of the jail and watched the sheriff pull away.

"Well, if everyone's down at the fire, nobody will be watching that storage building," Christine said.

I looked around the dark, empty streets. Other than the commotion across town the night was still and the streets around us were empty. We started walking across to the storage building. Chad didn't follow so I stopped and turned to him.

"Wait," Chad said. "I'm all for adventure, but I don't want to break into any buildings. The temperature of this town is already hot and if we get caught we might be joining Trevor in jail."

"You got a point there," I said.

"Who said we were going to break in," Christine said. "My ex is the mayor. He has a key in his office and I have a key to that office."

"You don't think he'll be there?" I asked.

"No, he'll be down at the fire as well," Christine said.

"Let's go," I said and the three of us joined arms and skipped down to town hall were we absconded the keys to the city storage building.

It wasn't long before we found our way into the storage building and headed down to the basement. I pulled my cell phone out and used the light to guide the way . We decided it was better to keep the lights off in the building so we didn't attract attention.

"It is suspicious that there is another fire and all," Chad said as we crept down the stairs."

"There are a lot of campsites set up for the festival," Christine said. "More chances for a fire than usual."

The long wooden staircase led down to a dusty, musty smelling room about thirty feet by forty feet that had old pallets of boxes stored but was otherwise empty. It was a wheelbarrow at the far end that caught my eye.

"Looks like someone's been digging around down here digging for something," Chad said as he used his phone flashlight to point to several locations on the floor where the ground had been disturbed.

We approached wheelbarrow that had a shovel leaning against it to find it parked over a piece of plywood.

"I bet you if we move that piece of wood we'll find a hole in the ground," Chad said.

"You think someone's already beat us to the gold?" Christine asked.

"Why not?" Chad said.

"Who?" Christine said.

"It can't be Trevor, he seemed surprised when we reminded him that the first hotel burned down," I said. "He realized he'd been looking in the wrong place."

"Unless it was a trick to throw us off," Chad said. "I wouldn't want to tell anyone where to find the hidden gold if I was behind bars."

"Trevor is prone to exaggeration," Christine said. "But he's honest to a fault."

"Well," I grabbed the shovel, "there's only one way to find out." I placed the tip of the shovel under the edge of the thick piece of plywood and pried it up. Chad grabbed the edge and we moved it out of the way. Underneath was a dark hole about four-feet wide and six feet deep. At the bottom of the hole, we could see pieces of wood flooring.

"Could that be the floor of the pirate's cabin?" Christine asked.

I was about to jump down into the hole when a sound came from the building above. Someone had entered and was walking across the floor toward the basement's entrance. The sound of steps creaking led me to pull on Christine and Chad's arms and we hid behind a set of pallets and turned of our lights. We ducked down and listened.

The beam of a flashlight scanned around the room for a minute and then came to a stop at the wheelbarrow which I could still see off in the distance. Another set of footsteps came down the stairs.

"Did you leave that open," a familiar voice said.

"For God's sake, Mike, turn the light on," another familiar voice said. Suddenly, the entire room was lit. "No, I didn't leave that open did you?"

"No, I think someone's been down here," the first voice said.

"That's exactly why I wanted to come down here and check. With all the craziness going on."

I looked at Christine as I finally placed the second voice, it was the mayor, her ex-husband's Rick's voice. Her face, taut and stern as her eyes stared at the ground. Then, she rose to her feet. "Mike, Rick, what is going on here?"

In a quick reaction, Mike had pulled his gun which was now pointed at the three of us as Chad and I stood on either side of Christine.

"Now, let's all calm down for a minute," I said.

Sheriff Mike Johnson holstered his revolver when he recognized the three of us. "What are you doing down here? This whole town has gone crazy tonight. Fires everywhere and now the alarm goes off here. What happened to my quiet town?"

"We were on the trail of the Dread Pirate's gold," I said. "It looks like we're not the first to realize everyone's been looking in the wrong place." I pointed to the uncovered hole in the ground.

"Are you responsible for this?" Christing asked as she approached Rick.

"Look," Rick said, "if we did find the gold it would go to the town, you've got to believe me."

"So, you've known all along that Trevor was telling the truth?" Christine asked.

"Well, sort of," Rick said. "We don't know about the curse or how much of it is true. The fires started years ago when we began searching for the gold."

"That's why you started having the festival?" I said.

Rick nodded.

"Trevor convinced you that it would appease the pirate."

"It worked until tonight," Rick said. "That medicine man was right."

"Did you find anything while you were digging?" I asked.

"Yes, all kinds of old furniture pieces," Rick said and pointed to some storage shelves across the room under the stairwell. "Most of it's broken and some of it's burned. But no gold yet."

Chad went to the shelves and started examining the items. The rest of us went over to the shelves.

"Look at this," Chad turned to me holding what appeared to be a thick, rudimentary cane with burn marks on it. "This isn't just made of wood," he said. "Look at the inset."

"The pirates leg," I said. "Someone inset it in the wood."

"What leg?" Rick asked.

"The leg that needs to be buried to put the pirate to rest," Christine said. "You see, according to the story, the pirate had lost his leg but carried it around with him."

"Well, what do we need to do?" Rick asked.

"Ask him," Christine pointed to me. "He's the ghost expert."

Chad laughed as he moved into the light to better examine the bone.

"I just write about and study that kind of stuff," I said. "I'm not expert."

"You know more than the rest of us," Christine said.

"Okay then," I said. "We need to bury the bone preferably with the rest of the pirates body." We all started heading toward the stairs. "Do we know where that is?"

"Trevor knows," Rick said. "We'll need to stop by the jail."

Suddenly, a flickering light came from behind us around the area of the dig. A spot on the basement floor had started on fire. Rick quickly grabbed an extinguisher that was hanging at the bottom of the steps and extinguished the flame. When he turned to join us, the fire started again.

"I'll handle this here, Mike," Rick said. "Take them to get Trevor and bury that bone before I run out of time."

Mike nodded and turned to me. "Let's go," he said and led the way to the jail with Christine, Chad and myself in tow.

"Your name sounds familiar," I said to the Sheriff. "When I was a kid, there was a sheriff Mike Johnson in Pueblo."

"That was my dad," Mike said.

"Is that right," I said and grinned at Chad.

"Yep," Mike said. "He told me about some kids that he dealt with who were trying to be ghost hunters. I read your book, *The Questor's Adventures*, was that you guys?"

"One and the same," I said. "What a small world it is."

We entered the jail and Mike went to the cell and unlocked it. Trevor stood and walked to the door. I grabbed the cane and showed it to Trevor. "We found the Dread Pirate's leg bone."

"You did," Trevor said as he reached out and touched it. "See, Sheriff, I'm not so crazy after all."

"Well, Louis here thinks if we bury the leg bone with the rest of the pirates body, we can stop the fires," Mike said.

"So, you admit I was right," Trevor said.

"We don't have time for this," Christine said. "We need to get going."

"We need to get that bone to Sunnyside," Trevor said. "But we need to stop by my shop first."

"Follow me," Mike said and led us to his police SUV. He and Trevor piled in the front while Christine, Chad and I took the back seat. Mike started the car and we could hear chatter on the radio as the fire chief reported yet another fire in town. "I hope this works or we're liable to have the whole town on fire before this night is over."

We pulled to the side of the road in front of the town museum and passed Trevor the keys as he exited and went into the museum. The museum used to a firehouse at one time and we heard the bell in the tower starting to ring. We all stepped out of the car and looked up to see Trevor in the tower yelling.

"Run for you lives," Trevor yelled. "Clear out of town before it burns. The end is here!"

"Oh, my," Christine said.

"TREVOR!" Sheriff Johnson yelled out. "We don't have time for this get your but down here."

Trevor stopped yelling and looked down at us. Then, he disappeared.

"Should I go in and get him?" I asked.

No one answered as Trevor came through the door and back to the car getting in the front seat. The rest of us got in and the Sheriff let the engine roar and the sirens wail as we headed to the town's historic cemetery.

"What the heck was that all about," Sheriff Johnson asked.

"Sorry," Trevor said. "I wanted to verify a reference on my map."

"And the yelling?"

"I've just always wanted to ring that bell and yell out a warning in desperate times," Trevor said.

"Well, you scared all of us. I hope you're satisfied."

Trevor turned around to look at us in the back seat. "Sorry, you all. Guess I got carried away."

"How sure are we that we know where the Dread Pirate is buried," I asked.

"How sure are we that we know that is his leg?" Mike asked.

"How many leg-bones cast in a cane that happened to be near a buried cabin do you think there are in this town?" Trevor said. "Of course it's his leg."

"Do you know where the grave is?" I asked Trevor.

"Well," Trevor said, "The site had to be disguised, see, because of all the treasure hunters. They thought the gold was hidden where he was buried."

"Now, who in his right mind would think that?" Chad said. "Did he come back from the grave and bury it after he died?"

"People get that gold fever and do crazy things, right sheriff," Trevor said.

"After what I witnessed tonight at the dig site, I'm not so sure what is possible," Mike said.

"Dig site?" Trevor asked. "What dig site?"

"Yes," Christine said. "Apparently my ex and the sheriff here were digging for the lost gold which is how they found the cane you're holding there."

"The cane that happens to house the pirate's leg bone?" Trevor said.

"YES!" Chad, Christine and I all responded at the same time.

We had arrived at the gate and Trevor directed the sheriff as we entered and parked toward the rear of the cemetery and exited the vehicle.

"Where to now?" Mike asked as he turned on a flashlight and handed one to Trevor. He then opened the back and took out a small, folded shovel.

"This way," Trevor said.

We started walking among the tombstones.

"As you said," I turned my head toward Chad, "at least it's a nice night out."

"I can't believe after all of these years and everything we done, we still can't do something together without ending up at a haunted house or in a graveyard somewhere."

"Kind of makes it exciting to be around me, doesn't it," I quipped.

We followed Trevor's lead to a large tombstone with the name "Adred Patier."

"Really, an anagram?" I said out loud to the group.

"This is where it's supposed to be," Trevor said and put out his hands. Mike handed him the shovel and he started digging.

"What if we're wrong?" Mike asked.

"I'm not sure it matters," I said. "As long as the bone is buried in consecrated ground we should be okay. Oh, and we probably only have until midnight to accomplish the task."

"Midnight? Why?" Christine asks.

"Don't know," I said. "It's in the literature for things like this."

"It doesn't have to be that deep," Mike said.

"Good point," Trevor said and stopped digging. He turned to me and I handed him the cane. He put it in the hole and filled it with dirt. He stepped back "I guess maybe we should say something. You're the official here, sheriff."

"What should I say?" Mike asked.

"I don't know," Trevor said. "Maybe something about we're sorry about the pirate losing his leg and then being burned alive by greedy people that wanted his gold."

"We're sorry you had such an unfortunate life," Mike said. "We aren't trying to steal your gold, but put it to good use for the town. Please rest in peace."

Trevor took two flasks out of his pocket. He handed one of them to me as he removed the lid of the other and sprinkled the content over the site.

"Holy water," Trevor said as he topped the flask, placed it in his pocket and grabbed the other one from me repeating the process with the second flask. He then lifted the second flask to his lips and drank. "Bourbon," he said and passed the flask to the rest of us as we took a drink in honor of the pirate.

Chad and I exchanged glances and bowed our heads as the sheriff said the final words. A gust of wind came across the cemetery and rattled the evergreens as it passed.

"We better get back to town," Mike said. "If this didn't work, they'll need help with the fires."

Mike drove us back to town and as we approached the cities Annex, a sigh of relief sounded from Christine and the sheriff when we could see the building still standing.

"No smoke," Trevor said. "That's a good thing."

We raced into the building and down the stairs where we found Rick sitting next to the open hole with the fire extinguisher to his side.

"What is it Rick?"

Rick, grinning from ear to ear, opened his hands and showed us several pieces of gold coins. "The fire started up several more times. The floorboards there," he pointed, "burned all the way through before I could put them out. It's then I noticed something shiny in the hole below."

"The pirate's gold," Chad said.

We all gathered around and looked at the bags of gold as Rick hoisted them out of the hole. There were two small bags of gold with one having a hole worn through it which allowed some of the coins to slip out.

"The pirate finally gave up his gold," Trevor said. "Let's make sure it goes to a good cause."

"It will," Rick said. "We are going to fix up this town and next year, we're going to have the biggest Steampunk festival ever."

"And buy a bigger fire truck so we can burn that pirate effigy no matter what the hazard is," Mike said.

"Amen," the group said in unison.

After we helped Mayor Rick get the gold to the sheriff's office, Christine, Trevor, Chad and I went back to the hotel. There at the bar, we stayed up well past midnight telling stories. Sheriff Mike Johnson came by to let us know the fires were out and the town had finally settled to state of calm. Chad and I said goodnight and that we would be checking out in the morning. We headed to the elevator and to our room.

The elevator rattled as it came to life and lumbered to the fourth floor.

"Pretty exciting weekend," I said. "Aren't you glad you came along?"

Chad looked at me and his face turned white as his mouth opened and he pointed behind me. I turned to see what he was pointing at and caught a glimpse of a construction worker, male with a beard and hardhat, that disappeared before my eyes.

"Was that a, ghost?" Chad asked.

"Okay," I said, "I need to tell you something so you won't be up all night. You know how sometimes its marketable to have a haunted hotel and sometimes it's not?"

Chad nodded.

"Well, in order to go with the history and make the hotel more appealing, Christine installed some projectors that, shall I say, make ghosts appear when they are triggered."

"You're kidding," Chad said.

The elevator came to a stop and we exited on the fourth floor.

"Nope, it's true, watch," I said and walked down the hall where I knew a sensor had been installed. "Now, look down the hall."

Chad and I both turned our attention down the hall and the outline of the ghost he'd seen the night before appeared.

The next morning, I woke early and headed down before Chad was up. Christine was there making pancakes and I sat down at the booth closest to the kitchen.

"So, when will you be back?" Christine asked as she brought me a plate of blueberry pancakes.

"I'll come up to see some of the plays, this fall. And then for sure, I'll be back for the next festival."

"Well, don't be afraid to call once in a while."

I smiled as she headed back to the kitchen. "Oh, I wanted to let you know your fake elevator ghost really got Chad last night. When did you install the projector in the elevator."

Christine looked up from the skillet she held and paused. "There's no projector in the elevator."

"AHHHHH!"

THE LUMBERING JACK

TABLE OF CONTENTS

CHAPTER ONE

THE VEIL OF CONSTRUCTION

It was late September, almost my birthday when I convinced the others to go to the mountains for one last camping trip. I asked my older brother, Eric, with the help of some presidential photographs on green paper, to drive us there and leave us off. He would return the next morning to pick us up.

In company were the Questors: My brother Mike, eleven years old with red hair like mine was the second tallest next to me. Our neighbor, Chad, also eleven, had shaggy-black hair and was the smallest in our group. He usually had some appendage wrapped in a cast. Chad was resourceful and usually got us what we needed. Finally, my best friend, Shane thirteen, with long, blonde hair was able to dodge anything with his lighting reflexes. Shane and I about were both about to turn fourteen.

We used our usual cover story and convinced our parents that we were staying at each other's houses and camping out in the backyard, which was cover for why we needed tents and sleeping bags. Life at this time in the rural part of Pueblo, Colorado was simple. As long as we kept our grades up and didn't get in trouble at school, our parents trusted us. This was a period before everyone could afford cable television and video games. A time before home computers and cell phones. Parents would push kids outside and say it was good to get exercise. We all knew it was also because they preferred some peace and quiet of their own.

It was the early eighties, when camping around the lake was still free thanks to the American Taxpayer and the lack of government interference or need to tax every single item in life. Something I didn't think about then as a teenager, but happens all of the time now. We were all under the age needed for a fishing license so the world seemed pretty good to us.

Chad brought extra gear for all of us while we had each packed our sleeping bags, extra socks and whatever provisions we could muster. One last stop at the gas station on the way there served as our dinner which consisted of everything a young body needs: carbs and sugars.

We climbed the winding road in our parents station-wagon to the lake finding traffic light. The weather was beginning to change and the nights would becoming too cold for most people to camp outside. Eric was going to drop us at a familiar point that we'd been too many times. However, as we approached, we found that the roads were closed.

"Construction?" Eric said. "Looks like you've come all this way for nothing." He pulled the old, blue, station wagon alongside the barricade and put the car in park. "You can always camp in the yard."

"Just means we'll have to walk farther, that's all," I said and looked at the others who nodded.

We shuffled out of the car and secured our gear.

"We'll meet you here in the morning," I said.

"If anything happens, don't call home," Eric said. "I'll be over Tom's house."

"Don't worry," I said. "What could possibly go wrong?"

Eric nodded and pulled away.

(Short note here. As a Questor's tip, whenever you are out at a place you are not supposed to be at, that is not in its normal state such as being under construction or closed for any reason, don't ever challenge fate by saying: "What could possibly go wrong." Because fate will answer that challenge!)

"What if there's construction workers up there?" Chad said.

"Not likely on a weekend," Shane said. "Besides, we can pretend we came over the mountain and were hiking down the trail and got lost."

We walked around the barrier and followed the road to the campground. The cool evening air was fresh and felt good on my face. The silence brought a sense of serenity and calmed the spirit. A calm that wouldn't last.

"I brought hot-dogs," Chad said. "I always like hot dogs around a campfire. They always taste better."

"I know," Mike said. "I got marshmallows."

"I picked up some chocolate bars at the last stop," I said.

"And I got graham crackers," I said. Everyone stopped for a moment. "See, we're already having fun."

We were soon at the campground and had our tents up, collected firewood and walked our perimeter. Our security consisted of strings tied to cans that would rattle if the string were pulled. Chad and Mike tested the device.

"I can hear it," I said as they both came into camp.

Our seats around the fire were big rocks that other campers had moved to the location over the years.

"You were right," Mike said as he put more wood on the pile. "No one is up here."

"In addition to the season changing, that construction barricade probably helped as well," I said.

We took our seats around the fire.

"The wood's a little damp," Mike said. "I'm not sure we'll get it to light."

"Chad?" I said.

Chad went to his backpack and pulled out some hairspray. "Luckily, my mom buys these in multiple quantities when they're on sale. He handed it to me but I gave it back along with a pocket lighter.

"Here, my dad smokes so there's always some of these around the house," I said. "You brought the hairspray; you do the honors. If you set yourself on fire we're throwing you in the stream."

Chad lit the mist of spray as he pointed it to the damp wood. A few minutes later, we, with singed front hair and eyebrows, were sitting around a warm campfire and the hotdogs came out with bags of chips and plenty of mustard. The hotdogs went down as easy as the sun and we found ourselves stuffed. The light of the campfire reflected off our faces and the perimeter of the world became the boundary lit by the fire.

"How is it you're never scared out here," Shane asked. "I mean, there's bears, mountain lions, wolves and all kinds of bugs that are creepy."

"I guess I never think about those things," I said. I prefer to think of how many stars I'm going to see or how beautiful everything is."

"I'm glad we came out here," Shane said. "I thought it was a stupid idea at first. I mean, we've snuck out before but not this far away. If I get caught, I'm in major trouble."

"Then, I'll give you a good reason why we took this chance but first, we need to go over a few things. Chad, you've got to be careful out here."

"He's talking to you, Stick," Mike said referring to a nickname we had come up with for Chad since he was so skinny."

"And Mike, I don't want any creepy crawlers in my tent tonight so, no collecting on this trip," I said.

Mike was an avid bug collector and new more about bugs than any single encyclopedia.

"Ok, Professor," Mike said. "Since we're using nicknames, are you going to keep us in suspense or tell us the real reason we are out here tonight?"

"Well," I said, "we haven't had any excitement in some time or any quests to go on."

"There's only so much ghost hunting or paranormal stuff you can do when everything has to be within the distance of our bikes," Mike said.

"I heard that jail in Canyon is haunted, maybe we should sneak in there?" Chad said.

"Right, sneak into a jail," Shane said and we all laughed.

"It's quiet out here, isn't it?" I said. Everyone nodded. "Too quiet, don't you think? Isn't it curious that there's all these construction signs around, but no sign of construction?"

"Ah, that don't mean nothing," Shane said. "My dad says there's always construction signs for miles with no sign of any work being done. He says it's all a conspiracy to keep raising taxes."

"True."

"Right."

"You got me there," I said. "But that's not the reason here. It's something more sinister. People were murdered here. That's why they don't want anyone camping here now. It was in the papers. See, I saw it when my dad carelessly left it open on the table when he went to go get more coffee. I read the article quickly and moved away from it when he came back. He looked at me suspiciously before closing the page and taking it with him. That's something he doesn't usually do unless he's trying to hide something."

"What was it?" Mike asked.

"It was a story about the lumbering Jack," I said.

"You mean a 'Lumber Jack?'" Shane asked.

"No," I said. "The Lumbering Jack is his nickname. Now, quiet down and listen close for the story I tell is real and it happened right here at this very campground. You see, broken hearts can lead to broken dreams and the tale they spin is of tragedy. That is the tale of Jack, the outcast, and Riley, the beautiful young girl who worked at a coffee café. Jack had given his heart to Riley. They were supposed to go on a camping trip to this very location. But, at the last minute, Riley said something had come up and couldn't make it."

"Let me guess, she lied," Chad said.

"Yes," I stated. "But worse, the reason she couldn't make it was that she had a new boyfriend and they came to the very same campsite and Jack found out. You see, Jack was known as odd. He could sense things, hear things, and so, he was an outcast. Riley was the only one who he felt could talk to him and he could talk to her. They met at the coffee shop where she worked because he went there to get away from the other teens.

"Right, teenagers don't like coffee," Chad said.

"It's kinda gross," Mike said.

"Tastes bitter," Shane said. "They need to add more sugar and flavors like caramel and amaretto and then it would be more popular."

I shook my head and the others stopped. "Can I finish now?"

"Sorry," Shane said.

"That night, he went to the cabin he'd rented with all the money he'd saved up for months. It was there the voices took over," I said.

"Wait, did you hear that?" Mike said.

We scrambled for some flashlights as we heard sounds off in the distance.

"Someone's coming, I can see a flashlight?" Shane said. "Is it the lumbering Jack? Is he coming after us already?"

"I don't think a killer would be holding a flashlight to sneak up on us," I said. "Everyone kept it a secret that we were coming her tonight, right?" I said as I caught a glance between Mike and Chad.

"Well," Mike said, "We might have invited someone."

"Right," Chad said, "But we didn't think they'd come."

Suddenly a girls voice called out, "Chad, Mike, are you there?"

I recognized Shannonee's voice.

"Over here," Chad said. Soon, three figures emerged from the rocky path to our campground. Mike's girlfriend, Shannone, a girl Chad was seeing, Pam, and Shane's sister, Tracey.

"How did you guys get here?" I asked.

"Pam's old enough to drive," Shannone said.

"You're just in time for the story," Shane said.

I signaled for Shane to come over to me.

"Look," I said. "I know I usually make up a lot of stories, but there's a reason I didn't want anyone to be out here, this story is REAL."

"Sure, it is," Shane said and patted my shoulder. "Don't worry, I'm sure we'll enjoy it. "Welcome to our campsite, there's plenty of room."

CHAPTER TWO

THE LUMBERING JACK

With everyone settled in and the sleeping bags stored, alongside a crackling campfire, I started my story:

"There he sat, alone in the wooden cabin. Alone and sulking. 'It wasn't supposed to be this way,' he said to himself. He had rented the secluded cabin for the weekend and planned a trip with his girlfriend. He was going to propose. Instead, she broke up with him the day before they were scheduled to arrive. The ultimate irony is that she was already with someone new and they were staying at the campground down below.

"He looked into the worn, full-length mirror hanging on the wall across from him. A worn wooden frame held the mirror which was attached to the wall. Jack moved to stand in front of it and it was in this movement that he spotted his reflection. His hair was thick and curly and looked unkempt although he'd combed it multiple times. His shoulders were big and burly but his legs looked too thin for his torso. Health problems kept him in bed when he was younger and he could never play sports or even get out of bed. Could that be why she left him? Did she suspect he was going to propose and after all these years she just couldn't bare being with someone who was so odd? It's true, people stared at him all of the time. Jack had long ago learned to deal with it. Maybe Riley hadn't learned.

"A moment of soft reflection was shattered when out of the corner Jack spotted the bottle of champagne he'd bought, well beyond his price range. Sitting beside the bottle, a small box with a ring; one he'd picked out himself. It would take him years to pay off the ring.

'I'll work it out, he thought to himself. The reflection told him different. 'Ha! They told you at the store it was a discount because it was not returnable remember. You fool, this is what you get. Riley was way out of your league.'

"But, she was so good to me all of these years,' Jack said.

"Was she? Or did she just pity you? Pity the fool who can't even speak in front of the class. Pity the kid with such weak legs you wouldn't even be able to carry her over the threshold. She needs a man. You're no man. You're a loser. Isn't that what your father called you?

"My father was a mean, self-centered alcoholic who drank himself to death,' Jack said. "I'm smarter than he ever was.

"Yes, Jack, you're smarter. So, what are we going to do about this Riley thing? Do you think she should just get away with it? Why don't you go down there and confront her? Why don't you go teach her a lesson about stomping on your heart.

"Why don't you shut up! Shut UP!' Jack raised the bottle of champagne and in a moment of anger threw it at the mirror. It smashed against the glass causing a large crack that ran the length of it. The bottle didn't break when it hit the mirror but ricocheted and broke when it hit the floor.'

"Oh no, what have I done?' Jack stepped toward the broken mirror and slipped on the spilled champagne. He blacked out when his head hit the table on the way down.

"Jack, you there? Oh, there you are my boy. Now it all makes sense doesn't it? What we've got to do. No one will know Jack boy. No one will know.

"Bleeding from the back of his head and in a haze, Jack headed down to the campground where he knew Ross and Riley were staying. Ross and Riley were setting up their site completely unaware that Jack was in the area.

"Honey, where did you put the axe?' Ross asked as he looked around the campsite.

"I didn't move it,' Riley said.

"Well, I left it right here and we are going to need it to chop more wood for tomorrow morning.' He looked back and Riley had tears in her eyes. 'What is it?' Ross said. 'You looked at that damn tree again? I thought it was over between you two.' He took out a pocketknife and went over to a peach-leaf willow tree where there were initials carved inside a heart. He started scratching them out and Riley tried to stop him.

"Don't," Riley said. "It doesn't mean anything but you don't need to destroy it.

"Ross stopped and threw the knife down. 'I'm going down to the lake to see if I left the axe there. You better make up your mind who you want to be with.'

"Riley ran her hand over the defaced initials Jack had carved on the tree more than three years ago. It was their first trip together away from the parents; away from society where they made the promise to be together forever and carved their initials in the tree. Suddenly she felt a deep burning pain in her arm. Her hand fell from the tree and she watched as it detached from her wrist. The axe that Ross had been looking for stuck in the tree after it sliced through her wrist. Someone pulled it out. Still in shock, Riley felt no pain as she turned, holding her bloody stump up with her left hand, to gaze upon her attacker.

"Jack?" the last word Riley would speak left her mouth as the axe sliced through her throat contacting the tree on the other side.

"What are you doing?' a voice rang out behind Jack. He turned to see Ross there. He went to pull the axe out of the tree and it came out but Ross tackled him before he could fully turn around. In the fall, the axe came down on his left heel and sliced through the back of his ankle. Jack struggled while Ross pelted him with fists. His hands reached out to grab a branch or rock when he felt the knife Ross had dropped. He gripped it tightly and stabbed it into Ross's neck.

"Ross stopped the attack and stumbled away from Jack as his hands went to his neck. He stood and stumbled around in a circle. He pulled the knife out but the blood was too much and he soon fell over.

"Jack came to his knees and watched the panic in Ross's eyes as he slowly went numb. Jack used the tree to brace himself as he leaned against it and looked down at the two bodies for a long time.

"What have I done?' Jack said as he noticed blood on his hands. He was shaking and looked around the campground to see if there was anyone else around.

"You taught them a lesson,' the voice inside said. 'A lesson that betrayal of the heart is the same as murder.'

"Jack wrought his hands together trying to wipe the blood off. He stopped and clenched them tight. He straightened his shoulders and took a deep breath and his face lost all expression.

"Yes,' Jack said. 'People shouldn't toy with love, it's dangerous.' He reached down to get the knife and as he stepped away from the tree he fell when his left leg didn't work right. He reached down to his ankle and felt the blood on the back of it. 'I'm bleeding.'

"Does it hurt?' the voice asked.

"No,' Jack said and pulled himself up using the tree for support. He took the knife and carved the initials back in the tree. 'There,' he said when he was finished. He looked down at Riley one more time. 'I had to let you go before your heart changed. Now, we'll be together.'

"He grabbed the axe in one hand and clenched Riley's hand with the other dragging her body with him. He slowly made his way back to the cabin, lumbering as his left leg didn't work right. He knew he wouldn't be able to stay long. He placed Riley's body on the bench by the fireplace in the cabin. He removed his boot and examined his ankle. It was still bleeding so he took the poker from the fireplace, heated it and used it to cauterize the wound. Then, he sat by Riley for hours until the sunlight coming in through the window woke him.

"I have to go now,' Jack said. 'But I'll be back.' He stood and lumbered out of the cabin.

"The next morning, a hiker found the body of Ross and called the police. The police followed the trail of blood to the cabin and found Riley's body along with Jack's blood, the broken mirror and champagne bottle. The only thing missing was the ring, the ring was gone and so was Jack. To this day, they haven't found him."

"Wow," Shane said. "A truly gruesome story. And you say it happened here?"

"That's why the campground is closed," I said.

Everyone remained quiet as the story I recounted sunk in. I knew some of the specifics but had created much of it for effect. It was working as the others fidgeted and scanned around the campground waiting for something to emerge from the darkness.

The crackling fire kept me company in the silence that ensued. The faces glaring into the fire were sullen and, for a moment, I thought I might have taken things too far.

Mike leaned forward. "Let me get this straight," he began. "You convinced us to sneak out of the house, travel all the way up here where it's sure to be cold tonight."

I nodded.

"Where we have no transportation or way out except on foot."

I nodded.

"To a campground that is supposed to be closed because an axe murderer may be on the loose?" Mike finished.

"That sums it up pretty good," I said. "Hand me the marshmallows."

"Your brother is so cool," Chad said.

"I know, right," Mike replied.

"So, what do we do first," Shane said.

"What do you mean, there's no way this story is true," Mike said.

"Look at that tree over there," I pointed.

Chad, Pam, Mike and Shannone all went to the tree and with a flashlight the spotted the carving.

"JL and RD," Mike said.

"And there's axe marks on the tree. Is that a red stain from blood?" Chad said.

Everyone came back to the campfire.

I plopped a marshmallow in my mouth. "You want to see the cabin where Jack went mad?" I asked.

"For real?"

"It's across the bridge over there," I pointed.

CHAPTER THREE

THE CABIN

With flashlights in hand, we all headed to the old, wooden bridge that crossed a small stream coming down the mountain. The bridge was twenty feet in length and was only about ten feet high but, the rocks below would make a rough fall.

"What's that?!" Chad said as his light reflected off a huge spider web over the bridge.

"That's a Hentz orb weaver," Mike said.

"Of course, you'd know that" Chad said.

Mike was a known bug enthusiast and often fascinated us with his knowledge of crawling things.

"Does anyone in the group have arachnophobia?" Mike said.

"Should we catch it for you?" Tracey asked.

"What's archnophobia?" Shane asked.

"He said 'arachnophobia'," I said. "It's the fear of spiders."

"I'm okay with them as long as I can see them," Tracey said.

"Me too," Pam said. "I just don't like going through a web in the dark."

"Right," I said. "Especially when you don't know where the spider is."

"Just better hope your mouth was closed," Shane said.

"Eeew, gross," Tracey said.

Mike moved to the head of the line, turned around in front of the spider web and raised his hand as we halted.

"This is not in our house, it's in its own element, we should leave it alone," he said. "We don't catch it or hurt it. It's helping us actually."

"Hey, the more mosquitoes it catches, the less to bite us right?" I said.

We all agreed and crouched under the spider web as we crossed the bridge to the other side.

"Everyone stay close now," I said as I took the lead with the flashlight. "The trees get thicker in this area because there's been less people back here. This cabin's been kind of a secret for years and I don't think the rangers like people visiting. Shane, you stay in the back since you have the other strong flashlight. That way if we need to turn around we're ready."

"Got it," Shane said as he moved to the back of the group and we headed single file down the dark, damp trail.

Due to the construction, the few lights that were usually present on the road or around the campground were not on. There were plenty of trails around this area with most leading down to the lake or the stream. Only one went forward to where the cabin lie. We managed to stay on the right trail using the sound of the stream running behind us as a guide.

"How much longer," Mike asked. "It's getting colder and were starting to lose any moonlight. It'll be harder to see."

I stopped and waited for everyone to group together.

"Look," I said. "I know you all think I tell a lot of stories, and I do. But we need to be prepared going into this. In case something happens."

"That's not the problem," Chad said.

"No?" I questioned."

"The problem is you make stuff up that sounds real," Chad said.

"That's not all," Mike said. "Sometimes you put stuff that's real into the story so it's hard to tell what's real and what's not."

"Oh," I said. "So, you think the story I told you isn't real even after you've seen the axe marks and bloodstains." I faced a group of shaking heads. "Well then," I pulled a folded-up newspaper article out of my pocket. "Hold this," I said to Shannone who stood to my left as I handed her the flashlight and proceeded to unfold the article.

"Murder at lake cabin," Shannone read.

"See," I said. "So, listen up. The rangers have been combing this area for weeks and found nothing so, I think it's safe to say Jack is gone. But, just in case, if we hear anything, follow Shane with all due speed back to the campground."

"What if he follows us?" Mike asked.

"We outnumber him," I said. "If worse comes, we take him out at the bridge. Agreed," I looked at Shane and Chad as we stood close enough to the light to see each other's faces.

"I mean, how hard could it be, he has an injured leg right?" Chad said.

"How long ago did this take place?" Mike asked.

"The article dates exactly a month ago," Shannone said.

"On what date?"

"The twenty-first," I said. "It took place on August twenty-first."

"So, you brought us here on the twenty-first, exactly one-month after?"

We started walking again.

"That's right," I said. "If we are going to see something it will most likely be a correlation with a date. I thought it would be our best option only..."

"What?" Chad asked.

I leaned into whisper to Mike and Chad, "you shouldn't have told the others. This might be dangerous if something does happen."

"Why, because we're girls?" Tracey said from behind me.

"Sorry, didn't know you were there," I said and we all stopped again. "No, that's not it. The Questors' took an oath. We know what we are getting into. You didn't sign up for this. I don't think it's right for us to drag you into something that's dangerous."

"So, what's this oath?" Tracey asked.

"I have it," Shane said. "Everyone put up your hand. We Questors do swear to help one another in all matters through rain, sleet, hail, snow, or fire and to keep all secrets between us and tell no one else unless tortured or threatened with exile. Agreed?"

"Yes."

"I do."

"Right."

"Uh, okay?"

"Now that we've all agreed," I said, "let's continue to the cabin." Hands slowly went down.

"Exile? Torture?" I heard Shannone say.

"He's just kidding about that part," Mike said. "But the helping each other part is real."

"It kind of sounds like the same saying..." Shannone didn't finish as Chad cut her off.

"As the Marines, I know, isn't it cool, oohrah!"

We started out in single file through the trees as the path became less clear. It wasn't long before Shane signaled with his flashlight.

"Everyone be quiet," I whispered as I made my way back to Shane. "What is it?"

"You didn't' notice these tracks on the path?" Shane said. "I thought it might be one of us, but I've figured out what shoes everyone is wearing and none of them match."

I looked down where Shane was shining his flashlight noticing the footprints.

"Which leg did you say he hurt?" Shane asked. "Doesn't that look like someone walking and dragging their left leg?"

The two of us headed to the front and scanned the trail with our flashlights.

"More marks," Shane said. "This is concerning," he pointed to another track by what would be the traveler's right leg. "What do you think that is."

"Someone dragging something along," I said.

"The axe?" Chad said coming up beside us. "Did you guys stage all of this?"

"Yes," Chad I said. "We drove our stealth car up here ahead of you guys and put all of this in place and then drove back in time to make it look like we're never gone."

"OKAY, just asking," Chad said. "It would be cool to have a stealth car though."

"Speaking of Stealth, I think it's time we go to stealth mode," I said. "We gathered together and checked each other for any clothing that might be loose or clang. Shane and I changed the lenses in our flashlights to a blue light so that it was less visible from far away and told the others to keep their flashlights off unless it was an emergency.

"Last chance if anyone wants out," I said.

"No way," Shannone said. "This is the most exciting thing I've done since school started."

Pam stepped forward. "Look, when I was growing up my dad was worried about me so I started training at a young age. I am a blackbelt in Butokukan and Kempo Karate. I can handle myself."

I nodded to Pam and turned to Chad. "Chad, I'd stick close to her if I were you."

The group started walking again at a reduced pace keeping close together. This was necessary due to the darkness and our need to reduce our profile. We soon found ourselves coming to a clearing. On the opposite side from where we emerged stood the single room cabin. A flickering light came from the front window.

The wood foundation had been built on a mound so it was taller than the ground surrounding it. Rocks bordered the foundation and three stone stairs led to the wooden porch that had a bench on it. The two front windows were single paned and evenly spaced on either side of the door.

"Is that a light inside?" Shane said as we faced the cabin.

"A flickering light," Chad said. "I'd say someone has a fire going in there."

"Should we throw a rock on the roof to see if someone comes to the door?" Shane asked

"No," I said. "We don't know who's in there. It could be anyone which means we need to be extra careful from here on out. Gather round."

Everyone got in a circle. After several adventures that hadn't gone well, we had decided that in the future, we would make sure we had a plan when going into dangerous situations. The main purpose of the plan was making sure we knew how to retreat.

"Okay," I started, "we might be facing an unknown, possibly an unpredictable killer or just someone we irritate if we go poking around. So, I think we need to make sure everyone is clear on what we do next."

"What's that?"

"We are going to sneak up there and look inside to see if we can see anything. We also need to prepare a fast escape in case we're noticed and need to run."

"What if we get separated?" Mike asked.

"The sound of the stream is behind us," I said. "Use it as your guide and try to make it back to the bridge."

No one made a sound or asked a question. Even I started to doubt if we were taking this a bit too far by seeking out a possible killer. "Chad?"

"Right here," Chad said.

"Tell me you have some fireworks," I said.

"Of course," Chad said and reached into a pocket of the small pack he had on his hip. "Black Cats, smoke bombs, zippers, spinners, whatever you need."

"Smoke bombs," I said and he handed me two. I gave one to Shane along with a lighter. Tracey also put out her hand.

"The more the merrier, right?" Tracey said. Chad gave her two smoke bombs and I handed her my last lighter.

"Did you take all of dad's lighters?" Mike asked.

"I just searched the couch cushions," I said. "Now, everyone listen. If someone comes after us, we light these to confuse him and cover our escape while we head back down the trail. Mike, you and Shannone stick close. Chad, you and Pam. Tracey, sorry, but your with your brother and me. Got it?"

"Got it," Everyone said.

"Okay, who's going up there with me?" I asked.

"I'd go, but I just got my leg healed and I don't want to take a chance of having to run off that wooden porch," Chad said. Chad was prone to breaking bones and usually had some appendage in a cast. Although, he never broke one in our presence, I decided not to test the odds.

Mike and Shane stepped forward.

"Anyone else," I asked. No one stepped forward. "Okay, keep quiet at all times. Watch where you're stepping and don't use your flashlight unless absolutely necessary. It helps you see but will give away your position. If you fall and hurt yourself, you need to suck it up and keep it down. If we do get chased, this will only help the attacker find you. Don't worry, we won't leave you behind."

"See," Chad said to Shannone. "Just like the marines."

"Anything I'm missing?"

Three brave ghost-hunters stepped headlong into the path of mortal danger and dared to look into the eyes of fate. We stopped at the base of the porch and gathered at the wooden, three-step stairway. There we paused for a moment and listened. Nothing.

Mike led as Shane and I followed up the stairs. The firelight coming from the window facing us was enough for us to tell where we were going. There, at the edge, four feet from the door we stopped.

Shane pointed. I followed and spotted the object that made my stomach churn. THERE, BESIDE THE DOOR WAS AN AXE LEANING AGAINST THE CABIN WALL.

Mike pointed his fingers to his eyes and then pointed to the window. I nodded as he crouched and headed toward the window to peek inside. He took a quick look and came back toward me. He raised his hand, finger to his mouth as an indication to be quiet and pointed back to the others. I followed as he went down the stairs away from the cabin. Here we could speak with the others.

"What did you see?" I asked Mike.

"There's someone in there alright," Mike said. "A large man lying back in a big, wooden rocking chair by the fire."

"That could be anyone," I said. "A park ranger or someone who owns it that we don't know about."

"Hey, look what I got," Shane smiled wide as he interrupted and held out the axe.

"Why did you take that?" I asked. His smile disappeared.

"Well, if it is Jack in there, he won't be able to use it if we have it," Shane said.

"He's got a point," Mike said.

"And a pointy object," Chad said giggling.

"Very funny," I said. "Good thinking," I told Shane. "So, how do we know it's Jack?"

"We're going to have to see him walk and see if he lumbers," Shane said.

"Rock on the roof," Chad said picking up a rock.

"Wait a minute," Mike said and turned to the girls. "Pam, how close did you park your car?"

"Right where the construction barricade is," Pam said. "Why?"

Mike turned to me. "Just in case," he said.

"Why?" Pam asked again.

"Listen," I said as everyone gathered around. "We need to be ready just in case."

"Ready for what?" Shannone asked.

"Ready to run for our lives," Shane said. "If things go bad, run to the car and don't stop."

"Uh," Chad started to say something but I cut him off.

"You're right, maybe we are getting a little too serious," I said. "Maybe we should just go back..."

Chad grabbed my shoulders and turned me so that my body faced the cabin where he was looking.

"I think it might be too late," Chad said.

In our moment of contemplation, the man inside the cabin had come out of the front door. Luckily, he didn't appear to notice us as he looked around the porch.

"What do you think he's doing?" Mike asked.

"He's lumbering, it's him!" Shane stated.

"Right, and he's probably looking for that," I said and pointed to the axe that Shane held in his left hand.

Our luck had run out as the man glanced in our direction. "Who's there!"

"Run," I said. "Back to the camp and don't stop. Mike, Chad, you lead. Shane, you're with me."

The group took off with their flashlights blaring while Shane and I watched the figure at the cabin. The lighting was too poor for us to see the look on his face but he started moving to the edge of the porch. It was apparent his left leg didn't work right as he drug it along instead of lifting it. I was hoping he would stop but he lumbered down the stairs and stepped in our direction.

"He's lumbering," I said as I moved and bumped into Tracey.

"Tracey, what are you doing?"

"You said I should stick with you guys?" Tracey said.

"Right," I said. "As soon as we get down the trail, let's use these to disguise it," I said and held up my smoke bomb.

"Should we give this back?" Shane said.

"You really think we should give a potential killer his weapon back?" I said as we started heading down the trail.

"Good point," Shane said. "I don't think he can catch up to us so."

"Ready?" I said and held up my smoke bomb.

"Ready," Tracey said and we lit the fuses and threw three smoke bombs behind us.

"Well, if the smoke doesn't help, maybe the smell will keep him from following us," Shane said.

"To the bridge, and don't trip over anything," I said. I thought with any luck, our eyes would be better adjusted to the night and we had the advantage of sight and speed. However, there was definitely pursuit as I heard a rattle of tree branches behind us. I then heard a whispery voice.

"My axe," the voice said. "My axe."

The voice sounded like it came from someone right next to me and carried with it an ominous feeling. I felt my body grow heavy and struggle against the sound. It was as though it pulled on us. Shane looked at me.

"Do you feel that?" Shane asked and I nodded. "What is it?"

"Something bad," I said. "It feels like the darkness has hands and is tugging at me." Suddenly, Shane tumbled down as he dropped the axe and tripped over it.

I reached down to help him up and he brushed himself off.

"What happened?" I asked. "Did you hit a bump?"

"I don't know," Shane said. "It's like the axe all of the sudden weighed a ton and my arm gave out. Where is it?"

Tempted to use my flashlight I hesitated. Shane pulled out his flashlight.

"No," I said and put my hand over Shane's light. "It will give away our position."

Tracey lit another smoke bomb and threw it behind us to disguise the trail.

"We can't just leave it," Shane said. "What if he gets it?"

"My AXE!" the voice grew closer.

Shane and I felt around the ground and I was about to give up when I ran my finger across the blade of the axe drawing blood. "Found it," I said and moved my hand down to the handle and grabbed it. "Let's go," I said and we hurried along the trail with Shane limping slightly.

We soon found ourselves at the bridge and close to our campsite. I could see flashlights up ahead. "We need to warn them," I said. "Quick, across the bridge."

We ran across the bridge when a flashlight hit us directly in the eyes and we froze.

"Don't forget to duck," Mike said as he pointed his light at the huge orb weaver's spiderweb that took shape across the bridge.

We crouched under the web and made our way across the wood-framed bridge.

"What are you all still doing here?" I asked.

"Waiting for you," Mike said.

"It's not safe, we're being followed," I said and started to move forward but Mike reached out and stopped me.

"We can't run," Mike said. "Shannone fell and hurt her ankle. You'd be proud though, she isn't crying."

"We'll carry her," I said. "We've got to get out of here."

"Too late," Shane said and pointed.

"Tracey, get the others out of here."

Mike and I turned around and there, on the opposite side of the bridge, a tall, dark burly figure stood. A white cloud of steam came from Jack's mouth as the warm air condensed against the cold night. Black eyes full of darkness started at us as Mike shined the flashlight on him.

"Great, we're going to die here," Chad said as he came up beside us. In his hands were some fireworks.

"Chad?" I said. "Where did you come from?"

"Pam and Tracey are guiding Shannone back to the car," Chad said. "I came to help you guys. My mistake."

"Come on," I said, "Let's make ourselves look big and hope he doesn't call our bluff."

The four Questors stood together at the edge of the bridge and made ourselves known.

"Hold up the axe," Shane said.

I held up the axe in front of me.

"My axe," the whispery voice came.

"Not anymore," I said. "You won't be hurting anyone anymore." I lowered my voice. "Chad, get ready with those fireworks.

Jack stepped forward and Mike directed his flashlight at his eyes. Jack's hand went up to block the light.

"Good idea," Shane said. "Blind him."

"I know," Mike said and took his light and positioned the beam so it highlighted the spider web coming down from the top across to the sides of the bridge. There, in the middle of the web was the large orb weaver. The shadow cast from the light toward Jack made it look bigger. The effect was noticeable as Jack stepped back and cowered at the sight of the eight-legged creature on the bridge. Chad lit the fireworks and hurled them down under the bridge. The bright flashing disoriented Jack and he turned and headed back the way he'd come.

"It's over Jack," I called out. "No more axe, no more killing," I said fairly proud of myself. I turned to Mike. "How did you know he had arachnophobia?"

"I suspected," Mike said. "People who have neurological disorders tend to be more prone to that kind of fear."

"You guessed?" I said.

"You do it all of the time, Professor," Mike said.

"Fair," I said.

"Hey," Shane said. "I know we're all celebrating here and stuff. I mean, we just faced down a killer and all. But, I was thinking, what if he knows another way over here instead of the bridge and is headed there now."

Scattered glances and defensive stances took form in our group as flashlights scanned the surrounding area.

"We should get the heck out of here," Mike said.

"What about the tents?" Shane said.

"Leave them," I said.

With our best pace given the darkness of the night, we went down the road and ran into the girls who were coming our way in Pam's car.

"Get in!" Pam yelled out of her open window. We all crammed in with five in the back and three in the front as Pam executed a U-turn and started driving away. The road went uphill slightly as it ran parallel to the lake and then leveled off before going back down toward the main road.

"Pam, pull over," I said.

Shane and I exited the car and went to the edge of the road. At this point, the road was elevated above the lake it overlooked. Mike and Chad got out as well and came up beside me. "Who wants to do the honors?" I asked holding up the axe.

"Shane found it," Mike said. "Let him do it."

I handed the axe to Shane. He backed up a few paces and took the axe in both hands. He moved it back like he was going to hit a home run and flung the axe out into the lake. We listed and heard the splash.

"Well, that should put it to rest," Shane said as we all piled back into the car.

Pam headed down to the main road that intersected the one we were on. The windy path made it difficult to go fast but once we were at the main road, Pam stopped. Shane and I got out to move the construction barrier back in place.

"Let's get out of here," I said as we took our seats in the car.

"This was one of my favorite places to go," Chad said. "How can we come back now?"

"I have an idea," Mike said. He had Pam stop at the small convenience store at the base of the mountain. "Anyone have change?"

"I don't think it costs anything to call the police," Shannone said. "That is who you are going to call?"

Mike nodded. He went to the phone and reported the sighting of Jack. When we headed down the road to catch the highway back to town, we spotted several police cars turning off the exit and heading toward the lake.

After a short drive, we found ourselves at Chad's house where we all quietly exited Pam's car, said our goodnights to her, Shannone and Tracey, and headed to the basement where we got at least a full two-hours of sleep.

The next morning, we watched cartoons, ate cereal and reveled in our security. We had logged another adventure for the questors.

Lumbering Jack was not apprehended that night at the campground and Winter set in. It was mid-November and Shane, Mike and I were up in the treehouse when we heard Chad down below.

"Hey guys, you've got to look at this," Chad said as he climbed up through the hatch. He handed me a newspaper as he came through.

"What is it?" Shane asked.

"The police have found a body they believe to be the killer of the summer massacre in a cabin not far from the scene. The young man, Jack, appears to have frozen to death in the cabin. Police say it looks like he ran out of firewood."

"Wow," Shane said. "That's Kharma for you."

I continued reading: "Police further stated that the murder weapon Jack had used, an axe, had not been recovered in the search and was still at large."

Prologue:

The cabin stood empty for years with the door and windows boarded shut. The fireplace cold, the rocking chair still and the mirror staring out at the emptiness. Then, a voice from outside.

"Here it is, this is it," a male voice said.

"This is the one they are going to tear down?" another voice asked, this one was female. "Let's look inside and see if there's anything worth saving."

The two entered the cabin. It was a young couple, maybe sixteen or eighteen.

"There's nothing here," the boy said. "That old rocking chair. Not even a bed."

"Look at that mirror on the wall," the young girl said. She had long locks of black hair that framed a kind face as seen in the reflection. Her brown eyes blinked back at her and the face smiled.

"It's a piece of junk," the male said.

"Take me with you."

"Did you hear that?" The female said.

"It's probably a ghost," the male said. "I heard this place is haunted. A murder or something like that." He raised the wooden rocking chair and crashed it down on the floor breaking it into pieces. "See, what a piece of junk. It's good they are going to burn it down."

"Kill him."

The girl reached down and grabbed what used to be one of the chair legs that had splintered. It was dull but sharp enough and she thrust it through the boys chest. Blood flowed out of his mouth as his hands clutched the piece of wood and he looked at her in surprise. He fell back and sputtered a few times before going quiet on the floor.

"He wasn't good for you anyway. He made fun of you wanting to help animals didn't he?"

Heather nodded.

"What's your name?"

"Heather," the girl said as she removed a set of matches from the boy's pocket and put the wood from the chair in a pile. She started the pile on fire close to the wall. The flames crawled up the wall.

"*Heather is a nice name. But I have a secret name for you. So, you will know it's me when we are talking.*"

Heather removed the mirror from the wall and headed out of the cabin and down the trail. "What is my new name?"

"*Your name will be* **Blood Lust.**"

THE MARSHAL

<u>Introduction:</u>

The Marshall was originally called the Gunfighter Series. It is a set of short stories I composed in poetic fashion that involve a man with an iron hand; a gunfighter. The gunfighter never instigates the action but responds to perceived unjust events around him.

From his introduction in the first to his exit in the fifth, we are introduced and learn of a man who stands up to bad guys but always leaves town in the end.

In the fourth of the series, Anatomy of a Gunfighter, The Marshal reflects on lessons he learned from other men in his trade that he has been around.

In the sixth story, we get to witness the perspective of the evil villain, Six Gun, the lawman, and the gunfighter.

The Marshall is a concept of an enforcer who stands for justice and transcends time. Maybe he was a man once but, now he is spirt brought forth by the prayers of those in need. An avenging angel.

What people should realize is that the spirit of The Marshal is in us all. We have the ability to stand for justice.

GUNFIGHTER I

No one had ever insulted him and got away with it
As this man did
I watched his teeth grit
He stood up
The situation looked grim
He prepared to draw as he had so many times before
But he only turned and walked out the door
As the man who challenged him passed out on the floor

I went out to him and asked why he turned away
This is what he did say

"You kill a man because he is a fool
and forgot to think before he spoke
or did something stupid
You may walk around feeling real proud
But as you look at the world
You find that nothing has changed by what you did
Only that somewhere there's children without a father
A wife without a husband
A mother without a son
A sister without a brother"

His face grew confused as he found no way
To finish saying what he wanted to say
Then the echo of a pistol did sound
As the man before me fell to the ground

There he lie
Shot in the back
By a mean looking gunfighter
All dressed in black

He was quick and steady
Stood seven feet tall
His friends backed him up
There were six in all

He looked at me in awe
As I reached for my gun
And prepared to draw

Six shots were fired
And six men fell to the ground
Because you see…
I'm the fastest gunfighter around

I rode out of town with the gunshots echoing in my head
And I remembered what he said

"You find that nothing has changed by what you did
only that somewhere there's children without a father
a wife without a husband
a mother without a son
a sister without a brother"

A friend without a friend
–The End

<u>Gunfighter II</u>

A stranger in a strange land
A man with an iron hand
Face to face
A game of chess
Power play
Who is best

Turning rivals
Running around
Looking scared
A new Sheriff's in town

A solitary man
A solitary job
Putting them to rest
Day after day
Here the ground's dug at night
Six foot down
When it's cool
Where in a pine box
will lay the next fool

Out on the street
Showdown began
Curiousness watched
Intelligence ran

The Sheriff stood sideways
Watching
Didn't matter who'd win

He'd shoot them in the back
Two gunslinger's dead
A days work done again
The solitary man
Finishing the grave holes
The priest in the chapel
Praying for the lost souls
Thunder and lightning
Fire flashed
Bone met steel
When the smoke cleared
One man left standing
The other lie still

The sheriff with his shotgun
Prepared to extend his law
But lightning flashed again
The stranger was too fast
And beat him to the draw

The solitary man appeared
Time to do his deed
The stranger made his way out of town
The priest had the last words
From the book he read
Putting them to rest
Before sundown

Post a sign
"Sheriff Wanted"
-The End

<u>Gunfighter III</u>

Three men and a young lady
Arrived on the stage
The lady a prize
In any man's eyes
The kind of face
That starts a fight

Seven crazy fools
Half drunk
Half lame
One saw the young lady
And decided to play games

Fists started flying
Outnumber three to one
The sore loser
Reached for his gun

Though drunk and distracted
A steady gunfighter still
Drew faster
Shot quicker
Got the first kill

Two men dead
Two wounded lay
Six drunken fools
Began to walk away

Then a sound
From behind the six men's back
Words of insult
Provoking an attack

The men turned around
To their total surprise
Only one man stood opposing
A badge on his chest
A fire in his eyes

The Sheriff didn't flinch
As he was shot all to hell
He killed one and hit another
Before he fell

I admired his courage
As I stepped out onto the street
The four drunken men
were sobering fast
As the wounded one
scrambled to his feet

My hand felt cold
When I first drew
But soon felt warm
As the bullets flew

What I remember most
Is the look in their eyes
At first the doubt
Then the surprise

For a few moments
Silence was the only sound
As disbelief reigned
Except in me
For you see
I'm the fastest gun around

I went to my horse
Mounted and turned to ride out of town
I stopped by the young lady
And as I looked down

She looked at me with eyes of thanks
For at least revenge
If not justice had been done
As I rode away
toward the setting sun
-The End

<u>Gunfighter IV</u>
<u>Analogy of a gunfighter</u>

"When you kill a man, eventually it will catch up to you"
The first one said this to me
He was hunted down
By a band of ten
Who left him cold
In the end

"If you ride alone, you better watch your back"
The second one said this to me
In an alley
Late at night
He was shot in the back
Guess he was right

The third one said
"sooner or later a quicker gun comes along,
and then you die without time to realize,
life wasn't worth living anyway"
this he did confide
Right before I killed him
His prized guns
Now at my side

"You can't write it all down and call it absolute law
someone will find a way to misuse it
you must stop the mentality
we know how to choose the foods we like and don't like

we know pleasure and pain
believe me, we know what's right and wrong"
The fourth one said this to me

He was taken in his sleep
Tried and hanged by a crooked Sheriff
(Rest in peace
you are avenged
I killed the sheriff
The hangman
And all their friends)

The story of a fighter
A will to stand tough
In a world where bullets are law

No one's your friend
No one you can trust
No place to call home
Just the trail and the dust

In one flash
You may end it all
One careless word
A careless deed
Can bring on the draw

Outlaw or hero
You tell the tale
When law is opinion
Enforced by words and fines

The barrel of a loaded gun
Keeps a straighter line

Sometimes there just has to be a better way
When the system falls short
Take your pick
Win lose or draw
In the Gunfighter's court

"Sooner or later, we all meet our end
but you don't have to take it lying down"
The final one said this to me
-The End

<u>Gunfighter V</u>
<u>The Story of Six Gun</u>

Another Town
Another Place
One more time
One more face

Ugly and distorted
Grim and Rank
Upright two legged
Even the sound of his name stank

"They call me Six Gun,
not because I carry a six gun
but because I carry six guns
One on each hip
That makes two
One in the back of my belt
One by each shoe
And one up my sleeve
Just to trick you
Life ain't never been no good
Me neither far as I can tell
I was born to be bad
Guess I'll be going to hell"

Uneducated unregulated
Unbathed and just plain no good
Even the grass died on the ground
Where he stood

When he walked into the saloon
All faces turned grim
Only one man
stood up to face him

"I'm the law
I keep the peace in this town
Get what you need
And be out by sundown"

With an evil grin
'Ol Six Gun laughed as he drew his gun
Blew away the sheriff saying,
"I'm just here to have fun"

No one dared challenge
As he moved to the bar
Two men picked up the sheriff's body
With a clink to the floor
Rolled the tin star

I said,
"Excuse me Roxy"
as I moved from my seat
walked over and looked down
at the star by my feet

I reached down and picked it up
Noticing the blood on the floor
Hearing the sound of panic
Heading for the door

I never have understood
What exactly happens to me
I get a feeling cold as ice
A killer instinct
Heading down a one-way street
I don't think twice

I tossed the badge onto the bar
In front of the slime's nose
He looked somewhat surprised
As he turned to me
Everyone else froze

"I'll kill you dead"
is what 'Ol Six Gun said
pointing with a crooked finger

He reached to draw
A flash of lighting was all anyone saw
Six Gun spun around
Pistol half cocked
He slid to the ground
Mouth open in shock
Silence reigned as the only sound
Cause you see
I'm the fastest gun around

One last shot of Whiskey
A kiss to Roxy
And time to ride
Me and my horse, a six gun by my side
-The End

Gunfighter VI

The Marshal

In a place where truth has fled
Gangs rule
freedom is dead
Men with guns roam the street
The quest for peace
Has met defeat
evil men reign
In places of darkness
Follow the path of the takers
Vulturous soul
Preying on the weak
Dark as the night
Blacker than coal

Cold eyes no longer human
Command blood and sacrifice
From innocent lambs
Who cannot defend
But pay the price
God did not create men like these
They use their free will
For violent gain
To feast on the flesh of those they kill
Their cowardice inflicts pain
When will this end

In the middle of the town

Lying on the ground
The mayor face down
A bullet in the back
Same story told
This time unsettling
a spirit of old
rise to take form
Justice brave and bold

Drinking and laughing
Celebrating their quest
for sin and lust
Bad men stand abreast
When slowly he arose
out of the dust
Carrying a gun
And a black rose
Facing the men
The night grew cold

He walked straight up to the men
Lifting his hand over the mayor's body
He dropped the rose and as it fell
Fire flashed
Sending demons back to hell

A look of surprise
As the bullets flew
The fear in their eyes
Each one rang true
The bodies turning to dust
As steel and iron went through

More gangs gathered
Revenge in their tone
Circling around
Who is this one who dares stand alone
Against us he will be taken
Our wrath will regain
When facing righteousness
Evil loses in vain

Clenched teeth
Long stares from within
They couldn't believe
They outnumbered him
In both men and machines
They went forward without reprieve
"Bring me his head"
The leader shouted
Each wave the marshal stood tall
Proved he wasn't human at all
As the evil men were routed

Watching them fall
Each meeting their fate
the avenging angel
From Heaven's gate

Six more shots rang
Six more fell
Over and over
Until no more were found
Just the leader and his lieutenants
They moved forward to meet

Standing there facing The Marshal
On the sinister, bloody street

"I don't know who you are
But I'll make this clear
No one kills my men
I'll make you pay dear"

The Marshal was quick
More guns flashed
The bullets were thick
The scene was unreal
Bad men's deeds
Met cold hard steel
As to the ground more bodies crashed

When the fight was over
The Marshal walked to the edge of town
He took off his hat and knelt down
Said a prayer for the one's he was too late to save
And asked for strength to be strong and brave
In the end there were many dead
Before he left he turned and said

"It's time for a change
It's time for real truth
It's starts with teaching
The right things to our youth
It's wrong to use your strength or your position
To prey on others or over them tower
Giving and serving because you can
That's the real power

What we build together
Will out measure what we own
When we stand as one
No longer alone

Until the time this is learned
Spread the word
For Evil will not rest
Each day a new test
Stand up, stand down, do it your way
Stand with me and we will see this new day

When evil arises, it should know
The Marshal will come wherever it can go
With lightning and thunder
A time of reconciliation is here
I'll put it six feet under
That much is clear"

The Marshal tipped his hat as his words came to an end
Turned and with a few steps faded
Like dust in the wind…

www.Literarylou.com

Home of Author Louis Paul DeGrado

www.ingramcontent.com/pod-product-compliance
Lightning Source LLC
Chambersburg PA
CBHW051503150726

47997CB00001B/95